Strawberry Sundaes
at the
Rockhopper Café

Strawberry Sundaes
at the
Rockhopper Café

Tony Hopes

Matador
9 Priory Business Park,
Wistow Road, Kibworth Beauchamp,
Leicestershire, LE8 0RX
Tel: 0116 279 2299
Email: books@troubador.co.uk
Web: www.troubador.co.uk/matador
Twitter: @matadorbooks

ISBN 978 1838592 844

British Library Cataloguing in Publication Data.
A catalogue record for this book is available from the British Library.

Printed on FSC accredited paper
Printed and bound in Great Britain by 4edge Limited
Typeset in 11pt Minion Pro by Troubador Publishing Ltd, Leicester, UK

Matador is an imprint of Troubador Publishing Ltd

In Memory of Jack
And happy times spent in reminiscence of
the golden days of our youth and childhood

INTRODUCTION

As with my first novel, *A Year at Nethercome Ley*, I am again indebted to my friend and mentor, Trevor Bannister; this time not only for his thoughtful and enlightened editing, but also for his invaluable help in developing the story and authenticating the background of the era in which it is set.

The story is fiction and neither refers to nor suggests any incident or occurrence which may actually have taken place anywhere, at any time. Fairhaven, Myrtlesham and their environs are imaginary. The characters in the story are not real people, nor do they represent anyone living or who has ever lived. Their beliefs and attitudes are intended to be characteristic of the time the story is set and are not those of anyone associated with this book.

It is set during the long, dry summer of 1959; a time when Britain was at last recovering from the ravages of the Second World War and finally showing signs of greater affluence, although the standard of living of most Britons lagged way behind that of their American cousins. The average wage for a working man was between £5 and £10 per week and virtually all transactions for working class families were made in cash. The majority of them did not own their own home and few had a car or a telephone. The cinema and radio, or wireless as it was commonly called, maintained cherished places in the nation's affections; although most families owned or rented a television set on which they could enjoy a choice of programmes offered by two channels.

In the story, I have tried to portray the stronger sense of community that prevailed in those days, even in the poorer areas, as well as a greater deference to authority. In that closer society, people's conduct was generally moderated; at least in public. What would now be considered a mild swearword could invite a reprimand in mixed company. Obscene language in public was likely to attract the attention of the local 'bobby on the beat', who was often a familiar and trusted member of the community. Lacking the affluence we now enjoy, and with the availability of alcohol limited and governed by strict licencing laws, drunken hooliganism was less prevalent than today, and neither excused nor tolerated by the public or the law. Off-course betting was illegal, which led to local 'bookies' employing 'runners' to collect illicit bets in pubs and clubs.

Before 1960, the National Service Act required physically able young men between the ages of 18 and 21 to serve for a period in one of the armed forces. Only those in defined essential services were exempt. For servicemen and servicewomen stationed in the far flung remnants of Britain's crumbling empire, or the British sector of occupied and partitioned Germany, a Sunday radio programme called *Two-way Family Favourites* provided a chance for contact with home by allowing them and their loved ones the opportunity to send a message and dedicate a song or a piece of music to each other.

In the 1950s, Rock and Roll achieved what Adolph Hitler had failed to do, and successfully invaded Britain. It was welcomed and embraced by a section of the population universally known for the first time as 'teenagers', who adopted new fashions and a vibrant culture and lifestyle of their own. Britain quickly produced home-grown rock and roll stars, such as Tommy

Steele, Marty Wilde and a young man who called himself Cliff Richard. The new phenomenon of the coffee bar was where many youngsters gathered to jive to the twang of the electric guitar, which was becoming the predominant sound of popular music.

But not all was sweetness and light. The superpowers' burgeoning arsenals of terrifying weaponry cast a shadow across a war-weary world desperate to avoid the horror of nuclear conflict. In Britain, class barriers were still firmly entrenched and the 'ceiling' restricting female career opportunities was often not so much 'glass' as 'concrete', with the aspirations of women of the so-called lower classes presumed to be no more than typically that of a typist, shop assistant or factory worker.

Strict censorship of films, TV and literature prohibited the use of most swearwords, the portrayal of excessive violence and anything more than an allusion to sex. The few films that were permitted to include such things were given X-rated certificates for cinemas, restricting them to adult viewing. Victorian attitudes to co-habitation and having children out of wedlock still lingered, as did the stigma attached to unmarried mothers and their offspring. Many people were less than comfortable with the idea of inter-racial marriage and relationships, and there were no specific laws to prevent narrow-minded bigotry denigrating or excluding anyone of a certain race or colour.

At the end of the fifties, British seaside resorts were enjoying *a last hurrah* before cheap air travel and package holidays began a decline in their popularity. Manufacturing still relied to a great extent on manual labour, and many factories closed for a week or fortnight in summer, when workers would flock to caravan parks and boarding houses in the larger seaside resorts, like Blackpool and Scarborough. A day-trip to the seaside by coach, or charabanc as they were still sometimes called, was a much loved treat, especially for less affluent families.

Smaller resorts provided the opportunity to enjoy a little time beside the sea in more relaxing surroundings. The seaside town of Fairhaven that I created for this story encapsulates the character and ambience of those small resorts that I remember from my youth and childhood. Inevitably, it is idealised to some extent by my own fond memories, but I hope I have at least conveyed a sense of 'how it was' in those bygone days.

In that time before easily affordable international travel and the social media, the experiences of most people, and hence their aspirations, were in many ways different from today. Opportunities were not as unlimited as those we now enjoy and, as a consequence, the average person's needs and expectations were usually more modest.

In this story, I have tried to ensure authenticity in the attitudes and way of speaking of my characters in the time in which it is set. Where the reader may feel I have not achieved complete accuracy, I can only offer the excuse that it is based on personal recollections of a time that, to an ever-increasing proportion of the population, is history.

Tony Hopes
May 2019

I

'Is there any more forlorn sight than an English seaside resort on a wet winter afternoon?' David wondered, as the single-decker bus turned onto the Esplanade. Wiping the condensation from the rain-flecked window with his sleeve, he gazed at the dripping sign over the entrance to the pleasure gardens, which seemed to proclaim *Welcome to Fairhaven* with more despondency than cheer. Beyond the promenade railings he could see the deserted beach and grey-green rollers heaving themselves listlessly onto the shore. The funfair, at one end of the sea front, looked just as desolate and forsaken; the lights of its displays lifeless and the rides hidden beneath heavy tarpaulin covers that sagged under pools of rainwater.

With its engine snarling irascibly, the bus slowed and came to a halt beside an ornate wrought-iron shelter; open on all four sides, but partitioned to provide all-round refuge from the fickle British weather. David retrieved his canvas holdall and guitar case from the luggage rack and turned to the conductor. "You wouldn't happen to know where the Seagull Café is, would you?"

The conductor shook his head, "Sorry mate. I'm new on this route."

"I'm told it's near The Packet Boat Inn," David mused. "So it shouldn't be too hard to find."

The only other passenger on the bus, an elderly chap wearing a flat cap and an old army greatcoat, pointed towards the far end of the promenade. "It's down by the harbour, son. You can't miss it. Just keep walking. If you wind up in the drink, you've gone too far."

"Thanks." Turning up the collar of his mackintosh, David stepped down into the rain and lowered his head against a curtain of drizzle being driven by an onshore wind. He regretted not owning a hat, but having to wear a school cap for most of his childhood and that silly RAF side-cap for the two years of his national service had put him off them for life. His hair was probably a little too long anyway; much to his father's disgust. Anything other than short back and sides with a proper parting was frowned on. In his dad's eyes, a DA or a quiff would have made him a teddy-boy.

His guitar case bumped against his leg as he walked, rattling the keys in his raincoat pocket and rekindling his curiosity. Why had Great Uncle Ralph left him a half share in a café, and why to him and not his brother, who was much more of a businessman? For some inexplicable reason, Richard had been left a hundred quid and a piano, which he couldn't play! Their parents had been unable to offer an explanation, other than the probability that Uncle Ralph had got them mixed up. Richard had no idea either, but he could hardly be expected to concern himself with such things in his present state of health.

David had been surprised to receive anything from their uncle's will. He could recall the family visiting Fairhaven before the war, when he and Richard had been children, but the memories were hazy. He could vaguely remember playing on the beach and going out on a boat with Uncle Ralph to catch crabs and lobsters. But he had no recollection of a café.

The other half of the business had been left to someone referred to by the solicitors as J.M. Lampeter. Their letter had given no clue to his identity, so David could only surmise that he had been Uncle Ralph's business partner.

"He doesn't know me from Adam," David murmured to himself. "So I suppose he's as unimpressed as I am about having a partner foisted on him." It reinforced his initial reaction, when he had received news of his legacy. 'What might it be worth to him to buy me out?'

A small harbour nestled between the seafront and a wooded headland. He could make out several masts spiralling against the backdrop of low cloud, as the hulls of craft hidden below the level of the quay rocked on the changing tide. Crossing the road to the promenade, his attention was captured by a rain-soaked poster peeling from a boarded-up kiosk. Above the exaggerated stage-smile of Loretta Dufray, an ageing ballad singer, and the vacuous grin of Saucy Stan Slattery, a comedian who had briefly been popular in the thirties, it exclaimed:

Fun in the Sun
at
The Wintergardens Palace Theatre

"So this is where old music hall acts come to die," he murmured. "Doesn't anyone here know its nineteen-fifty-nine? I wonder who they've got lined up for this year; Darby and Joan?"

The Packet Boat Inn faced the harbour at the junction of the Esplanade and a road that rose steeply towards the downs. Halfway up the hill, he could see a field with regimented ranks of caravans and one or two tents. "Good luck to anybody camping on a day like this," he muttered.

He didn't know what a packet boat was, but assumed it to be a kind of sailing ship; like the one battling through a storm on the sign hanging above the entrance to the pub. The timber and brick façade suggested the building was well over a hundred years old, although he wondered about the authenticity of the bulls-eye panes in the bow windows. In front of the pub was an area of water-logged turf, on which several heavy wooden tables and benches stood, dripping and deserted, in pools of muddy water.

Skirting the sodden patch of grass, he caught sight of the weathered blue paintwork of his inheritance. It was larger than he had imagined, with a faded sign above its double-doors declaring it to be *The Seagull Café*. It faced the harbour and was separated from The Packet Boat Inn by a cobbled lane, at the end of which the roofs of several large sheds and boathouses were silhouetted in stark relief against the steel-grey sky.

Lights were on upstairs in the pub, but like all but one of the other shops and establishments on the quay, it was closed. Peering through the grubby glass panes of the café doors, David could see chairs stacked on tables and rows of shelves lining the wall behind a counter.

So this was it.

Fumbling in his pocket, he pulled out the keys he had been given by the solicitor's clerk in Myrtlesham and inspected the buff label attached to them. It gave no clue to which lock each key fitted, only the name, address and telephone number of Uncle Ralph's executors: Graddistoke, Flockwood and Trumpleman.

"Why do solicitors have such daft names?" he chuckled, as he tried to identify which keys fitted the café door locks. Swinging the doors open, he was greeted by the musty odour of a building which had been closed up for some time, although it seemed surprisingly clean. The windows were smeared and dusty, but the floor appeared to have been swept recently and the tables and chairs were free of dust and dirt.

Putting down his holdall, he propped his guitar case against the counter and took out his handkerchief to wipe the rain from his face and mop his hair. The room measured about forty feet by thirty, with a high ceiling decorated with elaborately moulded cornices and scrolls, now yellowed with age and nicotine. He discarded his raincoat and draped it over the counter while he looked around. It took a few moments to locate the light

4

switches, which were on the wall of a short passageway that led to the kitchen. Flicking them on, he was relieved to watch all but one of the café wall-lights come to life; replacing the late afternoon gloom with a bright, amber glow.

A narrow flight of stairs led off the passage, next to which was a door that responded with an asthmatic wheeze as David pulled it open. He was met by a heady cocktail of odours, among which he could distinguish bleach, disinfectant and lavender polish. As if in gratitude for their release, the handles of a broom and a mop toppled slowly towards him. The cupboard was lined with shelves laden with dusty cartons and bottles and, high up on the rear wall, he could make out an electricity meter and switchboard. The broom and mop were entangled in a partly unravelled roll of carpet and seemed reluctant to return to their gloomy confinement. He had to force them back before he could close the door.

The kitchen, at the end of the passage, was barely ten feet deep, but it stretched the whole width of the building and, like the café, it was clean. A glass-panelled door led to a walled yard, which appeared to be accessible to all the harbour-side businesses. Against the far wall of the kitchen was a four-ring gas stove together with a couple of belfast sinks and a long, wooden draining board fixed below two tall sash windows. The space between the windows was filled by the large, enamelled cylinder of a gas boiler, which was adorned with a variety of labels and knobs. The other walls were tiled and lined with shelves, plate racks and cupboards; all well stocked with crockery and glassware. An assortment of pots and pans, a large multi-slice toaster and a couple of tea urns stood on the worktops above a row of floor-cupboards. An inspection of two wooden chests attached to the wall revealed a collection of cutlery of disparate styles and vintages.

He was thirsty after the long journey, but there was no sign of bottles of pop, tea, coffee, or anything else that might once have been on offer to customers. The idea of drinking tap water that might have lain in lead pipes for several months was decidedly unappealing, so he decided to wait until he could find somewhere that was open.

"I wonder if there's a café anywhere around," he chuckled.

He was distracted by the sound of a door opening and went back along the passage to investigate. A man wearing a frayed flat cap and a shabby, grey overcoat was standing in the entrance. His unshaven jowls and down-at-heel appearance made it difficult to estimate his age, but David guessed he was probably in his late forties. It wasn't until the man shuffled forward that David noticed the metal calliper protruding below his trouser turnup. It was clamped firmly around his ankle and shoe.

David pointed to the 'Closed' sign hanging on the door. "Sorry…" But he was given no chance to continue.

"Saw the light on. Thought I'd pop in an' say 'ello." The accompanying grin revealed several gaps between nicotine-stained teeth.

"That's very neighbourly of you," David replied. His spirits wilted, as the thought struck him. "You're not Mister Lampeter by any chance, are you?"

"You what?"

"Is your name Lampeter?" David repeated.

"No; Sammy."

"Oh, right," said David, still none the wiser. "I'm David … David Sheldon. Did you know my Uncle Ralph?"

"Knew Ralph; yeh. Used to work 'ere."

"Oh, I see," said David, coming to terms with Sammy's ability to dispense with pronouns. "What did you do?"

"Aw; this an' that. Bit a'cleanin'; bit a'washin' up … clearin' the tables when it got busy."

"Did it get busy?"

"Now an' then … durin' carnival week."

"When is that?"

6

"August. Kids're on 'oliday then."

David nodded. "Yes; I know. But, it doesn't look as if this place has seen any customers for quite a while."

"Shut last September. Few weeks afore ol' Ralph died."

"Didn't his partner keep things going?" David enquired.

Sammy looked puzzled. "You what?"

"His partner. Didn't he have a business partner; somebody called Lampeter?"

"Not that I know of. Vera from the Co-Op used to 'elp out servin' now an' agen. But never 'eard o'nobody by that name."

"Anyone else involved, at all?" David prompted.

Sammy wrinkled his brow in thought. "Couple o'blokes turned up once. Foreign one of 'em wuz. Didn't stop long. 'Ad their 'eads together with Ralph upstairs. But never 'ad nothin' t'do with this place, far as I know. Cussed ol' bugger wuz Ralph. Can't see 'im lettin' nobody else 'ave a say in 'ere."

"I see," said David; even more intrigued.

Sammy obviously considered the subject exhausted and gestured towards the kitchen. "Want me t'get that boiler goin' for yuh?"

"I don't think so. Thanks all the same."

"Right bugger t'light," Sammy declared, unbuttoning his coat. "Specially now it bin out fer six months. Gotta know what you're doin'. Can blow back at yuh."

It had already occurred to David that tackling the monstrous, bomb-like contraption might be tricky; if not downright hazardous. So Sammy's alarming revelation made his offer suddenly more appealing. "Alright; thanks. I don't have any matches though."

"S'alright; got some." Sammy patted his pocket and grinned, revealing another display of teeth that reminded David of an abandoned graveyard.

Both men turned to look out of the open door in response to a call of, "Hello Sammy!"

Sammy waved in reply to a woman who scuttled past, hunched beneath a green umbrella that bore the logo 'Gemma's Gems'. Leaning out of the door, he shouted, "Watcha Gemmer! Davy's 'ere! Me an' 'im's gonna get this place goin' agen!"

"Now, wait a minute…" David began, but realising that Sammy was too engrossed in whatever Gemma was saying to take any notice, he decided to save his breath.

"Wass that? Okey-dokey. Tell 'im that; yeh!"

"Tell me what?" David asked.

"Can't stop now, but sez to tell yuh she's gonna pop round tomorra an' say 'ello … Oh yeh; and to tell yuh Joe Lam … Lamper…"

"Lampeter?"

"Yeh; thass it. Anyway; come round at the weekend an' agen this mornin'. Done a bit a'tidyin' up … Comin' back later, so Gemmer sez."

"Did she mention who he was?"

"No; thass all."

David shrugged. "Well, I suppose we'll find out, all in good time."

Sammy nodded. "Spect so." Removing his overcoat, to reveal an equally shabby tweed jacket, he dropped it onto a table and, favouring his damaged leg, made his way towards the kitchen. "Right; let's get this bugger lit up."

David decided it was time to take a look upstairs. The steep staircase led to a small landing with four doors leading from it, one of which opened onto a large room with two windows overlooking the harbour. Two smaller windows at the back afforded a less appealing view of the service yard and the sheds beyond. Nevertheless, he could envisage the room's potential charm when filled with summer sunlight. It was bare except for a shabby armchair, a couple of wheelback chairs and a drop-leaf table with scratched and stained veneer.

One of the other rooms contained an old wardrobe with no doors and a brass bedstead, with no mattress. The other doors led to a toilet and a small bathroom, both of which smelled of bleach and looked as if they had recently been cleaned.

He was startled by what sounded like a muffled explosion, followed by Sammy's raised voice. "Come on yuh bugger! Don't play up!"

"Are you alright?" he called.

"Yeh. Damned thing don't wanna light!"

"Don't worry then," David shouted nervously. "Leave it for now!"

"No! Get it goin' in a minute."

Against his better judgement, David went down to investigate; his nose registering an unmistakeable whiff of gas before he reached the foot of the stairs. Peering cautiously round the kitchen door, he saw that Sammy had removed the front cover of the boiler and was poking about in it with a fork. The smell of gas was stronger in the confined space.

"Leave it Sammy; please! I don't need it at the moment," he insisted, with as much authority as his trembling voice could command.

Sammy ignored him and reached for the matchbox on the draining board. "Be alright now. Bit bunged up, thass all."

David's vision of an almighty explosion, resulting in both of them being dredged from the harbour, made the hair stand up on his neck, and he rushed to a window. "Wait a minute! Let me get this open and let some air in!"

Sammy looked puzzled. "Waffor? Won't make it light no quicker."

"No; but it might save us from being gassed or cut to pieces when we get blown through it!" David retorted caustically. Fumbling with the window catch, he almost left the ground at the sound of another sudden detonation beside him.

"There y'are; goin' a treat now," Sammy announced proudly.

The boiler rumbled, as if in agreement. But David decided he needed some air; great lung-bursting gulps of fresh air … and a drink. The pubs were closed, so he would have to settle for a good strong cup of tea.

"Where's the nearest grocers?" he asked.

"Co-op … Up the 'ill … near the caravan park."

"Right; the rain seems to have stopped, so I'm going to get a packet of tea and some milk and something to eat."

Sammy picked up the boiler cover. "Okey doke. Just get this back on while you're gone. Make sure it's warmin' up proper."

It was dawning on David that getting rid of Sammy, without being downright rude, was not going to be easy. Retrieving his damp raincoat from the counter, he shouted towards the kitchen, "By the way, if this Lampeter chap turns up, tell him I won't be long."

"Right-oh!"

Thrusting his arms into the sleeves of his mackintosh as he left, he almost collided with a pretty girl in a shiny, yellow raincoat. She was petite, with dark, wavy hair styled in a pixie-cut. But it was her large, sparkling eyes that held his attention. They were brown with long, curling lashes … and quite compelling.

David smiled apologetically. "I'm sorry; we're not open. Not even for a cup of tea, I'm afraid."

"That's alright. I don't want one," she said. "I'm looking for David Sheldon."

"You've found him," he replied. "What can I do for you?"

"I'm Jo Lampeter."

"What … J.M. Lampeter?"

"Yes." Her eyes widened. "Is there a problem?"

"No! It's just … well; you're … ah … not what I was expecting," he stammered awkwardly. "To tell the truth, I was expecting a man!"

"Sorry to disappoint you. Didn't you see my name in the will?"

Her smile was disarming and David grinned nervously. "I'm not disappointed; just surprised. My brother and I have never actually seen the will. He's been very ill and I didn't bother to ask. I took care of it all with the solicitors by post, and they only referred to you as J.M. Lampeter in their letter. Someone called you Joe, just now; so I just assumed. Sorry."

"No need to apologise; it's not the first time it's happened. My name is Josephine, but I've never liked it … or *Josie*. Everyone calls me Jo."

"Well; come in, Jo," he said and stood aside to let her pass.

Watching her unbutton her raincoat, he noted that she wasn't wearing a wedding ring. Still unsettled by the surprise, all he could think of was, "Well; we seem to be partners."

"Yes; for the moment," she replied pointedly. "Who's in the kitchen?"

"That's Sammy. He's been fiddling with the boiler and doing his best to blow us to kingdom come."

"Who's Sammy?"

"Apparently, he used to do odd jobs here, like sweeping and washing up. He just turned up and offered to light the boiler. It looks a bit daunting."

He was treated to another appealing smile. "How much do you know about running a café?" she asked, gazing around her.

"Well," David began gravely. "Let me fill you in on the full extent of my experience in the catering trade; all of which could be written on the back of a postage stamp, with room for your name and address." Her laughter was delightful and gratifying.

"That goes for me too."

"Oh! I see. I assumed you were my Uncle Ralph's partner, or had at least been involved in running this place."

"No; I'm a nurse. I work at Myrtlesham General Hospital."

"So, how did you know him?"

"I didn't. I'm as baffled as you must be. I have no idea why he left me anything in his will. I met him a few times when Aunt Ginny and I called in for a cup of tea, but I can't say I knew him. Aunt Ginny did, though."

"Aunt Ginny?"

"She's my mum's cousin. I live with her. It's a long story, but she took me in when mum died."

David nodded, as if enlightened.

She took a bunch of keys from her shoulder bag. "Aunt Ginny gave me these. Your Uncle gave them to her to look after, just before he died. She's got about a hundred and fifty pounds and a biscuit tin full of old papers he left with her, as well."

"I see," said David. "The solicitors didn't mention it."

"That's probably because they don't know," she suggested. "I get the impression from Aunt Ginny that your uncle was secretive about his affairs and liked to keep what he used to call *the revenuers* at arm's length."

"So Aunt Ginny got a nice little windfall."

Jo shook her head. "No; she insists its part of our inheritance."

They both turned towards the sound of Sammy making his way along the passage. He appeared, drying his hands on his jacket. "Get the tea did yuh?" He gestured over his shoulder with a raised thumb. "Runnin' the water fer a bit. Get the kettle on in a minute."

"No; I haven't been out yet," David replied. "This is Jo Lampeter."

"What; the bloke you bin on about?"

"Does she look like a bloke?" David asked tetchily.

"Was you what said it was a bloke," Sammy retorted.

Despite her amusement, Jo decided it was time to intervene. "Never mind; you both know I'm not a bloke, now." Turning to David, she said, "I was hoping we could talk. But if you're going somewhere…"

"I was just going to get something to eat and drink, but it can wait."

She motioned towards the counter. "I left some tea and sugar under there, and a tin of biscuits. I came in to tidy up a bit at the weekend."

"Oh, well done; thanks!" David exclaimed. "I haven't looked over there, yet."

Jo giggled. "Nurses are rarely without the means to make a cup of tea. It's what keeps us going. I'll go and see if Gemma can spare us a drop of milk."

Still bemused, David watched her pass by the window.

"Neat little party, that," said Sammy. "Bet you're glad she aint a bloke."

* * *

Lowering his head to negotiate the entrance to The Packet Boat Inn, David found himself and Jo in a narrow lobby, facing a half-open hatch that he assumed served as a bottle and jug. Doors on each side of the lobby led to bars identified by ornately lettered signs as: 'Wardroom' and 'The Mess'.

"Officers or other ranks?" David asked.

Jo balanced on tiptoe to peer through the glass pane in the right-hand door. "This will do. There are signs of life in here."

"The Mess it is then," said David, ducking his head again to avoid the lintel of the doorframe, as he followed her into the bar.

It was roughly the same size as the café with a low ceiling spanned by gnarled wooden beams that, to David's untrained eye, appeared to be original. Lights in the form of nautical lanterns lined the walls between ornately framed pictures of ships and ancient maritime posters. One or two contemporary notices were pinned to a varnished door, above which another hand-painted sign bore the word: 'Heads'.

A log fire flickered in a fireplace on the far side of the bar-room, on one side of which was a dartboard. On the other side of the fire, two men sat silently playing dominoes; the arrival of strangers not enough to break their concentration or arouse their curiosity.

The bar counter appeared to extend all the way through from the Wardroom and the bottle and jug to The Mess; where, halfway across the room, it met a sturdy, wooden pillar and curved towards an alcove on the far wall. 'Miss March', a generously-endowed young lady, who seemed perilously close to bursting out of her bathing costume, smiled and waved from a glossy calendar that was tacked to the pillar. Above it, a brass ship's bell gleamed in the glow of the bar lights.

On the other side of the pillar, a heavily built individual, with sagging jowls and a florid complexion, was perched on a bar stool, reading a newspaper. Despite the inclement weather, he was wearing a linen jacket over an oxford striped shirt and a red cravat. A panama hat rested on the counter beside an empty spirit glass and an ashtray containing the wrapper and smoking stub of a King Edward cigar. As Jo and David approached the bar, he looked up from his newspaper and smiled a greeting.

"You have customers, Hooky," he called towards the open cellar hatch.

"Right you are, Monty," came the echoing reply.

A moment later, a mop of wiry, greying curls emerged from the cellar, above the lean figure of a middle-aged man in a fairisle sweater. His weathered features creased in a smile. "Evenin'. You'll notice I didn't say *good evenin'*," he added. "The weather's bin like this all week. I 'ope you're not on 'oliday."

Unwilling to offer an explanation to someone he had only just met, David didn't reply.

Monty pushed his glass forward. "When you're ready, Hooky."

"Hooky?" Jo repeated quizzically.

"I was in the Andrew, love. That's the Royal Navy to you. I 'ad the fouled anchor on me sleeve, see. So that's what I got called … an' it's just stuck."

"I see," said Jo.

"You on 'oneymoon or sommat?" he asked.

Jobs eyes widened in astonishment. "No; we're not!" she replied hurriedly.

"We're here on business," was as much as David was prepared to divulge.

"Oh, Right," said Hooky; his grin suggesting he had his own idea of what 'business' it might be. "What can I get yuh?"

"I'll have a half of bitter, please. What about you, Jo?"

"Just a lemonade, please. I'm on duty later."

Hooky raised a bushy eyebrow. "On duty? You're not a copper, are yuh?"

Jo grinned in response. "No; I'm a nurse. I don't think I'm tall enough for the police."

"I was thinkin' the same thing," he chuckled.

"Do you have anything in the way of food?" David asked.

"Crisps … peanuts … nuts and raisins."

"Is that all?"

"Afraid so."

Both of them watched appreciatively as Jo took off her raincoat and settled herself, as demurely as her tight skirt would allow, on a padded bench by the window. David felt his cheeks redden as she looked up and met his gaze. She smiled as he delivered her lemonade and seated himself opposite her.

Monty seemed engrossed in his newspaper and the dominoes players continued to compete wordlessly; the only sound being the odd tap when one of them couldn't follow on. The muted bumps and rattles below them indicated that Hooky had returned to the cellar.

"Is that all you're having; crisps?" Jo remarked.

"It's all they've got," he said, fishing for the salt bag at the bottom of the packet.

"When did you last eat?"

"At breakfast."

She declined his offer of a crisp with a shake of her head. "That will hardly fill you up. You must be starving!"

"I'll get fish and chips or something later. When I've found somewhere to stay."

"Haven't you done that yet?" she exclaimed. "You're cutting it fine. There's not much open at this time of the year. The Grand Hotel is closed for refurbishment."

"I can't afford a hotel, anyway; least of all a grand one," he replied. "I hadn't intended to stay overnight. I didn't know you couldn't get here by train and the journey took a lot longer than I anticipated. I had to change at Cambridge to get to Myrtlesham; and then catch a bus from there."

Jo looked at her watch. "It's gone seven. You'll be lucky to find a bed and breakfast now; most of them are closed until Easter."

He shrugged. "I suppose I could stay the night in the café, if all else fails. If you have no objection."

Jo shook her head. "No; of course not. But it will be pretty uncomfortable. There's no mattress on the bed."

He shrugged. "Oh, I'll manage."

"What do you do for a living?" she asked.

"I've done a fair few things since national service, but I like to think of myself as a musician. I play guitar and piano … Not both at the same time," he added frivolously. To his disappointment, it received no more than the hint of a smile. He enjoyed being able to amuse a pretty girl, especially one with such a delightfully infectious laugh.

"Well, it explains the guitar. Where do you perform?"

"Oh, here and there."

She was nothing if not persistent. "Where are you performing at the moment?"

"I'm … ah … between gigs, as you might say."

Jo's brow creased in curiosity, "Between what?"

"Gigs; it's what musicians call a booking; a job."

"When was your last *gig*?"

"About two months ago," he murmured defensively. "I've been helping out a friend in his car showroom for the last few weeks. I'm going on from here to play a few sessions with my pal Archie's skiffle group … hopefully."

She sipped her lemonade. "It doesn't sound much like a steady way of making a living."

"I manage," he said nonchalantly. "Anyway; enough of me. Now we've managed to get away from Sammy, shall we get down to business?"

Jo nodded. "OK. I don't know what you have in mind, but I'm not interested in running a café."

"That's a shame; neither am I," David replied. "I was hoping you might offer to buy me out."

"On a nurses pay?" she snorted. "I wouldn't; even if I could! I'm at everyone's beck and call as it is. I don't fancy running around serving cream teas and what-have-you, as well."

David grimaced. "Nor me. Think of all that washing up!"

"So, have you any suggestions?" she asked.

"Selling it seems the best idea."

"Have you any idea what it's worth, or how to go about it?"

David shrugged. "I suppose we could advertise it in the local paper. Or perhaps we could ask Gravestones, Flotsam and Trumpet if they can help."

"Who?"

"You know; the solicitors."

To his delight, she giggled; her eyes twinkling with mirth. "Do you take anything seriously?"

"Not much. Unless it's dangerous; like TB."

Her smile faded. "Have you lost someone with it?"

David sighed. "Nearly. My brother. He's still in hospital. Thankfully, he's almost recovered, but it scared us all stiff for a while."

"I'm sure it did. I haven't come across it. I thought it was dying out; but it's an awful disease."

"We think he must have caught it when he was abroad. But, anyway…!" Unwilling to dwell on such an emotive subject, he said, "As you're a working girl and I, as they say in show business, am resting, shall I contact the legal beagles and have a word with the local paper?"

"If you like." Her eyes betrayed barely constrained mirth. "Resting?"

"I believe that's what they call it."

Jo's bottom lip trembled and she burst out laughing. Recovering her composure, she dabbed at her eye. "I can honestly say you're not at all what I expected."

"And neither are you, *Mister* Lampeter."

A bellow of, "Ello, ello, ello! What's all this hilarity then?" brought an abrupt halt to their mirth and made them turn their heads sharply towards the bar. Their startled stares were met by a pair of twinkling eyes and a broad smile set amidst the tawny mane of a full beard and moustache, which, with the hawk-like nose and greying locks of unruly hair, gave the stocky, broad-shouldered individual an almost piratical air.

"Sorry; we didn't know it wasn't permitted," David quipped.

"Don't mind me. It's nice to 'ear a bit of laughter on such a miserable evenin'."

"Are you the landlord?" Jo asked.

"Yes; that's right, my love. Wally … Wally Jarvis; that's me. What brings you young folks to sunny Fairhaven at this time o'year?"

David was about to answer in the same perfunctory manner he had with Hooky, but Jo beat him to it. "We've been having a look at the café, next door."

"Oh, right. You thinkin' of takin' it over, then?"

"We've been left it in a will," Jo explained.

Wally was visibly surprised. "I see. You related to Ralph?"

"David is. I hardly knew him. Neither of us really knows why he left it to us."

Wally's chuckle was a deep rumble. "That don't surprise me. Ralph did whatever 'e liked. Couldn't give a damn about what anybody thought. When're you thinkin' of openin' up, then?"

"We're not," said David.

"That's right," Jo concurred. "We don't know anything about running a café. We're going to sell it, if we can."

"Daltons Weekly," Monty murmured from behind his newspaper.

"I beg your pardon?" said David.

Monty lowered the paper. "Daltons Weekly, dear boy. It's a publication that specialises in advertising businesses for sale."

"Oh, I see. Thank you," David replied.

"Of course, there are agencies that will act for you," Monty expounded, "But I fear you might have precious little left after they've taken their pound of flesh."

"Thank you," David repeated. "That's very helpful."

"Monty knows a bit about a lot of things," Wally chuckled.

"I beg to differ," Monty replied loftily. "I know a great deal about many things."

"But not all of it useful, eh Monty, love?" The female voice came from somewhere behind the bar.

"I fear I must take issue with your observation, dear lady," Monty reposted, before returning his attention to his newspaper.

"Who are you talking to, Hun?"

The question, and the tap of approaching footsteps, heralded the appearance of a meticulously made up woman with platinum blond hair, whose cashmere sweater did little to disguise the contours of her impressive figure. Her face broke into a broad smile at the sight of Jo. "Hello love! How are you getting' on next door?" Noticing David, she added, "Is this your young man?"

Jo replied with a hurried, "No! This is David Sheldon. He's been left the other half of the café."

"That's nice. Pleased to meet you, David; I'm Avril. Jo and I met the other day, when she was cleanin' in the café."

Jo nodded her confirmation.

"Were you related to Ralph?" Avril asked.

"Yes," said David. "He was my great uncle. But I can't say I knew him; certainly not enough to expect him to leave me anything in his will."

"I don't think anybody knew Ralph well," Avril mused. "Kept himself to himself."

"That's right," Wally concurred. "Ralph could be an awkward beggar at times."

"How did he get on; business wise, I mean?" David asked.

Avril grimaced. "Not very well. It was all a bit hit and miss. You couldn't be sure when he was goin' to be open. Ralph suited himself. We tried to tell him that he needed to keep regular hours and brighten the place up, but he never took any notice."

"It got a lot worse last year," Wally added. "But I suppose that's understandable. We didn't know 'e was ill. 'E never said anythin'. But we could see the place was goin' t'pot. To be honest, it 'adn't bin any great shakes before. But it was especially bad last year."

"It'll need a lot of work to build it up again," Avril reflected.

"That's not their problem. They're gonna sell it," Wally declared.

Avril sighed. "That's a shame. The Seagull was a lovely place when we first took over here; wasn't it Hun? Two sisters ran it before Ralph. It was bright and clean…"

"When was that?" Jo asked.

"We moved in here eleven years ago … Monday; the twelfth of April, nineteen-forty-eight," Avril announced proudly. "Wally was just out of the navy."

"That's right; done time enough fer a pension," Wally chuckled.

Avril giggled. "Bein' a typical sailor, he'd always dreamed of havin' his own pub. This place was goin', so we jumped at it."

Wally pointed to David's glass. "Ready for the other 'alf?" Noticing that Jo's glass was still half full, he added, "Want that topped up, love?"

Jo looked at her watch. "No thank you. I don't want to miss my bus."

"Jo's a nurse," Avril explained to her husband.

"Yes, I am," said Jo. "They're short of night staff on men's orthopaedic, so I'm helping out on that ward for a week. The night sister on that wing is a bit of a tarter; she'll skin me alive if I'm late."

"Don't you have to wear a uniform?" David asked.

"Yes; but I usually change in my friend's room in the nurses' home. People want to tell me all about their ailments on the bus if they see I'm a nurse."

"I see. Well, I'll walk you to the bus stop."

"There's no need," she insisted. "Don't forget; you've still got to find somewhere to stay! You haven't eaten all day, either!"

"I haven't forgotten. But from what I've seen, most of the bed and breakfasts are at the other end of the bay. The bus stop is on the way, isn't it?"

"Hang on a minute; let me call my friend, Audrey," Avril suggested. "She's got a guest house just off Market Square. I'll see if she can take you."

"Thank you," David replied, and turned to Jo. "Can you wait while I go and get my bag?"

She nodded. "Yes; I need to powder my nose, anyway." Looking around the bar, she added, "If I can find out where."

Wally pointed to the door with the sign marked 'Heads'. "Through there; second on the left."

"Wouldn't tails be more appropriate?" Jo suggested mischievously.

"It's naval expression, my dear," Monty murmured disdainfully. "One of the more repeatable ones, I might add."

Wally responded with a broad grin and winked at Jo.

When David returned, the collar and shoulders of his mackintosh were dark with rain. Jo already had her raincoat on and was standing at the bar with her bag over her shoulder and her rain hat in her hand.

"It's tipping it down out there," he declared needlessly.

Avril returned, shaking her head. "Sorry, love. I couldn't get hold of Audrey. Now I think of it, I seem to remember her sayin' somethin' about visitin' her daughter."

"Never mind," said David. "If all else fails, the café will do for tonight. At least it's dry."

"You can't stay there!" Avril exclaimed. "It'll be cold and damp after bein' empty for months! Jo said there's no furniture to speak of in the flat, so what are you goin' to sleep on?"

"I'll manage," David insisted.

Avril's brows creased in contemplation and she turned her gaze on Wally. "We've got a room, haven't we, Hun?"

Wally's eyebrows rose. "We 'ave?"

"Yes; the spare bedroom at the back. If you clear out all the boxes of crisps and nuts and the cigarettes, I'll make up the bed. It's quite comfortable."

Interpreting Wally's expression as reluctance, David replied hurriedly, "It's extremely kind of you. But there's no need to go to all that trouble. I'll be alright; honestly."

"It's no trouble," Avril insisted. "You see Jo to her bus and then come straight back here! Wait a minute; I'll get you an umbrella."

Wally's laugh was a rumbling growl. "It's no good arguin', son. Once she's made 'er mind up, there's no changin' it. One thing I've learned from bein' married for fifteen years is; when they get a bee in their bonnet, you might as well give in … Especially when they've got a mind of their own, like my missus!"

"But, I'll be alright," David repeated. "I don't want to put you to all that trouble."

"It's no trouble. It won't take a minute. She won't take no for an answer, and I've got no beef about it. You'll 'ave a job findin' anywhere else this late, at this time o'year, I can tell yuh."

"He's right, David. Don't be silly." Jo declared. "Thank you, Mister…"

"It's Wally."

Avril reappeared with a brolly and handed it to David. "Here you are, love. Give us your bag, and we'll see you later."

"Thank you," David replied and took out his wallet.

"Put it away, son." Wally said gently. "Done yer national service, 'ave yuh?"

"Yes," said David. Mindful of Wally's naval background, he added, "RAF I'm afraid."

Wally chuckled mischievously. "Never mind. It can 'appen to anybody."

Jo took the umbrella from David's hand. "There's no need to come with me, now."

"No; I'd like to," he insisted. "It's pitch black out there and the weather's filthy."

"There's no need. I'll be quite alright."

Avril exchanged a knowing look with her husband. "Better safe than sorry, love."

II

The buffeting breeze tugged at David's jeans and borrowed seaman's sweater; moulding them to his body and tousling his hair, as he made his way along the grey-stone mole towards the harbour entrance. Inside its protective embrace, iridescent patches of surface oil glistened in the early-spring sunshine, and small craft jostled and pirouetted at their anchor buoys, as the incoming tide streamed beneath their keels. Above him, the plaintive squeal of gulls mingled with the rattle of blocks and pulleys and the snap of pennants flapping at the mast-heads of larger vessels moored against the quayside; their fenders creaking as they ground against the weed-encrusted stone.

Alerted by the sonorous thump of a large wave breaking against the end of the mole, David instinctively ducked as a shower of wind-borne spindrift swept over the retaining wall. He laughed; awed by the relentless power of the sea and enthused with sheer exuberance at the joy of the wind on his face and the tang of ozone and seaweed in the air. Leaning on a salt encrusted rail, he watched the silhouette of a large naval vessel glide soundlessly across the horizon. It felt good to be alive.

Reflecting on the joy of living brought his brother to mind. Richard had looked pale and thin when David had visited him in hospital the previous day. However, his doctors were confident that he was recovering satisfactorily and could soon be released for convalescence. Thankfully, illness hadn't dulled Richard's sense of humour. He had been amused to learn that David's mysterious business partner had turned out to be both female and attractive. They had been joking about the prospect of Richard being fussed over by their mother, when she and their father had arrived for one of their twice-weekly visits. A young nurse, who had found a bowl for the fruit they had brought, had inevitably prompted the comment that she was the sort of girl Richard should be looking to settle down with. David had stifled a chuckle; grateful that their mother's concern for the health and wellbeing of her firstborn had spared him a similar homily.

However, he had not been so fortunate later, when he had tea with his parents in a nearby café. Replying to his father's enquiry about Uncle Ralph's legacy, he had unwisely confided that he had no intention of becoming a char wallah. It had evoked an all too familiar sermon about lack of ambition and failing to take advantage of opportunities when they came along. His own acerbic observation that the so-called opportunity was, in fact, a half-share of a run-down dump in a coastal backwater had not helped.

He had fared no better when he tried to lighten the mood by revealing that the mysterious J.M. Lampeter was, in fact, a girl called Josephine. His mother's immediate reaction had been, "Is she single?"

On reflection, he regretted the way he and his father had parted and had to admit that, as usual, the argument had been his fault. He was all too aware that, unlike Richard, he had inherited little of their father's self-discipline and orderliness; attributes honed from wartime service as an RAF flight sergeant supervising ground crews.

Richard had put his degree in physics to good use and, although not yet thirty, he was the general manager of a successful engineering company. Whereas he, himself, had rejected a university education and had been called up for national service soon after leaving school. He wasn't proud of his record of drifting from one job to another, but he had never been able to arouse much enthusiasm for anything other than music.

Turning his back on another shower of spume, he surveyed the row of shops facing the harbour. Beside the dowdy and weather-worn façade of The Seagull Café, the candy-striped awning above the door of Sullivan's Novelty Confectioners looked bright and cheerful, as did the fresh, clean paintwork of Gemma's Gems, whose window display of jewellery and semi-precious stones sparkled as they caught the rays of reflected sunlight.

Even without the scrolled lettering across its windows, the varnished ship's wheel and polished wood and brass exhibited by E. R. Rolfe and Sons would have marked it out as a marine chandlery; unlike its other neighbour, whose shuttered facade gave no clue to its purpose. David's enquiries had revealed that it had once been a hardware store, but had been used for several other purposes in recent years, including that of a locksmith and a bicycle and mower repair business. The current occupant was a Polish refugee, who dealt in bric-a-brac and second hand furniture.

Tucked into the far corner of the quay, and set apart from the other premises, stood a white-washed building, which had once been a fisherman's cottage but now bore a crested, metal sign announcing that it was occupied by the harbourmaster. It appeared to be closed, prompting David to wonder how much mastering such a small harbour required.

'Not exactly Monte Carlo,' he thought ruefully. 'And unlikely to spark much interest in the café. Not from anyone willing to pay decent money, anyway.'

It was no surprise that few people were on the beach on such a blustery March morning. A couple were strolling arm-in-arm above the line of flotsam and seaweed deposited by previous tides, and a few bobbing bathing caps marked the progress of hardy souls taking a morning dip. The only other creature bold enough to emulate them was a labrador retriever that was bounding in and out of the surf, barking excitedly, while its owner prudently restricted his participation to throwing a piece of driftwood for it to recover.

It occurred to David that perhaps he ought to adopt a routine of a brisk morning walk along the beach; or at least a leisurely saunter. He was convinced that three days of Avril's epic meals were already having a detrimental effect on his waistline. It wouldn't take many more of her morning fry-ups; 'a sailor's breakfast' as she called them; followed by hot lunches with pudding; sardines or cheese on toast for tea; and one or two pints in the evening, to turn him into Billy Bunter.

He dreaded to think what his bill would come to. He had only intended to stay overnight, while he got the sale of the café under way. But he had discovered that the process of selling a business, especially a run-down café, was not as swift or simple as he had hoped. In addition to which his telephone call to his friend, Archie, had put a spanner in the works of his arrangements for the immediate future.

According to Archie's rambling and melodramatic account, his skiffle group was undergoing a transformation. "It's the new scene, man! We cats are into the beat ... Rock an' Roll, man!"

David had learned that the group had a new manager, who had convinced Archie and the others that skiffle and country and western music were dead; 'yesterday's scene'. Consequently, David's services were no longer needed. Archie had been fulsome with his insincere apology. "Sorry; mate. If it was up to me ... But you know how it is. My hands are tied. Gotta go with the guys."

"No need to apologise; I quite understand," David had replied. Having been billeted with Archie for eight months of his national service, he was well aware of his friend's fickle attitude to loyalty.

As a result of these setbacks, David had no immediate plans and, more to the point, nowhere else to go; except home to his parents. As much as he loved them, he had dismissed that option out of hand. The inevitable arguments with his father would upset his mother and lead to him feeling obliged to take a job he would hate; just to appease them.

Avril had refused to allow him to move into what she called 'That cold and empty barn of a place next door' until it had been made habitable. So he had stayed with her and Wally, making himself useful whenever he could, within the scope of his limited talents. The rest of his time had mostly been spent pottering around in the café, trying to avoid Sammy and playing his guitar.

The problem was that neither Avril nor Wally seemed in a hurry to discuss the cost of his bed and board. He hadn't got very far with either of them when he had tried to broach the subject. Avril's "Sorry luv; I haven't got time now," had been no more helpful than Wally's, "Not my department, son. Talk to the boss."

He had no idea what the going rate was, although he feared that what he already owed was enough to severely deplete his limited resources. Another few days would probably exhaust them entirely. There was no casual work available out of season, and he couldn't bring himself to ask Jo for a loan from the cash Uncle Ralph had left with her aunt. So he would have to risk upsetting Avril and explain that he could no longer afford to stay at The Packet Boat Inn … or anywhere else … and that he had no option but to move into the café.

His troubled thoughts were interrupted by the sight of a large limousine turning off the Esplanade; its polished two-tone grey coachwork and chrome trim glinting as it pulled up on the quay next to a sign that read *Strictly No Parking*. David recognised it as a Daimler Majestic saloon.

A huge, bull-like character emerged from it, attired in full chauffeur's livery; complete with peeked cap, leather gauntlets and polished riding boots. It brought to mind Erich von Stroheim in *Sunset Boulevard,* and it was all David could do to stop himself laughing, as he made his way back along the mole. It seemed a wise precaution, because the chap's face looked as if he had picked a fight with a bulldozer. A livid scar above one eye, an inexpertly reset broken nose and a missing earlobe gave his bovine expression a disturbing air of menace. Opening a rear door, with comically exaggerated deference, he stood aside as a slightly built, middle-aged man got out.

The brylcreamed hair, greying at the sides and parted in the centre, reminded David of the sporting heroes on the cigarette cards he used to collect as a boy. Brushing imaginary creases from his immaculately tailored grey suit, the man straightened his silk tie and looked along the row of quayside establishments, wrinkling his nose at the traces of diesel fumes and decaying seaweed that hung in the air.

A more modestly dressed cadaverous looking individual, wearing a dark blazer and cavalry twill trousers, got out of the other side of the car, clutching a leather document case. Both men looked directly at the café and a brief nod from the impressively attired individual sent the chauffeur striding towards it. His two ham-like fists gripped the door handles and, finding the doors locked, he began shaking them until the hinges rattled alarmingly.

"Hang on! No need for that; I've got the keys here!" David called; hoping his hand wasn't trembling too noticeably, as he held them up.

The well-groomed gent turned towards him, raising a bejewelled hand to shade his eyes from the low winter sun. "Are you David Sheldon?" he asked, in a surprisingly soft voice.

"Yes," David replied, keeping a wary eye on scarface as he approached. "Can I help you?"

"I understand you're looking to get shot of this place."

The local accent came as a surprise to David, who hadn't expected it from someone who appeared cultivated and affluent. He thought he also detected a slight lisp. "I'm looking to sell it; yes. But how do you know?"

"You put an ad in The Argus."

David was nonplussed. "That's right; but I only gave them the details yesterday. They said it wouldn't be in until Friday's edition."

"Not much goes on in Fairhaven that I don't know about, son."

"I see," said David, warily. "May I ask who you are?"

"Charlie McBride." He didn't offer his hand or volunteer any additional information.

The name meant nothing to David, but from the way it was expressed, he assumed he was expected to recognise it. "And you're interested in the café?" he prompted.

"I might be. I used to do a bit of business with the previous owner."

"That was my Uncle Ralph," said David.

"Oh, your uncle was he?" Charlie gazed disdainfully at the café's weather-worn façade. "Not exactly The Ritz, is it? But if it suits my other business interests, I might be prepared to take it off your hands."

"What other business interests do you have; if I might ask?"

Charlie waved a hand in the general direction of the town. "Seavista Holiday Park; you must've seen the caravans up on the hill. The Beach Café … The Copper Kettle … The Cascade Fun Palace … The Isle of Capri restaurant … one or two pubs, a hotel … and a few other enterprises."

"I see," David repeated, lamely.

"You're well advised to sell up," Charlie suggested offhandedly. "Fairhaven's pretty well served for this sort of thing. There's more than enough competition already. You'd never make a go of this place." He motioned to his companion, who had remained silent; seemingly lost in his own thoughts. "This is Mister Alan Turnbull. I brought him along to look the place over and do a preliminary business survey for me; to give me an idea if I could make anything of it."

Mister Turnbull roused himself to offer a half-hearted smile and stroke his narrow moustache with a finger and thumb. His comment: "I'll need to take a look around and ask a few questions," was accompanied by the faint click of ill-fitting false teeth.

"Want me to get them doors open, Char'… er Mister McBride?" scarface enquired hopefully.

"No; it's alright, Horace. Mister Sheldon's going to let us in. I shan't be needing you for a while. You can wait in the car."

"Horace?" David mouthed incredulously.

Charlie's smile revealed the glint of a gold tooth. "I know; but that's the name his mother gave him. He used to be a circus strong-man and a prize fighter in fairground boxing booths. He's as strong as an ox but he's got a heart of gold. He's quite harmless, really … as long as you don't upset him."

David grinned uneasily. "Heaven forbid!"

"He's very protective." Charlie added meaningfully, and gestured towards the café. "Why don't you open up and let the dog see the rabbit."

Settling himself on a bar stool, David watched Wally lever the best bitter pump several times and hold up a half-full pint glass to the light. He could hear the theme tune of *Housewives' Choice* coming from the radio, and Molly's accompanying, "Ladida-di-dadida-di-dadida…" as she cleaned in the Wardroom. The overnight odours of nicotine and stale beer had largely been expelled by the fresh breeze from the open front doors and replaced by the pungent aromas of Mansion Polish and Ajax.

"That looks clear enough." Wally smiled with satisfaction and emptied the glass into the ullage tray. "What d'yuh reckon of this ban the bomb march they're 'avin' at Easter"? Think it'll do any good?"

"No, I don't" said David. "But, I can sympathise with the people involved. The thought of a nuclear war doesn't bear thinking about."

"We've got to 'ave our own bomb, though, 'aven't we?" Hooky interjected from the step ladder, where he was changing a light bulb. "If Russia's got it, we've got to 'ave somethin' to make 'em think twice. Stands t'reason."

"I can't imagine even the Russians are daft enough to start another war," Wally mused. "They saw what the Yanks did to Hiroshima and Nagasaki, so they know what they could do t'Moscow."

"You never know with them commies!" Hooky retorted. "Look what they done in Hungary. But anyway; I can't see a few people walkin' to London from that weapons place, whatever it's called, is gonna make any difference."

"It's The Atomic Weapons Research Establishment," David explained, "It's at Aldermaston in Berkshire."

"Right. Well, wherever it is; they won't make a blind bit o'difference."

"Perhaps not," said David. "But they probably feel that someone has got to do something to make people stop and think. Nobody would come out of a nuclear war unscathed. Not us; not Russia; not America. You'd think the politicians would have learned that from the two wars we've already been through. Nobody benefits from a war."

"I dunno about that," Wally chuckled. "From what I've 'eard, one or two round 'ere did very nicely out of the last one."

"I assume you mean people like Charlie McBride," David suggested. "I take it you don't like him."

"I don't know 'im. So I can't say whether I like or dislike 'im. All I know is what people tell me. And that is: you wanna watch yourself where Charlie McBride is concerned."

"He seems to have done very well for himself," David suggested.

Wally grunted dismissively. "All the more reason to keep your wits about yuh. If 'alf of what's said is true, you'd do well to count your fingers after shakin' 'ands with 'im."

David grinned at the thought. "He was friendly enough."

"That's what Chamberlain said about Hitler," Hooky chuckled.

Avril appeared from the doorway to the living quarters and took a pack of Pall Mall from the cigarette shelves. "Have you put that new barrel on, Hun?"

Wally nodded. "Just done it, Pet. Bit lively at first, but it's settled down now." Gesturing towards David, he said, "Fill 'im in about Charlie McBride, will yuh?"

"Charlie McBride? You're not gettin' involved with him, are you?"

"He might be interested in buying the café," David said hesitantly.

"I wouldn't have anythin' to do with him, if I was you!" Avril exclaimed. "Anybody that does, ends up regrettin' it!"

"I don't intend to *get involved*," David replied. "All I'm interested in is selling the café. But I'll bear that in mind."

He was distracted by the sight of a passing cyclist, incongruously clad in what looked like a heavy leather jacket, plus-fours and a deerstalker. He could have sworn it was a woman, but she, if it was a she, disappeared from sight before he could be sure. "Did you see that?" he exclaimed.

"See what?" Avril asked.

"The cyclist that just went past! A woman ... at least I think it was ... dressed in a deerstalker and golf trousers!" His puzzled expression was replaced by a smile, as another cyclist appeared behind her. "Here's Jo," he said, half to himself. "But, who the heck is that with her?"

"You never know; it might be yer future mother-in-law," Hooky chuckled.

David's immediate inclination was to hotly deny any interest in Jo, beyond their business relationship. But realising that Hooky was fishing for a reaction, he ignored the comment. Nevertheless, his cheeks were burning as he slid off the stool and left the bar.

Jo greeted him with a smile as she rested her bicycle against the front of the café. She was wearing a pale blue windcheater over a thick woollen sweater and tight, dark, corduroy slacks with stirrups that fitted under the arches of her feet. She was bare-headed and her raven locks had been ruffled by the stiff breeze during her ride along the Esplanade.

Her companion was, as David had supposed, an elderly woman. She was sitting astride an old, heavy-framed bike, still wearing the deerstalker and with the bulky leather jacket zipped up under her chin. Its fleecy collar framed her narrow face like a ruff, giving her the look of an eccentric Elizabethan courtier. She wore thick, woollen socks, pulled up to knee-length plus-fours and a pair of sturdy, brown brogues. The thought: 'Did she get dressed during a fire alarm?' crossed David's mind.

Recognising his bemusement, Jo gestured towards her. "David; this is my Aunt Ginny."

"I'm very pleased to meet you," said David, unsure how to address the woman.

Aunt Ginny smiled a greeting and removed the deerstalker, to release an unruly mane of frizzy hair that fell to her narrow shoulders in a grey cascade. Aware of David's curiosity, she spread her hands in front of her. "This is my winter cycling outfit. When you get to my age, you feel the cold a lot more."

"I see," was all David could think of as a response.

She looked at him closely. "So, you're Ralph's nephew?" It sounded more like an accusation than a question.

"Great nephew, actually," David explained, warily. "Did you know him?"

A sudden gust ruffled Aunt Ginny's hair and she brushed errant strands from her face. "Yes, I did. He had some business dealings with my late husband. So I got to know him over the years."

"I got your message about that McBride chap," Jo interjected. "Sorry I couldn't get here before. I did a longer shift to cover for a colleague."

David unlocked the café doors. "Don't worry; there's no rush. He hasn't got back to me yet."

Jo glanced nervously at her aunt, who was leaning her bike against a bollard. "Aunt Ginny thinks we should avoid him like the plague."

"Yes; I do!" Ginny exclaimed. "I've already spoken to Jo, but I think you should be aware of what you could be getting into."

David cocked a thumb towards The Packet Boat Inn. "Avril and Wally have been saying pretty much the same thing. I appreciate your concern, but all we're doing is selling this place. It's not as if we intend going into business with him. It can't be worth a lot. As he said, it's hardly The Ritz."

"That's as maybe. But you'll be lucky to get half of what it is worth from Charlie McBride," Aunt Ginny snorted, as she followed Jo and David into the café.

"Good grief it feels colder in here than outside!" Jo exclaimed.

"The boiler's gone out. So there's no heating," David explained. "To tell the truth, I don't really know how to light it, but I'm loath to ask Sammy. He's hard enough to get rid of as it is. There doesn't seem much point, anyway."

Pulling off her woollen gloves, Aunt Ginny settled herself at a table and unzipped the fleece-lined jacket, revealing the intricate pattern of a tight, fairisle sweater that accentuated the sparseness of her figure.

Embarrassed at being caught staring, David exclaimed hurriedly, "I can't help admiring your jacket. It looks like a flying jacket."

"It is. It belonged to an American airman," she explained. "A lot of them were stationed at the aerodrome on the downs, during the war. They used to come into the Crown and Anchor near where I live, so I got to know some of them. Just young boys really … lonely and homesick. Ernest, my late husband, and I used to give them tea on Sunday afternoons, when they could get away. It was something different from the pub; somewhere they could relax, away from the stress and strain, and play their records on my gramophone. They called it a home from home. They used to bring us chocolate … candy they called it … and cigarettes; as well as little luxuries we couldn't get here.

She hesitated, as if savouring the memory. "Anyway, one Sunday, one of them forgot his jacket when he left … Roy, his name was. He was a nice little chap. He came from a place called Kearney, in Nebraska; I remember that. We'd celebrated his twenty-first birthday, the previous week."

The look in her eyes became distant and wistful, and her voice faded to almost a whisper. "He'd never been out of Nebraska before the war."

"And he didn't come back for his jacket?" David prompted.

"He never came back at all," she sighed. "An awful lot of them didn't."

Jo broke the ensuing silence. "Shall I make us a pot of tea?"

"Good idea," said David, grateful for her intervention.

"Anyway; about Charlie McBride!" Aunt Ginny exclaimed, as Jo made her way to the kitchen. "He never went short of anything in those days; rationed or not. It was no secret that he was well in with somebody at one of the American airbases. He knew people in London, as well. He could get you anything … at a price. Charlie did very well out of the war."

"I see," said David, although he felt it had little relevance to the sale of the café.

Reading his expression, Ginny asked pointedly, "Did you know that he tried to get your uncle to sell him this place?"

"No; I'm afraid I had very little to do with Uncle Ralph."

"Well, he did. Even when Ralph was terminally ill, he didn't stop hounding him. He probably thought Ralph wouldn't have the stamina to stand up to it. But your uncle was made of sterner stuff."

"Why wouldn't Uncle Ralph sell to him, if he knew he was dying?" David asked.

"Well; he couldn't stand Charlie, for one thing. He knew him before the war. I remember Ralph saying he knew why he wanted the café."

"Why was that?"

"He didn't say." Ginny hesitated, as if pondering the question. "Ralph only told you what he wanted you to know."

"Well, if Mister McBride wants it that badly, perhaps we have a bargaining point," David suggested.

"I would be very careful, if I were you," Aunt Ginny cautioned. "You don't realise what you're dealing with. You could get your fingers badly burned."

"So what do you suggest, we do?" Jo asked, placing a tray, laden with crockery, on the table beside her aunt.

"Sell this, by all means; if that's what you want. But not to Charlie McBride!"

"What; even if he makes a better offer than anyone else?" David asked incredulously.

Ginny rested her elbows on the table and looked at him intently; making sure she had his full attention. "Shall I tell you what happened to the Lawsons when they sold him their souvenir shop?"

Daunted by the intensity of her gaze, David hesitated. But Aunt Ginny neither expected nor waited for a reply.

"Sue and Phil Lawson are dear friends of mine. They'd had their shop, The Trinket Box, since before the first war. But about ten years ago they decided to retire and move near to their daughter and grandchildren. They did exactly as you suggested. Charlie McBride made them an offer that was below their asking price and they naturally refused it. When they received two better offers, Charlie increased his, so the Lawsons accepted and went ahead with buying a lovely bungalow."

"What's wrong with that?" David asked.

Ginny held up a hand. "Wait a minute; I'm coming to that. McBride's offer depended on a quick sale, and didn't include their stock, so they sold it off quickly … They got less than it was worth, of course … and that's when the problems started."

"Problems?" Jo queried.

"All of a sudden, Mister McBride wasn't in such a hurry to complete the purchase. He claimed he'd had a business survey done that left him with reservations about the Lawsons' valuation of the business. Not only that, but according to him, his surveyor was warning him about wet rot, as well as possible problems with the damp course and goodness knows what else."

Jo lifted the lid of the tea pot and began to stir. "So, what happened?"

"What do you think?" Ginny sighed. "Charlie was full of apologies, but surprise, surprise; he decided to withdraw his offer. However, he was willing to buy the business at the price he originally offered."

"Why didn't they go back to the other people who'd made offers?" David asked.

"One of them had already found another shop and the other had *somehow* got to hear that there were *problems with the premises.*"

"That's despicable!" Jo exclaimed

"Couldn't the Lawsons have told him to get lost and carry on looking for another buyer?" David asked.

Aunt Ginny smiled ruefully. "Think about it. They would only have got what they wanted if it was a going concern, which would have meant restocking the shop from scratch. They were desperate and in danger of losing the bungalow they had set their hearts on. I advised them to take legal advice, but they found that the conditions of McBride's offer allowed him to withdraw it in circumstances just like those he claimed."

"So what did they do?" David asked.

"What could they do? It would have taken time and money to take Charlie to court, with little chance of winning. So they took his offer and retired with a much smaller nest-egg than they'd hoped for."

"That's it!" Jo snapped, knocking over a cup, in her anger. "I'm having nothing to do with that devious swine!"

"Well, we know how he operates, so we could play him at his own game," David suggested flippantly.

The irate reaction of both women startled him.

"Forget it! Jo retorted.

"You're joking!" Aunt Ginny exclaimed. "He'd eat you alive! And I have no intention of allowing you to involve Jo in any shenanigans like that!"

"I *was* only joking!" David insisted, suspecting that ruffling Aunt Ginny's feathers might be as unwise as upsetting Horace.

Perched on the high stool, with his guitar across one raised knee, David shaped the chords and contentedly sang the late Buddy Holly's '*Everyday*', relishing the unseasonably mild evening breeze that wafted through the open doors of the café.

Crimson banners of evening cloud streamed across the horizon, and the rippling water in the harbour was laced by the elongated shadows of masts and rigging. Beyond the harbour wall, he could see the dark silhouettes of serrated rocks at the tip of the headland rising above the surface of the gentle swell like the snouts of mythical sea monsters.

As the last chord of the song faded away, he was startled by a sudden burst of clapping outside. A moment later, Hooky's head appeared around the doorframe. "Hey, Buddy! Ready for a pint?"

David grinned and laid his guitar on a table. "Give me a minute to lock up and I'll be right with you."

"You've got quite a little audience out 'ere," Hooky chuckled.

And he had. When David emerged from the café, he received another ripple of applause from people sitting at the wooden tables outside The Packet Boat Inn. Among them, he recognised Avril and Gemma, and smiled diffidently in response. A group of youths, perched on the railings overlooking the beach, raised a ragged cheer and he received an appreciative thumbs-up from a young couple who were returning from an evening stroll along the mole.

A lad with curly, ginger hair called, "When you openin' up agen, mate?"

"It depends on the new owner," David replied.

One of the youths was wearing a short, fitted jacket cut in the newly-fashionable Italian style. Running a comb through his Elvis quiff, he asked, "Who's that, then?"

David shrugged. "I don't know yet. I'm afraid the café is closed until whoever-it-is takes over."

"Just our luck," one of the girls exclaimed. "We thought this wuz gonna be somewhere wiv some decent music."

David noted that she would have been quite pretty, were it not for the pock marks disfiguring her cheeks. "You've had Loretta Dufray at the Wintergardens," he suggested mischievously, which evoked a chorus of, "You what!? ... Give over! ... You gotta be jokin'!"

"Isn't there a coffee bar or something around here?" he asked.

"Nah; there ain't nuffink!" Ginger snorted in disgust. "Everywhere's shut at this time a'year. An' if yuh takes a trannie radio in somewhere, like Lenny did, they make yuh turn it off!"

"Can't you ask if they'll switch their radio on?" David suggested.

"Wot; an' 'ave t'listen to Billy Cotton an' 'Enry 'All!?"

"He's right," Avril declared. "There's nothin' much for youngsters to do in Fairhaven, in the winter. There's not a lot more in summer, come to think of it. Only the funfair or The Cascade; and the machines in there go through your money in no time."

It was greeted by a growl of agreement from the youths and a murmur of accord from some of the people sitting at the tables.

David nodded in sympathy. "Charlie McBride owns The Cascade, doesn't he?"

Avril wrinkled her nose. "Need I say more?"

Gemma grasped his hand, which he found disconcerting. At first glance, she could be taken for a teenager. She was wearing a red and white checked shirt and light-blue slacks, and her honey-blonde hair was drawn back in a pony-tail. However, closer at hand, she was obviously past her teens and possibly in her thirties. "You're good, David!" she enthused. "It's nice to hear someone doing up-to-date songs, for a change."

"Thank you." David felt himself blush and eased his hand away. To mask his awkwardness, he said, "While I think of it; could I have a word with you, Avril … when you've got a minute?"

"Of course, luv. What's it about?"

"I'd rather it was in private, if you don't mind," he said hesitantly.

The plucked eyebrows of the woman sitting opposite Avril rose above her false eyelashes and heavy eye-shadow. "Looks like your luck's in, Avril," she quipped suggestively.

David felt his cheeks burn and he deliberately avoided eye-contact with the woman.

"Behave yourself, Betty!" Avril admonished, although the tremor in her voice betrayed her amusement. "Take no notice of her, luv!"

Betty leaned towards him and patted his arm. "Don't mind me, darlin'. I didn't mean to embarrass you."

David could only manage a feeble grin, distracted as he was by the amount of cleavage revealed by her low cut blouse and the realisation that she was well aware that it had not escaped his notice.

"I'm just going in for a pint with Hooky," he mumbled, edging away from the table.

"Celebratin' your pools win?" Avril suggested.

"You've won the pools?" Gemma exclaimed.

"Yes, but it's nothing too exciting," David declared. "We didn't manage eight draws, or anything like that. Hooky thinks it won't be much more than a couple of hundred quid ... and split between eight of us..."

"It's not bad, though. It's still a nice win," Betty insisted. "You didn't use the Infra-Draw Method, did you?"

It prompted her and Gemma to chant the jingle regularly heard on Radio Luxembourg: "Horace Bachelor's Famous Infra-Draw Method ... Department One ... Keynsham ... spelt K-E-Y-N-S-H-A-M ... Bristol!"

"Not as far as I know," David chuckled, enjoying their infectious giggling. "As Hooky says, if it's that good, why haven't Vernons and Littlewoods gone bust before now?"

"You obviously brought them luck," Avril suggested. "Wilf's been runnin' that syndicate for over four years, and they've never won a sausage before. And now they go and get a win the first week you join it!"

"Beginner's luck, I suppose." It sounded odd to hear Hooky referred to as Wilf. Avril was the only one he had heard call her brother by his proper name.

A lively discussion, or more correctly an argument, was in progress when David entered The Mess. Frankie Laine, the skipper of The Emerald Star fishing boat, appeared to be the only one who believed that Brian London would beat Floyd Patterson in the forthcoming contest for boxing's heavyweight championship of the world. Frankie's real name was Sam, but inevitably the Packet Boat regulars had dubbed him with the name of the country and western singer, Frankie Laine.

"Not a chance! Cooper beat 'im, so 'e won't beat Patterson!" snorted Tiny Blackman, who at six-feet-four and *'built like a brick karzy'*, as Wally once described him, looked capable of giving both boxers a run for their money.

"Brian's a tough lad ... and Patterson's not that big!" Frankie insisted.

"Big enough," Wally retorted. "What d'you reckon, David?"

"I'm not that well up on boxing," David confessed. "Where's the fight taking place?"

"Iss in India," Johnny Cline announced. He was about David's age, slightly built and, in Frankie's words, "A dependable deckhand ... but a bushel short of a full catch."

Johnny's crewmate, Bill Grainger, paused in the process of feeding a Rizla paper into his cigarette roller. "India?" he queried, his weathered features screwed into incredulity. "Why the 'ell are they 'avin' it there?"

"Dunno. Thass wot the bloke on the wireless said!" Johnny insisted.

"I think you'll find he said *Indiana*," Monty suggested dryly. "It's in the United States of America."

"Never 'eard of it!" Johnny retorted irritably; stung by the laughter all around him.

"In that case, I'd go for Floyd Patterson," David declared.

His prediction was met by a chorus of accord. The only dissent being Frankie's exclamation, "You dunno what you're talkin' about!"

Avril's arrival rescued David from a melee of raised voices and vociferous opinions, which drifted from boxing to the merits of the teams in the FA Cup and the bets they had placed on the next day's Grand National with Shifty Barnes, the local bookie's runner.

"Come on then, luv," she called. Leading the way behind the bar to the living quarters, she gestured towards the chairs around the kitchen table. "Now; what is it you want to talk about?"

David was pretty certain she knew, but taking a sip from his glass to moisten his palate, he began hesitantly. "Well; it's about me staying here. I've been looked after like royalty for the past week or so..." He stopped, as Wally's face appeared around the doorframe.

"What did you do with that change you got from the bank, Pet? We're runnin' short of silver in the till ... Sorry; am I interruptin' somethin'?"

Avril pointed to one of the kitchen cabinets. "It's in my bag, on there."

"Actually, what I want to say concerns you too," said David.

Wally folded his brawny arms, revealing the fishy tail of a mermaid tattoo below his folded cuff. "Fair enough; fire away."

"It's about my keep. I can't go on living like a lord and eating like there's no tomorrow, without having paid a penny for it..."

"So, 'ave we asked you to?" Wally interjected deliberately.

"No; but that's just the point! I can't go on sponging off you. Goodness knows what I'd have to pay in a bed and breakfast." David was aware that nervousness was making him gabble, but he was desperate to get it all out. "I've got some money ... and with our pools win..."

"*Spongin'!?* Don't talk such nonsense!" Avril's outburst startled him, but she continued more gently. "It's a pleasure, David. You've found yourself in a situation you weren't expectin' or ready for. I wouldn't want a son of mine left to fend for himself in somewhere like that cold, draughty place next door. We've all had times when we needed a helpin' hand."

"But, I feel I'm taking advantage…"

"Of course you're not! It's what friends are for … I hope you think of us as your friends."

David took a deep breath. "Of course! But, at least, let me give you my share of the pools win."

"You 'eard Avril," Wally said quietly. "We don't want your money, son. What's it comin' to, if we can't do each other a good turn now an' then, eh?"

"But…" David couldn't find the words to express his feelings.

"Tell you what, though." Wally's eyes twinkled and a broad smile appeared amongst the thicket of facial hair. "If it's botherin' you; you can always sing for your supper."

Avril and David looked at him with puzzled expressions.

"You can't 'alf play that guitar and you've got a good voice. So, if the fancy takes yuh, you can always do a turn or two in the bar."

David's face lit up with pleasure. "Yes! Of course; I'd be happy to!"

Avril clapped her hands in delight. "That's a smashin' idea, Hun!"

Wally winked at her affectionately. "I do get 'em, now and agen."

III

David took the manila envelope held out by a short, balding man in a gabardine mackintosh, and inspected it with suspicion. "What's this?"

"I believe it's a final notice to pay the non-domestic rate charged on these premises," he replied flatly.

"But we're closed! The place has been empty since the middle of last year."

"I'm afraid you'll have to take that up with the rating assessment officer. I'm only authorised to deliver this communication."

David tore open the envelope and read aloud: "Further to the unpaid assessment relating to … blah, blah … As a business currently registered with this authority, you are required … blah, blah … Have failed to reply to our previous communications … blah, blah, blah … Final notice is hereby given to pay the sum of … *What? You must be joking!*"

"What is it, David?" Jo called from the kitchen.

He thrust the notice towards her as she emerged from the passage. "It's a 'pay-up-or-else' from the council."

Jo's forehead creased with concentration as she read the document. "It says here that we haven't replied to their communications."

"I understand you have received previous reminders," the council official declared loftily.

"I haven't seen any; have you, David?"

He shrugged, "Not that I know of. I thought the solicitors took care of that sort of thing."

"Well, they obviously haven't," Jo asserted. "Come to think of it, we don't seem to have had any post. At least, I haven't seen any."

David's mouth suddenly felt dry. "Um … there's … ah … some in a cardboard box under the counter."

Jo disappeared below the counter top, only to reappear almost immediately. "My God! There's a heap in here … nearly all unopened!"

Replacing his trilby on his threadbare pate, the council official backed out of the café doorway. "I'll leave you to it, then. Good day to you."

"What are these doing in here?" Jo demanded. "Why haven't you opened them?"

"I'm allergic to brown envelopes," David replied; instantly regretting it, as he noticed the glint of anger in her eyes.

Ignoring his flippancy, she began sorting through the contents of the box. "A lot of these are bills! Electricity Board; Gas Board; Insurance; Chalgrove Commercial Waste Disposal … whoever they are; Fairhaven Harbour Services…"

"Harbour services? We haven't even got a boat!" David exclaimed.

Jo tore open the envelope. "Well, we appear to have a mooring permit for one; and we also have to contribute to the maintenance of the quayside and harbour facilities. If you'd taken the trouble to open this *and read it* you would know!"

"What facilities?" David bridled.

"How should I know? … Oh look; here they are; the rate demands we never received!"

"Sarcasm is the lowest form of wit," he mumbled defensively.

"And thinking you can ignore things by burying your head in the sand is nothing but stupidity!" she countered.

It occurred to him that he ought to add her to Aunt Ginny and Horace on his list of people to avoid upsetting. "Sorry."

"I should think so! There's a bulky one here from your uncle's solicitors."

"What does it say?"

"Let me see… They've sent us a reminder they received from Tralford Estates. The next quarter's rent is due on the twenty-fourth of March. Apparently they've paid the rent and what they call ancillary charges up until then from the assets of your late uncle's estate. They point out that the responsibility for settling on the designated quarter days now falls to us. They've sent a schedule of: *services rendered and disbursements incurred in administering the estate*; and an invoice for: *such expenses and disbursements which the realised assets of the estate are insufficient to satisfy*."

"How much?"

"Eight pounds, five-and-nine."

"No; I meant how much is the rent?"

"One hundred and forty-five pounds!"

"Jeez!" David whistled though his teeth. "The twenty-fourth? That's the day after tomorrow! … What does all the rest come to?"

"I don't know; I haven't added it up yet."

David paced the room while Jo listed the bills on the back of an envelope. "It looks like we're in it up to our necks! Thanks a lot Uncle Ralph!"

"Quiet! I'm trying to add up!"

"Sorry."

Jo looked up from her calculations, her brow furrowed with concern.

"How much?" he all but whispered.

"All told; I make it three hundred and thirty-six pounds, eleven-and-eight."

48

"My God! We haven't a hope of paying that!"

"There's the money your uncle left with Aunt Ginny."

"That's not even halfway there." David pulled his wallet from his back pocket. "Let's see; I've got four pounds ten and some loose change on me, plus ten quid in my coat, next door. By my reckoning that still leaves us a hundred-and-seventy-odd short."

"You'll need something to live on," Jo suggested. "What about your pools win?"

"Ah, yes … that."

"Don't tell me; you've already spent it, haven't you?"

"Afraid so. I bought a guitar and amplifier. I got it from that second-hand shop in Gladstone Road … It was a real bargain."

"But you've already got a guitar!"

"Yes, but this one's got electric pick-ups. I'll need amplification if I play in the pub."

"I see," she sighed, unable to hide her frustration.

"Well, I didn't know about all these bills, did I?"

"You wouldn't would you? They've just been chucked in this box, unopened!" She heaved a sigh of resignation. "I've got a savings account at the Midland. It's nowhere near what we need, but…"

"No, Jo; you can't! You're not doing that! This is my fault." Gesturing towards the bills on the counter, he added, "You're right; I was stupid to ignore them."

"It makes no difference. We still wouldn't be able to pay them."

"I know. But the thoughtless old twit who dropped this mess on us was *my* uncle. I know how hard you have to work for your wages. I'm not letting you suffer for something that's none of your doing." He paused for a moment. "I'll just have to take the guitar and amp back to the shop, but I won't get what I paid for them. I'm sure my brother would lend me the rest, but I've no intention of bothering him in his present state of health. I'll just have to eat humble pie and ask my dad to bail me out, and hope my share of Charlie McBride's offer is enough to pay him back."

"David; don't be silly!" Jo declared. "This is no more your fault than mine. How can you play in the pub without this other guitar?"

"I can't. I'll have to move out of there, as well. But I'm determined to give Avril and Wally something for my keep."

"Where will you go?"

"Home to my parents, I suppose; once we've got shot of this place. I can't see any alternative to that … and winding up in a dead-end job."

"There is another option."

They both turned their heads sharply in response to the familiar voice.

"Aunt Ginny!" Jo exclaimed. "What are you doing here?"

In contrast to her previous visit, she was dressed more conventionally in a tweed winter coat worn over a navy blue dress. A tartan beret crowned her unruly grey mane.

"I wanted another word with you both, before you do anything silly; like allowing yourselves to be cheated by Charlie McBride."

"Do you think there is another option?" David asked hopefully.

Aunt Ginny hoisted herself gingerly onto the high stool and, satisfied that it was not about to collapse under her, put her handbag on the counter. "Yes, I do. You could run this place … for the summer, anyway."

"What!?" they exclaimed simultaneously.

"We don't know anything about running a café!" Jo asserted. "And I've already got a job! How am I supposed to cope with another one?"

"I was thinking more of David."

"Me?"

"Yes." Ginny's penetrating gaze was becoming uncomfortably familiar. "I heard what you and Jo were saying … By the way, you ought to close those doors if you want to talk privately … You said yourself; you've got nothing else planned, other than living with your parents and taking a dead-end job."

"Like Jo said, neither of us knows anything about running a café," David protested.

"I'm sure you could learn, if you put your minds to it. You're going to have to pay the rent and rates and what-have-you for the time being, anyway. Jo can't be expected to work here and at the hospital, of course. But she's perfectly capable of taking care of the finances. I know the manager of Flemmings Tea Rooms, on the corner of Station Road in Myrtlesham. I've had a word with him; and his advice is that you should identify your core clientele, decide on a simple menu and then work out how to cater for it. After that, it's all about hard work and trial and error. He's offered to have a chat with you and give you a few tips."

"That's very good of him ... and you," David replied. "But, to be honest, I really don't fancy sloshing gallons of tea about and doling out wads of sandwiches."

"Of course not!" Jo retorted acidly. "You're resting ... and you have so many other options, haven't you?"

Unsettled by her sarcasm, he shrugged, but recovered his equilibrium as a thought came to him. "Anyway; it won't get us off the hook. In fact, we could be worse off! Getting this place up and running will take time and even more money on top of all the bills we're being chased for."

"Alright; let's talk about finance," Ginny said firmly. "Have either of you read the terms of the lease you have on this place?"

Jo looked bemused.

David shook his head. "Good Lord, no. All I did was sign the bumph the solicitors sent me and send it back like they told me to."

Jo nodded. "That goes for me, too."

Aunt Ginny smiled knowingly. "That's what I thought. There's a copy of the lease in the papers Ralph left with me. It makes very interesting reading."

"If you say so," David muttered doubtfully.

"I do ... and it does. Your uncle managed to negotiate a very unusual lease with surprisingly favourable terms, which is why

I'm suggesting you hang onto this place for a while. It might turn out to be well worth it."

"In what way?" Jo asked.

"Well, for a start: if your landlords want you to surrender the lease, they have to compensate you according to an agreed scale, which diminishes as the lease runs out."

"Are they likely to?" David queried hopefully.

"They might, if someone wanted to redevelop this site. There was talk of it around this time last year, although I've heard no more about it since. Charlie McBride seemed to be involved, which might be why he wanted your uncle to sell him the business."

"Does he know about the lease?" Jo asked.

"I shouldn't think he knows all the details. Ralph kept his private business very much to himself. But Charlie's no fool. He probably realises there would be something on offer as an incentive to surrender it. Being involved in the redevelopment as well, he would stand to benefit both ways, wouldn't he?"

Jo nodded in response. "How generous is the compensation?"

"The lease expires in September nineteen-eighty, so it's still got over twenty years to run. If you were asked to surrender it now, I think you'd be due about three thousand pounds, plus compensation for your legal fees and costs of relocation."

"Crikey! Where do we sign?" David quipped.

Ginny smiled indulgently. "That's not all. You have an option to buy the freehold of the premises at any time after the first five years of the lease have expired, at the original valuation plus the average inflation rate up to the date you purchase. The first five years will have expired in September, next year."

"How did Ralph get the landlord to agree to all that?" David asked.

Ginny hesitated, as if uncertain how to answer. "Only he could tell us that," she said guardedly. "And it's too late to ask him now, isn't it?"

"That's very nice, but it's all a bit academic," Jo observed. "We can't even pay the bills on this place, let alone buy it."

"All I'm suggesting is: it's worth hanging on and building the business back up again. Don't rely on getting a quick offer from Charlie McBride. He knows you're anxious to sell, so if he thinks you're desperate, he'll make you sweat. And even if nothing comes of what I've just said, you'll have a better chance of getting a decent offer if the business is a going concern."

Ginny, opened her bag and took out a bulging envelope. "And as for your pressing debts; I assumed there would be bills to pay. There should be enough in there to pay this quarter's rent and those other bills."

"No, Aunt. We can't take it!" Jo exclaimed.

"Jo's right," David concurred. "It's really kind of you, but…"

"Don't talk such nonsense; both of you. I've redeemed an old insurance policy with Home and Empire Mutual. I've had it for years. God knows why! Ernest, my late husband, talked me into it. It's no good to me; it wouldn't have paid out until I was dead. You'd have got it then, anyway, Jo. So you might as well have the benefit of it now, when you need it."

Jo's eyes welled with tears. "Oh, Aunt Ginny! I don't know what to say!"

"That goes for me too," said David. "Thank you. I'll pay you back, as soon as…"

"You'll do no such thing!" Ginny insisted. "All I ask is that you do me the favour of considering what I've suggested. You ought to be able to do well enough out of this place to at least make it pay its way."

Jo kissed her aunt's cheek. "Thank you. We will, won't we, David? … *David!*"

"OK; I'll think about it."

'What a difference a little sunshine makes,' David thought, as he strolled through the Wintergardens towards the sea front. Fairhaven was waking from its winter hibernation. Men were painting railings, trimming the grass and hedges and tending the ornamental flowerbeds. On either side of the ornate entrance to the Wintergardens Palace Theatre, bright new posters announced the coming season's attractions.

He recognised the smiling face of Jenny O'Dell; a pretty Irish girl once proclaimed as *the next Ruby Murray*. A year or two ago, her plaintive ballad, 'Don't Leave Me 'Til Tomorrow', had made it into the Hit Parade, although her later releases hadn't fared as well.

'Still; she's an improvement on Loretta Dufray,' he thought. It was a pity that the same couldn't be said for Eddie Gilbert, whose banal patter was, in David's opinion, as stale and tedious as Stan Slattery's. However, at the foot of the poster, the beaming smiles of the Mervin Devine Dancers radiated youthful exuberance and enthusiasm. He had never heard of Danny and The Drumbeats, but whoever they were, their inclusion was a welcome nod towards the changing face of popular music.

Reaching the Esplanade, he crossed the road to the promenade, where the Punch and Judy booth had already been erected. Heavy, winter shutters were being taken down from the kiosks and stalls overlooking the beach and, at the far end of the bay, the covers were off the fairground rides, revealing them in all their garish splendour. Even the sea seemed revitalised by the promise of summer. Sparkling in the sunlight, its blue-green rollers swept across the bay to tumble onto the shore in a flurry of foam and spray.

Hooky was removing the padlock from the doors of a large wooden shed that stood at the end of a row of beach huts. His shouted reply to David's wave was lost amid the screech of swooping gulls and the sibilant roar of the sea, as he swung open the doors to reveal stacks of deckchairs and windbreaks, carefully stored 'neat and navy fashion'.

The end of March seemed too early for Easter, but if the good weather held, Hooky would be busy, from Good Friday onward, issuing Fairhaven Town Council's green and white striped deckchairs and windbreaks in exchange for three bobs and one-and-a-tanners from holidaymakers eager for a first taste of the sea and the sun. The thought reminded David of a blustery day at Weymouth, just before the war, and Grandpa's increasing frustration as he had struggled to set up a deckchair for Grandma. It was a bitter-sweet reminder of the carefree days of his childhood.

What had happened to the dreams he had cherished as a boy? He was going to be a test pilot, like Neville Duke, and fly the new jets; he had pictured himself partnering Denis Compton to win The Ashes for England; and as a spaceman flying a rocket to the moon. Now; here he was; twenty-four years old and about to become a glorified waiter!

His fortunes had sunk to the point where even a legacy was a millstone round his neck. Waiting hand-and-foot on a hoard of holidaymakers was the last thing he wanted to do. But having accepted Ginny's help, he had no choice but to make an attempt at running the café. He had no idea how he was going to cope and dreaded the dire consequences of making a hash of it.

However, there was some consolation; he would be spending the summer by the sea. Fairhaven was quite pleasant, really … and there was Jo. He couldn't deny that those beguiling brown eyes had influenced his decision to stay; even though he had already learned that they could blaze with anger, and that Josephine Mary Lampeter was not inclined to suffer fools gladly.

A month ago, he would never have believed that he would even consider running a café; opening a joint bank account with someone he had known for less than three weeks; agreeing, or more precisely being instructed, to paint the place; and winding up with a daunting list of things that needed to be done before it opened.

He had left the keys to the café at the pub, but found its doors locked when he arrived back at the harbour. He was about to rap on a glass pane to attract attention, when they were opened by Molly, the cleaner. As usual, a colourful headscarf covered her hair like a turban. He had never seen her without it or her wrap-around pinnie. 'Does she sleep in them?' he wondered mischievously.

"Are you off then, Molly?"

"Yeh; I'm done fer today. See yuh tomorra," she replied, hitching the handles of her bag up her arm.

Avril had gone into town and he could hear Wally moving things around in the cellar, as he went in. His keys were not in the drawer of his bedside cabinet, where he usually kept them, so he searched his bedroom thoroughly; turning out all his pockets, but to no avail. He was on the brink of panic, when he suddenly remembered leaving them on a worktop in the kitchen.

Emerging from the pub, he was surprised to see Jo straddling her bike and talking to Sammy, who was sitting on one of the wooden benches. "I thought you said you were going home after we left the bank."

Jo took his wallet from the basket on her handlebars. "You left this on the bank manager's desk."

"Oh, thanks. That's very honest and public spirited of you, miss," he said, unlocking the café doors. "You could have run off with my entire fortune."

"So I could," she giggled. "I could have gone somewhere far away and exotic."

"That's right. Who knows; you could have made it halfway to Margate!"

He was rewarded with a delightful little giggle.

Something was obviously troubling Sammy. His usual jauntiness was missing.

"Are you alright, Sammy?" David asked.

"Yeh; be alright. Got no work, thass all." Sammy gestured towards the cobbled lane. "Nothin' for me no more at the boatyard. Got a new bloke now."

"What did you do for them?" Jo enquired.

"This-an-that. Bit a'sweepin' an' tidyin' up. Said it's too dangerous for me now."

"It couldn't be more dangerous than lighting that boiler!" David quipped.

Sammy grinned ruefully. "Fell over a coupla times. Lot o'rope an' wood layin' about, see?"

"I can imagine," said David. "The boiler's out again. You don't fancy having another go at lighting it, do you?"

"Yeh; course." Sammy rose to his feet and shuffled into the café.

David was about to follow him, but Jo put her hand on his arm. "Have you noticed? He's not right."

"He seems a bit down," David suggested. "But I suppose that's understandable; losing his job at the boatyard, like that."

"It's more than that," Jo asserted. "His eyes aren't right … They're not clear. His stomach was rumbling like thunder while he was talking to me."

"I expect he's hungry."

Jo's forehead creased with concern. "I'm certain of it. I think he's half starved. I wonder if he's got any money."

"Really? Surely he would've got paid-off by the boatyard."

"Don't bet on it. They probably only paid him by the hour."

"I'd better get some food into him, then," David proposed. "What do you think would be best?"

"Nothing too heavy. And don't let him bolt it down." Jo paused, as a thought came to her. "I'll tell you what; why don't I cycle up to the Co-op and get something for us all for lunch … I take it that cooker works."

"We'll soon find out," said David. "Let me give you some money."

"There's no need. I've got a bit left over from Aunt Ginny's insurance money."

"Hello you two!" Avril called. Smartly dressed, as always, in a red winter coat, kid gloves and 'in full warpaint', as Wally would say, she came along the quay towards them, with not a strand of her lacquered blonde hair out of place. "So, how are you gettin' on?" she asked.

Jo held up her crossed fingers. "So far, so good. But it's early days yet."

"It's excitin', isn't it?" Avril enthused. "It'll be lovely havin' the café open again."

"Frightening is how I'd describe it," Jo replied, hoisting herself onto the saddle. "Back in a jiffy," she called, as she pedalled away.

David watched her until she disappeared around the corner of the pub, his cheeks flushing as he noticed Avril's knowing smile.

"Well, I'd better get behind the bar, ready for openin' time," she sighed. "Wilf's not doin' the lunchtime sessions now he's back on the council deck chairs."

"I'll come in with you," said David. "I need a packet of Weights or Craven A for Sammy. I don't think it matters which … and a bottle of stout."

* * *

Sammy leaned back in his chair and belched contentedly. All that remained on his plate was the ash he had flicked from his cigarette. "That 'it the spot!" he declared, revealing his unsightly fangs with a broad smile.

Draining the dregs from the Mackeson bottle into his glass, he studied the label wistfully before replacing it on the table. "S'posed t'be good for yuh," he mused. "Rather 'ave a pint o'mild an' bitter, but if you reckon it's doin' me good."

58

David bit back a remark about a little gratitude being appropriate. "They say stout is good for building you up."

"That's right, Sammy," Jo concurred. "You must make sure you eat properly." Collecting up the dirty plates, she made her way to the kitchen.

"Little cracker you got there!" Sammy declared. "Cooks as good as she looks. Fell on yer feet gettin' that one as part o'the deal."

"She's not part of *any* deal!" David insisted. "We're business partners; that's all."

"If you say so," Sammy muttered. Taking another cigarette from the open packet on the table, he lit it and drew on it slowly. "That right you're openin' up agen?"

"Possibly," David replied guardedly.

But Jo, returning from the kitchen, interjected with, "Yes; we are. As soon as we can get this place in a fit state."

"Gonna want some 'elp then," Sammy proposed hopefully.

"Yes; we will," Jo replied, forestalling the anticipated denial from David. "My shifts at the hospital won't give me time to do much; and David can't do… Well, he won't be able to do it all on his own, will you, David?"

She returned David's glare with a mischievous, but no less challenging, gleam in her eyes. But, acknowledging her motive and implied mistrust of his capabilities, he grinned ruefully. "I suppose not."

"We'll need to get the place looking bright and cheerful before we start serving customers," she asserted. "Do you think you could manage to help with the painting, Sammy? We'll pay you, of course."

Sammy's face lit up with his ragged smile. "Yeh; can do that! Can get yuh some paint, if yuh like … dead cheap!"

"That would be marvellous!" Jo exclaimed.

"As long it hasn't fallen off the back of a lorry," David cautioned.

Sammy shook his head. "Don't think so. Bloke what's got it does paintin' and decoratin' fer a livin'."

"We'll need to do something about these tables," Jo insisted. "Look at them! They're dreadful; all stained and ingrained with heaven-knows-what! They need rubbing down and varnishing!"

"Can't we just put tablecloths on them?" David suggested.

"No; they're unhygienic! And look at the legs; they're all scratched and scuffed. We'll need to paint the outside of the place, too. People won't come in if it looks scruffy and neglected."

"I don't suppose you know where you can lay your hands on a whip, do you, Sammy?" David asked.

Sammy looked perplexed. "Whaddya want that for?"

"For the boss-lady to crack!" Ducking to avoid the tea towel flicked at his head, David gazed around the café pensively. "I suppose it's time I moved in here. Apart from the fact that I can't expect Wally and Avril to go on feeding and housing me indefinitely, it makes sense if I'm going to be working here all the time. I'm told the insurance costs more if it's unoccupied, as well."

"That's a good idea. But you'll need some furniture if you do," Jo insisted. "That rickety old bed upstairs doesn't look safe and there's no mattress."

David sighed deeply. "That'll cost a fair bit."

"Yes, it might," Jo replied. "You'll need a chest of drawers and a wardrobe, as well."

David shook his head. "We can't afford to spend money on things like that. I'll have to make do."

"See Polish Stan," Sammy suggested.

"Polish Stan?"

"Yeh; down the end!" Sammy gestured along the quay. "Got furniture an' all sorts o'stuff in there."

"What; the place that's closed up?"

"Yeh. Don' open much in winter. There now though; saw 'im s'mornin'. Gets stuff they don't want from big 'otels and posh 'ouses, and that. Sells it to the boardin' 'ouses and bed and breakfasts. Gawd knows where 'e finds it all, but a lorry-load turns up now an' agen for 'im."

"That's not a bad idea," said Jo. "Why don't you go and see what he's got, David."

"Right; I'll go and have a look."

Sammy chuckled. "A job to understand 'im, though. Polish see? Come over after the war. Don't mix a lot. Lives on 'is own. Do yuh a good deal, I reckon."

"Anyone fancy a cup of tea?" Jo asked.

"Yes please," said David.

"Sammy stretched and scratched his stomach. "Yeh; be nice that. Three sugars." Flicking the ash from his cigarette, he watched Jo disappear along the corridor. "Wanna get yer feet under the table there, afore somebody beats yuh to it."

* * *

David returned from a foray into town for sandpaper, paintbrushes and turpentine just as Jo's attractive rear was appearing, as she backed out from the cupboard under the stairs. Her blue dungarees and tattered straw hat, smeared with dust and strands of cobweb, reminded him of illustrations in a Mark Twain novel. Looking cute enough to make his heart skip a beat, she gave him a coy smile as she dropped a stack of cardboard onto the heap of rubbish in the passageway.

"I like your hat. Where did you get it?" he chuckled.

"Hanging up in there. It stops the cobwebs getting in my hair." Peeling off what looked like a pair of gardening gloves, she switched off Workers Playtime, as a gale of laughter and applause greeted Ken Platt's doleful greeting: "I won't take me coat off. I'm not stoppin'."

David pointed to the pile of flattened cardboard boxes on the rubbish heap. "I've never noticed those before. Where did you find them?"

"In that other cupboard."

"What other cupboard?"

"There's another one under the stairs. There's a door to it in this one. Come and see." She took his hand as he gingerly stepped over partly unravelled roles of lino and moth-eaten carpet. "There you are!"

Squatting on his haunches, David peered through the low doorway set in the wall of the passageway cupboard. "Well I'm blowed! I had no idea that was there! It seems to go back quite a way … and it's got lights."

"Yes; look." Jo crouched beside him and reached under a low shelf. "There's a switch under here." The glow from two naked light bulbs was extinguished as she flipped it. "That's how I found it. I must have knocked the switch when I was pulling that old carpet out. I could see light round the edge of the door. It took me a while to find the catch to open it, though. It's right down there, nearly on the floor. All those empty cardboard boxes were in there."

David switched the lights on again and pushed his head and shoulders through the doorway. "There's room to stand up when you get right in here. It goes all the way back under the staircase and partly behind this cupboard. I can see some lobster pots, but there doesn't appear to be anything else, except dust and cobwebs."

"The lobster pots might be useful to some of the fishermen," Jo suggested.

"They might. We've got no use for them." Pulling his head back from the low doorway, David pointed to the heap of rubbish in the passage. "I presume all that's just junk."

"Yes, it is. I found a broom and a dustpan and brush that'll come in handy, but the cleaning stuff is no good any more. I've already put a lot out in the yard with the other rubbish, ready for the commercial waste people to take away when they come on Thursday."

"I wonder what was in all those cartons," David mused, when they had re-emerged from the cupboard.

"I think it was cigarettes," Jo explained. "I could smell tobacco when I pulled them out. The writing on most of them is in French, I think."

David lifted one of the flattened boxes. "That's French alright. Gitanes are French cigarettes. Look at that one … Montecristo … they're cigars!"

Jo pursed her lips pensively. "I didn't think your uncle sold cigarettes. I never saw any when I came here with Aunt Ginny."

David's brow furrowed in contemplation. "If that's the case, he must have smoked himself to death. There must have been hundreds of cartons of cigarettes and cigars in those boxes!" He looked into the cupboard again before gazing back at Jo. "Are you thinking what I'm thinking?"

Jo's eyes widened as the penny dropped. "Oh, good grief! You mean?"

David nodded affirmatively. "That's right. It all adds up. A hoard of foreign cigarettes and cigars in a hidey-hole … with a hidden light switch and door catch. I think my dear departed uncle was dealing in contraband tobacco!"

"Oh, David!" Jo gasped. "What are we going to do?"

"I suggest we shut the door on that cubbyhole and keep it and our mouths shut!"

"What about the lobster pots?"

"Leave them where they are!"

Jo peered anxiously into the cupboard. "Do you think anybody else knows about it?"

"I'm sure Sammy doesn't," David mused. "He'd have said something; and Wally would have warned us, if he knew."

Jo put a forefinger to her lips. "I can think of somebody who might know."

"Who?"

"Charlie McBride."

David stared at her intently. "My God, you're right! He mentioned he'd done some business with my uncle. That could be why he wants to get his hands on this place!"

Voices accompanying David faded; only to erupt in a burst of cheering and clapping, as he damped the guitar strings with his palm to bring *Hang Down Your Head Tom Dooley* to a close.

The apprehension he had felt during the short walk from the café to The Packet Boat Inn had long since been dispelled by his enthusiastic reception and the euphoria of applause. The youths at the outside tables had joined the crowd thronging The Mess and the 'overflow' in the Wardroom in singing the popular numbers they knew; or thought they did. The perspiring faces of Wally and Hooky bore testimony to their effort to keep so many vocal cords lubricated, although Avril still seemed cool and unruffled.

"We're goin' to need Linda to help out, next week!" Avril shouted.

Wally pushed a glass under an optic and bellowed, "Too right, Pet!"

"Ready for a break?" Hooky called and placed a foaming pint on the counter beside David, who was perched on a stool in the alcove at the end of the bar. He laughed, gesturing at the crowd. "This is all your ruddy fault, Davy boy! We're rushed off our feet!"

"Blame yourself, for putting those posters up!" David yelled back.

"Where's yer girlfriend?" Hooky called.

David was about to rise to the bait, but replied, "Jo's working."

Lifting his pint, he was distracted by a shout from a woman sitting nearby. "'Ere; d'you know that one … aw, wass it called?"

She turned to her companions, who were squeezed together around a table that was almost completely covered with bottles and glasses. "You know the one I mean!"

They obviously didn't, because they looked at her with blank expressions.

"You know … The one that bloke sings!"

"What bloke?" several asked at once.

The woman flapped her hands in frustration. "That bloke. You know … 'E wuz on the telly."

"D'you mean Tommy Steele?" the girl beside her suggested.

Hoping to jog her memory, David sang the opening lines of 'Singing The Blues'.

"No; not 'im!" the woman snapped. "You know. 'E's bin on telly … in that show. Aw, wass 'is name?"

"Perhaps if you sing it?" David suggested.

A chap in a flat cap guffawed loudly. "Gawd blimey, mate! You aint 'eard 'er sing! She'd clear the place quicker'n a fire alarm!"

Everyone around the table responded with a burst of laughter, including the woman herself.

"You're not thinking of Elvis, are you?" David prompted. But she appeared to have already lost interest, because she started a rambling discourse on Sunday Night at The London Palladium.

It seemed no time before Wally called, "Last orders!" and, taking it as his cue, David announced, "Last one, ladies and gentlemen." The groan of disappointment was gratifying, as he launched into the Everly Brothers' 'Bird Dog'.

The final chords were drowned by shouts, whistles and applause, augmented by banging on table tops.

"Time ladies and gentlemen, please!" Wally bellowed, ringing the ship's bell. "Come along folks; drink up. He'll be back next week. Same time; same place!"

Responding gratefully to compliments and thanks as the crowd slowly dispersed, David replaced his guitar in its case and blew out his cheeks. A sheen of perspiration covered his forehead and his clammy shirt clung to his shoulders. "That went a lot better than I feared," he said, half to himself.

"You're a star, my love!" Avril exclaimed. "You were terrific!"

Despite her non-stop evening behind the bar, she looked as well-groomed as when she had started; with not a hair or a false eyelash out of place.

"I'm surprised at how many were here," David remarked. "I thought Hooky's posters might bring a few in, but…"

"Some of 'em were from the caravan park," Wally explained. "Seein' it's Easter."

"Pity Jo couldn't be here," Avril sighed.

Hooky thumped a pint mug on the counter. It was more than half filled with silver and copper, as well as a couple of ten-shilling notes.

"What's that?" David asked.

"Yer fans 'ad a whip round for yuh."

David pushed it back towards him. "That belongs to Avril."

"It does not!" she retorted. "You earned that."

"We agreed that I'd do this to repay you," David insisted.

"You 'ave!" Wally declared. "I can't remember a night like this, out o'season. Avril's right; you earned it fair an' square. Put it in yer pocket, son."

"Do you still want me to do it again next week?" David asked.

Wally's laugh rumbled in his broad chest. "Too right! We might get lynched if we don't. As long as you're 'appy with it!"

David nodded. "Of course. I enjoyed it."

"Do that one by that bloke! … Wass 'is name? … On the telly!" Hooky squawked, leaving Wally and Avril bemused, as he and David burst into laughter.

Jo pointed at the plywood figure glaring at her from the counter top. "What's that?"

"It's a penguin," David grunted, struggling to hold up his end of a chest of drawers.

"I can see that. But what's it doing here?"

"I found it in Stan's shop. I thought we could chalk a menu on it … or something."

"Mind back, lady! Where you want?" Polish Stan asked, as he and David manoeuvred the bulky piece of furniture into the café.

"It needs to go upstairs," David gasped. "But can we put it down for a minute?"

"You two will never manage to get that upstairs!" Jo declared.

"Need turn up, arse-end," Stan suggested, pointing at the narrow staircase.

Jo held up a hand. "Wait a minute; I'll go next door and see if I can get some help."

Stan sat on a table while they waited and surveyed the café with evident curiosity.

"May I ask what your real name is, Stan?" David asked tentatively.

Stan looked at him for a moment, as if his thoughts were elsewhere. "I Stanislaw," he said quietly. "Stanislaw Mierzejewski." He laughed soundlessly. "English not say. Now I Polish Stan."

"Do you mind?"

"No; why mind? No matter."

When David had ventured along the quay earlier in the day, the metal shutter of Stan's establishment had been rolled up, but the doors were locked. Peering through the dusty window, he had made out the glow of a light, somewhere in the gloomy interior, and rapped on the doors two or three times before a voice had demanded, "Who make blastiks noise?"

"My name is David Sheldon," David had called back. "I've been told you may be able to help me. I'm moving into The Seagull Café and I need some furniture."

A few moments later, one of the doors had been opened by a man wearing baggy, corduroy trousers and a grey, woollen cardigan over a collarless shirt. He was well over six feet tall and slim. Tightly-curled, reddish-grey hair hung over ears which were conspicuously long. David would have assumed him to be in his late forties, had he not learned from Monty that Stan had been barely out of his teens when he had arrived from Poland, soon after the war.

Piercing blue eyes, above an aquiline nose, had regarded David with undisguised curiosity. "Come," he had said, beckoning him in.

David had been amazed to find the interior of Stan's 'emporium' crammed full of furniture, household equipment and curios of all description. Much of it of obvious quality, although mostly of styles no longer fashionable.

Stan had gestured around his poorly-lit premises. "See ... all things. Look; maybe you want. I make good price."

He had left David to browse and retired to a small, glass-panelled cubicle at the rear. Mooching amongst Stan's eclectic accumulation of furniture and bric-a-brac, David had come across an old-fashioned wind-up gramophone, complete with a large ceramic horn. It seemed to be in working order and even had a small compartment containing a tin of unused 'Songster' needles and a velvet record buffer. Beside it had been a pile of dusty 'seventy-eights', many bearing the labels of obscure recording companies.

'What would Jo say if I came back with this?' he had thought. Pretty certain he could make an accurate guess, he had reluctantly allowed his head to overrule his heart and resisted the temptation to ask Stan how much he wanted for it.

It had been while he was exploring a narrow space between two lines of wardrobes that he had been startled by a face glaring at him from beneath what had looked like wildly dishevelled hair. When his heart had stopped racing, he had made it out to be a wooden blackboard in the shape of a penguin, which stood on its own base on top of a bureau. Laughing quietly to himself, he had made his way to Stan's 'office'.

The cubicle had contained a metal filing cabinet, a table littered with papers and a banker's chair; its leather seat sagging with age. A kettle had been steaming on a single gas ring that stood on a tin tray on top of the filing cabinet.

Stan had been pouring a measure from a bottle of Camp Coffee into an enamel mug when David approached. "You find?" he had asked, topping up the mug from the kettle.

David had led him to a chest of drawers, a book case, a single wardrobe and a bed; all of which were recognizably of good quality. "How much for those?" he had asked tentatively.

Stan had stroked his unshaven chin for a moment and tapped the wardrobe. "Good … last long time."

David had nodded his agreement, waiting for him to deliberate.

"You take Ralph place; yah?"

"Yes," David had replied. "He was my great uncle."

"Ah!" was all that was forthcoming for a few moments. "Yah," Stan had said eventually. "I say eight quids … you like?"

"Is that for the wardrobe, the bed … or what?" David had asked.

Stan had looked at him puzzled. "No; I say for all things!"

David had been taken aback. "What; *all* of it?"

"Yah; I sink price blastiks good; no?"

"It's a very good price!" David had exclaimed.

"Ach; good for me, good for you. Come; I make paper."

Stan had rummaged about on the table that served as his desk before muttering something unintelligible and disappearing through a doorway behind the cubicle. Left to his own devices, David had inspected the old notices and newspaper cuttings pinned to a wall; some in what he took to be Polish. Two framed photographs, both faded and grainy, had caught his attention.

One had been of a couple who looked to be about Stan's age. The man's features had resembled Stan's and, from their dress, David had assumed the photograph to have been taken well before the war. The other one had been of a smiling group; apparently at a wedding.

Fascinated by the photographs, David had been unaware of Stan's return, and had looked up to find him standing at the entrance to the cubicle, watching him. "Sorry, I didn't mean to pry," he had said contritely. "Is this your family?"

Stan had simply nodded. Seating himself at the table, he had begun to laboriously prepare a simple bill of sale in immaculate copperplate script.

Unsettled by a silence broken only by the scratch of Stan's pen-nib, David had asked tentatively, "Is your family still in Poland?"

Stan had stopped writing and looked up at him impassively. "No family ... No more," was all he had said.

However, it had been enough for David to understand that he should enquire no further. To change the mood, he had asked, "How much do you want for the penguin?"

David was stirred from his thoughts by the cry, "The navy's 'ere!" bellowed from the café doorway. Wally was accompanied by Bunny Warren, another of the Packet Boat's ex-navy regulars.

"We could do with some help moving this and a few other bits of furniture from Stan's place and getting it upstairs," David explained.

"Right you are," Wally replied. "Bunny; get on the other end. Stan; you stand by, ready to 'elp turn it on end. Right; lift ... Gordon Bennett, Stan! What's in 'ere, bricks?"

"No brick; iz wood ... blastiks good!" Stan reposted, patting the top of the chest.

"Why don't you take the drawers out first?" Jo suggested. "It'll be lighter and easier to carry."

Wally grinned at David. "Now, why didn't we think o'that?"

"Because you're men!" Avril exclaimed from the doorway. "It takes a woman to do the thinkin'."

"Can't argue with that," Wally chuckled.

"Where do you want me?" David asked.

"You bring the drawers when we've got this upstairs. Right lads … up she goes."

"Whatever are you goin' to do with that penguin?" Avril asked.

David grinned impishly. "Stan gave it to me. I'm thinking of training it to be a waiter."

"It's a Rockhopper," said Gemma, as she appeared beside Avril. "They're recognisable by those head feathers."

David was beginning to wonder if he should sell tickets. "He reminds me of a mad sax player I used to know," he said.

The bumps and muted cursing coming from the staircase, suggested that Wally and his crew had manoeuvred the chest of drawers as far as the landing.

"You'd better go up and show them where you want it," Jo suggested. "I take it you've bought a bed?"

"Yes. I've ordered a brand new mattress too; from Turners in the High Street. They're delivering it tomorrow."

Later, after more sweating, grunting and cursing, David's furniture was in place in his bedroom, and he and his removal men were seated with Jo, Avril and Gemma around one of the tables in the café, enjoying a well-earned cup of tea.

"We're goin' to miss you," Avril declared wistfully.

"Thanks Avril. But I'll only be next door. You're not getting rid of me completely."

She patted his hand. "Just remember; you're welcome to come round for a bite to eat whenever you like."

"And don't forget Avril's fortieth birthday do, next Friday," said Wally.

"Go on! Tell the whole world my age!" Avril protested archly.

Wally responded with a chuckle. "We're closin' for the evenin' … Invited guests only. That includes you lot … You too, Stan."

Stan shook his head. "No good, party. I look; they look. I smile; they smile. Make talk; no understand … No more talk."

"You know us Stan," Avril insisted. "It's only goin' to be a drink and a get-together with a few friends. You'll enjoy it."

Stan pursed his lips. "I sink. Maybe yes; maybe no."

They all looked up at the ceiling in response to a creak above their heads. "Blimey! The place is haunted!" Bunny quipped.

Jo rose from her chair. "I'll go up and see what it is."

"It's probably the wardrobe door," Wally suggested. "The catch needs tightenin'. I noticed it was a bit loose." He chuckled mischievously. "But then agen; Ol' Ralph might've come back."

"If he has, shove a paint brush in his hand!" David called.

IV

For the second time since his arrival in Fairhaven, David woke, somewhat disorientated, in a strange bedroom. Above his head, the ceiling was alive with dancing reflections from the sunlit water rippling in the harbour and, lulled by the sibilant sigh of the sea and the cry of a seagull outside the open window, he yawned and stretched contentedly. Voices were calling on the quay and the guttural snarl of a diesel engine springing to life settled to a steady rumble as a boat was made ready to leave.

Fairhaven was stirring for a new day, and so must he. The refrigerator was being delivered that morning. Ralph's old Prestcold smelled of mould and was dented and speckled with rust, so Jo had insisted that it had to go. The Frigidaire wasn't brand new; she had seen it advertised in the Myrtlesham Chronicle, but she was satisfied that it was clean and in good working order. It had a separate chiller compartment, too.

What on earth was wrong with him? Getting excited over a fridge! "It must be the sea air", he mumbled, as he made his way down to the kitchen.

Seated at a table in the window of the café, he munched a bacon sandwich and watched two draymen lower barrels into the cellar hatch outside The Packet Boat Inn. There had been no need to get his own breakfast. Avril would have been only too pleased to provide him with one of her 'sailor's specials', but from now on he had to prove to himself … and to a certain staff nurse … that he could stand on his own two feet.

He was still brooding over his second performance the previous night, which he could hardly describe as a triumph. In contrast to his first appearance, The Mess had been half empty and the atmosphere nowhere near as raucous and enthusiastic as before. To add insult to injury, Wally and Avril had taken on an extra barmaid to cope with the expected crowd, only for them all to spend long periods with little to do.

A small audience would have been disappointing enough, without the embarrassment of having Jo there to witness it. Wally and Avril had tried to reassure him that it was not his fault, but he had wanted to impress Jo with the one thing he could do well. Typically, he couldn't even manage that. It had been a relief when she had left after an hour, because of her early shift the next morning.

Hooky had provided solace and a crumb of comfort, when he returned from collecting glasses from the tables outside and declared, "You know what we forgot, don't yuh? Go out an' 'ave a listen. It's the funfair's season opener, tonight."

Wally had explained that the fairground had an official opening night each year, when all the rides were half price and, to use his words, "They roast a ruddy great pig on a spit an' lay on a firework display later on."

It had mollified David's disappointment to some extent, and having received one or two requests, he had started the second half of his performance with Marty Robbins' *A White Sport Coat*.

"You're not serious about standing that thing outside?" Jo exclaimed.

David frowned with feigned gravitas. "What have you got against Rocky?"

"Well; there's that spiteful look on its face, for a start … and with those wispy things sticking out of its head, it looks mad."

"So would you, if you'd been locked up in the dark in Stan's place for God-knows how long. I'll tell you what; I'll ask him to smile at bit more … and get a haircut."

"You're an idiot," she said, unable to prevent herself smiling.

"Have tea with Rocky the Rockhopper!" he exclaimed. "That could be our slogan."

"So could: Have tea with a mad penguin and his loony pal!"

"You can be quite wounding, at times Nurse Lampeter. I shouldn't care to be a patient on your ward when you're in this mood."

"You'd feel out of place; it's a women's ward," she chuckled; adding, "You'd like it even less if I had to give you an injection!"

He screwed up his face in a pained expression, which vanished as the notion came to him. "Hang on a minute! I've got an idea."

She rolled her eyes. "Oh, good grief; not another one!"

"How about changing the name of the café?"

"Why?"

"Well; let's face it, The Seagull Café is a bit old hat, isn't it? It's what nearly every other seaside café is called. And, from what we hear, this place has had a bit of a seedy reputation for some time. We'll need to change its image and reputation if we're going to make a go of it."

"What have you got in mind?"

David hesitated, fearing he already knew what her reaction would be. "Hear me out before you say anything. I've been thinking over what Ginny said about customers and a menu."

"And?"

"Well, I can't cook, you haven't got the time; and, be honest, would you want to put anything in your mouth that Sammy's had his hands on?"

Jo giggled. "Go on."

"So we're going to have to keep it simple. I was thinking: we should do cream teas, sandwiches and buns and that … Ice creams, as well, if we can. But why not try doing hot dogs and milk shakes? You know; something a bit more modern. Like you see in American films. I think the kids would go for it. Milk shakes are a doddle, and a hot dog can't be that difficult. It's only a banger in a roll. As far as I can tell, none of the other places round here do them."

Jo looked at him, expressionless; her eyes conveying no reaction. Waiting for her reply made him feel like an errant schoolboy standing outside the headmaster's office.

"OK," she said quietly. "I suppose it's worth a try. What are you thinking of changing the name to?"

"My first thought was Rocky's Cave," he said tentatively, but observing her less than encouraging expression, he continued, "But, in keeping with our new image, how about The Rockhopper Café?"

"So you want to name it after your mad penguin chum?"

"It would make him very happy."

"You … are … an idiot!" she chortled and picked up her coat. "I have to go. I'll see you tomorrow."

"So; can I go ahead and get the sign changed?"

"Yes; I suppose so. But try and persuade Rocky to cheer up a bit!"

The sound of voices outside caught their attention. "The lights are on, so he must be around somewhere," one of them declared.

Hardly able to believe his ears, David yanked open one of the doors. "Rich! Have they let you out? Hello Mum … Dad. What brings you to sunny Fairhaven?"

His mother kissed his cheek as he hugged her. "Your postcard made it look so nice. So we thought we'd come and see how you're getting on."

"I'm out on parole," Richard chuckled. "They think I'm nearly cured, so they're letting me out for a day or two at a time, before they release me for good."

"That's marvellous! … How are *you* Dad?"

"I'm fine David. It looks like you're keeping busy."

"We are," he said, ushering them inside. "This is Jo; my partner. Jo this is my mum … my dad … and my brother, Richard."

Richard's grin and raised eyebrows made the need for comment unnecessary, as they watched Jo exchange greetings with their parents.

"I'm glad you're recovering well, Richard," she said. "David's been so worried about you."

"That's very kind of you, Jo," Richard replied. "I'm touched by your concern, Little Brother," he added with an impish smile.

"I understand you're a nurse, Jo," said David's mother. "So you'll know what Richard's been through and how worried we've all been."

Jo nodded. "I haven't nursed anyone with TB, but I know how dreadful it can be. I can appreciate how relieved you must be now that Richard's recovered." She looked at her watch. "I'm so sorry; I hope you'll excuse me. It's been lovely meeting you, but I have to fly. I've arranged to meet my aunt in Myrtlesham, and I'll miss the bus if I don't hurry."

"Well, well," said Richard, as they watched Jo make her way towards the Esplanade. "So that's the mysterious J.M. Lampeter. I take it you're still none the wiser about why Uncle Ralph left her a half share in this place."

"That's right," David replied. "Neither of us has a clue. Other than the possibility that he once had something going with her aunt. And that's a question only a very brave man would dare ask."

"I can't imagine you're unhappy about the situation, though," Richard chortled.

"She's a nice girl, isn't she?" their mother observed. "And such a pretty little thing."

"She lets you know if you've upset her, though," David declared.

His father laughed and patted his shoulder. "Keeps you on your toes, does she?"

* * *

"Not a bad day," David mused, as he watched his father's Ford Anglia turn out of Market Square and onto the Myrtlesham Road. His family's visit had been an unexpected pleasure, culminating in high tea at The Copper Kettle restaurant.

Richard's appetite was understandably not as hearty as it had been, but he was looking healthier each time David saw him. Thankfully, their mother had refrained from referring to Jo's marital status, and he had avoided any acrimony with his father.

His mother had insisted on meeting Avril and Wally to thank them for their kindness, which, characteristically, they had dismissed as "no more than anyone would do for a young man alone in a strange town." Avril had seemed particularly taken by what she perceived as the likeness between David and his brother, despite Richard's hair being fairer and he an inch or two taller than David.

It had been fascinating to observe the exchange between the two women; given the reserve and unadventurous nature of one and the gregarious and less inhibited personality of the other. Although their conversation had been a little formal and stilted at first, by the time David and Richard returned from a stroll along the seafront, they were chatting convivially and addressing each other as Annette and Avril. Their father had quickly found an affinity with Wally, as they exchanged wartime experiences over a half of bitter.

Jo's agreement to his proposal to change the name of the café *and* experiment with the menu had put the icing on David's cake. And, of course, there was the new fridge.

According to the ornate clock above the entrance to the Town Hall, it was almost ten-to-seven, and the sun was beginning to dip below the summit of the downs, as David crossed Market Square and turned into Victoria Street. *Carry On Nurse* was showing at The Regal cinema and he was tempted to escape from reality for an hour or two of bawdy humour and smutty innuendo. But it seemed a pity not to make the most of such a lovely April evening, so he continued on to the seafront.

He could hear the reedy notes of a pipe-organ before the funfair came into view. Tucked in the corner, at the junction of Victoria Street and the Esplanade, its entrance was hidden from view by a bend in the road, until he reached the imposing Edwardian facade of the Provincial Bank. As he approached it, he began to sing to the music: "*All of a sudden a bloomin' great pudd'n came rolling down the hill.*"

It was too early in the season for the whirling rides and garishly painted stalls to be anything but sparsely patronised, but the illuminated sign arcing above the entrance still proclaimed it to be a *Wonderland of Fun*. The pungent aromas of fish and chips, fried onions and candy floss hung on the air, as diesel generators whirred, barkers enticed and cajoled, and girls screamed to attract the attention of young lads, who were flaunting their bravado on the rides or combing their Elvis quiffs and looking on hopefully.

David stopped to lean on the promenade railings and gaze out over the almost deserted beach. The tide was out; leaving low, languid waves to lap listlessly onto a wide expanse of ridged sand that glowed, golden, in the evening sunlight. The elongated shadows of seafront hotels and cafés were creeping inexorably across the Esplanade, cloaking it in their enveloping mantle and, behind the harbour, the pale crescent of a new moon had already revealed itself above the headland.

"Where else in the world would you find this?" David murmured, as boyhood memories came to mind. He could remember helping Uncle Ralph prepare his lobster creels with Richard on the deck of a boat called the Lily May. He also seemed to recall building a huge sandcastle with Dad down there on the beach, and Mum being stung by some unseen creature she had disturbed while paddling.

"There's nothing quite like the British seaside," he sighed.

When he reached the quay, the raised voices wafting from The Packet Boat Inn suggested that yet another argument, or discussion as the regulars would insist, was in progress. Above the general furore, he heard Frankie yell, "I'm tellin' yuh; it's a cert fer the two-thirty at Kempton!"

Forgoing the dubious pleasure of joining them for a pint and a pointless dispute, he looked up at the faded sign above the café, trying to envisage the new one.

"The Rockhopper Café," he said. "I like the sound of that."

Surely the younger generation would too? It sounded modern; 'with it', as the saying goes. "The Rockhopper Café," he drawled in the best American accent he could manage. It brought to mind Peter Sellers' comic travelogue, *Balham – Gateway to the South* and made him laugh out loud.

Another thought sprang to mind. What if…? No; Jo wouldn't go for it. Or would she? She had gone for the change of name and hotdogs and milk shakes. So what were the chances of persuading her to let him have a juke box? He shook his head. None at the moment! But it was an idea worth nurturing for the future.

David watched the Bedford lorry pull away from the café and gestured towards two large, wooden containers sitting inside the doorway. "You're sure this stuff hasn't been knocked off, Sammy?"

"No; told yuh. Got it from Sid Bowker."

Inspecting the containers more closely, David remarked, "These boxes have been knocked about a bit. They look like they've had a soaking at some time, too."

Sammy shrugged. "Don't matter. Paint's in tins, ennit? Water can't get in them."

"I suppose not." David pointed to some tables and chairs by the window. "I've made a start on those. While I'm away, you can finish rubbing them down, if you like." He tapped the box bearing a faded stencil that read: *McCloskey Marine Varnishes.* "After that, you can give them a coat or two of this stuff; OK?"

"Right you are."

"I won't be back until Friday evening. Jo's got my parents' telephone number in case I'm needed. Make sure you lock up properly when you go; and don't forget to leave the keys with Wally, next door."

"Okey dokey."

David picked up his holdall. "By the way, has Jo given you any money?"

"Yeh; paid me yesterday."

"Good. See you on Monday, Sammy!"

He was looking forward to spending a day or two at home, before Richard returned to the convalescent ward. They had spent little time together over the past year-or-so and the anxiety of Richard's illness had brought home how much his brother meant to him.

"David! Come ... see!"

Closing the café door behind him, David looked up to see Stan beckoning to him. "I'm in a bit of a hurry, Stan," he replied. "I've got to get to Myrtlesham by half-past-eleven to catch my train."

"Moment ... Come see," Stan insisted.

Reluctantly, David hurried towards him.

"Look … Good for you?" Stan suggested, indicating a glass cabinet that was resting on top of a chest of drawers."

"I don't know, Stan," David replied doubtfully. "I'm not sure what we'd put in it."

Stan picked up the trailing cable attached to the metal base of the cabinet. "Make lectrics; see? Foods good cold."

"Oh; I see. It's a chiller cabinet!" David exclaimed. "I see what you mean. I suppose we could stand it on the counter. Does it work?"

"Yah! Course blastiks work! I try. Make good cold."

"Alright. How much?"

"No; I give you."

"You can't do that, Stan!" David protested.

"Whyfor? I pay nothing. You pay nothing."

David smiled reticently under Stan's intense gaze. "I don't know what to say. It's very kind of you. Just remember: tea and coffee is free at the Rockhopper Café."

Stan's brow creased in bemusement. "What rock?"

With difficulty, David stifled the urge to laugh. "Rockhopper! It's a penguin."

"Whyfor blastiks penguin in caff?"

"No; it's going to be the café's new name! Remember the penguin you gave me?" David looked at his watch. "Sorry, Stan; I've got go. I'll explain it when I see you again."

He was still chuckling when he boarded the Myrtlesham bus.

Aunt Ginny's house was larger than David had imagined. It stood on a hill, at the end of a cul-de-sac overlooking The Wintergardens and the seafront below. Twin bay-windows flanked the front door, above which was a multi-coloured fanlight in the form of an arc of sunrays. David whistled softly to himself, as the rap-rap-rap of the wrought-iron knocker echoed in the confines beyond the door.

Several neighbouring residences were bed and breakfasts, and he was amused by the grandiose names on their sign boards: Buena Vista; Sunnybank House; Riviera Lodge; Shangri-La. He was about to knock again, when the door suddenly opened.

"You're late!"

His intended quip was swept away by the sight of Jo in a white, sleeveless dress; its skirt flared by layers of net petticoats. Her bobbed waves and curls shone in the reflected glow from the fanlight, curving around her delicate ears, from which diamond studs flashed as she turned her head. Her bewitching brown eyes sparkled as she gazed at him.

"Well?"

"Sorry. I stopped off in Myrtlesham on the way back. I've been doing the rounds of wholesalers and what-have-you, and … Jo; you look terrific!"

"Is that supposed to get you off the hook?" she replied, although her cheeks flushed and the hint of a smile played at the corners of her mouth.

"No; but if you'll let me explain."

Grinning impishly, she moved aside. "Come in."

The narrow hallway was dominated by a large coat rack and umbrella stand. Putting down his holdall, David recognised Ginny's flying jacket and Jo's yellow raincoat hanging from the overloaded pegs. He followed her into a large sitting room furnished with one or two side tables; a large polished sideboard; a collection of venerable, but well-upholstered, armchairs and a settee.

"How's your brother?" she asked, lifting a pink mohair cardigan from the back of a chair.

"He's fine, thanks. Raring to get out of hospital for good. Where's your Aunt Ginny?"

"It's her bingo night. Or housey-housey, as she calls it. They have one every month at the British Legion club."

"Can I freshen up and change?" he asked. "As I'm late, I came straight here from the bus. It'll save Wally and Avril having to find my keys so that I can change at home."

"Yes. The bathroom's the second door on the right at the top of the stairs."

Unzipping his holdall, he said, "Is it alright if I leave this here and pick it up when I bring you home."

"Yes; that's fine."

"Thanks. I'll tell you about my day on the way to the party."

Fairhaven was bathed in mellow evening sunshine when Jo and David descended several long flights of steps to The Wintergardens. As they passed the floral clock, he pointed to the gift-wrapped package she was carrying. "What do I owe you for my share of that?"

"Call it a fiver, including the card."

High heels made her an inch or two taller. With her dress hugging her narrow waist and shapely figure, and the flared skirt swaying with each step, he could hardly take his eyes off her. She had made up her eyes and mouth just enough to accentuate their appeal; as if that were necessary. With a single string of pearls at her neck and the fluffy, pink cardigan draped around her shoulders, she looked a picture.

"So, how did you get on with the wholesalers?" she asked, stirring him from his trance-like state.

"So-so. Bullers Wholesale Supplies didn't want to know. It wouldn't surprise me if Charlie McBride hasn't been shoving his oar in there."

"Do you really think so?"

"From what we've been told, I wouldn't put it past him. The bloke I spoke to was pretty evasive. I got the impression he'd been warned off from dealing with us."

"You said you got on so-so," Jo prompted. "From that, I take it you had better luck elsewhere?"

David nodded. "Dale Farm Dairy want paying weekly and Stern Brothers will only deal with us on a cash basis for the first six months; after which, according to the pompous twit I spoke to, they'll review our creditworthiness. The Corona dealers were more helpful, but would only give us limited credit if we could provide references. Wally has offered to help out with fizzy drinks to start us off, but he's got to be careful. He's not supposed to allow stuff he gets from the brewery to be re-sold by anybody else."

"It seems to be getting more and more complicated," Jo sighed. "And expensive."

"I had one bit of luck though," David added. "I've arranged a meeting with a salesman from Delrio; you know, the local ice cream company. He called at Flemmings Tea Rooms while I was there, picking Selwyn's brains."

"I take it Selwyn's the chap Aunt Ginny told us about. Was he helpful?"

"Yes; very. He thinks our ideas are basically sound, but he thinks we'll struggle to cope without another pair of hands. He was even more convinced of it when I explained about Sammy's limitations. I made a list of some other things he suggested we should think about."

Jo sighed deeply. "It seems never ending. Do you think we should take whatever Charlie McBride offers and call it quits?"

"No; I don't!" David retorted. "Whatever he offers … if he makes an offer … you can bet it won't be a lot, and we'll still be out of pocket with what we've already shelled out. So, the way I see it, we may as well grit our teeth and *keep buggering on*, as Mister Churchill would say.

Jo's eyes sparkled mischievously. "The bulldog spirit, eh?"

"We'll fight McBride on the beach; on the Esplanade and in the harbour!" he growled, before adding apprehensively. "Unless you really want to accept his offer?"

She shook her head. "No; I'm prepared to stick to our plan, such as it is. If that's what you want."

"Of course I do!" At that moment, he was willing to commit to anything to be with her.

They could hear the party when they reached the end of the promenade. People on the quay were gazing inquisitively towards The Packet Boat Inn, from which music and a babble of voices were occasionally punctuated by a shout or a peel of laughter. One or two people approached to peer at the notice on the doors: *Closed for Private Function ~ Invited Guests Only.*

Ignoring wolf-whistles from a group of young men, Jo returned a wave from Gemma, who was sitting by a window in The Mess. As expected, the front doors were locked, but one of them opened almost immediately in response to David's brisk knock.

Hooky's grinning face appeared around the doorframe. "Sorry; this is a private party!"

"We're the cabaret," David announced. "Marvelo the Magician and Fifi the Fan Dancer!"

Hooky cast a mischievous glance at Jo. "Where's 'er fans then?"

David patted his jacket pocket. "She's only little. She doesn't need very big ones."

Hooky's chortle was accompanied by Jo's sharp slap on David's arm and followed by Avril's command: "Pack it in you two! Behave yourselves!"

As usual, she was impeccably turned out in a pale blue dress that did justice to her impressive figure. Her platinum locks were brushed up off her forehead, falling in waves to a pageboy curl at chin level, and a gold, teardrop earring dangled from each earlobe, matching the chain and pendant that hung at her throat. Her eyelids fluttered like blue shutters, as her lips parted in a broad smile of welcome. "I'm ever so glad you could come!" Pushing her grinning brother aside, she opened the door wide. "Come in!"

Jo held out their gift, as Hooky closed the door behind them. "Happy birthday, Avril," she said, raising her voice above the noise from The Mess.

"Yes; Happy birthday!" David repeated.

Avril kissed them both on the cheek and took the birthday card from its envelope. "Thank you; both of you. But you shouldn't have!" she protested.

Jo pointed to the gold watch glittering on her wrist. "Is that new?"

Avril held out her arm; beaming with delight. "Yes; it's my present from Wally. It was a complete surprise. I had no idea!"

"It's lovely," Jo exclaimed. "He has good taste!"

Avril chuckled. "You'd never think it, would you?"

Another rap on the doors heralded more guests and turning to answer the knock, Avril asked, "Is it alright if I open your present later? There's so much goin' on; I'd like to open them all when I've got a moment to appreciate them properly. Just get yourselves a drink from the bar. It's all on Wally, so have whatever you like."

David peered into the Wardroom; three walls of which were lined with tables laden with food hidden beneath white, linen cloths. The caramel-smooth voice of Nat King Cole was extolling the pleasures of *Walking My Baby Back Home* from a portable record player that sat on the bar beside stacks of plates and trays of cutlery. Neither Jo nor David recognised any of the people conversing in small groups or standing around in isolated pairs, watching two couples glide around the floor to the music.

The relative calm contrasted sharply with the raucous clamour coming from the other, more crowded, bar. They were greeted by several cheers and shouts of welcome as they went in, as well as one or two whistles of appreciation for Jo. Wally appeared from a group of men by the fireplace, grinning broadly and clutching an empty pint glass. His habitually unruly locks and whiskers had been neatly trimmed and he was wearing a tie, albeit with the knot hanging several inches below his unbuttoned collar.

"There you are!" he bellowed, his flushed features suggesting he had been celebrating for some time. "You made it then! We was afraid you wasn't comin'!"

"It's my fault," David confessed. "I got held up in Myrtlesham."

Wally patted his shoulder. "Never mind; you're 'ere now." Glancing around the room, he added, "Avril's around 'ere somewhere."

"We've just spoken to her," said Jo.

Wally's eyes twinkled as he gazed at her. "Don't you look a treat, my lovely! A sight for sore eyes."

"Not 'alf!" one of the group behind him shouted. He appeared to be about the same age as Wally and his smile was more in the nature of a leer, as his gaze lingered on Jo. His comment was repeated by another of the group.

Recognising her discomfort, Wally ushered her away. "Take no notice. They're just a bunch of sad old matelots … like me." Gesturing towards the bar, he said, "Let's get you a drink."

"What have you got to be sad about?" David asked.

Wally's chuckle was a deep rumble. "Well, me missus is gettin' old, for a start!"

Reaching around the pillar from behind the bar, Avril slapped him on the back of the head. "Just watch it, you!"

Wally burst out laughing; his eyes twinkling, as she tugged at his beard. "I'm still more than enough woman for you, sailor!" she chuckled, before turning to one of the bar staff who was hovering for her attention.

"I don't know what you're worried about. She doesn't look forty," Jo remarked.

"You're right there!" Wally exclaimed. "She's a cracker aint she? My right arm! The luckiest day o'my life when I met 'er. Though God knows what she saw in me!" He looked at David, meaningfully. "It's what every bloke needs; a good woman. We're no good without 'em."

"Jo; David; what can I get you?" Linda called across the bar.

"Good girl, Linda. Look after these two, an' a pint fer me," Wally replied. "Well look who's 'ere!" he exclaimed. "Come an' get yerself a drink, Stan!"

Shepherded by Hooky, Stan approached nervously through the crowd, looking very different from the last time David saw him. He had done his best to slick down his wayward curls and was wearing a paisley tie, a white shirt and a blue, double-breasted suit that, although slightly old fashioned, gave him a distinguished air. He had bottles tucked under his arms and he held a velvet box in his hand.

"Stan! I'm so glad you came!" Avril exclaimed and reached across the bar to take the box he held out to her. "Is this for me? Thank you!"

"Wszystkiego najlepszego z okazji urodzin," he replied.

"Bless you!" someone shouted facetiously.

"That mean, Good wish for birthday," Stan explained and placed the bottles on the counter.

"What're they for, Stan?" Wally asked. "This is a pub, fer Gawd's sake. It's full o'booze!"

Hooky laughed. "Coals to Newcastle."

Stan looked bemused. "Why bring blastiks coal? Iz warm … No need fire!"

Amid the laughter, Jo tried to explain. "It's a saying, Stan. It's what we say when someone brings something that…"

"*Oh my goodness!*"

All heads turned to Avril, who had lifted the lid of the box and was gazing into it, wide-eyed.

"Iz no good?" Stan asked apprehensively.

"Oh, Stan; it's beautiful!" she gasped and took out a thin, silver bracelet, delicately inlaid with blue and white enamel. It shone in the overhead light, as she slipped it over her hand;

eliciting a murmur of appreciation from those close enough to see it.

Wally blew out his cheeks. "Stone me!"

"Stan, it's lovely," Avril exclaimed. "But I can't take this. It's too much … It must have cost a fortune!"

"No! No fortunes!" Stan insisted. "Old lady die; I buy all things in house. Find in box. I sink maybe you like!" He turned to Wally with a concerned expression. "Not good I give Avril?"

Wally patted his shoulder. "If it's OK with you, it's fine by me, Stan." He nodded towards Avril, who was holding out her arm to several women who were straining to see the bracelet. "Anyway; never mind what I think. I'd like t'see anybody try an' get the bloody thing off 'er!"

Gemma appeared from the melee around Avril. "Hello Stan. What's in the bottles?"

"Iz good. I make. You try?"

Gemma called for a wine glass and watched as Stan half-filled it. She took a tentative a sip and smiled with pleasure. "That's nice!" she exclaimed. Taking a larger mouthful, she called to Jo. "Come and try this. It's really good!"

Jo put down her Babycham and sniffed warily at Gemma's glass, before venturing to drink. "Oh, that's lovely!" she exclaimed. "I can taste peaches."

Stan's face lit up with a broad smile. "Yah; piches … and wódka. I get more glass."

The sound of Hooky ringing the ships bell lowered the volume of noise considerably, as Wally moved through a haze of tobacco smoke to the centre of the room.

"Can you lot in the Wardroom squeeze in 'ere fer a minute?" he bellowed. "Thass right; close up! Give 'em some room." Gesturing to the girls holding trays loaded with bubbling glasses, he declared, "Grab y'selves some champagne, if you aint already done so. We're gonna drink a toast t'the birthday girl … Where are yuh, Pet?"

He slipped a brawny arm around Avril's waist, as she came to him. "Now; I'm no good at speeches, so all I'm gonna say is: please raise yer glasses an' join me in wishing 'appy birthday t'the best thing that's ever 'appened to me; or ever will … 'Appy birthday Avril, my Pet!"

Glasses were raised; everyone endorsing Wally's toast, as Avril planted a kiss on his cheek. On cue, a young chap gingerly made his way through the crowd with a large cake that blazed with candles. Accompanied by a rowdy chorus of *Happy Birthday to you!* Avril managed to blow out all the candles in two attempts, before the cake was taken away to be cut.

"Thank you ever so much!" she exclaimed; her voice thick with emotion. "Thanks for comin' and for all your cards and presents … I don't know what else to say; except to thank my lovely Wally for all this! Thank you, Hun; for everythin'!" Producing an embroidered hanky from her sleeve, she dabbed at her eyes. "My mascara's smudged. I'd better see to it or I'll look like Bela Lugosi."

"Right! There's plenty o'grub next door," Wally announced. "So, don't stand on ceremony; tuck in."

Jo, Stan and Gemma disappeared in the throng that shuffled out to swarm around the buffet tables. The queue quickly stretched back to the doorway of The Mess, so David decided to wait for the crowd to thin. Among others who did so was Monty, who was in conversation with a group at the far end of the bar. Sporting his customary linen jacket, a bright pink oxford shirt and what looked like an MCC tie, he was in full flow on a subject he obviously found absorbing; seemingly regardless of whether his captive audience concurred.

Frankie and his crew appeared to have jumped the gun, because they emerged with overloaded plates while the queue was still forming and made their way to a table beside the fireplace. "Aint you 'ungry, Dave?" Johnny Cline called,

91

cramming a sausage roll into his mouth. "You better get in quick. There won't be nuffink left if you don't 'urry up."

"I can believe that," David remarked, glancing meaningfully at the food piled on Johnny's plate.

"You gonna give us a song, tonight?" Frankie asked.

"No; he's not! He's a guest!" Avril interjected. She had restored her eye makeup and was wriggling her way through the crowd in the lobby, holding a cigarette between the fingers of one hand and a champagne glass in the other. "Don't worry; there's plenty more food. It hasn't all been put out yet," she announced pointedly. Taking David by the arm, she said, "Come and meet my mum and dad," and led him towards a group sitting around a table by a window.

"This is David," she announced. "He and Jo ... the lovely girl in the white dress ... have taken over the café, next door."

David would have recognised Avril's mother, even if he hadn't already seen her photograph in the sitting room upstairs. The resemblance was unmistakeable. He knew that she was in her sixties, but like her daughter, she took care over her appearance. She was slim and wore a lilac fitted suit, the jacket of which was unbuttoned, revealing a white blouse with a lacy collar. The grey in her ash blonde hair was only conspicuous where the roots were exposed by a parting on one side and, apart from the frown lines on her forehead and around her eyes and mouth, her complexion was relatively clear. She smiled a greeting, displaying teeth, which, whether or not they were her own, were obviously well cared for.

However, Avril's father was less well preserved. What there was of his thinning hair was completely grey and his features bore creases and blemishes consistent with age. He was smartly dressed in a dark suit and a white shirt, the collar of which hung loosely around his wrinkled neck, reminding David of a tortoise.

Sitting next to him was his brother, Norman, whose reputation David was already aware of from Avril's tales of how she had learned to stay clear of Uncle Norman's 'wandering hands' during her youth.

Gesturing to a dapper, grey-haired man with a Ronald Colman moustache and a woman with tightly permed, almost white hair, Avril said, "Have you met Victor and Grace, David? They own the sweet shop next to you."

David accepted the invitation to join the group more from politeness than choice, but found their company both agreeable and enlightening. Having been intrigued by the fact that there was little resemblance between Hooky and Avril, he was interested to learn that Wilf, as the family called him, had been adopted when he was a baby. David picked up one or two other fascinating pieces of information too, during the course of an hour or so.

He had little contact with Jo during the evening. She was with Gemma for most of the time, among a group of people he didn't know, and he found it almost impossible to get near her. On one occasion, he caught sight of her dancing with a chap wearing a blazer with a badge embroidered on the pocket. Despite having no claim to her affection, it still aroused a pang of jealousy.

For a while, he drifted around the room with Hooky; holding brief, inconsequential conversations with groups and individuals they were acquainted with, while trying to avoid being drawn into one of Monty's 'symposiums' or the embarrassment of being teased by Betty. He failed to achieve either, although he managed to escape quite quickly from Monty's observations on the European Economic Community.

Despite his protestations that he couldn't dance, he was eventually coerced onto the Wardroom dance floor by Betty, whose dress was too figure-hugging and disconcertingly low-cut for comfort … his especially. It took an accidental collision with Wally and Avril, in the crowded and confined space, to help him relax and overcome his self-consciousness; or as much of it as was possible in such close proximity to Betty's exposed cleavage.

It was late, and the party was drawing to a close, by the time David remembered that all he had eaten was a piece of Avril's birthday cake. A few couples remained smooching to Glenn Miller's *Moonlight Serenade* when he went into the Wardroom, only to find that the buffet tables had been cleared. All that was left were some unappetising scraps and a few curled and dried-up sandwiches. He was resigning himself to the fact that he would have to provide his own bedtime snack, when Jo came in.

"I am right; I did have a cardigan when we came, didn't I?" Her words were slightly slurred and her eyes heavy lidded.

"Yes, you did; a pink one," David replied.

"I thought so … but I can't find it!"

"Forget it. You can come back and get it tomorrow," called the chap in the blazer, as he followed her into the Wardroom.

"No; I've got to find it," Jo insisted, gazing around the room. "It's not here. So it *must* be in the other bar, somewhere." Taking another, defining look around, she made her way unsteadily out again.

"You don't need it, sweetie. I've got the car outside!" the Blazer called after her.

His familiarity made David's hackles rise. "She said she wants to find her cardigan," he said slowly and deliberately.

"Mind your own bloody business!" the Blazer retorted. "I'm talking to Josie."

Trying to control his temper, David replied, "It is my business. I brought her."

"Well, hard luck, chum! Because I'm taking her home."

"Now then, lads!" Hooky called from the lobby. "We've all 'ad a good time. There's no need for any o'that!"

"You're right," said David; aware that the dancers had stopped and were watching them expectantly. Avril and Wally appeared behind the bar and, fearing that he was making a fool of himself, he decided that an apology was necessary. "Sorry, Avril. I didn't mean to spoil your party."

"Too bloody right!" the Blazer sneered.

"Stow it, you! An' watch yer language!" Wally growled. "I'll tell yuh if your opinion's needed … and what it is!"

"Don't be silly, love!" Avril said soothingly. "You've done nothin' of the sort."

Jo appeared in the doorway, carrying the errant cardigan. "Found it," she giggled. Sensing the tension, her smile faded. "What's up?"

"Oh, nothing to worry your pretty little head about," the Blazer smirked. "Just this oik chucking his weight about."

"He was not!" Avril snapped.

Wally leaned across the bar. "Who d'you think you are, sunshine; callin' a good friend of ours an oik?"

"He started it!" the Blazer asserted petulantly.

"An' if you don't watch yer mouth, sonny-jim, I'm just liable t'finish it!" Wally snarled.

"Alright; everybody calm down," Avril entreated. "You were just makin' sure Jo was alright, weren't you, David?"

He nodded self-consciously. "Well, I'd better be off. Thanks; it was a smashing party." Turning to Jo, he said, "I'll pick my bag up tomorrow…"

"Right; come on, Josie!" the Blazer exclaimed airily and draped an arm around her shoulders.

To his obvious surprise, she pushed it away. "Take your hands off me!" Losing her balance, she reached out to steady herself on the bar. "And *don't* call me Josie!"

The Blazer's eyes widened and he gave her a mocking smile. "Oh dear; touchy aren't we? What's come over you, all of a sudden?"

"Nothing's come over me!" she replied, flatly. "You're taking too much for granted!"

His expression darkened. "You what!? You've been fluttering your eyelashes and giving me the come-on, all evening!"

"*I have not!*" she retorted, her eyes suddenly coming to life with anger. "Whatever *you* may think; a couple of dances *is not* giving you the come-on!"

"Oh so that's the way it is!" the Blazer sneered. "I know your type. You lead a bloke on and…"

"E*h! Eh!*" Wally bellowed.

David opened his mouth to intervene, but Avril beat him to it. "Gordon!" she snapped, adding more calmly, "I think you'd better apologise to this young lady and leave."

"Apologise? Oh, alright. I'm s-o-o-o sorry *young lady!*" he smirked. "Sorry I wasted a whole bloody evening on a little tart like you!"

David took a step forward, bunching his fists, but Wally forestalled him by slamming back the counter flap. "*Geddout!*" he bellowed. "Go on; sling yer 'ook!"

Gordon fled, bouncing off the door frame in his haste.

"Are you still taking me home?" Jo asked, unsteadily. "Or have you changed your mind?"

"No; of course I haven't!" David replied. "I thought you were going with Gormless Gordon."

As he had hoped, she rewarded him with a snort of laughter, although she had to lean against the counter.

"Who is he, by the way?" David asked. He was about to use the term obnoxious twerp, but stopped himself as it dawned on him that he might be one of Avril's relatives.

"His father's the chairman of the area Licensed Victuallers Association," Avril explained. "He works in their offices in Myrtlesham. He seemed a nice, friendly lad; that's why I invited him."

"I need some fresh air," Jo announced tremulously.

"I'll get a taxi," said David.

"We haven't got money to waste on taxis," she insisted. "A walk will do me good."

David's suspicion that she was being overoptimistic was borne out when they said their goodbyes and she tottered out onto the quayside beside him.

"Whoops!" she chortled, as she stumbled against him.

Steadying her, he asked, "What have you been drinking?"

She patted his cheek, playfully. "Only Babycham … and some of Stan's peachy drink … Oh; and Avril's birthday toast. I've never had champagne before … *I like it*! Gordon gave me some of his, as well."

"I'll bet he did," David muttered, easing her upright. "Champagne is quite potent if you're not used to it. And you do realise what was in Stan's drink, don't you?"

"*Piches!*" she exclaimed, mimicking Stan.

"And vodka!"

"And wodka!" she giggled.

"Vodka is powerful stuff!" David insisted.

A breeze was blowing off the harbour and she shivered. "It's chilly," she murmured drowsily and drew her cardigan tighter around her.

David took off his jacket and draped it around her shoulders, relieved that there was no protest when he lowered her onto a bench. "Sit here for a minute, while I get another coat. Then we'll see about getting you home."

He was about to hurry towards the café, when Wally came out from the pub, waving the keys. "You'll need these. Sammy left them with us." He pointed to Jo, who was slumped across a table with her head resting on her arms. "She'll never make it 'ome on foot."

David nodded. "I know. I'll just get another coat and then sort out a taxi."

"Bill Roberts is pretty reasonable," Wally suggested. "I'll give 'im a bell."

"Thanks," David called and hurriedly unlocked the café doors.

The overpowering odour of paint and turpentine suggested that Sammy had been hard at work. It was a reminder to be careful not to brush against anything in the dark. Flicking on the lights, on his way to the stairs, he stopped in his tracks … and stared in disbelief. "*Sammy!*"

His anguished yell brought Wally scurrying to the doorway. "What's up?"

"I'll bloody kill him! I'm gonna strangle him with my bare hands!"

V

David stood outside the café and took a deep breath. Opening all the doors and windows over the weekend had dispelled the worst of the cloying odour of paint, but it was still invigorating to savour a fresh, sea breeze.

His anger had abated somewhat, but he was still determined to have it out with Sammy, who had yet to put in an appearance. Not that Sammy's absence was especially significant. He was not an early morning person, nor was he inclined to feel constrained by fixed hours of work.

It was a relief to spot Jo cycling along the Esplanade towards the harbour. She had been in no condition to exonerate him when he had taken her home and he had been disinclined to risk more of Ginny's displeasure by telephoning over the weekend to enquire how she was. Jo's eyes were hidden behind the dark lenses of a pair of white-framed sunglasses, but she had colour in her cheeks as she came to a halt and dismounted.

"How's the patient today, Nurse Lampeter?" he asked.

She wrinkled her nose as she unzipped her blue windcheater. "As well as can be expected, thank you. Sorry for being a nuisance."

David shrugged. "Forget it. You weren't. It was quite amusing. At least, it was until I got you home. Am I still in the dog house with Aunt Ginny?"

She chuckled. "Not any more. I explained what happened, so you're off the hook."

"That's a relief."

Pushing her sunglasses up onto her head, she said, "I ought to apologise to Avril and Wally."

"I'm sure there's no need," David insisted. "If anyone should apologise, it's me. It was me who made a fool of myself over that twit in the blazer."

"I'm glad you did. Thanks for protecting me from that lecherous creep."

David swept his arm across his body with a courtly bow. "At your service, mademoiselle!"

"Idiot!" she giggled. "What have you been doing over the weekend?"

"Nothing compared to what I'm going to do to Sammy … when he gets here!"

"Why, what's he done?"

David took her by the arm and ushered her towards the café. "There you are. What do you think of his handiwork?"

"Good grief!"

"Exactly! I left him to make a start on varnishing the tables and chairs, while I was away … and look!"

Jo gazed, open-mouthed, at the tables Sammy had painted; one canary yellow; one dazzling white; and one bright scarlet. Beside them stood six, equally colourful chairs. To David's surprise and annoyance she started to giggle.

"You can laugh. Take a look in that crate. It's full of useless little tins of paint; all different colours, as far as I can tell! I doubt if there's a drop of varnish in any of them."

"As far as you can tell?"

"Yes; hardly any of them have got labels. They've been washed off by the look of things. Most of those still on the tins are so water damaged they can't be read!"

"So, what are you going to do?"

"I'm going to get one of those tin baths from Stan's place, pour all the paint in it and drown that stupid…"

"David! Be serious!"

"What makes you think I'm not? I gave him ten quid for that lot!"

"Can't we use it?" she asked.

"How can we? The tins are too small to be any use and we'd have to open them all up to find out what's in them."

"Here comes Sammy, now," Jo warned. "Whatever you do, don't lose your temper and say something you'll regret."

"I can't think of anything I'd regret!" David growled.

"David, please!"

"Mornin." Sammy shuffled in nonchalantly, with a smouldering dog-end hanging from his lips.

"Oh good; Picasso's turned up, at last!" David exclaimed caustically.

Jo greeted him more cordially. "Good morning Sammy."

David gestured towards the newly painted tables and chairs. "Care to explain this?"

Sammy's brow wrinkled in puzzlement. "Whass up? Done what you told me to."

"I told you to *varnish* them!"

"Never did! Slap a coat o'what's in them boxes on 'em, you said."

"But you've heard me say that I was going to varnish the tables and chairs!"

Sammy remained unfazed. "Coulda changed yer mind. 'Ow was I t'know? Ent got no varnish, anyway."

"I know that … now! It says varnish on the crates, so I naturally assumed that's what's in them!"

"Can't 'elp that. Shoulda looked first, shouldn't yuh?"

Forgetting Jo's entreaty, David yelled, "How the hell could I? The tins have got no labels … none you can read! What was going on in your excuse for a brain that made you think I wanted you to paint the furniture all the colours of the rainbow!?"

"Calm down!" Jo pleaded.

Sammy pursed his lips. "Done what you told me. 'Ow was I t'know what you 'ad in mind?"

"I'll tell you what I had in mind!" David retorted! "In case you haven't noticed, this is a café! Strange as it may seem, that's what I want it to look like. Not a flaming chimps' tea party!"

"Stop shouting!" Jo demanded.

"Alright; I'll say this quietly … and clearly," said David. "Your services, Sammy, such as they are, are no longer required."

Sammy looked bemused. "You what?"

"You're fired … sacked!"

"Hang on a minute!" Jo exclaimed, her eyes flashing. "Don't I get a say in this?"

David blinked; startled by her anger. "Yes; but…"

"I thought this place belonged to *us!*" she snapped. "And that Sammy works for *us!* So, don't you think I deserve to be consulted about who gets taken on or sacked?"

"Well, yes," David spluttered.

Turning her attention to Sammy, she asked. "Where did this paint come from?"

"Told 'im. Got it from Sid Bowker."

"And who did he get it from; *Moby Dick*?" David exclaimed acidly. "Those tins have obviously been in water, haven't they? And long enough to soak the labels off."

"Dunno. Didn't ask. Told yuh I could get yuh paint, cheap. Thass what I done."

David waved his hand at the crates. "It says they contain varnish. As for the tins…"

"Actually, it doesn't."

"What?"

Jo pointed to the lid of the unopened container. "Take a look. It says: *Property of McCloskey Marine Varnishes*. It doesn't say that's what's inside."

"Never said nothin' about varnish," Sammy muttered. "Said you wanted paint."

"Well; whatever it is, it's useless!" David snorted. "Piddling little tins like that are no good, and there's no way of telling what's inside without opening them."

"Is; if yuh looks proper."

"How?"

Sammy picked up an unopened tin and turned it over. "Stamped on the bottom, see? *B* means blue. Number next to it tells yuh what shade. Four different colours in this lot; I looked."

"OK., Sammy. Carry on sanding the tables down, for now," Jo suggested and tugged at David's arm. "Come in the kitchen. There's something you should know."

"Still work 'ere, do I?" Sammy asked uncertainly.

Jo looked at David meaningfully.

"I suppose so," he replied and followed her along the passage. Reaching the kitchen, he said, "What's so important that I should know?"

"Do you know why Sammy's leg is in a brace?" she asked.

"Club foot? Polio?" David suggested.

Jo nodded. "Polio ... when he was twelve."

"So?"

"His father cleared off soon after he was born. His mother died when he was fourteen. He's got a sister ... Ivy. She's three years older than him. Apparently, she's not quite right in the head. *Not all there* is how Gemma described her. She's never been able to hold down a proper job, apart from an odd bit of cleaning now and then."

"That's rough," said David. "But what's that got to do with the paint?"

"Nothing directly. But this job is all they've got now the boatyard have done the dirty on Sammy. He's had to look after his sister since their mother died. He's been the sole bread-winner from the age of fourteen ... and with that leg! He makes sure Ivy comes first. If they're short of money, he's the one who goes without."

"Gemma told you all that?" David asked.

"Yes. She got it from Grace Sullivan. She and her husband own the rock shop next door. They've been there for donkey's years."

"I know; I met them at Avril's party."

Jo continued undaunted. "Sammy and his sister live in one of the council prefabs in Waterloo Road. That's behind here; between the boat yards and the warehouses in Gypsy Lane. According to Aunt Ginny, the prefabs were thrown up in a rush at the end of the war, to cope with the housing shortage. Guess who she thinks was involved in building them."

"Charlie Boy?"

She nodded "From what I hear, they're in a bit of a state. The council was going to pull them down a year or two ago, but nothing's happened."

David shrugged resignedly. "So, I … we … can't sack Sammy."

Jo's expression softened. "He obviously misunderstood what you wanted. I know he can be annoying; and he's not always terribly hygienic, but he means well … and he is useful."

"Alright, boss-lady. You win."

"Don't call me that! I'm not being bossy," she insisted. "And it's not a case of winning. I'm just asking you to appreciate how hard things are for Sammy."

"Fair enough." As a conciliatory gesture he called, "Ready for a brew, Sammy?"

"Yep." Sammy's response came from the passageway, and a moment later his head appeared round the kitchen door. "Bin thinkin'. If you wants varnish…"

Despite his promise, David couldn't resist temptation. "Don't tell me! For a tenner I can have the next crate that comes floating in the harbour." He was relieved to hear Jo chuckle, as she filled the kettle.

The irony was lost on Sammy. "No; was gonna say: 'ave a word with Jock, up at Cameron's Boat Yard. See yuh right, 'e will."

"Thanks Sammy," Jo replied.

Sammy nodded in acknowledgement. "An' that paint. If t'other crate's the same as the one thass bin opened, reckon there'll be about enough blue t'do the doors and windas in the caff. Will be if we trims 'em with the white, anyway."

"That's not a bad idea," David exclaimed. "Good thinking."

The heavy tins of emulsion paint he had just bought for the café's ceiling were making David's arms ache and the wire handles were chafing his hands. So the row of benches midway along the promenade offered welcome relief. Putting the tins down, he mopped beads of sweat from his brow and temples. Not many people were on the beach or the promenade now that the Easter bank holiday was over, which was how he preferred it. He sat down contentedly and stretched out his legs, lowering his eyelids as he enjoyed the warmth of the sun on his face and the invigorating sea air.

Opening his eyes with a start, he realised that he had fallen asleep. It could only have been for a minute or two, but he felt guilty. Here he was snoozing in the sunshine, while Jo was hard at work getting the café ready for opening day. What would she say if she knew? Would those lovely eyes flash with anger, or would she tease him about dozing off on a bench, like an old man? It was amusing to think that, when he had tried to imagine who the mysterious J. M. Lampeter might be, it never occurred to him that it could be a girl; least of all one like Jo.

If he hadn't already been perspiring when he reached the harbour, the sight of the grey Daimler parked on the quay would have made him break out in a cold sweat. There was no sign of

Horace, which meant that he was probably inside with his boss; and Jo was having to face them both, alone.

He winced when one of the tins caught his shin, as he hurried towards the café. Putting them down, he rubbed his leg and wrenched open the doors. But instead of the disquieting scene he had expected, what greeted him was the incongruous sight of a petite girl and a great bear of a man sitting at a table by the window, drinking tea.

"Oh, there you are!" Jo exclaimed and held out an envelope. "This gentleman has brought this for you."

Horace's battered features creased into a smile, as he gazed at her. "Horace … call me Horace," he said bashfully.

David nodded a circumspect greeting to him and took the envelope from Jo. "You can guess what this is. Why didn't you open it?"

"It's addressed to you. And it would have been rude while Horace and I were chatting."

To David, the idea of a brute like Horace chatting and sipping tea seemed bizarre. He couldn't get over how different he looked 'out of uniform'. The hair erupting from his ears and billowing from the open collar of his shirt was in stark contrast to the lack of it on his head. His biceps were the size and consistency of branches on the apple trees in the Sheldon family's garden and the seams of his brown, corduroy trousers seemed in imminent danger of splitting under the strain of his enormous thighs.

"Your boss isn't expecting an immediate reply, is he?" David asked tentatively.

Horace shook his head. "No. Charlie … er, Mister McBride 'as gawn t'Jersey … Thass in the Channel Islands," he added confidentially to Jo. "I've just took 'im an' Yvonne to catch the plane. 'E told me t'bring that 'ere on me way back." He stood up slowly, towering over the table. "Well, I better be on me way. That wuz a lovely cup o'tea, Miss. Just what I needed."

Jo rewarded him with a smile. "You're welcome, Horace."

Tearing open the envelope, David suddenly remembered the tins of emulsion he had left in the doorway. He was about to call out a warning, when Horace picked them up as easily as if they were china teacups and placed them on a table. "Gonna do some paintin'?" he asked.

Deeming it wise to forget the facetious reply that came to mind, David replied, "Yes. As you can see, the ceiling badly needs a coat of paint."

Horace nodded sagely. "Gonna be busy then."

"Yes we are," said Jo. "Bye-bye. Horace. It was lovely meeting you."

David raised his eyebrows as Horace left. "Lovely is not a word that springs immediately to mind about coming face to face with an ugly brute like that."

"David; that's unkind!" Jo exclaimed. "He can't help how he looks. He's quite sweet really ... and shy."

"If you say so," David chuckled. "Seeing you two together, put me in mind of Beauty and the Beast."

"Really? Which one am I?" she enquired archly.

"Oh, Beauty, of course," David replied. "Although you can be quite scary when you're angry."

"What's McBride offering?" she asked, peering over David's shoulder as he sat down to read the letter.

David's brow creased. "I'm not sure I know what to make of this? What do you think?"

"It looks like his lawyer's written it," Jo observed, taking the letter from him. "But if I'm understanding it right, he wants to give us five hundred pounds now, as *a retainer*, in return for us giving him the sole right to take over the lease and purchase the goodwill of the business at an agreed valuation."

"Agreed by who?" David enquired.

"Who do you think?" she replied caustically. "I'm not sure I know what goodwill is. But, what I do know is: there won't be much of it from McBride. Whatever it is, he won't give us what it's worth. If we take the five hundred, you can bet the agreed valuation will be his."

"Do you suppose he knows about that other cupboard?" David asked.

Jo shrugged her shoulders. "I don't know. But, like Aunt Ginny said, he's cunning and devious. So, he might. But, even if he doesn't, he's probably guessed there must be something on offer for surrendering the lease. This retainer offer might be his way of trying to find out how much."

"Do you think we should ask Monty what he thinks?" David suggested.

Jo tossed the letter onto a table dismissively. "No! I think we should tell Charlie McBride what he can do with his five hundred quid!"

Carefully prising open the lid of a tin of wood stain, David looked up at the sound of familiar voices outside the café. Hooky was staring at the newly painted sign above the doors. "The Rockhopper Café ... Well, it's different, I suppose."

Jo propped her bike against the café windowsill and stepped back to follow his gaze. "It wasn't my idea."

She was wearing the faded dungarees she had worn when she had cleared out the cupboards under the stairs. Remembering how cute she had looked with that straw hat perched on her head brought a smile to David's face.

"Don't you like it, then?" Hooky asked.

"I don't mind. But changing the name was Boy Wonder's idea. He's never short of those."

Hooky laughed. "You're not wrong, there. Our Davy's got the bit between his teeth these days."

"I'm not deaf!" David called mischievously. "Do you mind not talking about me as if I wasn't here?"

Hooky responded with an impish grin. "You shouldn't be earwiggin' other people's conversations! We're talkin' *about* you, not *to* you!"

"That's right; get on with your work!" Jo giggled. "We've only got a few more days before we open."

David tugged at his forelock. "Yes, boss! Whatever you say, boss!"

"Just think of all that lovely lolly jinglin' in the till," Hooky chuckled.

The smile faded from Jo's face. "That's a thought; have we got a till, David?"

"Not that I know of." Wiping his hands as he stepped out onto the quay, he added, "I haven't seen one."

"Well, you're gonna need somethin' to keep your float in," Hooky suggested.

"Our float?" David repeated.

"Yeh; you'll need a cash float. What yuh gonna do if somebody gives you a ten-bob note for sommat that comes to 'alf-a-dollar, an' you can't give 'em change?"

Jo's eyed widened. "We never thought of that, did we David?"

"Of course I did!" he replied loftily. "I was just waiting to see how long it would take you to think of it." He winced as she slapped his arm.

"Well, I gotta go," Hooky declared. "I've left Bunny dishin' out the deckchairs on 'is own. See you kids later."

"Bye, bye Hooky! Thanks for the advice!" Jo called after him, and turned to David. "So, where are we going to get a till?"

"We could see if Stan's got one," David suggested. "Do you want to come with me? If you flutter your eyelashes, you might get another glass of peach vodka."

Jo shuddered. "No thanks! Anyway; I want to give the cupboard in the hallway a thorough clean, so that we can keep our stock in there. Connie's coming to see us this morning, too."

"Oh good; I like her."

Jo looked puzzled. "Really? I didn't realise you knew her."

"Of course! Doesn't everybody?" he declared, before breaking into *Who's sorry now.*"

"You will be if you don't stop acting the fool!"

"Not Connie Francis, then? That's a shame."

Undeterred, Jo persevered. "I'm talking about Connie Jennings. She did the buffet for Avril's party. She might be interested in doing cakes and sandwiches for us."

"Oh, right. Well then; carry on nurse! I'll just wash my hands and go and see if Stan has such a thing as a blastiks till."

David looked around the café with a mixture of pride and trepidation. Admittedly, the colour scheme could be more stylish and coordinated, but they couldn't afford to waste the paint Sammy had acquired. At least the paintwork was fresh and clean; the ceiling was white and no longer nicotine stained; the floorboards had been scrubbed and varnished; and the windows were clear and sparkling. Jo had even washed the shades on the wall lights and made sure they all had a bulb that worked.

To his credit, Sammy was taking pride in helping with the renovations. He had proved especially useful in the kitchen; demonstrating his ingenuity by getting some of the more aged equipment to function efficiently.

Even after being stained and re-varnished, some of the furniture still looked past its best. But Jo had covered the tables with cloths, setting them with menu cards in porcelain holders. The condiments sets on raffia trays were Woolworth's finest.

Aunt Ginny had helped by washing seat covers and repairing one or two that had seen better days. Moth-eaten window blinds had been disposed of and the three garishly coloured tables were stacked in the alcove beside the doors, awaiting a similar fate.

The chiller cabinet, overhauled by Sammy and thoroughly cleaned by Jo, now stood on the counter-top and displayed a selection of Connie's tarts and cakes. Dominating the space between that and the wall adjoining Sullivan's Novelty Confectioners was a monstrous brass till with large keys mounted on cumbersome levers that needed some effort to depress. The *clang*, as the cash drawer sprung open, could alarm the unwary and had prompted Wally to comment that he'd heard quieter warning buoys. Stan hadn't been able to help with a till, and aghast at the prices of new ones, David had found this one in a shop selling various jumble and bric-a-brac. The proprietor had wanted a fiver for it, but it had obviously lain unwanted and collecting dust for some time, so he had accepted David's offer of fifty-bob, plus ten-bob for delivery. However, Jo had been less than impressed; expressing the opinion: "You've been had!"

They had augmented the display of soft drinks, packets of biscuits, crisps, sweets and other assorted snacks on the shelves behind the counter with stand-up displays advertising such delights as Pepsi Cola, Corona, Robinson's Barley Water and Fry's Peppermint Cream. Jo had found a blackboard in the passage cupboard, which Sammy had screwed to the wall between the two windows that looked out onto the cobbled lane beside the pub. It would announce *Today's Specials*; if and when there were any.

"D-Day … zero hour!" David exclaimed, hoping that bravado would help to calm the butterflies in his stomach. Taking a deep breath, he turned the sign to *Open* for the first time and unlocked the café doors. "No pushing! Please form an orderly queue!" he called to the deserted quay, as he placed Rocky outside.

The morning was bright and clear, with an azure sky almost devoid of cloud that promised another warm and sunny day. Seagulls were swooping over the mole; their plaintive shrieks accompanying the rhythmic sigh of rollers gently breaking on the shore. Breathing deeply to settle his nerves, David looked out across the harbour to the heart-lifting sight of vessels rocking gently above their sparkling reflections.

How would he cope? Would he make it through the day without spilling something on a customer; getting an order wrong; or giving somebody the wrong change? At least Jo was there, for which he was grateful. She was taking a few days of her annual leave entitlement to support him during the first week of their new venture. He doubted he would have been able to face it without her steadying influence. She was quite a girl; something he was coming to appreciate more and more.

His concern that they might be rushed off their feet turned out to be unfounded. After spending a week renovating the outside of their premises, the Sullivans had finally opened-up next door and seemed to be doing business. But, by mid-morning, The Rockhopper Café was still awaiting its first genuine customer. One or two people had glanced inside or been amused by Rocky, but none had been hungry or thirsty enough to be tempted in. Perhaps we need a slogan, he thought. 'The Day Is More Fun with Tea and a Bun.'

He was in the kitchen, doing just that; drinking tea with Jo and tucking into a slice of Connie Jennings' victoria sponge, when he heard voices. Glancing along the passage, he could see a man and a woman with a boy about ten years old standing in the café doorway.

The woman could have been anywhere from her thirties to forties; he couldn't guess from her pale, grim-set countenance. She wore an unbuttoned blue coat over a pink summer dress and a straw hat with a latticed brim that, on anyone with a less dour expression, might have looked quite fetching. The chap beside her looked older than her. He wore a grey, double breasted suit, a starched collar and tie and a brown trilby. The shopping bag he carried looked heavy and his demeanour suggested weary resignation. The boy was dressed in a white, short-sleeved shirt and khaki shorts. He had scuffed one of his brown sandals and there was a ragged hole in one of his socks, which was wrinkled around his ankle. A handkerchief was wrapped around one hand and his eyes were red from crying.

David approached them with what he hoped was a welcoming smile. "Good morning."

Ignoring his greeting, the woman declared, "I was told there's a nurse here."

Nonplussed, David replied, "Yes, there is."

She gestured to the boy, who was whimpering and clutching the bloodstained handkerchief covering his hand. "Eric's cut himself on that rusty fence behind the harbourmaster's office, and I'm frightened it'll turn septic. The woman in the jewel shop told me the nearest chemist is at the other end of the bay, but she said you've got a nurse here."

David's immediate reaction was to wonder why Eric had been somewhere that was clearly marked *Private – No Entry* and, more to the point, why wasn't he at school? However he thought better than to ask. "Yes; there is a nurse here," he said. "She's in the kitchen. I'll call her ... Jo!"

The morose looking chap, who David assumed was Eric's father, remained silent and gazed absently round the room; apparently content to let his more forthright spouse deal with the situation.

"Yes? What is it?" Jo asked, as she appeared from the passage.

"Are you a *proper* nurse?" the woman asked.

"Yes; I'm a staff nurse at Myrtlesham General Hospital," Jo replied, with an enquiring look at David.

"This poor chap's cut himself," he explained.

"Let's have a look, then," she said, and reached out to take Eric's hand.

Snatching it away, the boy glared at her malevolently.

"I can't help you if you won't let me see it," Jo coaxed.

"You're not a nurse!" he exclaimed petulantly. "Nurses wear blue frocks and funny hats!"

"I don't wear my uniform when I'm not on duty," she chuckled.

"Let the nurse see," his mother insisted, nudging him forward.

Jo sat the boy at a table. His muted whelp, as she carefully unwound the handkerchief, seemed more a reflex reaction than the result of discomfort. "Right; let's get this cleaned up first," she said soothingly.

"Please sit down," David suggested to Eric's parents. "Can I bring you a pot of tea or anything?"

"No thank you. We've brought a flask and our own sandwiches," the woman replied. "We're not paying the prices they charge round here, are we Edgar?"

Edgar shook his head. "No, dear."

"No offence intended," she added.

"Oh; none taken!" David replied, not daring to catch Jo's eye.

Fortunately, Eric's wound was not deep or extensive and, apart from one or two flakes of rust that Jo wiped away, it appeared to be clean and uninfected. His parents watched impassively and, except for the odd whimper from Eric, the five minutes-or-so it took her to wash it, daub it with Germolene and bandage it passed in almost complete silence.

"There you are," said Jo, tying off the bandage. "Make sure you keep it clean." Looking up at the boy's mother, she added, "I'm sure it's not infected and it doesn't need stitches, but I'd keep an eye on it for a day or so."

"Thank you," the woman said with obvious relief. "What do you say to the lady, Eric?" But Eric was already on his way out; drawn to the sight of a fishing boat entering the harbour.

"Well, cheerio; and thank you again," the woman called, as she left. Her husband doffed his hat and offered a wan smile, before following her out onto the quay.

"Thank you for your custom. Do come again," David murmured, as he watched them make their way towards the promenade. Turning to Jo, he sighed, "Our first customers."

Her eyes sparkled and her laughter echoed around the empty café. To David's surprise, she rested her forehead on his arm, still shaking with mirth. With her so close, he instinctively made to put his arm around her shoulders. But she pulled away, avoiding eye contact. Picking up the tin of Germolene and the dish she had used to wash Eric's wound, she disappeared along the passageway to the kitchen.

Their first bona fide customers appeared a few minutes later, when a gaggle of ladies 'of a certain age' filled the café with their animated chatter and laughter. David assumed they were from one of the daily charabanc excursions. But wherever they were from, they were clearly determined to enjoy themselves.

A rotund woman in a green dress was clutching her rear and laughing almost uncontrollably. "I've just had my bum pecked by your penguin!" she shrieked. Noticing David's bemusement, the woman beside her explained, "She backed into it on the way in."

"I'll bet you thought your luck 'ad changed, Doris!" cried a thin, elf-like woman wearing a sun-hat with a wide band declaring *Sailor Beware*. It evoked a gale of laughter, as the six women noisily arranged themselves around a window-table.

Somewhat unnerved, David allowed them to settle before approaching uneasily. "Good morning ladies. What's your pleasure?" he enquired; immediately regretting his choice of words.

"Ooh! We've got a saucy one 'ere!" the woman in the Sailor Beware hat exclaimed. "Your 'air would stand on end if I told you, darlin'!" she squawked.

"Stop it Ethel. You're making the poor lad blush!" cautioned the more soberly dressed woman beside her.

David felt his cheeks glow. "I meant: what can I get you to eat and drink?" he stammered.

A woman with a blue-rinsed perm came to his rescue. "I don't know about anybody else, but I'm gasping for a cup of tea." Her suggestion was greeted with exclamations of agreement. The heavy costume jewellery around her neck and wrists rattled as she reached out to pick up a menu card. "Would you bring us some tea, dear … while we're making up our minds about what we want to eat?"

"Of course!" David replied, relieved to see that Jo had appeared beside him.

"Why don't I look after these ladies?" she suggested; her eyes twinkling playfully. "You serve the other customers."

Grateful for her timely intervention, David turned to a young couple entering the café.

"Your waiter's very nervous, isn't he?" he heard one of the ladies remark. "Is he new?"

"Yes; we've taken him on as a trainee," Jo replied, biting her lip in response to his startled glare.

A group of four followed the couple in and two others were studying the menu displayed in the window.

'The noisy old birds have drawn attention to us, if nothing else,' David thought.

* * *

Propping open the café doors, David moved aside to allow two perspiring men to manoeuvre a chest-freezer into the café. The last customer had left, leaving him and Jo drained and relieved at the end of their first day in business. But the chance to relax had been denied them when a garishly ornamented van had drawn up outside, bearing the multi-coloured legend: 'DELRIO ICES ~ The Exotic Taste of Summer'.

The salesman accompanying the delivery men was tall, slim and sun-tanned, with a pencil moustache and luxuriant, wavy locks that gave him a slightly raffish air. His cream slacks were neatly pressed, with razor-sharp creases, and the bow-tie at his throat matched his pink and yellow striped blazer, which had 'Delrio' emblazoned across the breast pocket.

Pointing to the giant model of an ice cream cone adorning the van's roof, Jo asked, "Does that thing light up?"

To her surprise and amusement, the salesman replied, "Yes it does." Placing his straw boater on the counter, he asked, "Would you like me to show you?"

"No thank you; I just wondered." In more serious mode, she tapped the agreement she held in her hand. "Let me get this straight; we're renting that freezer, but we don't have to pay anything?"

The salesman nodded. "That's right. As long as you meet your annual minimum order value, we waive the rental charge."

She flipped over a page and pursed her lips. "Do you really think we'll sell this much ice cream, David? We've only got the summer months."

"The Candy Cabin turns over twice that amount in summer," the salesman said. Adjusting his bow-tie, he added, "The Beach Café sells a lot more."

"They would, wouldn't they?" she replied. "One of them is in the middle of town and the other's on the promenade … and there's the Walls kiosk right on the beach, as well. *We* won't get the amount of custom they do."

"We'll do alright," David insisted.

"We'll have to, now you've signed this agreement." she retorted.

"You agreed to it!" he countered defensively. "And don't forget; it won't only be cornets and wafers. People will want ice cream with Connie's tarts and fancies, won't they?"

"I suppose so," she conceded. "What happens if we don't meet the sales target?"

"As I explained to your husband…"

"He's not my husband," Jo interjected. "We're business partners."

The salesman's eyed widened. "Oh, I see. So you're not married … or a couple?"

Jo shook her head. "No; we just run this café together."

"Well; as I explained to your colleague, I'm afraid you'd be charged for the rental of the freezer and ice cream dispenser, and we would have to recharge you with the discount we've allowed you." He pointed to the large cardboard box at his feet. "But, to put your mind at rest; with all this display material, I'm sure you'll have no problem attracting customers. Delrio fully maintains the freezer, free of charge."

They were distracted by the sound of Hooky's voice outside on the quay. "Blimey! What's this? It's not carnival week already, is it?"

Jo went to the doorway to greet him and Wally. "We've got a new ice cream freezer and a thing-a-me-bob for filling cornets," she announced, pointing to the men who were removing the packaging.

"Where d'yuh want this?" one of them asked.

"Against the wall; just inside the doors, please," David replied. "The soft ice cream dispenser can stand between the side windows. Just let me move these damned things." Dragging aside the gaudily painted tables and chairs, he pointed to the skirting board. "There's an electricity socket down there."

Wally pointed to the van. "I thought you'd bought yourselves a little Sunday runabout."

"What's 'e supposed t'be then?" Hooky asked, gesturing towards the salesman.

"He's from Delrio; the ice cream company!" Jo exclaimed, her eyes twinkling.

Hooky grinned mischievously. "Strewth! You're not gonna lose 'im in a crowd, are yuh? The Man from Delrio, eh?"

"Yep; the fastest gun in town," said Wally.

"Dressed like that you'd 'ave to be!" Hooky declared.

"Stop it you two!" Jo giggled.

Wally patted her arm. "Sorry, my lovely. We've just come round to see 'ow it went today."

"Not too bad," she replied. "A bit slow at first, but it picked up as the day went on. I'll need a Charles Atlas body building course to manage that till, though."

"It's a bit of a monster, ennit?" said Hooky.

"I represent The Delrio Ice Cream Company," the salesman announced as they came in.

"I'd never a'guessed!" Wally replied, inspecting the business card held out to him.

"If you're interested in selling our products..."

Wally was quick to forestall the anticipated sales pitch. "I'm the landlord of the pub next door. We don't get a lotta call for ice cream. An' anyway, I don't reckon it'd do us any good if we was in competition right next door to each other, d'you?"

The salesman smiled ruefully. "No; I suppose not." Turning to David, he said, "Right; they've plugged the freezer in and got it going. There's a label on the back showing the ideal running temperature. This operating manual explains everything, but I'll set the thermostat. Just leave the lid closed overnight for it to run up and maintain the right temperature. Make sure you don't overfill it or you'll risk some of the contents spoiling. Your first delivery will be here in the morning. After that, we'll deliver every other day, except Sundays, during the summer months. They'll be as you require out of season. I'll call in tomorrow to make sure you're happy; if that's alright."

David nodded. "Yes; that's fine."

The salesman turned to Jo. "It was nice meeting you. My name's Lance."

"Nice to meet you too, Lance," she replied. "I'm Jo."

Hesitating, as if about to say more, he smiled and made

to follow the delivery men to the van, but had to step aside as another visitor appeared in the doorway.

"Wowee! What a transformation! I *love* the décor! Who's your designer?"

The improbable exclamation came from a lean, wiry chap, no taller than Jo. His features were tanned and bore the healthy glow of youth, although his heavily veined hands and the crow's-feet at the corners of his eyes and mouth suggested he was older than he seemed. A peeked yachting cap was perched jauntily on one side of his head, revealing a stubble of fair hair, closely cropped in the style beloved of the US Marine Corps. His hooped Breton shirt clung to his sparse frame above tight, white slacks that hugged his narrow hips. Completing the outlandish picture were a red kerchief knotted around his neck and a pair of blue, canvas deck shoes adorning his sockless feet.

Hooky's eyebrows rose. "Gordon Bennett; they're all out, today!"

"Mervin Devine," the visitor announced. "AD of the WGPT." In response to their bemused expressions, he added, "Artistic director of The Wintergardens Palace Theatre ... So, you're open again!"

"Yes," David replied, not daring to look at the others. "I'm David Sheldon. Today's our first day open."

"I *just love* what you've done here, David!" Mervin enthused, with an exaggerated wave of his arm. "It's so vital ... so invigorating! The dominant blue and white, with the red and white panels on the counter-facing works so well! Especially with those yellow and white flower motifs. Who did it? ... No; don't tell me. It's Julian Van Drewe, isn't it? Don't you just adore him? As you know; he did the revamp of The Myrtlesham Art Gallery. Have you seen his atrium?"

"No; but I'll bet you 'ave," Hooky murmured.

"Actually; we did this ourselves," David replied, feigning a cough to stifle a chuckle.

"No! You can't have! You're pulling my leg!"

"It's true," David insisted, battling suppressed mirth.

Jo had sidled behind Wally, whose face remained expressionless. Only his twinkling eyes and a raised eyebrow betrayed his amusement, as he glanced at Hooky.

Regaining a measure of self-control, David added, "Jo and I did it, with help from Sammy, our handyman. It was the only paint we had. The motifs were Jo's idea."

"Oh you clever things!" Mervin exclaimed. "You must introduce me to Joe."

"Here she is," said David, taking her elbow and shepherding her into view.

"*Oh! You're a girl!*" Like everything else, Mervin's surprise was expressed dramatically. "Is Joe your professional name?"

"No; my name is Josephine, but I prefer Jo." She managed to keep a straight face, although the slight tremble of her shoulders gave her away.

"Oh, quite right dear! I always think of Josephine as being associated with that ghastly oaf, Napoleon!"

"I used some old stencils I had when I was a little girl to trace the motifs," she explained, and clamped her teeth on her bottom lip.

"Clever you! Oh; I see you're going for a bistro ambiance!" Mervin enthused, as his eye caught the brightly coloured furniture. "How marvellous! The continental look is so in! They'll look wonderful outside ... Under an awning, perhaps?"

His exuberance was stemmed by the return of the Delrio salesman. "Sorry; I forgot my boater." Retrieving it from the counter, he added, "I couldn't help overhearing your conversation. I might be able to get you one or two parasols to go with those tables, if you like, Jo."

"That's kind of you, Lance; but I'm not sure we'll have any use for them," she replied.

"Hang on; that's not a bad idea!" David exclaimed.

"It's a marvellous idea!" Mervin chimed in. "Chic! ... Well, for around here, anyway. It'll give the place style and pzazz!"

Jo looked unconvinced. "Won't the wind blow them away?"

"We can bring them in if it gets really windy," David declared.

"You could drill 'oles in the tables to take 'em and anchor the ends in blocks or sommat," Wally suggested.

"They're quite sturdy and they have their own stands," Lance explained. "Leave it with me, Jo. I'll see what I can do for you. See you in the morning, then."

Wally slapped Hooky on the shoulder. "Come on matey; it's time we cleared off, too. These two 'ave 'ad a long day. They could do with a bit o'peace, I expect."

"Bye Wally; bye Hooky!" Jo called.

Mervin's eyes widened theatrically. "Hooky?"

"It's a nickname he picked up in the navy," she explained.

"Oh, I see," Mervin sighed. "For a moment, I thought he really *had* a hook." Giggling boyishly, he added, "It would have come in handy if we ever did Peter Pan." Making his way to the doorway, he said. "I won't take up any more of your precious time, dear hearts. I heard you'd re-opened, so I thought I'd pop in to say hi and bon chance!"

"I'm glad you did," said David. "Thanks for suggesting a use for those tables."

"Oh, mon plaisir!" Spreading his arms theatrically, Mervin started to sing 'If I Can Help Somebody' and took a final lingering, gaze around the café. "Wait 'til the kids in the chorus line hear about this place. They'll love it. Toodle–oo!"

David and Jo had to stifle a fit of giggling when Mervin's head suddenly re-appeared around the doorframe. "By the way, David; word is getting round that you sing like a nightingale."

"I wouldn't go that far. I sing and play guitar occasionally in the pub next door."

"I'm sure you're too modest. I must pop in and catch your act, sometime. TTFN!"

Wary of him reappearing yet again, David and Jo fought the urge to give way to hilarity. Trembling with barely restrained amusement, Jo went to the doorway and looked out. Assured that Mervin really had gone for good, she subsided onto a chair. "What a day!" she exclaimed.

* * *

David stood at his bedroom window, gazing out at the dark silhouettes of vessels moored in the harbour. His mind was too filled with his first day as a café proprietor to allow him to sleep. It had been an eventful day, but he had got through it; although he appreciated that he couldn't have done so without Jo. He could hardly believe how much his life had changed; all because of an unwanted legacy … and a girl who was now very much part of his life.

He was about to turn away from the window, when he noticed a pin-prick of light glow fleetingly in the darkness. A moment later he saw it again, and a shadowy figure move beside the steps leading to the mole. Whoever was out there was smoking a cigarette and apparently trying to keep out of sight.

Suspecting it might be a would-be burglar, David switched off the light and peered round a curtain. After a few moments, he saw someone move out from the shadows and toss his cigarette into the harbour. The light from the nearest lamp was too dim for David to see his face clearly, but he could make out that it was a slightly built individual, wearing what looked like a short jacket or windcheater with the collar turned up. For a few moments the man remained motionless, staring up at David's bedroom window, before he moved off towards the Esplanade.

Hastily drawing the curtains, David made a mental note to make sure all the doors and windows were locked at night and when the café was unoccupied.

The sound of an altercation outside aroused David's curiosity. Putting down his razor, he wiped the residue of shaving soap from his face and went into the bedroom to look out of the window. Below him on the quay, Ken Rathbone, the harbourmaster, was remonstrating with someone David didn't recognise. They were standing beside an A-frame advertising board and a narrow wooden hut shaped like a sentry box. Behind them, a pleasure boat was moored at the quay; its blue and white paintwork gleaming in the sunlight. The upper deck was draped with coloured bunting, and behind the varnished wheelhouse a passenger seating area was shaded by a white canvas awning.

The harbourmaster stood ramrod straight; legs apart, with his hands on his hips. "I don't care what Ben Thomas let you do! I'm in charge now he's retired! And I'm telling you; you can't put them there!"

"Why not?" the chap demanded. "They're not in anybody's way! 'Ow else can I let people know about my trips when I'm out at sea?"

"That's not my problem. You're not allowed to obstruct the quay and you can't erect anything on it without written permission from the Harbour Authority. And, what's more, you can't moor alongside the quay without a permit!"

"I've got a permit and a commercial operator's licence."

"Fair enough. But that only gives you permission to operate from this harbour, subject to my authority. It *does not* include the right to put up structures and advertising boards."

"Where can I put 'em, then?"

"I don't know. That's your problem."

The vociferous exchange was interrupted by Wally. "What's all the noise about? What's the problem, Danny?"

It was the harbourmaster who answered. "I was just telling him; he can't put that booth up and leave that board on the quay."

Wally frowned disapprovingly. "Why not? It's where Danny's trippers board 'is boat and come ashore. Ben never minded, an' nobody's ever complained before."

"I don't care what anybody used to do. It's against regulations. Ben's not the harbourmaster anymore. I am … and I'm not having my quay obstructed by every Tom, Dick and Harry whenever it takes their fancy."

Pulling up the bottom window sash, David leaned out, relishing the invigorating morning freshness. All three looked up as he called, "Morning Wally. What's up?"

"The admiral 'ere's givin' orders," Wally replied.

"There's no need for sarcasm!" Ken rasped. "I'm just acting in the best interests of the harbour and the people using it."

David had never had dealings with Fairhaven's harbourmaster, but having watched him strut along the quay in his roll-neck seaman's sweater and peaked cap, with its crown and gold-leaf badge, the word martinet had sprung to mind. What he was now witnessing did nothing to dispel that opinion. Always immaculately turned out, Ken Rathbone seemed to delight in any opportunity to display his authority. Broad shouldered and a little below average height, he reminded David of Kenneth More, although with none of the actor's charm or affability.

"So, 'ow is stopping people makin' a livin' in their best interests?" Danny retorted.

"I'm not stopping you operating," Ken insisted. "But my harbour is going to be run efficiently and seamanlike."

"What would you know about seamanlike?" Hooky scoffed. "I 'eard, you wuz a shore based shiny-arse, navigatin' a desk … HMS Collingwood trainin' base, wasn' it?"

David couldn't see Hooky, who was standing in the pub doorway, but his jibe had obviously struck home, because the harbourmaster's tone became more strident. "I wasn't shore based all the time. I did time at sea … in frigates and corvettes!"

"Whose? Ours or Adolph's?"

"Very funny!" Ken snapped. "You can take the mickey all you like. But while I'm in charge, this harbour's going to be run properly and according to regulations!"

"What about over there; where them tables and benches are?" Danny asked. "Are you in charge o'that?"

"No; I am," Wally interjected. "That belongs t'my pub."

"So, I could put my cabin there, then?" Danny suggested hopefully.

Wally combed his fingers through his beard. "I'd like to 'elp yuh, Danny. But it'd make it difficult for people to get in an' out o'the tables. Especially if they 'ad a sprog in a pram or a pushchair."

Danny looked crestfallen. "So, that's it then. I'm buggered!"

"You're welcome to put your board outside here," David proposed. "That paved area in front of our window is our property; it's not part of the quay. I haven't got room for your booth, but your board wouldn't be a problem."

Danny looked up, shielding his eyes with a hand. "Thanks for the offer, mate. But I'd still 'ave nowhere to sell tickets."

"It was just a thought."

"Why don't you take the money when the passengers get on board?" Ken suggested.

"That's no good!" Danny replied dismissively. "I need to be sellin' tickets all day for the next trips."

Ken straightened his cap and turned to walk away. "Suit yourself."

Danny thrust his hands into his pockets disconsolately, but his gloomy expression faded and he looked up at David again. "You wouldn't be interested in a little business proposition, would you?"

"It depends. Hang on; I'll be right down."

* * *

126

"Mind yer back darlin'!" the deliveryman called, as he wheeled a sack truck loaded with cartons from the Delrio lorry.

Jo moved aside as she studied the board outside the café doors. "Two hour cruise to the lighthouse – Viking Point – Smugglers Hole – Day-trip to Great Yarmouth every Sunday. So we're the booking office for Blue Ocean Cruises, now."

"That's right." Pausing from loading the freezer, David pointed to a large ledger on the counter. "That's the ticket book. We write out a ticket, take the money and give the white copy to the customer. The yellow carbon copy stays in the book. At the end of each week, we tally our yellow copies with the white copies that Danny takes from the customers and hand over the money, less our five percent agent's fee."

"And this Danny chap is happy with that?"

"Yep. We have to keep a record of the money we've taken, of course. But it's a pretty simple process. We're selling tickets for him all-day-long, so he's happy enough with the arrangement. He thinks that giving us five percent is no more expensive than paying people to man his kiosk."

"How much is our agent's fee likely to be worth?" Jo enquired.

"Well; the boat's licensed for a hundred and twenty passengers, but Danny reckons he gets an average of around eighty for each trip when the kids are on holiday. It can be more if the weather's really good. He can do three a day; sometimes four in midsummer. The Sunday one to Great Yarmouth is an all-day affair."

Studying the prices on the advertising board, Jo did some mental arithmetic. "If that's right, we won't do at all badly. Well done!"

"Thanks; but it was none of my doing, really. Obergruppenführer Rathbone did us a favour by stopping Danny putting his booth on the quay."

"Is that what they call the harbourmaster?" she giggled.

"Hooky's got another name for him, but I couldn't repeat it to you."

A Ford Prefect pulled up by the mole, and Lance, 'The Man from Delrio', got out. He was more soberly dressed than the previous day, in dark grey trousers, a tweed sports jacket and a blue open-necked shirt.

"Everything OK?" he called, as he unloaded three large parasols from the back of his car.

"Yes thanks," said Jo. "David's filling the freezer before we open for the day. As you can see, we've used your window stickers, but we're trying to decide how best to use the rest of the advertising stuff you gave us."

Lance dragged the brightly-coloured parasols and their heavy bases to the café and stood them beside the doors. Even though they were furled, Jo could see that the Delrio emblem was prominent.

Lance watched David change his mind several times in the process of filling the freezer, before asking, "Need some help?"

David grinned sheepishly. "It's tricky getting it all in."

"There's a knack to it. Let me show you."

"Thanks," said David, adding good-humouredly, "I see you're out of uniform."

Lance grinned. "It's my day off." Turning to Jo, he said, "I just popped in to deliver the parasols and make sure you're happy with everything."

Installing the carton of soft ice cream in the dispenser was a simple process and filling the freezer was more straightforward once David had been shown the best way to do it. However, Lance seemed reluctant to leave and spent the best part of an hour with them discussing different ways to display the Delrio promotional material. Eventually he made up his mind to go and picked up his jacket from the counter stool. Pausing in the doorway, he hesitated, nervously toying with his car keys.

"Would you happen to be free next Saturday evening, Jo?" he asked. "There's a dance at our social club."

Taken by surprise, she replied, "It's very kind of you, Lance; but I've got a boyfriend."

He smiled wistfully. "I thought you probably would have."

Jo pointed to the '*Staff Needed*' card in the café window. "Have you had any response to that?"

David shook his head. "Not yet."

"I put one in the post office window, near us," she said. "I thought there was more chance of people noticing it there."

"Good thinking."

Jo's brow furrowed with concern. "You'll never manage on your own, you know. But I can't take any more leave at the moment; and we can't let Sammy deal with customers."

"I know. Avril's going to ask Linda if she'd be interested."

"The Linda who helps out behind the bar in the pub?"

"Yes. Apparently she could do with a bit of extra cash. The only problem is Avril thinks she can only work evenings during the week."

"That's not going to be much help then, is it?" Jo sighed.

"Something will turn up," David assured her; with more conviction than he felt.

Unfortunately, something did turn up. David was arranging the multi-coloured tables and chairs outside the café window when a familiar grey Daimler purred to a halt on the quay.

"Uh-oh!" he exclaimed. "That's all we need."

"What's up?"

David gestured towards the car as Jo came to the doorway. "We've got a visitor."

Clad in his comically ostentatious uniform, Horace got out of the car and performed his meticulous ritual of opening a rear door.

"Good morning, Horace," Jo called.

For a moment, he seemed unsure if he should respond or remain aloof. But his grim expression creased into a smile once his employer had emerged from the limousine and walked past him. As always, Charlie McBride was immaculately turned out. His white shirt, blue blazer and light grey slacks were as crisp and pristine as the window display at Edwin Ford, the gentleman's tailor in Myrtlesham.

Eschewing preliminary greetings, Charlie stopped and stared at the café and the colourful tables. "Good God! What the hell have you done?"

Stung by his outburst, David replied, "We've re-opened."

"What as? The place looks like a Turkish knocking shop!"

Bridling with resentment, David retorted, "That might be your opinion Mister McBride, but it's in pretty poor taste! I'd appreciate it if you'd watch your language with a lady present."

Charlie glared at him; his eyes narrowed with anger. But his expression immediately softened. "I'm sorry. I forgot you were there, Miss er…"

Jo ignored the invitation to introduce herself. "What can we do for you, Mister McBride?"

"It's more what *I* can do for *you*, young lady. I came to see if you've considered my offer."

"Yes, we have," she said. "Thank you; but we're not interested in selling at the moment."

"I made you a decent offer," Charlie insisted. "Let me explain it clearly. I pay you a retainer now, and we finalise the deal later. This way, you get cash right away; cash that I'll bet you could do with, and…"

"We understood your offer," Jo interjected. "But the answer is still: no thank you."

Charlie looked at David questioningly, but received a nod of confirmation. Uttering a loud sigh, he blew out his cheeks. "For God's sake; be reasonable!" Frustration was making his lisp more noticeable. "Do yourselves a favour! Just look at this place! Unless you see sense you'll live to regret it, I can promise you."

"That sounds like a threat!" David suggested.

"It's not a threat. It's a sound piece of advice for your own good! It's as plain as a pikestaff that you know nothing about running a catering establishment. *Rockhopper Café!* God knows where you think a daft name like that's going to get you … And with the place looking like that! The glare of that paint's enough to blind people! You'll lose your shirt, son; believe me! They're talking about redeveloping the harbour. Did you know that? Where will you be then? I'll tell you. You'll be left high and dry … Up to your neck in debt!"

David resisted a flippant response to the concept of being high and dry in a harbour. "As it happens, we know there are plans to develop the harbour, and we realise how little we know about running a café. But we're learning. We're getting good advice; and what's more, we're determined to give it a go. So, as Jo said, our answer is: thank you for your offer, but no thanks."

"Alright; be it on your own head. Don't come running to me when you're in trouble!"

"We won't, I can assure you," David replied.

Aware that Horace was taking an interest in the altercation, Jo walked towards him. "How are you Horace?" she called cheerily.

"Careful, Jo!" David cautioned.

But Charlie held up a hand. "It's alright Horace. If I need you, I'll call."

Horace took off his cap and ran a hand over his bald pate. "I'm very well, thank you Miss. 'Ow are you gettin' on with the paintin'?"

Before Jo could answer, Charlie snapped, "Come on, Horace. I haven't got time to waste on people too stubborn for their own good."

"Bye, bye Horace. Pop in for a cup of tea again, sometime," Jo called.

"That's very kind of you, Miss," he replied, as he saw his boss into the Daimler. "I'd like that."

A window slid down and Charlie's head appeared. "Get in and drive, for Christ's sake!"

"I don't think our Mister McBride knows how much the compensation is worth in our lease," David mused, as he and Jo watched Horace reverse the Daimler onto the Esplanade.

"What makes you think so?" she asked.

"He may have been bluffing, but he was going on about us being up to our necks in debt if the harbour redevelopment goes ahead."

"Did he mention knowing about the secret cupboard?"

"No; but that's not to say he doesn't know. If he had dealings with my uncle, he might well know about it; or suspect there is one!"

As Jo and David soon discovered, becoming the booking agent for Blue Ocean Cruises was going to test their ability to cope. They had hoped to benefit from people coming in to buy tickets, but what they hadn't anticipated was how convenient The Rockhopper Café would be for those disembarking from the Ocean Queen or waiting to board it.

The effect was hardly noticeable at first. It was still early in the season and one or two days of overcast skies and intermittent showers meant fewer visitors and, consequently, little demand for Danny's cruises. However, the warmth and sunshine returned at the weekend and with it the appeal of the beach and the sparkling ocean.

Steadily increasing sales of ice cream and ice lollies was an indication of what lay ahead. At times, the queue for cornets and wafers caused congestion in the café, until the problem was eased by Avril's suggestion that they use the small side-window nearest the quay as a serving hatch for ice creams and lollies. As Mervin had predicted, the coloured furniture and parasols proved popular with the customers, who took full advantage of the sunshine to eat and drink al fresco.

However, the situation reached breaking point around four o'clock on Saturday, when the well-loaded Ocean Queen returned and disgorged its passengers, many of whom made straight for The Rockhopper Café. Sammy, aproned and rubber-gloved, was kept busy washing up, while Connie remained fully occupied making sandwiches and slicing cake.

It was just as well that they hadn't had time to add hot dogs to the menu, because there was no respite for David and Jo, who were relentlessly waiting on tables and serving ice cream at the hatch. The echoing clang of the till, constantly cutting through the babble of voices and the music of Joe Loss on the radio, was a source of amusement to many of their clientele. At one point, it even silenced a crying baby.

They had to apologise to several customers who were waiting to be served. Thankfully, most reacted with typical British patience and understanding, although there was one notable exception. The sour expression on the red, peeling face of an individual in a white flat cap, who was gesticulating to David from a window table, reminded him of a corporal who had tormented him and his fellow erks during the first weeks of national service.

Beckoning to him aggressively, the chap pointed at the thin, mousey-looking woman sitting opposite him. "Me an' the missus bin waitin' over twenty minutes for us tea and sandwiches," he exclaimed. "Where are they?"

"I'm terribly sorry, sir," David replied. "As you can see, we're very busy."

He was given neither the chance to continue nor any sympathy. "Then you should 'ave more bloody staff on lad! Makin' folk wait all this time; it's not on! We want us bloody teas now; not next week!"

Conscious that all eyes were on them, David was at a loss for words. But, to his relief, he heard disapproving murmurs.

"Will you please stop swearing!" an elderly lady called from a nearby table. "Some of us find your language offensive … and there are children present!"

"Leave off the young man!" another woman exclaimed. "They're doing their best. You can see the poor kids are rushed off their feet!"

The chap's chair scraped noisily over the floorboards as he rose abruptly. "Come on Cissie!" he barked. "We're goin'!" Fixing his gaze on David, he snapped, "You can forget about us teas and them sandwiches … an' we'll not be back!"

With a silent Cissie to heel, he strode towards the entrance, almost colliding with a tall, golden-haired girl who was coming in carrying a pile of dirty cups and plates. Her long, flaxen locks spilt over her shoulders and, lit by the halo of light from the doorway, she appeared angelic.

"Where would you like me to put these?" she asked in a gentle, almost child-like voice.

Transfixed by her bright blue eyes, David stammered, "Oh … thank you. Let me take those from you."

"I saw your card in the window," she declared. "Do you still need someone?"

"Yes, we do!" David replied eagerly. "As you can see we're having a job coping."

"Oh good!" she exclaimed. "My name is Tilly and I'm looking

for some work for the summer."

"Then you're just what we're looking for," said David. Clutching the pile of crockery, he added, "Tilly; that's an unusual name."

"It's Matilda really," she giggled. "But everyone calls me Tilly."

"Oh, I see … I'm David."

"Shall I take those; *if you're so busy*?" Jo suggested deliberately.

"Jo; this is Tilly," he explained. "She's interested in our advert … Tilly; this is my partner, Jo."

"Hello Tilly. Have you had any experience of waiting on tables?" Jo enquired.

Tilly turned on a dazzling smile. "A little. I helped a friend in his bistro for a week, last summer."

"A bistro? Where was that?"

"Near Nice … in the south of France. I looked after some chalets for a while, too, in St Moritz."

"Wouldn't Fairhaven be a bit of a come-down?" Jo suggested pointedly.

"Oh, no! This will be fine," Tilly insisted. "Daddy wants me to earn a little money of my own during the summer, before I go back to school in Switzerland. I'm staying with a friend near here, so this would suit me very well."

Jo looked at David meaningfully. "I'm afraid we're very busy at the moment, *aren't we David?* But if you're still interested, perhaps you could come back when things are a bit quieter. We can discuss it then."

"I can see how busy you are," Tilly replied. "But I have nothing planned for today, and the tables outside needed to be cleared, so I thought I'd help. There are cups left on the wall too. I'd be happy to collect them for you … and help in any way I can, if you'd like to try me out."

Connie appeared from the passageway with two plates of toasted teacakes. "Who wants these?" she asked.

"Oh; good grief!" Jo exclaimed. "I forgot them. Sorry Connie! They're for the lady and gentleman in the corner." Turning to Tilly, she said, "Thanks; that would be very helpful."

David switched on his amplifier and looked round him with pleasure and relief. It was the therapy he needed after the stress and anxiety of his new role as a café proprietor. His fear that he would once again be performing to a sparse audience had been dispelled as soon as he and Jo left the café. The Packet Boat's windows were wide-open, the tables outside were crowded and he had been greeted with a rowdy ovation by his teenage 'fan club'. The sight of them lining the railings and the adjacent harbour wall reminded him of a flock of roosting starlings. He had been welcomed by more cheers from the patrons packed into both bars and broad smiles from Avril and Wally.

Hooky's beaming face appeared across the bar, as David tuned the strings of his guitar and settled himself on a stool in his now customary place in the alcove. "There y'are. Yer fans're back!"

"You don't suppose it could have anything to do with all the posters you plastered everywhere?" David suggested; to which Hooky grinned impishly.

"It's bank 'oliday ennit? But yeh; they could've 'elped. And I might 'ave mentioned it when people come for a deckchair."

David watched Jo settle herself between Gemma and Grace Sullivan on a window seat, as he sang the opening lines of Conway Twitty's *Only Make Believe*. She had barely made herself comfortable when a young chap with dark curly hair, a 'loud' sports jacket and a 'deafening' tie, sidled over to her. David smiled as she looked towards him, rolling her eyes disparagingly, as the would-be lothario tried to chat her up. He didn't expect a Flash Harry like that to get anywhere with her, but it was still a relief to see the chap's expression register disappointment. David felt a tingle of pleasure, as Jo's eyes met his again.

Listening to the volume of his accompanying 'choir' begin to swell when he reached the chorus, it was all he could do to contain his hilarity, as the register ascended and male voices fragmented and degenerated into raucous bellowing.

Elated by the eruption of cheering and applause when the final chords faded, David immediately launched into Ricky Nelson's *Poor Little Fool*; his audience joining him to bellow "*Oh, Yeh!*" in the chorus.

An hour later, he finished his first set with the Packet Boat's favourite, *Bird Dog*, and settled his guitar on its stand, before taking a long pull at the fresh pint Hooky had placed on the counter next to him. Looking out of the window, he was delighted to see Tilly sitting at one of the benches engrossed in conversation with a strikingly attractive redhead.

Following his gaze, Hooky chuckled. "Taken a fancy to one o'them, 'ave yuh?"

"The blonde girl's called Tilly," David explained. "She's our new waitress … Well; she will be if Jo agrees."

"Reckon she will?" Hooky asked dubiously.

"Why wouldn't she?" David asked. "We've been rushed off our feet all day. She got stuck in and helped us out. Besides which, there hasn't been anyone else interested."

"I dunno," Hooky sighed. "There's no tellin' with women; especially when there's a looker like that involved. It can spell trouble."

"Jo's not like that," David insisted.

"Not like what?" Jo enquired, appearing unexpectedly at his elbow.

"Oh nothing. I was just telling Hooky that we might have found a waitress."

Jo shrugged. "Do you think so? I doubt she'll stay long. Fairhaven's not exactly Nice or St Moritz, is it?"

"What other options have we got?" David declared. "Even if she doesn't stay, it's better than nothing."

Jo smiled archly. "And she's *a lot* better than nothing, isn't she, David?"

"What do you mean?" he exclaimed, although he was well aware of her inference.

"Come off it! You've hardly taken your eyes off her since she turned up!"

"Don't talk rubbish!" he snapped defensively. "Anyway; what about you and all your admirers. You've had Gormless Gordon after you; the milkman obviously fancies you; you've got Lance from Delrio mooning over you, and now that spiv over there. Did you fob him off by telling him you've got a boyfriend, as well?"

"As a matter of fact, I did," she said calmly. "Because I have."

"What!?" David felt his scalp tingle. "You've never mentioned it before! Who is he?"

"He's in the Royal Army Medical Corps. He's stationed in Germany at the moment."

Dumbfounded; all David could think of was, "What's his name?"

"His name is Colin. You'll meet him when he comes home on leave."

* * *

Unable to sleep, David got up and went downstairs for a cup of coffee. He was tempted to take another look at Uncle Ralph's hidey-hole, but decided against it. There might be a perfectly reasonable explanation for it, although he couldn't think of one. Were they obliged to report it, and if so, who to? Monty might know, but getting him involved might well create more trouble than it was worth. Perhaps it was better to keep quiet and hope that no-one else knew about it; especially Charlie McBride.

So Jo had a boyfriend. What a fool he was! Why hadn't it occurred to him to wonder why a girl like that wasn't spoken for? He couldn't remember her ever mentioning her boyfriend; even in casual conversation. "She probably thinks it's none of my business," he mused. And he supposed it wasn't. But evenso, it was strange that she hadn't said a word about him.

"Get over it!" he told himself, as he filled the kettle. "She's just another girl."

But she wasn't *just another girl*. She was part of his life ... An important part. If he hadn't realised that before, he did now. As well as the fact that she was, to a great extent, the reason he had subjected himself to all the problems and aggravation of trying to resurrect the fortunes of a neglected café, instead of grabbing whatever he could get for it and clearing off as fast as he could.

Charlie McBride was right: they knew next to nothing about running a café, and could find themselves with insurmountable financial difficulties. So why bother?

What was Colin like? Was he tall, dark and handsome? Was that the type Jo went for? "You can be sure of one thing," he murmured to his reflection in a window pane, "Whatever type she does go for, you're not it!"

So, why did it matter? As an old jazz pianist once proclaimed: "The world is full of good-looking chicks. Why lose sleep over one? Another one will come along soon enough."

But it did matter. And another Jo wouldn't come along soon ... or at any time.

VI

Hooky placed a pint of Guinness on the counter in front of Frankie Laine, who was studying the racing pages of the Daily Mirror. "Wastin' more money on sick animals, Frankie?" he quipped.

Johnny Cline paused in the process of lifting his glass to his mouth. "What sick animals?"

"Them 'e keeps backin," Hooky declared.

Johnny frowned in bemusement. "Why's 'e backin' 'em if they're sick?"

Hooky leaned over the bar confidentially. "Frankie don't know they are 'til they stagger in last."

"Leave off!" Frankie growled and flicked half an inch of cigarette ash into an ashtray without lifting his eyes from his newspaper.

Johnny still looked puzzled and stared at the glass hovering in front of his face. He opened his mouth, as if to speak, but seemed to change his mind and took a swig.

"I'll bet Len Garrett sends Shifty round with a Christmas card every year," Wally called from the Wardroom. "I should think Frankie's payin' 'alf the mortgage on Len's new bungalow."

David grinned, enjoying the banter. Everyone knew that Len Garrett ran an illicit 'book' under cover of his haulage company,

140

and that Shifty Barnes was his 'runner'. Everyone, it seemed, except those responsible for enforcing the law.

"I do alright!" Frankie asserted.

"You do alright? Is that what you call losin' money on that nag they 'ad to put down in the Grand National?" Hooky snorted.

"It could a'bin a decent each-way bet at undred-to-one!" Frankie insisted.

"It could if it 'ad made it to the finish!" Hooky retorted. "You 'ad a fiver on Brian London to beat Floyd Patterson, too, didn't yuh? … An' you bet Dusty Miller that Luton'd win the Cup Final, when they were two-nil down at 'alf time."

"They could a'won it!" Frankie exclaimed defensively. "The Forest only 'ad ten men! Roy Dwight broke 'is leg."

"Ten was enough the way Imlach was playin'," Bill Grainger remarked. Having crewed The Emerald Star for more than ten years, he was accustomed to his skipper's inability to resist a bet … and his talent for 'picking a wrong-un'.

Wally appeared from the other bar and winked at Avril. "Frankie Laine; the bookies' best friend!" he chuckled.

Frankie ignored the taunt and drained his glass.

"Is that the Daily Mirror?" Johnny asked. "Can I 'ave a look at the cartoons? I wanna see what Jane's up to."

"Whatever it is, she won't have much on," Avril snorted. "She never does."

Wally pushed an envelope across the bar to David. "You'd better take a look at this. It came this mornin'."

David picked it up and took out a letter bearing the embossed crest of Fairhaven Town Council. It began: *Dear Sir, It has come to our attention that you are permitting musical performances to take place on your premises in contravention of local bylaws…*

"So that's it, then."

Wally nodded. "It looks like it. Sorry, son."

"I see they don't like people dancing outside either," David commented wistfully.

"They don't like people enjoyin' themselves at all!" Avril snapped. "It's a cryin' shame! It's why this town's always been behind the times; and always will be, with the council we've got."

"Do you think McBride put 'em up to it?" Hooky suggested.

Avril shrugged and lit a cigarette with the silver Dunhill lighter he had given her for her birthday. "I wouldn't put it past him!"

"You could be right," Wally concurred. "From what I 'ear, McBride's got one or two councillors in 'is pocket."

"Do you really think he'd do that?" David asked dubiously.

Avril exhaled a plume of blue smoke. "I wouldn't put it past him … out of spite, because you turned him down."

"Much as I sympathise, I fear your suspicion of a conspiracy may be a little melodramatic, dear lady," Monty pronounced. Lowering his newspaper, he added, "I would imagine it's more likely to be the work of some officious council johnny going about his business of meddling in our lives."

"You're probably right, Monty," Avril sighed. "But I still wouldn't put it past that crafty beggar, McBride."

Monty held out a hand. "May I see the letter?"

"Why not?" said Wally.

Monty's brow creased in concentration as he began to read. "Hm; very keen on their byelaws, but not terribly specific about which ones."

"Does it matter?" David replied despondently. "They've put a stop to me playing in here; and that's all there is to it."

Monty passed the letter back across the bar. "Not necessarily, my boy."

David drained his glass and slid from his bar stool. "Thanks for letting me know, Wally. See you later."

He needed fresh air and time to think. Disappointment was once again blighting his life; just when things had appeared to be looking up. His performances in the Packet Boat were important to him; therapeutically and for his self-esteem. The customers' whip-round came in handy too. With no particular destination in mind, he made his way along the promenade and down the wide semi-circular steps to the beach.

The ebbing tide had retreated from the patches of seaweed and flotsam it had discarded at its high point and the sun, sinking below the crest of the downs, was casting grotesque shadows across the gleaming expanse of wet sand. On the horizon, the deepening blue sky was streaked with rose-tinted banners of cloud and, behind the harbour, the headland was becoming dark and featureless; the trees shrouding its slopes no longer distinguishable.

He still hadn't got over the probability that Uncle Ralph had been involved with contraband tobacco. It was unlikely that he had been doing it on his own, so was Charlie McBride involved? Or was there another accomplice … or accomplices?

Snatches of a tune from a pipe-organ reached him; carried on the breeze from the fairground at the far end of the bay, where the tops of the big wheel and scenic railway were still bathed in sunlight. He stopped and smiled wistfully at a group of children, who were laughing and shrieking as they splashed through sun-warmed pools left by the receding tide. What he wouldn't give for that carefree innocence again.

Telling himself that it was pointless to fret about Jo's boyfriend didn't dispel the empty feeling it gave him. He had no right to feel possessive about her. Their relationship meant nothing more to her than a business partnership. So why bother? Why not just get over it and move on with his life?

He was pretty sure of one thing: he and Colin were not going to get on!

David's demeanour didn't improve the next morning when he opened a letter from the local authority's Health and Hygiene Inspector. It was addressed to: *The Proprietor(s) of The Seagull Café* and was headed: *Food Hygiene Regulations 1950.* The letter began, *Dear Sirs. Under the provisions of the Health Act 1947...*

"That's all we need!" he groaned, tossing the letter onto a table. "I wouldn't be surprised if this is more of your doing, Mister McBride."

He desperately wanted to discuss it with Jo, but she was working a few late shifts, deputising as night sister on another ward. So he made himself wait until late afternoon before telephoning.

* * *

'Why do they make these things so heavy and stiff?' David wondered, as he dragged open the door to the phone box. A notice above the receiver urged: *Please Be Brief.* As if anyone would stay any longer than necessary in somewhere so spartan and inhospitable, with a lingering odour that suggested some unidentifiable animal had been the last to make use of it. It was fortunate that he knew Jo's telephone number, because the directory was missing. While he waited for his call to be answered, he read the business cards tucked into the metal frames of the notices. Most were dog-eared, and the only one that wasn't grubby suggested it was offering a service that was.

"Hello; seven-five-two-four!"

David pushed button *A*; relieved that it was Jo and not her Aunt. "Jo; it's David."

"Hello, David. What's up? Is there a problem?"

"You could say that. We've had a letter from the local hygiene inspector. Apparently we should have an official certificate authorising us to sell food to the public."

"How do we get that?"

"We have to fill in an application form."

"So, what's the problem?"

"The letter quotes a load of gobble-de-gook about food hygiene and the requirements of the Health Act, but the gist of it is: he's coming to inspect the premises to decide if he's prepared to issue us a certificate."

"What happens if he doesn't?"

"I don't know. He'll probably close us down, I suppose."

"When is he coming?"

"It doesn't say. I presume it's any time he feels like it."

"Is there a telephone number to contact him?" she asked.

"I think so. I haven't got the letter with me."

"Why don't you telephone him and see if you can put him off for a few days? It will give us more time to get ready. If you haven't got his number, phone the council and get it from them. In the meantime, we'll have to go all-out to make the place as spick and span as possible."

"We'll have to keep Sammy out of sight," David quipped. "He probably rates as a health hazard in his own right." Her giggle brought a smile to his face.

"I'll see you tomorrow, before I go on duty," she said.

"There's no need!" David exclaimed. "You haven't got time to do your job and work here."

"I'll have to make time, won't I?" she insisted.

"OK, then; but only to talk about what we need to do! You're not doing any more than that. You'll wear yourself out."

"We'll see. I'll see you tomorrow."

Nothing had changed or been resolved, but he left the telephone box feeling that the air had been cleared, in more ways than one. Somehow, talking problems through with Jo made them seem more straightforward and manageable.

To add to David's woes, several days of wind and showers deterred visitors from visiting the beach and harbour. Lack of interest in sea cruises kept the Ocean Queen berthed at the quayside for most of the week and, consequently, there was very little agent's commission to supplement the cafe's meagre takings. Nonetheless, deliveries from Delrio continued uninterrupted. Eventually, there was no more room in the freezer, which heightened Jo's concern about the contract and triggered their first serious quarrel.

"So, what do you propose to do with all the ice cream?" she demanded.

"We can put some of it in the fridge freezer-box."

"I meant; how are you going to get rid of it all?" she replied impatiently. "We won't get much in the freezer-box, anyway!"

"How am *I* going to get rid of it?" David exclaimed. "Not *we*?"

"You signed the contract with Delrio!"

"You agreed!"

"I didn't realise you'd commit us to all this!" she snapped. "I was foolish enough to think you'd do something sensible!"

"Thank you so much for your confidence in me!" David retorted. "I suppose the lousy weather is my fault, as well!"

Jo's heavy sigh was laden with frustration. "Don't be stupid! But even if the weather wasn't so bad, we still wouldn't sell enough to cope with these deliveries."

"Things will pick up!" he suggested hopefully. "They're forecasting a decent spell of sunny weather from the end of the week ... and the school holidays will make a difference."

"They're nearly six weeks away!" she declared, exasperated. "We're getting deliveries three times a week! We'll be up to our necks in ice cream and ice lollies by then!"

"You could always flutter your eyelashes at Lance and persuade him to stop them." Her hostile glare left him in no doubt that his attempt at humour had been ineffectual ... and unwise.

"So; that's my function, is it?"

"No! I'm sorry Jo."

Jo's eyes narrowed angrily. "So, I'm supposed to flutter my eyelashes and butter up Lance and whoever else it takes to get us out of whatever mess you get us into. Is that it?"

"Jo; please. I didn't mean it like that. It was a joke!"

"That's just it, David. Everything's a joke to you, isn't it?"

"No it's not!" he insisted. "It was a stupid thing to say. I *am* concerned; honestly. I'll get in touch with Lance and see if there's anything he can do."

"Yes; why don't you do that?" she said brusquely and picked up her coat. "The rain seems to have stopped, so I think I'll get off home before it starts again."

Disturbed by her uncharacteristic terseness, he said, "Thanks for coming to help clean up."

She shrugged her shoulders, "That's alright."

He watched her open the door with deepening despondency. "Jo!" he called. "I'm sorry."

"So am I," she said flatly and closed the door behind her.

Lack of customers at least brought the consolation of allowing more time to prepare for the hygiene inspection. David hadn't managed to speak to the inspector in person when he telephoned his office, nor had he been able to discover the exact date of the inspection, but he had learned that it wouldn't be before the following week.

In the meantime, he set Sammy to scrubbing the sinks and kitchen work-surfaces and buffing up and de-scaling the kettles and urns, while Connie pitched in and gave the crockery and cutlery a thorough wash. David concentrated on the café; his rigorous cleaning and polishing only occasionally interrupted by customers. Tilly's help would have been useful. But in view of the inclement weather, it was fortunate that they had put her off until the following week. Her wages would have been an added burden. "Unless she's willing to be paid in ice cream," he thought mischievously.

The deterioration in his relationship with Jo had hardly been out of his mind for the past couple of days. He shared her concern about the contract with Delrio, so why had he stupidly made things worse with that ill-judged remark about Lance? The look on her face as she had left still haunted him.

Ominously, he hadn't heard from her since then. She was doing a stint on the night shift again, but that hadn't stopped her calling in at the café before. He had lost count of the times he had stepped outside, hoping to see her cycling towards the harbour. How would things be between them from now on? If, as he feared, he had lost her respect and trust, how could he hope to sustain the enthusiasm to keep things going until they could sell up?

Another glance out of the window confirmed that the rain had stopped and a stiff breeze was parting the clouds to reveal patches of blue sky. Enough to make a sailor a pair of trousers, as his grandmother used to say.

"I'd better phone Lance again," he sighed. "I hope he's managed to get his manager to agree to stop our deliveries for a while." Checking his pockets to make sure he had change for the coin box, he called to the kitchen, "Can you keep an eye out in case we get a customer, Connie? I won't be a minute. I'm just popping out to the phone box."

When he returned, he found a swarthy individual, in a blue donkey jacket, sitting at a window table. He was gazing with an amused expression at Rocky, who glared back at him from just inside the doors. The cup and saucer on the table confirmed that Connie knew he was there.

He looked up as David came in. "Hello; are you David?" he asked.

"Yes; I am," David replied guardedly.

The chap stood up and held out a hand ingrained with faded smudges of paint. "Christos Vasilakis," he announced. "But I answer to Chris. Mervin from the Wintergardens Theatre suggested I have a chat with you." His upper class drawl was in marked contrast to the foreign heritage his name implied. Interpreting David's expression, he added, "My father came from Crete. My mother is English, though."

"Oh; I see," said David, grasping the extended hand.

"The reason I'm here, David, is: Mervin thought you might like your window painted. You know; with the name and perhaps one or two little caricatures or what-have-you. It's what I do when my paintings aren't selling terribly well … which is much of the time, I'm afraid."

"I'd like to say yes, but I don't think we can afford it," David replied apologetically.

Chris took a deep breath. "Ah; yes. I thought that might be the case. Mervin said you haven't been open long. So I was wondering if I might put a proposal to you."

"What sort of proposal?"

"Well; something in the way of: I do your window for a nominal fee and you display my paintings on your walls, with a view to your customers being overcome with the urge to part with large amounts of cash to possess them."

"How nominal a fee?"

"It depends what you want on the window and how long it takes. But I'm not looking for much. Just enough to ensure my stomach doesn't make the acquaintance of my backbone. What I really need are places to display my work. Getting local art dealers and galleries interested is nigh on impossible, unless you're already sought after."

"What sort of things do you paint?" David asked.

Chris reached down to retrieve a canvas satchel from beside his chair. "Landscapes and seascapes mostly. But I'll happily oblige if anybody's prepared to pay to have their likeness preserved for posterity."

"These are good!" David exclaimed, admiring two seascapes and a rustic scene as they were handed to him.

"Allow me to congratulate you on your impeccable taste," Chris replied, his eyes twinkling impishly. "I could throw in one of this café as part of the deal, if you like."

David's resolve was wilting; and not just because he was impressed by the paintings. He found Chris likeable and engaging. "I presume we would get a commission on any sales?"

Sensing that David was teetering on the brink, Chris spread his hands in a gesture of acquiescence. "I'm sure we can come to an arrangement."

David stroked his chin thoughtfully. "I'll have to discuss it with my partner."

"Of course. Mervin mentioned you had one. She kindly offered me a cup of tea while I was waiting for you."

David shook his head "No, that was Connie. My partner's not here at the moment; she's a nurse."

"I see. Well, I'll leave you to talk it over with her, then." Chris, glanced meaningfully at the freezer.

Taking the hint, David asked, "Would you like an ice cream?"

"It's hardly the weather for it, but I'm very partial to a choc-ice."

David smiled apologetically. "Here's your change," he said, handing it to one of three young men sitting at the red table outside the café. "Sorry about the mix-up with your sandwiches. Our waitress only started yesterday. She's still learning the ropes."

"We don't mind," the young man replied and handed him a shilling. It took David by surprise; the practice of tipping being unfamiliar to most customers. "That's for Tilly," the young chap explained pointedly.

"Is she here every day?" another of the lads asked.

"Yes. Well, most days. For the summer, anyway." David replied.

"Good!" they exclaimed, almost in unison.

Tilly was serving at a table inside, and to the delight of all three young men, she noticed they were leaving. "Bye-bye, boys!" she called. "See you again soon!"

Watching them wave to her like star-struck schoolboys, David didn't doubt that she would.

Tilly's effect on the male customers was at least a diversion from his anxiety over the hygiene inspection that had taken place earlier. The chap who had arrived around ten o'clock, and introduced himself as Brian Forbes, was not the chief hygiene inspector, which probably explained the way he had been dressed. His corduroy trousers, suede shoes and tweed jacket, with leather elbow patches, had made him look more like an art teacher than a council official. A green knitted tie, tightly knotted at the frayed collar of his grey shirt, had completed what, to David, was a most un-official look.

Although affable and polite, he had been unforthcoming when David had nervously enquired, "How's it looking?" He had begun by inspecting the outside of the premises. Patrolling the service yard, he had examined the drains and rubbish bins; writing his observations on various sheets of paper attached to his clipboard.

Next, he had asked if any toilet facilities were available for customers, which, like the outside inspection, David had not anticipated. Fortunately, the influence of Corporal Flanagan's fanatical obsession with the cleanliness of the flight's *hablushuns*, during the early days of David's national service, had remained with him, and the toilet was thoroughly cleaned each day and kept well-provided with fresh towels and all the necessary toiletries.

Having paused in his deliberations long enough to accept a cup of tea, the inspector had lifted the lid of the freezer and peered inside, before checking the nozzle of the soft ice cream dispenser. Running a finger along the counter and shelves had all but completed his interest in the café itself, although Tilly's rear, as she had leaned across a chair to pick up a fallen paper napkin, had not escaped his scrutiny.

His final inspection had been the kitchen, where Connie had been preparing sandwiches and rolls for customers' orders. Despite David's efforts to persuade him to take the day off, Sammy had been washing up, swathed in a large white apron. David's heart had sunk when Sammy had exclaimed, "Watcha Brian! 'Ow are yuh? 'Ow's yer dad?"

* * *

Lulled by the rhythmic surge of waves breaking on the beach, David propped his elbows on the yellow table and rested his chin in his hands. The harbour was bathed in the tawny glow of evening sunlight and crowded with a motley collection of vessels belonging to summer boaters; 'fair-weather commodores' as Wally referred to them. Lacking the resolve or energy for anything more taxing, he tried to outstare a seagull that was gazing at him intently from a bollard. Realising there was no chance of an opportunistic snack, the bird flew off.

"It's alright for you," David called after it. "You can clear off whenever you like ... wherever you like."

It had been a long day in the café, and a busy one. Connie had generously stayed for most of it, helping to serve the customers when needed; which was quite often, because Tilly had been more than willing to engage them in conversation. They and Sammy had now gone and the other harbourside businesses had closed for the day. With few people remaining on the quay, David had time to indulge himself in gloom and despondency.

If there hadn't already been enough to worry about, there was now the aftermath of the hygiene inspector's visit to contend with. How had he got himself into this mess? Why would any sane person choose to run a café? There seemed no end to unforeseen problems and interference from officialdom, and no respite from *rushing around like a blue-arsed fly*, another of Corporal Flanagan's choice expressions. He didn't even have the consolation of playing and singing in the Packet Boat, anymore. He was nearly broke and Jo had lost confidence in him. So why not just give up and clear off?

"A penny for them!"

For a moment he thought his mind was playing tricks, but lifting his chin from his hands, he saw Jo astride her bike; smiling at him.

"Jo! I didn't hear you coming."

She leaning her bike against a bollard. "I'm not surprised. You were miles away!"

"I'm sorry, Jo…" he began, but she raised a hand to stop him.

"No; David; there's no need. I shouldn't have gone on at you like that. You only did what you thought was for the best. After all, you're having to run this place and deal with everything that crops up."

Heaving a sigh of relief, he replied, "You've got enough on your plate with a full time job!"

"Well, perhaps. But that's not the point. I'm sorry I was so bitchy. I've had a lot on my mind lately, but I shouldn't have taken it out on you."

"I don't mind," he lied. "Is there anything I can do?"

"No; but thanks for asking. We've been rushed off our feet on the wards. Several of our nurses were on leave or off sick. We couldn't get enough temporary staff, so the rest of us had to work longer shifts to cope."

"I was wondering why I hadn't seen you. I thought … Well, let's just say I thought you'd given up on me."

Sitting down beside him, she put a comforting hand on his. "No; of course not. I might well think the same about you."

"Not likely. You're the brains of the outfit," he quipped, enjoying her touch and proximity. Her giggle was infectious and made him chuckle in response.

"So, how are things?" she enquired. "Do you know when the hygiene inspector's coming?"

"Yes; it was today. This morning, actually."

Her eyes widened. "Really? How did it go?"

"Perhaps we'd better go inside."

Hoisting herself onto the stool at the end of the counter, Jo took the two official-looking documents he handed her and read aloud: "You are in breach of hygiene safety regulations in the following respects: cracked wall tiles surrounding food preparation areas; mildewed tile grout around food preparation areas; food preparation surfaces damaged and unsterilized; cold water tap encrusted with lime scale; inadequate hand washing facilities for kitchen staff…" Too shaken to read on, she looked at David, her brow furrowed with anxiety. "My God!"

David massaged his chin wistfully. "It was a shock. We worked like mad on cleaning the place; Connie's been wonderful. I thought there might be one or two minor points, but not all this!"

"Does this mean we've got to close?" she asked apprehensively.

David shook his head. "Not right away. That top sheet is the list of things we've got to do. The other list is apparently advisory. We've got twenty-eight days to comply. They're going to inspect us again after that." He sighed wearily. "To be honest;

even without the advisory stuff, I don't see how we can manage it all in time. That's if we could afford it."

"We've got very little in the bank to play with," she sighed. "The rent's due before the end of this month. We can pay that, and there's probably just about enough for this month's bills, too. But that's about all."

"What have I got us into?" David groaned.

"*You* haven't got us into anything!" she declared. "We both decided to take this on; remember? Neither of us knew what to expect or what we were doing, really. But it was *our* decision!"

"Perhaps we should've taken Charlie McBride's offer."

"No we shouldn't. Anyway, it's too late to worry about that, now! Don't forget there's my savings account."

"No!" he said sharply. "Sorry; I didn't mean to shout; but we've been through all this before. If this place folds, then so be it. But you're not throwing your hard-earned savings after it!"

"What else *can* we do?" she pleaded.

David shrugged. "Just at this moment, I don't know. I'd rather not ask my parents to bail me out, unless it's as a last resort. I'm sure my brother would, but I don't want to worry him, with all he's been through.

Jo nodded. "Of course not. I suppose I could ask Aunt Ginny."

"No! She's done enough for us, already. Perhaps it's better if we just let them close us down."

"And lose everything?" she retorted. "After we've come this far? We can't give up, just like that!"

Her pugnacious expression amused him. "Do you fancy a Pepsi?" he asked. "It's on the house."

Her laughter lifted his spirits. "Perhaps we should share one as we're so hard up," she chortled.

"I think we can stretch to one each." he said and flipped the cap off a bottle. "I've got some more news for you."

"You're not still being watched, are you?"

"No. At least, I don't think so. I haven't been handed the black spot, or seen anybody with a parrot and a wooden leg hanging around."

Jo's eyes sparkled. "They were pirates in Treasure Island, not smugglers."

"It wouldn't surprise me to know that my devious uncle was up to that, too," he muttered. "But, anyway; we can put a hold on the Delrio orders for the rest of the month."

"That's wonderful!" she exclaimed. "Well done!"

"Yes; but there's a catch. We've got to make up the shortfall over the remainder of the contract."

Jo took a straw from the jar on the counter and dropped it into the neck of her Pepsi bottle. "I see. Well, I suppose we'll just have to cross that bridge when we come to it."

David grinned self-consciously. "I have a confession to make. When I explained the situation to Lance, I told him you were very worried about it. He obviously fancies you, so I laid it on a bit thick, I'm afraid."

"Oh; you did, did you?"

"Yes. I thought I'd better tell you, in case he mentions it the next time he sees you."

Taking the straw from her mouth, she grinned archly. "I forgive you ... this time!"

"We sold a fair bit of ice cream yesterday and today," he said. "Danny's running his trips again, so we're beginning to shift it. It's just as well, because the health inspector didn't like us keeping it in the fridge next to the ham and unpacked food."

"How's Tilly coming along?" she asked.

"She's willing enough. But she's a bit feather-brained. She got the orders mixed up once or twice and she spends a lot of time chatting to the customers. But she gets away with it. They seem to like her; especially the men."

"I don't doubt that," Jo exclaimed.

"Do you want to hear the rest of my news?" he asked.

"I don't know," she said warily. "Do I?"

"Well; there's Christos."

"There's what?"

David picked up Chris's canvas satchel from under the counter. "Mervin, from the theatre in the Wintergardens, sent this artist chap along to see me. His name is Christos; he's half Greek." David carefully removed the paintings from the satchel and laid them on the counter. "He did these."

Jo studied them appreciatively. "They're really good. But this is the last thing we can afford to spend our money on, in our present situation!"

"That's not why he left them. He wants us to display them on the walls and hopefully sell them for him. We'd get a commission on each sale."

"We're getting to be a proper little tycoon, aren't we, Mister Sheldon?" she giggled. "So we're an art gallery, now. What next?

"I haven't said yes, yet. I wanted to see what you thought, first."

"I can't see why we shouldn't ... Assuming we manage to stay open."

"There's one other thing," he said quietly.

"What's that?"

"I can't sing in the pub anymore. Apparently it's breaking local bylaws."

"Oh, David!"

Stan, stroked his chin pensively. "No; I no got tile."

"I just wondered," David said resignedly.

"How many you want?"

Conjuring up a picture of the café's kitchen in his mind, David counted the row of tiles above the worktop. "About forty, I think."

Stan pursed his lips. "I look; maybe I find some place I go. You need other thing?"

"I need a tap and new kitchen worktops."

"No got tap. Have bath one time. Sell to football team."

"Fairhaven United?"

Stan nodded affirmatively. "Ja. No good. All time lose."

"At least they can console themselves with a nice bath afterwards," David chuckled.

Stan's grin faded to an expression of concern. "You think blastiks council make you shut caff?"

"They will if we don't do everything they tell us to."

Stan frowned; deep in thought. After a moment, he gestured for David to follow him. "Come see," he said and led him through a labyrinth of narrow gaps between furniture and bric-a-brac. In a gloomy far corner, he switched on a dim light and pointed to two large kitchen units. "Good for you?" he suggested, tapping the laminated worktops.

"They're just the job!" David exclaimed enthusiastically. "If they'll fit in our kitchen."

Stan pulled a tape measure from his pocket. "I see how big … write on paper. You see if good for you."

"Thanks, Stan. You're a real friend."

Stan replied with a smile. "Yah; you good friend … and Jo." Extending his tape measure along one of the cabinets, he added, "Jo; she pretty girl."

David nodded. "Yes, she is. She's smart, too."

"You marry her?"

Taken unawares, David stammered. "No … she's got a boyfriend. He's in in the army … in Germany."

Stan's expression darkened and he muttered something unintelligible, which David assumed was in Polish. "This big," he said, handing David a scrap of paper. "Both same."

"Thanks Stan," said David. "I'll go and measure up in the kitchen. If they'll fit I'll come back and settle up with you." He had almost reached the door, when Stan called to him. "Yes, Stan; what is it?"

"You marry her, David!"

* * *

"Just my luck," David sighed, inspecting his tape measure. "They're too tall."

Sammy looked at him enquiringly. "What, them cupboards you bin on about?"

"Yes. They won't fit under these wall cupboards."

"Chop 'em down, then," Sammy suggested.

"Don't be silly," David retorted. "It'll make a hell of a mess of the wall. We'd break even more tiles in the process."

"Not *these* cupboards!" Sammy exclaimed. "Them that Stan's got. In two bits, I expect. Most of 'em are. Top an' bottom comes apart. Thass 'ow they makes 'em."

"What; you mean we take the top cupboards off them and…?"

"Thass right. Fit the bottoms in 'ere. Can do that ourselves."

"If that works, Sammy, you're on a bonus!" David exclaimed. "Those units in Stan's place are as good as new!"

Sammy's laugh gurgled like a blocked drain. "Can do the tiles an' all, if yuh like."

"Could you?"

"Course! Done a bit o'tilin' in me time. Can 'ave a go at the groutin' y'self … dead easy that is."

"Thanks, Sammy! I need to get hold of some tiles first, though."

"Randolph's, in Gypsy Lane," said Sammy. "Sells the stuff they takes outta places they bin workin' on."

"Right; I'll try them. Do you know any plumbers?"

Sammy shook his head. "Ol' Charlie Greenaway used t'do a bit. Died last year though."

That's a shame," David sighed. "But if those units come apart, we're off to a flying start."

"Hooky said someone was in here asking about the café. Who was it?" David asked.

Wally shrugged dismissively. "Dunno. Didn't give 'is name."

"Was he a little chap in a bomber jacket?"

"No; it was a tall fella with dark wavy 'air. Seemed pretty sure of 'imself. 'E came in last night an' started askin' about your place."

"What did he want to know?"

Wally's brow creased in thought. "Well; where you come from ... do you own a boat. 'E knew Ralph was dead, though."

David felt his scalp tingle. "What did you tell him?"

"Nothin' that 'e didn't already know or couldn't see with 'is own eyes."

"Thass right!" Hooky concurred. "I asked 'im why 'e didn't come an' talk to you, if 'e was so interested."

"What did he say to that?"

"Nothin'. Just finished 'is drink an' left."

"There was a bloke hanging about on the quay the other night," David explained nervously. "But he was short and wearing what looked like a bomber jacket. I thought it might be someone looking for the chance to break into a boat, or pinch one. But he seemed to be watching my café."

Hooky's eyebrows rose. "What; you mean casin' it for a break-in?"

David shrugged his shoulders. "I don't know. He was in the shadows by the mole when I looked out of the window. He only

160

came out when he thought I'd gone. I could have sworn he was watching the café!"

Wally shook his head. "That don't sound like the bloke that was in 'ere."

David decided it was time take them into his confidence. "I'm wondering if it has something to do with the secret cupboard Jo found."

"Secret cupboard?" Hooky exclaimed.

"Keep your voice down!" Wally cautioned, although the other customers seemed too absorbed with their own conversations to have noticed.

David lowered his voice to almost a whisper. "Yes; Jo found it when she was clearing out the cupboard in the passageway. There's another one leading off it under the stairs. She found a lot of empty cardboard boxes and cartons in there. They'd all had foreign cigarettes and cigars and what-have-you in them."

"Well, I'm blowed!" Wally murmured. "So Ralph was up to that, was 'e?"

"We didn't know what to do about it," David explained. "The boxes were all empty and there was nothing else in there except lobster pots, so we decided to keep quiet about it."

"Not a bad idea," Wally declared. "But, it looks like somebody knows about it … Somebody Ralph was involved with, I shouldn't wonder. We'd better keep an eye out for this bloke. I'll 'ave a word with Tommy Bowyer, as well; if yuh like."

"What, the local bobby?"

"Thass right."

"Don't say anything about the cupboard, though," David warned.

"Tommy's alright," Wally insisted. "But I won't say nothin' about it if you don't want me to."

"I'd appreciate it if you didn't," said David. "The fewer people who know about it the better, in my view."

A sudden hiatus in the clamour of voices around them indicated that someone who could command attention had arrived. Looking round, David could see that all eyes were on two strikingly attractive girls who were standing in the doorway.

"Evenin' ladies," said Wally, eying them appreciatively.

"May we come in?" Tilly asked hesitantly.

"Course you can, my lovely," Wally replied. "Make yourselves at 'ome."

Tilly greeted David with a delightful smile. "Hello David. I saw you through the window. I hope we're not intruding."

"No, of course not," he said, uncomfortably aware that they were the centre of attention.

"We could only see men, so we weren't sure if we are allowed in here. Ladies aren't allowed in the bar at Daddy's golf club." She turned to her companion. "This is my friend Arabella ... We all call her Bella. I'm staying with her for the summer. Bella; this is David ... my boss," she added with a giggle.

Although not as tall as Tilly, Bella was just as eye-catching. Her grey-green eyes fixed David with an appraising, almost feline, gaze that hinted at something more worldly than Tilly's air of innocence. Luxuriant waves of auburn hair tumbled to the shoulders of her black, turtle-neck sweater, which he couldn't help noticing was more amply filled than Tilly's.

"Nice to meet you, Bella," he said. "Or should I call you Arabella?"

Her eyes sparkled. "No; Bella is fine." Her voice was deeper than Tilly's girlish trill. "I've heard a lot about you, David ... and Rocky."

David laughed nervously; relieved that previously interrupted conversations had resumed around them. Amid the increasing volume of noise, he heard Hooky's voice: "Fer Gawd's sake; somebody give Johnny a nudge, before 'e gets stuck like that! 'Is eyes are stickin' out like organ stops!"

"What would you both like to drink?" David asked.

"Oh; Kir, if I may," Tilly replied.

"Kir," Wally repeated, deadpan. "Let's 'ave a look." Scratching his beard pensively, he turned to inspect the shelves behind him. "Sorry my lovely; I think we've run out."

It was all David could do to stifle a laugh, but Bella came to their rescue. "Aperitifs and cocktails aren't often drunk in English pubs, Tilly," she cautioned, her eyes twinkling with amusement. "Crème de Cassis is not that popular here."

Tilly giggled. "Silly me. I've spent so much time in France and Switzerland, I forgot."

"I can do you a port and lemon," Wally suggested.

They were distracted by Monty's arrival. Removing his panama hat, he settled himself on his customary bar stool and smiled benignly at the girls. "I'm afraid this establishment is very much what one would describe as an ale house, my dear," he declared. "Tendering more sophisticated refreshments would merely be casting pearls to swine."

"I should watch who you're calling a swine, Monty," Hooky quipped and pointed to the towering figure by the fireplace. "Tiny's in a funny mood."

"It was merely an allegory, Hooky," Monty replied wearily. "Another way of putting things."

"Good job you told 'im that," Wally chuckled. "Hooky might o'thought it was a skin complaint."

Tilly flicked a lock of her long, blond tresses from her face. "Is Hooky your real name?"

"No, darlin'. It's a name I got from me time in the navy. Everybody 'ad one. Wally was 'the Buffer'; chief bo'sun's mate."

Both girls looked at him blankly. "Are you and Wally brothers?" Bella asked.

Hooky shook his head. "No; Wally's married to my sister, Avril."

"Oh, I see," she said. "Are you married?"

"No; I was once. Never agen!"

David had learned about Hooky's marriage from his mother, at Avril's party. In her words, his wife had 'run off with a yank' during the war; while Hooky had been in Haslar Hospital, recovering from a wound.

"Once bitten twice shy, as they say," Hooky declared, as he placed a dimpled beer mug under the best bitter tap and levered the handle. "But it's nice of you to offer."

Bella laughed; totally at ease with his banter.

"You should be so lucky!" Avril asserted, appearing from the Wardroom. As usual, she was impeccably dressed and made up, without a hair out of place. "Don't take any notice of this lot," she cautioned. "They're all talk. I'm Avril, by the way."

Introducing herself and Bella, Tilly added, "I work for David."

"So I hear. How are you likin' it?"

"It's fun," Tilly enthused. "I love meeting people. One does get a little mixed up sometimes, but David has been awfully sweet about it."

Feeling a flush to his cheeks, David avoided eye contact with Wally and Hooky.

Wally pointed to a top shelf. "I've just remembered; there's some of Stan's peach vodka up there. The girls really took to that at Avril's party."

"Go careful with that stuff, girls," Hooky cautioned. "David got Jo pie-eyed on it."

"I did no such thing!" David retorted; immediately cursing himself for rising to Hooky's bait, yet again.

"I don't suppose either of you thought to ask the girls if they're old enough to drink!" Avril remarked.

"We are," Bella replied. "Tilly's nineteen and I'm nearly twenty-one."

"In that case, I've got some white wine in my fridge," Avril suggested. "A nice sauvignon, if you'd prefer that."

"Yes, please," the girls replied enthusiastically.

Wally picked up Monty's brandy balloon and pushed it under an optic. "This one's on the 'ouse, Monty."

Monty nipped the end from a King Edward Imperial with a silver cigar cutter. "Much appreciated, Wallace."

"I forgot to tell yuh, David," Wally declared. "Monty's bin lookin' into that letter from the council."

"I have indeed," said Monty, carefully drawing on his cigar. "I managed to acquire a copy of the local bylaws. It makes for very interesting reading."

"If you say so," Wally replied. Winking at David, he gestured towards Tilly and Bella, who were perched on bar stools chatting to Avril; both with a glass of wine in one hand and a cigarette between the fingers of the other. "I'll bet them two give the lads the run around," he chortled. "Especially the red 'ead."

David responded with a grin. "Tilly certainly seems to be attracting young blokes to the café."

Monty cleared his throat noisily to regain their attention. Glass in hand, he assumed his familiar oratory pose. "I identified one or two clauses which seem to have some relevance. One in particular makes reference to 'activities and pursuits in public spaces and establishments licensed by the local authority'. So we may assume it is to this that the said N. D. Chapman refers in his recent correspondence. However, the wording of the clause is somewhat imprecise. It simply makes reference to 'professional performances' and denotes 'organised entertainment and recreation.'"

"Isn't that what we're doing?" David suggested.

"In the wider sense, perhaps," Monty replied loftily. "But more specifically, no."

David looked enquiringly at Wally, who shrugged. "Don' ask me!"

Monty ignored the interruption. "While your performances, dear boy, may be deemed entertainment by those who appreciate what is described as modern music, it is my considered opinion that they are not professional."

"You might not think so, but the customers think 'e's damned good; so do I!" Wally asserted.

Monty waved his cigar airily. "Don't misunderstand me. Although David's repertoire is not to my personal taste, I am not refuting the undeniable fact that he is an accomplished musician. My point is: he does not receive a fee for his services, and is therefore *not* performing professionally according to the precise definition."

"Don't forget the customers make a collection for me," said David.

"A moot point," Monty countered. "It is a gratuity voluntarily made; an expression of appreciation. There is no requirement for your audience to purchase a ticket or make payment in in any form in order to gain access to your performance. Nor are you recompensed by the proprietor of this establishment."

"So what can we do?" Avril asked, revealing that she had been taking note of Monty's rhetoric.

"I would suggest you reply to Mister Chapman in those terms, my dear."

"We'll 'ave t'think about it," Wally said doubtfully. "I don't reckon we'd manage to get all that down on paper, d'you Pet?"

"Don't go to all that trouble for me," David insisted. "It's a waste of time, anyway."

"Don't be silly, love!" Avril declared. "It's worth a try! Everybody's goin' to be really disappointed. They look forward to your music nights."

"Yes; you're really good," Tilly exclaimed. "Isn't he Bella?"

"Absolutely," Bella enthused. "One was privileged to be present at your concert the other evening. You're very talented, David!"

David felt his cheeks redden. "Thank you," he mumbled diffidently.

"Perhaps I might make representations on your behalf," Monty suggested.

"Would you? Bless you, Monty!" Avril exclaimed.

"Are you a lawyer?" Bella asked.

"I was in another life, my dear," Monty declared. "For more years than I care to recall, I was a barrister-at-law. Now gratefully retired."

"How are you gettin' on with all the work in the kitchen, David?" Avril asked.

"We've got Stan's cupboards and worktops fitted in," David explained. "We even found some brand new chopping boards in one of them. Sammy's been a tremendous help. He's going to do the tiling, as well. I was hoping to get some second-hand tiles, but no such luck. So it looks like we'll have to shell out for new ones."

Avril nodded understandingly. "Let me know when the inspector's due back and I'll get Molly to come round and help with the cleanin.'"

"Thanks, Avril; that'll be a great help. I've still got to find a plumber to fit a new tap."

"Perhaps I might ask my father," Bella proposed. "Men are always working at the house. I'm sure Daddy could arrange for someone to help."

"I'd be very grateful," said David. "Where do you live?"

"Abbots Hempley," she said casually, as if he should be familiar with it.

David shook his head. "Sorry; I don't know where that is. I'm afraid I don't know the area very well at all."

"Charmingly picturesque," Monty proclaimed. "Duck pond; late Norman church; village green; rustic pub … called The Ploughmans Arms, I believe. The village is four or five miles along the Raddiston turn-off from the Myrtlesham Road."

"Yeh; there's that ruddy-great mansion 'ouse there!" Dusty Miller interjected, as he passed three pint mugs across the counter for Hooky to refill. "It's where that Lord Whassname lives. Now; whassit called?"

"Huckfield Hall," Bella replied.

"Thass it! Live near there do yuh?"

"It's my home," she said calmly.

"Gordon Bennett!" Dusty exclaimed. "What you doin' in 'ere then?"

"None o'your business, Dusty," Wally declared. "The young lady's entitled to slum it with the likes of you, if she's a mind to."

"So, you're related to Lord Anthony de Tenneaux?" Monty enquired.

"He's my father. Do you know him?"

"I once made the acquaintance of your grandmother, Lady Alice. A most charming and gracious lady. I met her in the late twenties, on one or two occasions when she visited our chambers with your grandfather. She took tea with us once, while your grandfather was instructing our Head of Chambers, Sir Henry Povery Q.C."

"Grandpapa died ten years ago," Bella said wistfully. "But Grandmama's still very much alive. She's such fun! We all adore her. What's your name? I'll tell her I met you!"

"My name is Montague Barrington-Lyons, my dear. It's kind of you to offer to remember me to your dear Grandmama, but I fear it will mean nothing to her. I was but an insignificant junior barrister; unlikely to have made a lasting impression."

"She probably does remember you. She never forgets anything!" Bella declared. "She has the memory of an elephant!" Turning to David, she said, "I'll ask Daddy if he'll get his estate manager to find you someone who knows about taps."

"That's kind of you, but please don't bother him," David insisted. He didn't doubt her sincerity, but he could hardly expect a peer of the realm to concern himself with the plumbing of a seaside café.

VII

Gemma sipped her coffee in the shade of a parasol, and watched Chris add a beak to the cartoon penguin he was painting on the café window. Unlike Rocky's irascible scowl, the expression on his rockhopper was cheery and welcoming.

"That's amazing!" she exclaimed.

Peering around the doorframe, Chris called, "Thank you. The approbation of a lady whose excellent taste is matched by her beauty is praise indeed."

Gemma's cheeks flushed and she responded with a coy smile, although her eyes sparkled.

"You certainly know how to turn on the flannel, don't you?" David chuckled. "Here's your tea."

"I speak it fluently," Chris replied. "It must be my Greek blood. But I do find the accusation a bit rich coming from someone with his own little harem. An attractive brunette in the kitchen; a delightful dizzy blond waitress; and a cutie, with adorable doe eyes, for a business partner. Who else have you got hidden away that I don't know about?"

"Sorry to spoil your fantasy," David chuckled. "But the brunette in the kitchen is married with two kids; the doe-eyed cutie has got a boyfriend in the army; and the dizzy blond is only nineteen and has tastes way beyond my means."

"How unfortunate for you. Where are they all?"

"Connie's probably at home, baking. She'll be in a bit later. Tilly's taking the day off and Jo might call in later, after work." David gestured towards his only customers, an elderly couple sitting at a table in the far corner of the café. "Mondays are usually slow; especially the mornings, so I can just about cope."

"Rather you than me," said Chris. "If you have no objection, I think I'll take my tea outside and make the acquaintance of your charming neighbour."

"None at all. Her name is Gemma."

"I know," said Chris. "May I take it, from the absence of a ring, that she's not married or spoken for?"

David nodded. "From what I know of her, I'm not aware that you have any serious competition."

"Just thought I'd check. It wouldn't do to get on the wrong side of some hulking-great brute of a husband or boyfriend."

"There's no-one I know of," David reassured him.

Chris paused in the doorway. "By the way; you haven't said what you think of the window."

"It looks marvellous from in here," David enthused. "Let's have a look at it the right way round."

Chris led the way outside, and while he introduced himself to Gemma, David walked to the edge of the quay and looked up at the window. Bright blue letters with gold shadowing spelled out *The Rockhopper Café* in a shallow arc across the upper half of the window. Below it, Rocky II waved a joyful welcome.

"That's terrific!" he exclaimed.

"Isn't he clever?" Gemma trilled.

To David's surprise, Chris accepted the acclaim with a modest shrug. "Glad you like it. I thought I might add a couple of smaller penguins playing guitars. You know, to play on the 'rock' in rockhopper. I also thought I'd put little silhouettes of things from your menu along the bottom; like a cup of tea, a bottle of pop, an ice cream cone and perhaps a milk shake."

"That would be marvellous!" David exclaimed. "I wasn't expecting all that."

"Well, you're doing me a service by displaying my pictures, and I've been looked after rather well by your bevy of beauties," Chris replied. "And, of course, it has allowed me to meet this charming young lady."

If Gemma was trying to disguise her pleasure at being so lavishly flattered, it wasn't evident, David thought. But, what the heck! He knew from Avril that she had once been engaged, but her fiancé had been killed in a motor cycle accident. So, if romance was in the air, good luck to them both.

"Wait till Jo sees this window." he said.

Jo saw the window the following afternoon. When David first noticed her, she was standing beside her bike; her eyes hidden behind her white-framed sunglasses, and her face expressionless. His eagerness for her opinion faltered as he went out to greet her. "Well, what do you think?" he asked apprehensively.

She pursed her lips, as if seriously considering her reply, but when she removed her sunglasses, he could see that her eyes were twinkling. "It's amazing!" she exclaimed. "It's beginning to look like a proper café!"

David sighed with relief. "You had me worried for a moment; I thought you didn't like it. But anyway; whaddya mean: *Beginning to look like a proper cafe?* It *is* a proper café!"

"Alright," she giggled. "It's a proper café."

"We'll, take a look," he said. "There are only two tables free and the Ocean Queen is due in any minute." Taking the box she lifted from the basket on her bicycle, he asked, "What's this?"

"Be careful," she cautioned. "It's full of strawberries from our garden. Don't squash them. Aunt Ginny thought we might like to put them on the menu with cream or ice cream."

"What a good idea! Well done Aunt Ginny."

"Who's that in there with Tilly?" she asked.

"That's Bella. Or I should say Lady Arabella de Tenneaux," he announced loftily. "She's the friend Tilly's staying with. She came to have lunch with her, but we've been rushed off our feet, so she pitched in clearing tables instead."

In reply to Jo's raised eyebrows, he added, "She's made herself useful. Tilly and I have more time to concentrate on serving customers. I think they find the girls entertaining. Some are actually tipping them. One chap left *five bob*, and a Scotsman in a kilt gave me half a crown for 'the bonnie posh lassies'."

"Be careful it doesn't cause arguments," Jo cautioned.

"Don't worry; it won't," David insisted. "All the tips go in that old glass bowl under the counter to be shared out equally; Connie and Sammy included. It was Avril's suggestion, for the reason you just mentioned. Tilly's perfectly happy with it."

"You really are getting organised, aren't you?" she chuckled.

"We need to be. We've been rushed off our feet at times."

"Hello Jo!" Tilly called; an angelic smile lighting up her face.

"We've got strawberries," David called, tapping the side of the box on his way to the kitchen.

"Oh, how super!" Tilly cried. "Golly; I'm so glad to see you, Jo!" she exclaimed. "We're so busy. This is Bella; she's helping us out."

"It's very good of you, Bella," said Jo. "I understand you came for lunch but got a job instead."

"Yes; rather!" Bella laughed. "It's quite fun … if a little hectic."

"It certainly is," Jo chuckled. "Don't feel obliged to do it, though."

Bella started stacking a tray with crockery and cutlery from a nearby table. "Oh; I don't mind. But I'm afraid you can only have me today. I'll be competing from tomorrow."

"Competing?"

"Yes; jumping my horses in gymkhanas and shows."

"Oh; I see!" said Jo. "Well, good luck."

"Oh, goodness. Here comes the boat again!" Tilly exclaimed.

"All hands on deck!" David called, as the bell sounded at the serving window.

"Allow me to attend to that, Jo, while you serve the customers," Bella suggested, placing the tray on the counter. "Tilly has shown me how to work the ice cream machine. I'm afraid I wouldn't be terribly good at serving at table. I'm sure one requires tuition and heaps more experience to cope when it's so busy."

Stifling a giggle, Jo replied, "Yes; alright." As she passed David, she murmured. "May one enquire who's in charge here?"

* * *

As the last customers walked out into the evening sunshine, Jo changed the sign on the doors to *Closed* and turned to David. "So, someone's been asking questions about us … Why?"

"Search me. From Wally's description, it doesn't sound like the bloke who was lurking about on the mole the other night." He had been in two minds about telling her. He didn't think they were in any danger. In fact, he was still convinced that Charlie McBride had something to do with it. Charlie probably knew about the hidey-hole and might surreptitiously be trying to discover how much they knew about his and Uncle Ralph's nefarious activities. But, having told Wally and Hooky, he knew she would be angry if she found out from them or anyone else.

"We ought to tell the police!" she insisted.

"I told Wally and Hooky about the hidden cupboard," he confessed. "I felt it best to in the circumstances. But I told them to keep it to themselves. Wally's already had a word with PC Bowyer about the lurker. He and his mates are going to step up their patrols around the harbour at night. Wally's told the local fishing boat skippers to keep an eye out, too."

"What do Wally and Hooky think about the cupboard?" she asked.

"They were as curious as we are. But I don't think they were altogether surprised."

"Do you think that's what this creepy business is all about?" she asked nervously.

"I can't think of any other reason," David mused. "Why would anybody be interested in you or me? It has to be something to do with my uncle."

Jo pursed her lips in thought. "Do you really think Charlie McBride's behind it?"

"Who knows? He's the prime suspect; and, from what we know of him, it's the sort of underhanded thing he's capable of. He told me that he had dealings with my uncle, so perhaps he knows about the cupboard and is trying to find out if we've found it."

"So, why hasn't he just asked us?" she queried.

"Perhaps he doesn't want his dealings with Ralph becoming known, for obvious reasons. If he were to ask us about the cupboard, it would be as good as an admission of his involvement. He might even wonder if there's stuff still in there."

"So, why leave it until now to find out?"

David shrugged. "I don't know. Perhaps he's getting desperate. Perhaps that's why he wants this place. Perhaps he didn't think we would manage to get the place going again and would have to accept his offer. Or, perhaps he thinks there's a hoard still hidden away that we haven't found, and decided it was safer to wait for us to sell him the café than trying to get it out any other way."

"That's an awful lot of *perhapses*," Jo observed.

David grinned sheepishly. "I know. But I can't come up with anything better."

"What if it's not him?" she suggested. "Who on earth could it be?"

"Who knows?" said David. "So, until we find out, be careful and keep your wits about you."

"You too!" she exclaimed. "You'll be here on your own if anyone tries to get in at night!"

"Thanks for reminding me!"

Sammy pointed to the box of wall tiles David had placed on a kitchen worktop. "Get a cutter with 'em, did yuh?"

"A cutter?"

"Yeh; gonna need t'cut some of 'em, so they fit in that recess over them cutlery boxes."

"Oh, I see what you mean," said David. "No, I didn't think of that. I remembered the adhesive and grout though."

"Never mind; can rent one from Easton's."

"What, the hardware shop in Market Street?"

"Thass right. Jack Easton's got proper cutters like the trade uses. Rents 'em out by the day."

"Another expense," David sighed. "This is costing more than I expected."

"Cost a lot more if yuh got somebody in t'do it."

David nodded. "You're right. I'm grateful for all you're doing Sammy. Things are bit tight at the moment, but I'll make good on my promise of a bonus as soon as we can manage it."

"Nah! Don' want no bonus! Bin good t'me, you two."

They were distracted by sharp knocking on the café doors. "I wonder who that is," David mused. "It's time we opened up for the day, but the customers can't be that desperate."

He found two men in blue overalls on the doorstep. Parked behind them was a green Austin van bearing the legend *T.D. Llewellyn & Son, Plumbing and Electrical Services.*

"Would you be Mister Sheldrake?" the elder of them asked; the lilt of his Welsh accent in keeping with the name on the van.

"It's Sheldon actually."

"Oh; sorry about that m'n. But that's the name they gave me, see? I'm Thomas Llewellyn, an' this is my son, Bryn. I take it you've got a plumbin' job needs doin'. Mister Coleman asked us to come by an' take a look at it, like."

"Mister Coleman?" David asked, curiously.

"That's right. The estate manager on the 'Uckfield Estate."

"Oh, I see! Bella obviously mentioned it to him."

"I don't know nothin' about that. All I know is Mister Coleman asked me if I'd call in, like."

"I'm glad you did. Come in," said David, beckoning them to follow him to the kitchen. "That's the problem," he said, pointing to a brass tap that was tarnished green and encrusted with a thick chalky deposit around the spout.

"Limescale," Bryn Llewellyn observed.

"Water's 'ard roun' yere, see," his father explained. "It clogs up your kitchen and bathroom fittings if you don't flush 'em through regular with a descaler."

"Can you do that?" David asked.

"I can, but it won't do much good for anythin' in that state. Your best bet is to replace it and that bit o'pipe feedin' it."

"What will that cost?" David asked cautiously.

"It depends. If you're lookin' to keep the cost down, I'm pretty sure I've got a tap that'll do for that back at the yard; unless you particularly want a new one."

"No; that would do perfectly well. I'm told we ought to have separate facilities to wash our hands, too."

Mister Llewellyn stroked his jaw and glanced around the kitchen. "I reckon the only place you could put another wash basin, without too much extra pipe work, is in that corner; on the end of the other sinks." He looked up at the boiler pensively.

"It'll need its own water heater, too. It'll be 'ell of a job tryin' to plumb something off that thing."

"How much will that cost?" David enquired nervously. "It's not essential. But I've been advised we ought to do it."

Llewellyn the elder pursed his lips. "It depends on 'ow much work's involved. What do you think, Bryn?"

"If it's only for washin' their 'ands, I reckon a little Sadia heater over the sink would do," Bryn proposed. "We can spur off that electric point under the window to save time and money."

His father nodded his agreement and turned to David. "Bryn's right. That's the best way to go about it, if you're lookin' to keep the cost down. Let me go away and work it all out. I'll phone you back with the best price I can come up with, and you can make your mind up then. How's that?"

"Thanks," said David. "But we're not on the phone."

"Oh; right. Well, you'd better phone me then." Delving into a pocket of his overalls, he produced a business card. "That's our number. Give me a day or two to get some prices together before you phone me. In the evenin' is best."

David took the card, "OK; I will. Thanks for coming. Can I offer you a cup of tea or coffee?"

"A nice cup o'tea would be just the job, eh Bryn?"

The Llewellyns were sitting in the sunshine outside the café, when the pop-pop of Tilly's Mobylette announced her arrival. Peering over the rims of their tea cups, they watched her sweep around the wooden tables and benches and disappear into the lane between the café and the pub; her golden hair streaming out behind her and her skirt billowing above her knees.

"Classy little article is that," said Thomas.

"Yeh; the bike's not bad either," Hooky quipped from the shadow of the Packet Boat doorway.

It brought a chuckle from Bryn, although it seemed lost on his father, who remarked "Handy little things them mopeds. Saves a lotta pedallin."

"That one's French," David explained. "Tilly brought it over with her a month or two ago."

"Anyway!" said Thomas, draining his cup. "Better get on, like. Thanks for the tea. Ring me in a day or two, an' if you want to go ahead, we'll come back next week."

"Thanks; that's fine," said David, shaking hands with both Llewellyns as they stood up to leave.

"Big job?" Hooky asked, as he and David watched them drive away.

"Big enough," David sighed. "But we've got to get it done if we want to stay open."

"Don't take this the wrong way," Hooky began. "But, I've got a few bob put away; and I'm sure Wally…"

"Thanks Hooky, but no," David interjected. "We've got to stand on our own feet, if we're going to make this work."

Hooky held up his palms in front of him. "No offence meant. All I'm sayin' is, the offer's there."

"None taken, Hooky. I appreciate it; I really do," David replied. "Brave words," he murmured to himself. "God knows where we're going to get the money from."

Bert Weedon's *Guitar Boogie Shuffle* was twanging from his transistor radio when he went back into the café. He smiled ruefully, as the solution came to him.

* * *

"What's good, Honey?" the young chap asked in a distinctive American accent, as he studied the menu card.

"We have fresh strawberries," Tilly announced proudly.

"Are they as fresh and sweet as you, sugar?" he drawled, bringing a titter from his companions.

"She's not on the menu," David growled.

"Just a joke. I wasn't trying to put a move on your girlfriend," the young man replied.

178

Tilly giggled and swept strands of hair from her face.

"She's not my girlfriend," David said hastily. "But Tilly has to put up with blokes trying it on at least a dozen times a week."

The chap grinned knowingly. "I can sure believe that."

"David was just being protective," Tilly explained, her eyes twinkling.

The chap smiled up at her engagingly. "My apologies, Tilly. Just having a little fun. My name is Bernard," he added, placing the emphasis on the second syllable.

Tilly rewarded him with a disarming smile of her own. "That's alright. Well, Bernard, we can offer you strawberries and cream, strawberries and ice cream, or a strawberry ice cream sundae."

"Oh; an ice cream sundae! Yes please!" exclaimed the slim brunette on the opposite side of the table. "Me too!" called the blonde beside her.

"OK Tilly; you made a sale," Bernard declared. "You can get me a sundae, too."

The three girls and two young men seated around a window table were all lean, with well-toned bodies that radiated fitness and the healthy glow of youth. Their faces seemed vaguely familiar, and David suddenly remembered seeing them on the poster outside the Wintergardens Palace Theatre. "You're The Mervin Devine Dancers, aren't you?"

"Some of them," the brunette chuckled.

"Sorry to disappoint you, but Tilly's getting carried away," David explained. "I'm afraid we don't do ice cream sundaes. To tell the truth, we don't know how."

"I do!" Tilly insisted, her blue eyes sparkling.

"Really?" David asked.

"Yes, of course!" Turning her attention to her order pad, she said, "One does get a little muddled sometimes, so let's make sure one has it all right. That's three strawberry sundaes; one banana and vanilla ice cream with chocolate sauce; one arctic roll with Neapolitan ice cream; three Pepsis; one Tango and one lemonade. Is that right?"

"Yeh. That's right. OK," came the responses from around the table. "How much are the strawberry sundaes?" Bernard asked; at which Tilly gazed at David questioningly.

"Four bob," he replied off the top of his head. To his surprise and relief, no-one questioned it.

"I'll go and get on with them, then," Tilly declared.

David's expression must have betrayed his astonishment, as he watched her weave her way between the tables, because Bernard drawled, "Tilly's quite a gal. I guess she's full of surprises."

"You can say that again," said David.

He served the dancers their drinks while he and they waited for Tilly to return; in his case not without apprehension. Going out to retrieve crockery from the outside tables, his attention was drawn to two uniformed 'squaddies' who were chatting to a group of girls on the Esplanade. It was another unsettling reminder that Jo's boyfriend would soon be putting in an appearance.

However hard he tried, he couldn't rid himself of the dejection the thought aroused in him. It didn't help to tell himself that Jo regarded him as nothing more than a colleague; perhaps a friend. But no more than that. He sighed wistfully. Just when he felt he was getting to know her; to like Fairhaven; and to get the hang of running a café. It brought to mind Flight Sergeant Dyer's stock reply to any whiner or malingerer who had the temerity to bemoan his lot: "Not fair? *Life's* not fair, laddie!"

Making sure that no customers were trying to attract his attention, David allowed himself a few moments to savour the fresh air and sunshine, while he attempted to clear his mind of dispiriting thoughts of Jo's boyfriend, health inspectors and sinister prowlers. Ken Rathbone was patrolling the mole with his characteristic strutting gait; stopping now and then to peer down officiously at one of the pleasure craft moored against the quay.

'Probably looking to tear the owner off a strip for being an inch out of position', David thought. He was being uncharitable, he would admit. The harbourmaster had his job to do. But why was it that a peaked cap and a uniform so often turned a perfectly reasonable and affable character into an obdurate stickler for the rules.

It was his mother's birthday in few days' time. He made a mental note to buy a card and have a word with Avril to see if she could come up with an idea for a present; something suitable *and* within his limited means. His 'harem', as Chris referred to them, had assured him that they could cope if he took a couple of days off to visit his parents. Jo had suggested that the break would do him good, but concern over the mystery prowler made him uneasy about leaving the café unoccupied at night. In the end, Avril's promise to keep an eye on the girls, and Hooky's offer to stay in the café overnight had persuaded him that it was safe to go.

Gasps and exclamations in the café jolted him back to reality, and he turned to see Tilly and Connie approaching Bernard and his companions carrying loaded trays. Connie's tray bore the banana and vanilla ice cream and the arctic roll, while Tilly's was loaded with her creations, which she carefully placed on the table.

The strawberry sundaes were nothing if not colourful and served in what David was convinced were glass mixing bowls, about the same height and diameter as breakfast cereal bowls. Each sundae included layers of chopped strawberries and cream, together with other fruit, on what looked like a biscuit or sponge-cake base, although the layers were not uniform in order or depth. A generous spiral of whipped cream, studded with chopped nuts, a swirl of chocolate sauce and a whole strawberry topped each one. Tilly had even crowned them with a fan wafer.

Exclamations of "Good grief! … My God! … Look at that!" came from around the café, as Bernard and his companions stared at each other with their spoons hovering over their sundaes, as if unsure how or where to start.

"How the heck did you manage all that in such a short time, Tilly?" David asked.

She brushed away an errant wisp of hair with the back of her hand, leaving a streak of something white beside her eye. "Oh, I had to hurry. I didn't want to keep everyone waiting."

"She's not kidding," Connie murmured, taking the tray of crockery from David. "Wait till you see the state of the kitchen."

Connie hadn't exaggerated. The worktop, just inside the door, was covered with spoons, knives, a whisk, discarded ice cream wrappers, overturned bottles of fruit flavouring and the assorted debris and crumbs of chopped nuts and sponge cake. Smears of cream and splashes of coloured flavouring speckled the new wall tiles, and a white trail from a split bag of caster sugar had spilt over the edge of the worktop and onto the floor.

"My God! Who set the bomb off?" David exclaimed.

Tilly appeared at his shoulder, looking anxious. "I'm sorry, David. I was in such a hurry. You keep telling me not to keep the customers waiting too long. I couldn't find anything to put them in … and there weren't any proper spoons … I got flustered and panicked!" The words tumbled out as her eyes brimmed with tears.

Female distress was something David had never been able to cope with. Unsettled and out of his depth, he replied as soothingly as he could, "It's alright Tilly; please don't cry."

Tears spilled down her cheeks, as she fussed with the messy spoons. "I'll clear it all up; really I will!" she whimpered, gripping his arm. Following his gaze, her eyes widened in horror at the sight of her sticky fingerprints on his shirt sleeve. "Oh, David; I'm so sorry!" she wailed.

Connie was battling suppressed mirth and, to Tilly's bewilderment, she and David burst out laughing.

Raised voices in the café caught their attention and Tilly clasped her hands to her mouth. "Oh goodness! They don't like them! What shall I do?" she gasped. "Should one apologise and bring them back … or clear up in here first?"

"I'll go and see what's up," David replied reassuringly. "Wash your hands and get those smears off your face … And dry those eyes before they get all red and puffy."

She managed a weak smile. "Alright. Thank you. I'll clear this mess up first, though."

"Leave that to me!" Sammy commanded. "Take care o'that in a minute, when I've took the rubbish out t'the bins. No need fer all the waterworks. Go on, girl. Go an 'ave a wash, like you bin told," he added gently.

Making his way apprehensively towards the hubbub in the café, David began mentally rehearsing a damage-limiting apology. As he emerged from the corridor, he could see that a great deal of attention was focused on the dancers' table, where brows were furrowed and spoons and fan wafers were being waved over the sundaes.

"I can definitely taste pineapple," the brunette insisted.

"No; I'm sure it's grapefruit," the blonde girl replied and held out her loaded spoon to the girl across the table. "What do you think, Lynn?"

Lynn cleared the spoon and closed her eyes. "Mmm," she crooned. "I can taste the grapefruit."

"I'm getting lemon," Bernard declared. "What the heck's going on here?"

"Is there a problem?" David began anxiously.

"Problem? You gotta be kidding!" Bernard exclaimed. "Tilly's an angel! These are great!"

"Heaven in a bowl!" the little blonde cooed.

The brunette took another mouthful and chuckled. "The only problem is; we can't make up our minds what's flavouring the sponge."

"There's only one way to find out," David chortled. Silently heaving a sigh of relief, he called, "Tilly! You're needed out here."

All around the café heads turned towards the corridor. However, they had to wait a few moments before Tilly cautiously emerged from the staircase, with her hair tied back off her face and her expression a mixture of anxiety and distress.

David crooked a finger. "Come on. Come and take a bow!"

Tilly's expression changed to momentary surprise and then delighted wonder as she received a round of applause from the dancers; the accolade taken up by customers at one or two other tables.

Bernard sprang to his feet. "Attagirl, Tilly!"

"This is the best ice cream sundae I've ever had!" the blonde girl exclaimed. "But you've got to put us out of our misery. Is it grapefruit, pineapple, or lemon you've put in them?"

"I don't know. They might all be different. One was in such a hurry!" Tilly replied, and burst into tears.

David instinctively put a comforting arm around her and she buried her face in his shoulder, appearing to laugh and cry at the same time. Amid the amusement and sympathetic murmurs around them, Bernard exclaimed, "Here's to Tilly's unbeatable, never-the-same strawberry sundaes!"

"Excuse me, can I get by?"

David turned towards the familiar voice. "Jo! We weren't expecting you."

"Evidently," she replied pointedly. "Don't let me interrupt."

"More strawberries." Taking his arm from round Tilly's shoulders, he said, "Let me take those."

"I can manage!" With a sway of her hips, she avoided his attempt to take the box from her and strutted towards the kitchen.

"Storm warning; someone's upset Jo," he murmured.

Tilly dabbed at her eyes with a paper napkin. Still curiously disconcerted, she was looking at him strangely and biting her bottom lip. She seemed about to speak, but was distracted by a woman sitting at a table behind her. "Excuse me. How much did you say your ice cream sundaes are?"

"Four shillings," David repeated.

"That's a bit steep," the woman replied.

"I can assure you they're worth it!" the brunette dancer declared.

"Alright. We'll have two, please."

David was already contemplating the potential benefit of adding them to the menu, as he followed Jo to the kitchen. Should he encourage Tilly to go on preparing them ad hoc, with no fixed recipe? He chuckled to himself at Bernard's description: '*Tilly's Never-The-Same Strawberry Sundaes*'.

The damp promenade paving suggested that Fairhaven had received a shower of rain, although David had seen none during his journey home. The rain had stopped, but Fairhaven Bay was still brooding under a mantle of sombre evening cloud when he stepped down from the bus.

He could only hope that Jo wasn't doing the same and that her mood had improved during the two days he had been away. She had been 'tetchy', for want of a better word, before he had left, and less than forthcoming when he had tried to discover the reason. He had been told to mind his own business when he had hopefully asked if she had fallen-out with her boyfriend.

She hadn't shown much enthusiasm for Tilly's ice cream sundaes either, despite their immediate popularity and how profitable they were. In fact Tilly had seemed to be the focus of much of her irritability. 'Tilly spent too long chatting to customers – Her *silly me* act was annoying – They ought to know what she was putting in the sundaes'.

Reminding her that Tilly was popular with the customers had had little effect. Nor had pointing out that she was a sweet natured girl, who was anxious to please, and that the mystery of her sundaes was part of their appeal. He had stopped short of using the phrase, 'Get off her back', which a little voice somewhere in the more prudent region of his brain had cautioned him to avoid.

At least his parents had been pleased to see him. So had Richard, whose health had visibly improved in their mother's care. However, he had confessed to David that he was finding her fussing and pampering stifling and couldn't wait to get back to having his own flat. She had been delighted with her birthday present; a silver brooch, which Avril had found in the flea market in Myrtlesham.

To his parent's relief, Richard had recently sold the piano Uncle Ralph had left him. Neither they nor Richard could play it, and all it had done was take up space in their dining room. David had refused Richard's offer to give it to him, on the grounds that there was no room for it in the café and no easy way to get it into the flat above. He wouldn't be staying there long, so it wouldn't be worth the effort, anyway.

Their father had seemed fascinated by what David had branded, *Tales of The Rockhopper Café* and had been impressed by its increasing success. "How are you getting on with Jo?" he had asked pointedly.

'Not you, as well!' David had thought. 'Mum's bad enough.' But he had replied, "Pretty well. We get along fine." To forstall any further curiosity, he had added, "Her boyfriend's coming home on leave from Germany, soon."

Despite the pleasure of two days with his family, David was happy to be home; if he could call Fairhaven home. However, he was anxious about what may have gone on between Jo and Tilly during his absence. He wasn't concerned about Jo sacking her without consulting him. His fear was that she might have antagonised Tilly enough for her to decide she'd had enough.

"Women!" he sighed. "Why do they have to be so complicated?"

The doors were open and the lights were on when he reached the café, but there were no customers. Jo was perched on the high stool with her back to the doors and a magazine open on the counter in front of her. Her turtle-neck sweater and straight skirt accentuated the delightful curves of her figure and, standing in the doorway, he allowed himself the pleasure of watching her for a moment; until she sensed that someone was there and swivelled round to face him.

Caught off guard, he grinned sheepishly and dropped his holdall onto a table. "Can you spare a few coppers for a poor, starvin' beggar, lady?"

"Idiot!" she replied, before a smile lit up her face … and his heart. "How are Richard and your parents?"

"All well, thanks. How have things been here?"

"Busy," she said. "Hooky hasn't seen anyone hanging about at night, and Tilly's strawberry sundaes have been selling like hot-cakes. Word seems to be getting round. I've had to buy proper sundae glasses and long spoons for them. We had a reporter from The Myrtlesham Argus in here yesterday morning wanting to know all about them. He brought a photographer with him."

"For a photo of Tilly?"

"He wanted one of all of us, with one of Tilly's strawberry sundaes. He took one of Rocky and a few of the café, as well. Fortunately, it was pretty full at the time."

"What about Sammy?" David prompted. "Don't tell me we're going to see his enchanting smile splashed across the front page!"

Jo giggled. "No; you needn't worry. They weren't interested in the kitchen. They never went in there, and Sammy seemed more than happy to keep out of their way."

David rubbed his hands together. "So, we're getting some free publicity."

"Hopefully," she said. "By the way, the plumber called in and left an envelope for you. It's under the counter."

"I assume it's the estimates. What do they come to?"

"I don't know. I didn't open it; it's addressed to you."

"But it's meant for both of us; you know that." Making his way behind the counter, David retrieved the envelope and tore it open. "Hm; not as bad as I feared. Not good, but not terrible." He slid the plumber's quote across the magazine towards her.

"It's bad enough," she declared. "Tell me; if you won't let me contribute, how do you imagine we're going to pay for this?"

He tapped the side of his nose with a forefinger. "Trust your beloved partner."

"You're not going to do anything silly, are you?" she asked apprehensively.

"As if I would!" Enjoying her chuckle and to forestall any further inquiry, he said, "We *are* alright, aren't we, Jo? I mean; you and me. I'm sorry if I did something to upset you. Whatever it was, it wasn't intentional. If there's anything I can do to make amends."

She shook her head. "No; it's not your fault. It was just … Well; I was fed up and in a bad mood, I suppose."

"How are things between you and Tilly?" he asked cautiously.

She grinned knowingly. "Fine. She's been a brick. Rushed off her feet; especially with the sundaes. But she's stayed disgustingly cheerful. You're right; she *is* willing and anxious to please. So don't worry. I won't mess things up for you with her."

"What do you mean?"

"Come off it, David. Don't pretend you don't fancy her. All the men do. Young lads come in just to moon over her."

"That's as maybe. She's a very attractive girl, and I'll admit to being fond of her. But I don't *fancy her!*"

"I couldn't blame you. I don't think she'd be too unhappy about it, either. She didn't seem at all put out when you had your arm round her."

"Will you please listen!?" David exclaimed hotly, his voice echoing around the room. "I *do not* fancy Tilly! She's a delightful girl, but don't forget she's only nineteen! She was upset and I didn't know what to do. I've never been able to cope with girls crying."

"You seemed to be managing pretty well."

"I told you; she was upset … and happy… and God knows what else besides. All at the same time. Don't ask me why. You lot … females. I'll never understand what goes on in your heads. But what you saw wasn't what you're suggesting. Ask Connie, if you don't believe me!"

Jo's shoulders trembled and her eyes sparkled with mirth.

"What's so funny?"

"You! Stop shouting. People on the mole are looking over here."

"I couldn't care less! I can't win, can I?"

"Well, don't shout at me, then." Her eyes twinkled mischievously. "Or I'll cry."

"David … Jo! Have you seen this?"

They both looked towards the doorway, where Gemma was holding up the evening newspaper. Its banner headline proclaimed: *Fairhaven Council Gives Go Ahead For Harbour Redevelopment.*

"Does it say when they're going to start?" Jo asked.

Gemma pursed her lips. "No; it just says they've given approval to start the planning stage. Apparently, they're sending us notices in the near future."

"What are they thinking of doing?" David asked.

"I don't know; I haven't read it all. I couldn't bear to." Visibly distressed she held out the paper to him. "Here; look for yourself."

"Well; whatever it is, it's put the kybosh on us selling this place," he murmured.

Gemma's eyes brimmed with tears. "It's taken me ten years to build up my business! And now this!"

Jo patted her arm. "Come and sit down and let David see what it says in the paper. Shall I make us a cup of tea?"

"I could do with something stronger," Gemma sniffed. "I wonder what Avril and Wally will say."

"It doesn't affect them," David explained. "The Packet Boat Inn is a listed building. They can't do much to it. But I see the redevelopment includes the sheds and boathouses behind us. So it's going to affect a lot of businesses"

"It's not fair!" Gemma exclaimed petulantly. "They shouldn't be allowed to do this to people!"

David continued reading. "It says here that there's going to be public consultation; whatever that is. But there's not much information about what they intend to do."

"We ought to fight it!" Gemma declared. "We should all get together and tell them we're not just going to take it lying down!"

David handed the newspaper back to her. "I don't know how much good that would do. But they'll have to compensate us. So those affected will at least be able to start up again elsewhere."

"That's not the point!" Jo declared. "No amount of compensation can make up for all the disruption and distress it's going to cause. Some of those businesses behind the harbour have been there for generations. Gemma's right; we should all get together and fight it!"

"How?" David contended. "We're up against big business interests. What can we do against the likes of Charlie McBride and their lawyers?"

Jo's eyes flashed angrily. "I don't know! But we've got to do something. We can't just lie down and let them walk all over us! Why don't we ask Monty what he thinks?"

"That's a good idea," Gemma replied and stood up to leave. "Well, I'd better close up and get ready. Chris is taking me dancing tonight, but I don't feel much like it."

"It'll do you good," Jo asserted. She shook her head as she watched Gemma pass by outside the window. "Poor Gemma."

"Surely she'll get compensation," David suggested. "If she owns the freehold, the council will buy it from her by compulsory purchase. Or, if she has a lease, I would imagine her landlord will have to compensate her for terminating it. Much like ours."

"I doubt if that's much consolation to her at the moment," Jo sighed.

Whistling cheerfully, David swept into the kitchen and almost collided with Tilly, who was leaving with a tray loaded with strawberry sundaes.

"Frankfurters," she exclaimed.

"The same to you!"

She giggled. "I mean frankfurter sausages. One uses them for hot dogs."

"Does one? How does one know?"

"Bernard told me. I asked him, when I saw him yesterday evening."

"So you're seeing Bernard?"

"No; not that way. Bella and I met him and a few of the other dancers in The Cavendish Hotel. There aren't any shows at the theatre on Mondays until July."

"Oh, I see. And you and Bernard had a romantic tête-à-tête about sausages?"

Tilly giggled again. "Not exactly. But I took the opportunity to ask him about hot dogs. Being an American, one assumed he would know. I thought it might be useful."

"And?"

"Well, basically it's a frankfurter sausage in a soft roll with fried onions and garnished with mustard or tomato ketchup; perhaps with an option of a relish. Bella says American-style diners are becoming popular over here. Bernard suggested one might offer french fries, which are basically thinly-cut chips, or a small salad, as a side order."

"That's good of him," said David. "And well done you!" he called, as she disappeared into the passage.

Connie gazed around them pensively. "With ice cream sundaes and everything else you've taken on, there's not much room … or time … to do hot dogs, or anything else."

He stroked his chin thoughtfully, "I see what you mean. Perhaps we'd better put a hold on the hot dogs for a while."

"We're going to need extra help … with or without hot dogs," she asserted. "We're not into the high season yet, and already there are times when we're just about rushed off our feet; especially at weekends. Don't forget, I'm supposed to be part-time; and you've got to think of Tilly! She's a young girl. She's getting precious little time off to enjoy herself."

"You're quite right," he said. "Where do you think an extra pair of hands is needed most; in here or out there serving?"

"If you want my honest opinion, we need both! At least, we will when the kids break up from school. Fairhaven gets quite crowded in late July and August; especially during carnival week."

David pursed his lips. "I'd better talk this over with Jo."

The short, stockily built chap held out a wad of banknotes with a smile that displayed an array of small, even teeth. "There yuh go guv; 'undred an' twenty quid, like we agreed!"

David guessed that he was no more than a year or two older than himself, although the crown of his head was bald, giving him the look of an uncommonly well-developed monk.

"Thanks." David took the money and placed it on the red table beside him.

"Aintcha gonna count it?" the chap asked casually.

"Do I need to?"

"Nah; it's all there. Benny Jeavons wouldn't short-change yuh. Ask anybody." He grasped the handle on the amplifier one-handed, his biceps bulging impressively, as he hoisted it into the back of a black A35 van. "Decent bit a kit, this. I 'andle a fair few Selmers."

"I've been very pleased with it," David replied. Handing him a guitar case, he added wistfully, "I'll miss this more, though. It's got an easy feel to the fretboard and a really nice tone."

"Yeah; real nice guitar, the Hofner Club."

David nodded in agreement. "I hope you find a good home for it."

"I don't reckon it'll be a problem. You don't come across second 'and ones in such good nick, that often." Benny held out a bear-like paw. "Nice doin' business with yuh, Dave."

"You too," David replied, wincing as he felt his knuckles grind in Benny's grip.

"You know where I am," Benny called, slamming the van doors shut. "Whenever you're in the market for some decent gear, I'm yer man. Guitars, strings, amps … whatever. See yuh around!"

David lowered the parasols for the night and, settling himself on a chair, gazed at the money on the table. Parting with his Hofner was a wrench, but he wouldn't be needing an electric guitar for a while, and now he had enough money to take care of the hygiene inspector's demands. He had been fortunate enough to make a surprisingly good profit on the sale. The chap in the second-hand shop, where he had bought it, hadn't known anything about guitars or what it was really worth. But, luckily, Benny had recognised its quality and, more importantly, its value.

Dusk was quenching the blaze of sunset; turning the crimson haze on the horizon to deepening shades of purple and gradually unveiling the stars overhead as pin-pricks of twinkling light. David stretched out his legs and gazed across the forest of overlapping masts and spars rocking gently in the harbour. In the gathering gloom, their rigging resembled the sinister web of a monstrous spider. At the far end of the bay, the funfair was a blaze of light, and the pavements along the Esplanade were already dappled with light reflected from windows and the illuminated signs of hotels and pubs. On the promenade, he could see shadowy figures strolling beneath the chains of coloured lights that glowed ever brighter as twilight faded into darkness.

Light, spilling from the windows of The Packet Boat Inn, was deepening the shadows and distorting the profiles of the deserted wooden tables and benches into eerie, unworldly forms; and, above the whispering sigh of the surf, he could hear the muted drone of voices wafting from The Mess and Wardroom.

"What earth-shattering issue is The Mess debating tonight?" David muttered sardonically.

There had been no sign of the mysterious prowler recently, so he allowed himself to relax and drift and into drowsy contemplation. He could hardly believe how much his life had changed in such a short time. Four months ago, he would have scoffed at the very idea of spending an entire summer running a seaside café, and dismissed the notion that anything ... or anyone ... could motivate him to do so.

It wouldn't be long before Jo's boyfriend was home on leave; a thought that was never far from his mind. If the chap had a grain of sense he'd marry her straight away. David swallowed to ease the constriction in his throat. Soon, it would all be over and gone; the summer, his new life ... and Jo.

What then? The harbour redevelopment plans had put an end to any chance of selling the café as a going concern, so there was no point in hanging on beyond the end of the season. Charlie McBride might still be prepared to buy the lease from them, if they came clean about the compensation clause. But he wouldn't offer them anything like the amount their landlord would have to pay to redeem it; certainly not enough to make it worth their while. There was no way of knowing when the compulsory purchase orders would be issued. All they could do was make as much money as they could over the rest of the summer, and hope to cover the rent and other expenses for as long as possible.

His dilemma was: what to do while they waited for the axe to fall? His heart wouldn't be in trying to carry on running the café without Jo. So he would move on again; playing guitar or piano in pubs and clubs, doing a few gigs here and there with various groups or combos, and making ends meet by occasionally working as a waiter or serving behind a bar.

He had no illusions about his chances of making a living as a musician or, more-to-the-point, how long his share of the lease compensation money would last him. Returning to his old way of life, he would get through it far too soon, and eventually have to settle for the tedium of clocking in and out every day in some dreary factory or office.

He laughed bitterly. "Oh, David! Is that all there is? Is that all you've got to look forward to?"

Avril placed a copy of The Myrtlesham Argus on the bar in front of David. "Have a look at page five."

Beneath the headline: *Strawberry Sundaes at The Rockhopper Café*, was a picture of his 'bevy of beauties', as Chris had labelled them; each with a captivating smile. They were grouped in front of the tables and parasols outside the café, with Tilly in the centre holding one of her creations.

The article covered the upper half of a broadsheet page

and, beneath the picture, it began: *The old Seagull Café on the harbour-side at Fairhaven has seen a remarkable transformation since it came under new ownership earlier this year...*

David read on and suddenly grimaced. "Jo's not going to like that!"

"Why's that then?" Wally asked. "I would've thought it's good publicity; especially with that picture of them three little crackers."

"Have you read it?" David queried.

"I 'ad a quick shufti when it was delivered, but that's all."

David turned the paper around and pointed to the line that read: *David and Jo Sheldon have renamed and completely refurbished what was previously the shabby and neglected Seagull Café...*

Avril peered over Wally's shoulder. "I didn't notice that! But I'm sure Jo will see the funny side of it."

"I wouldn't bet on it!" David snorted. "It'll be my fault, of course; even though I wasn't there at the time."

Wally looked up from the paper and grinned. "I've got a feelin' you're about to find out."

David followed Wally's gaze to where Jo was standing in the doorway of The Mess.

Greeting Wally and Avril, she hoisted herself onto a stool beside him. "What will be your fault?"

"We're in the Argus," he said cautiously. "They've given us quite a large spread."

"I know; I've seen it. Aunt Ginny showed it to me. Apparently, it isn't only the café's name that's changed."

"Well, that's one thing you *can't* blame me for," he asserted.

"I can if I want," she teased; her eyes twinkling. "But Tilly was the cause of it, really."

"So poor Tilly's to blame! If it's not me it's her."

"Wait a minute," she giggled. "Don't get all uppity. She was the cause of it, but it wasn't her fault. The reporter was asking *me* questions, but his attention was on *her* the whole time. I don't think he took in half of what I was telling him. I suppose he just jumped to conclusions when I told him we inherited the café."

"Never mind. No 'arm done," Wally pronounced. "What can I get you to drink, my lovely?"

"Just a lemonade, please. I need to keep a clear head if I'm going to be in conference with our tycoon, here." Her eyes sparkled impishly. "Or should I say *typhoon*? He can cause nearly as much havoc."

David grinned resignedly. "I see; that's the mood we're in, is it?"

"Aunt Ginny told me you'd phoned. I take it you need to talk to me."

"That's right." Gesturing to a window seat, he added, "Shall we move to the boardroom?" He waited for her to settle comfortably before he continued. "Connie thinks we need to take on more help … if we can get it."

"Go on."

"I think she's getting fed up with doing more hours than she agreed to and, as she pointed out, Tilly's working all hours. The way things are taking off, Connie's convinced we won't be able to cope in the high season."

Jo nodded. "She's right. I've been thinking the same thing. She and Tilly have been absolute bricks. So has Sammy. I don't know how we'd have coped without them."

"It's extra cost though, isn't it?" David sighed.

"I think we'll manage," she said. "We're not doing at all badly. The business is picking up nicely. Tilly's sundaes are really going well and boat ticket sales have been good, too."

"I sold one of Chris's pictures today," he declared.

"Oh good! He'll be pleased. So will Gemma. It looks like things are progressing very promisingly with those two."

"Well you know what they say in the song," he declared and launched into *Love Is A Many Splendored Thing;* causing heads to turn in their direction, and Jo to roll her eyes at Avril.

"What do you suggest we do about getting some help," she asked.

David took a long pull at his pint before answering. "Well; Connie's convinced we'll need help in the kitchen *and* with serving. Tilly hasn't complained, but Connie thinks she should have more time off. She's as willing as they come, but as Connie pointed out, she's still only a teenager. What do you think?"

"Hmm." Jo pursed her lips. "I agree with Connie. But where are we going to get the extra staff? We didn't get much response the last time we tried. We can't expect another Tilly to turn up out of the blue."

"I've just thought of another problem," David declared. "If we give Tilly more time off, what happens about the sundaes when she's not there?"

Jo shrugged dismissively. "That shouldn't be a big problem. She could make a few to keep in the fridge for when it's her day off. Come to think of it; I think it would be good if she did that every day; before it gets busy. It will save her having to make them up in a hurry every time one of us takes an order!"

David nodded enthusiastically. "Good idea. Although that's the main reason they're always different."

"We still ought to get her to show one or more of us her method," Jo suggested. "The way things are going she won't be able to keep up with the demand on her own, anyway."

"My little genius!" David exclaimed. "As Chris would put it; brains as well as beauty!"

"Well; you're not Chris, so don't get carried away."

"True. But if my name was Davidos Sheldonaikos, you would be swept off your dainty little feet." He picked up her glass. "Another? How about ouzo? You know what the Greeks say: Ouzo is jolly good boozo!"

"Idiot!" she giggled. "By the way. You know what you were saying about Richard getting frustrated at home?"

"Yes."

"Well, perhaps some sea air would do him good."

"You mean here, in Fairhaven?"

"Yes. You're always saying you don't see enough of him. I wouldn't have thought there was room or the facilities for both of you over the café, but I mentioned it to Aunt Ginny, and she's willing to consider having him to stay with us for a week or two."

"What about when your boyfriend's here?" David queried. "Won't he need the room?"

Jo wrinkled her nose. "We've got two spare rooms. But Colin usually stays with his godmother when he's here. She lives in Lathering; that's about twenty-odd miles north of here." Her eyes sparkled mischievously. "She's a straight-laced old Victorian lady and very religious. She doesn't consider it *proper* for him to stay at our house, when we're not even engaged. Colin's the apple of her eye; he thinks she's leaving him some money in her will. So he doesn't want to risk upsetting her."

"I see," said David.

"So, there's room for Richard," she declared. "At least, there will be when we've cleared out all Aunt Ginny's clutter from one of the bedrooms."

"Thanks. It's a nice thought. I'll phone Richard later. He's still on probation, as he calls it. Mum's mollycoddling is getting him down, so I think the idea might appeal to him. Say thanks to Aunt Ginny for me."

"What about the hot dogs," she called, as he made his way to the bar. "Or have you forgotten about them?"

He grinned awkwardly. "Ah; yes. In the present circumstances, it might be best to keep that idea on ice for the time being.

VIII

David knew that Mervin was in the vicinity before he saw him sitting under a parasol at the white table. Not only was his voice louder than those around him, but its theatrical flamboyance was unmistakably Mervin. He was wearing his trade-mark yachting cap and a gaudy Hawaiian shirt patterned with a design of migraine-inducing vividness. "Hello, Mervin. What can I offer you?" he asked.

"Oh, your golden-haired angel is taking care of us," Mervin declared. "Malheureusement, we only have time for coffee. I'm just dying to experience one of your world-famous ice cream sundaes. The boys and girls are simply raving about them! But alas, some other time." He gestured to the woman sitting at the table with him. "Allow me to introduce Dorothy Quinlan, our theatre manager.

"It's nice to meet you, David," she said in a voice coarsened with the rasp of a heavy smoker. "I've heard so much about your café."

She was slim and angular, with dyed-blonde hair lacquered into a series of waves that framed her long, thin features. David guessed her age to be somewhere north of forty. A pale blue cardigan was draped around her shoulders and the tails of a large bow flowed from the wide collar of a diaphanous blouse, through which he could see more of her than he cared to. An extra-long cigarette smouldered between her bony fingers; its tip smudged by scarlet lips, which now drew back in a smile to reveal an expanse of large teeth and prominent gums.

Mervin gestured for David to join them. "May we prevail upon you for a few moments of your precious time?"

The café was only half full and no-one seemed in need of attention, so he sat down. "Yes, of course. But I'll have to leave you if Tilly needs help. I've got plumbers working in the kitchen, too."

All male eyes followed Tilly, as she appeared from the corridor and made her willowy way to their table with a tray bearing two coffees, a sugar bowl and a small plate of fancy biscuits.

"Bless you, dear girl!" Mervin exclaimed, as she carefully arranged the contents of the tray on the table.

Tilly rewarded him with a sunny smile. "Would you like me to bring you a cup of coffee, David?"

"No thanks, Tilly," he replied. As likeable as Mervin was, David couldn't allow himself to be distracted for long.

Mervin reached into his pocket and smiled at Tilly. "How much do we owe, my dear?"

David shook his head. "Nothing; it's on the house."

Dorothy Quinlan treated him to another display of equine teeth. "Thank you, David. That's kind of you."

"Are you a dancer, by any chance, Tilly dear?" Mervin asked.

"I like jiving," she replied. "And I can manage a waltz and a quickstep."

"No; no. What I meant was, have you ever danced on stage?"

"Goodness, no. Daddy would never allow it," she giggled.

"Such a pity," Mervin sighed. "Such grace and poise. I'd love to do things with you."

Clearly nonplussed, Tilly looked at him warily.

"It's alright, dear. Don't be alarmed," Dorothy interjected. "He means professionally."

"Oh; no, no, no, dear child!" cried Mervin. "What I meant was; I could choreograph amazing routines for you! I'd make you a shining star!"

"Thanks, Tilly," said David, signalling that she could leave them and spare her blushes. Turning to Mervin, he said, "You wanted a word with me?"

"Oh, yes!" Mervin exclaimed, as if just remembering the purpose of his visit. "Dorothy and I have come from a très sérieux pow-wow with Donald Finsbury-Crouch, The Council's Recreation and Entertainments Director. And he's not a happy chappie! We've been badly let down by our rock and roll boys. You know; Danny and … ah…"

"The Drumbeats," Dorothy prompted.

"In what way?" David enquired.

"Where do I start?" Mervin exclaimed dramatically. "Two of them are in the pokey, would you believe! Locked up … in Germany, of all places! Their agent phoned Dorothy yesterday. He can't contact the others. Apparently, they've gone missing. Vanished without trace, if you please!"

David's eyebrows rose.

"The agent was cagey, but I suspect it's to do with drugs," Dorothy suggested. "They've been entertaining our troops out there and performing in night clubs. They were due here for rehearsals at the end of this week."

"You being musical; I wondered if you had contacts in the business, or could suggest someone who might be able to throw us a lifeline," Mervin implored.

"Can't their agent find you a replacement?" David suggested.

Dorothy snorted dismissively. "To be honest, I don't think he's much cop," she rasped, with a meaningful look at Mervin.

"Don't go all Bette Davis on me, dear!" he whined. "I was reliably informed that Danny and the Doodahs were on the brink of making it big."

"Who told you that?" David asked doubtfully.

"Well; their agent did actually," Mervin mumbled into his coffee cup.

Ignoring Mervin's outburst, Dorothy continued, "He couldn't offer us an acceptable alternative and didn't seem to know anyone who could. We've phoned all our own contacts, but no-one can come up with anything suitable at such short notice. Nothing we can afford, anyway."

David tapped the table pensively. "What about local groups?"

Dorothy shook her head. "All the decent ones have signed up with the Kool Kookie Klubs, for the summer season. A chap called Rob Driver has opened a series of them in some of the bigger resorts."

"The rest are all greasy quiffs and excruciating crash-bang-twang!" Mervin groaned. "We've auditioned some of them in the past. A *ghastly* experience! I'm sure they fondly imagine that an ear-splitting racket is a substitute for talent."

"I can't promise anything," David warned. "But if you can give me a day or two, I'll see what I can do. Does it have to be rock and roll? Trad jazz is popular."

"Anything you can come up with would be better than nothing, dear heart," Mervin replied. "As long as they're available at short notice and can tootle away in tune!"

Dorothy blew a plume of blue smoke into the canopy of the parasol. "To tell the truth, David we've spent quite a lot of our publicity budget promoting the fact that our production includes the kind of music that youngsters go for. They see our shows as fuddy-duddy and square. As you probably know, the Wintergardens and the theatre are owned by the council, and they're putting us under a lot of pressure to make our shows financially viable. To have a chance of achieving that, we've got to move with the times and attract the teenagers."

At the sound of a familiar boat horn, David rose from his chair. "That's the Ocean Queen coming in. I'm terribly sorry, but

Tilly's going to need some help. Leave it with me for a day or two and I'll let you know if I've had any luck."

David wrung his hands nervously. "So, what's the verdict? Can we have our hygiene certificate today?"

This inspector was older than the first one; his business suit and manner suggesting that he was more senior. He looked up from completing an official form. "I'm afraid not," he said quietly.

David felt the blood drain from his head. "Why?" he gasped. "I thought we'd done everything you wanted us to?"

A smile began to play at the corners of the inspector's mouth. "You have. In fact, you've done more than is required. But I can't supply you with a certificate here and now. You'll get an official printed one posted to you in about a week. I'm just making out my report and the authorisation."

David blew out his cheeks and sank onto a chair. "You had me worried for a moment!"

"I do apologise. I didn't mean to alarm you," the inspector replied. "You've done remarkably well. It can't have been easy bringing this place up to scratch given its age and, from what I remember, its previous condition."

"Thank you," said David. "We've had a lot of help."

The inspector nodded. "Well, it has obviously been worthwhile." Looking up from tucking papers into his briefcase, he added, "My grandchildren have been pestering my daughter to bring them here to see the penguins. You appear to be acquiring quite a reputation, especially for your milk shakes and ice cream sundaes."

David could hardly wait for him to leave, so that he could give free rein to his elation. Rushing to the kitchen doorway, he called, "We've done it! We've got our certificate!"

"Oh; how super!" Tilly trilled.

"That's marvellous!" Connie called. "I'm so pleased for you!"

Sammy responded by displaying his unedifying fangs with a broad grin.

"Thanks to all of you for what you've done to make it happen," David exclaimed. Unable to contain his excitement, he added, "I must call Jo and tell her." With a shout of, "Somebody keep an eye out in here, will you!" he rushed past curious customers on his way to the phone box.

"Where are you off to in such a hurry?"

Jo's oh-so-welcome voice stopped him in his tracks. He turned to face her and, without thinking, lifted her off her feet and swung her round. "We've done it, Jo! We've got our hygiene certificate!"

With her face hovering above his, he found himself gazing into her lovely eyes; their long, curling lashes fluttering beguilingly as she smiled down at him. It was all he could do to stop himself kissing her. Coming to his senses, he self-consciously lowered her back onto her feet. "Sorry," he mumbled. "I got a bit carried away."

"Well, I certainly was!" she giggled. "Well done; you deserve it."

"So do you," he countered. "You … and everyone … did a heck of a lot towards it."

"All I did was some cleaning and tidying up," she insisted. "It was you who made it happen. You've worked so hard to make sure everything was done in time. I'm proud of you!"

Elated by her praise, he followed her through the café to the kitchen, smiling diffidently in response to the amusement of customers who had been watching them."

"I hope you've got proper bills for all the work we've had done," she remarked. "The takings have been good, but I still need to account for the money you've taken from the till." As an afterthought, she added, "I presume that's how you paid for it?"

"Of course."

The line was faint and David had to press the telephone receiver closer to his ear to make out what his friend, Archie, was saying.

"I dunno, Dave. We're pretty booked up. We're called The Jet Stream now. We're in big demand!"

"OK Archie. It was just a thought. Like I said, the local theatre is looking for a replacement group, so I thought of you. But if you're booked up..."

Archie suddenly became more animated. "No; wait. Hang on! We're *pretty* booked up, but I'll see what I can do. Let me talk to our manager and the boys. After all, it's for a mate. We've got a lot lined up, but we might be able to re-arrange our touring itinerary ... seeing it's you that's asking."

Struggling to disguise his amusement, David replied, "Thanks. That's really good of you." Having been cooped up in an RAF billet with Archie for several months, he could read him like a cheap novel.

"For the whole summer, you reckon?" Archie queried, trying to sound casual.

"Yes; for August and September, anyway."

"What kinda bread are we looking at? You know, spondulicks ... money."

"I don't know, you'd have to negotiate that with the theatre manager if your audition goes well."

"Audition? We've got to audition? I thought you said they were desperate."

"No I didn't. I said they've been let down and are looking for a replacement. It's a proper theatre production. They're not just going to book anybody on trust."

"Oh, right," Archie muttered. "Will there be crumpet on the bill?"

"Well; there are dancers … and Jenny O'Dell."

"What; that little Irish sort?"

"Yes … Oh, and a nude fan dancer."

"*A nude fan dancer?*" Archie all but shrieked. "What; like *naked* nude!?"

Battling outright laughter, David replied, "What other kind is there? You should see her act. You wouldn't believe what she does with two turtle doves."

"*Really? … A naked fan dancer?*"

"No; only kidding."

"*You ratbag,* Sheldon!"

Anxious to end the conversation, David said, "Anyway; it was nice talking to you again, Archie. I must get back to the café. You've got the phone number of the theatre manager. Ring her if you're interested."

"Wilko. What's she like? You know; bit of alright is she?"

"A real stunner … and mad about guitarists. See you Archie!"

"You've 'ad one of these, I take it?" Wally enquired, handing David a leaflet headed: *Meeting of the Harbour Redevelopment Protest Group.*

"Yes, I have. I see you're holding it in the Wardroom."

Wally nodded. "Well, it's the obvious place, really. We're gonna shut it off. Hooky and Linda can look after the customers in 'ere. Gemma's organisin' the meetin' with Martin Winsor, from Rolfe's, the chandlers."

"I don't see much of him or his father," David replied. "I've only ever exchanged an odd hello or good morning with them."

"They're main place is near Southampton," Wally explained. "They do a lot of business with the ship owners and bigger

207

boatyards down on the Solent. They don't do a lot in Fairhaven these days. Old Dan Townsend looks after what trade they get in the shop."

"This pub's a listed building, isn't it?" David suggested. "I didn't think the redevelopment affects you."

"It don't, directly," Wally replied. "But me an' Avril reckon we ought t'show a bit a'solidarity with everybody. After all, we're all in this together; an' what 'appens to the 'arbour affects all of us."

"Who's coming?" David asked.

Wally picked up David's glass. Holding it under the best bitter tap, he pulled slowly and evenly on the pump handle. "Just about everybody, as far as I know. Victor and Grace are comin'. I think Stan will be 'ere and Gemma and Martin, of course. From what I can gather most of 'em from the sheds an' boatyards are on board with it. So is Frankie and the other workin' boat skippers. You an' Jo are comin', I take it?"

"Yes; of course," David replied, hoping he sounded more enthusiastic than he felt. He didn't believe the protest would make the slightest difference. It seemed to him that being compensated for surrendering the lease of the café would be more lucrative and possibly quicker than if they had tried to sell it as an ongoing business.

"Of course, we'll 'ave our legal beagle on tap." Wally announced, as Monty arrived and settled himself on his favourite bar stool.

"You will indeed," Monty replied and removed his panama hat to place it and his newspaper on the counter.

"Don't tap too 'ard, though," Wally chuckled. "You never know what might fall off."

"Very droll, Wallace," Monty murmured dryly. "It's fortunate that David is here, because I am able to announce that there have been developments regarding his musical performances."

Wally pushed a brandy glass under an optic twice and placed it on the counter in front of Monty. "Good or bad?"

Almost half the contents of the glass disappeared before Monty responded. "An extensive study of the local byelaws leads me to the opinion that the council's position is far from unassailable. I have taken the liberty of consulting with an old colleague of mine, who, I might add, is something of an authority on such matters. As a result, I am convinced that the local council is vulnerable on certain elements of their assertion; one of which is the extent of their authority pertaining to the regulation of the harbour."

"So, what can we do about it?" Avril asked, as she appeared from the doorway to the living quarters.

Monty clipped off the end of a King Edward Imperial and lit it with an impressively long cigar match. As if pausing for effect, he carefully ensured the cigar drew evenly before continuing. "On your behalf, I requested a meeting with the appropriate council representatives. To which the reply was initially, shall we say, less than constructive. However, I informed them that my professional opinion is that their interpretation of the said byelaws and the extent of their authority are erroneous and that, as your counsel, I have advised you that there are grounds on which to challenge their decision. I also intimated that, while any intransigence on their part may hinder our endeavour to seek redress, it would not affect our determination to do so."

"I assume they replied with the equivalent of two raised fingers," David suggested.

"Not at all, my boy," Monty replied loftily. "Mister Davenport, who introduced himself as the Town Clerk, has contacted me by telephone to inform me of his intention to discuss the matter further with the relevant officials and their legal advisors. He promised to communicate the result of those deliberations to us in due course."

"So, you think you've got them worried, then?" Avril suggested.

Monty allowed himself a satisfied smile. "It would suggest that they are prepared to be less uncompromising. My opinion is that the intervention of the Town Clerk indicates that he considers the council's position to be less than assured and, perhaps to avoid the possibility of expensive litigation, he is quite probably advising his colleagues to reconsider and be prepared to negotiate."

"What's to stop them just changing the law?" David asked.

"Nothing; in theory, dear boy. But, in my experience, the process of amending byelaws is not necessarily simple or swift. In some circumstances it may require an Act of Parliament. But, even if they should decide to go to the trouble, they would be aware that the decision might still be challenged in court."

Wally's chuckle seemed to start as a rumble in his chest. "Better get yer guitar tuned up, son."

A gentle breeze and the warmth of the sun had brought a smile to David's face as he strolled along the promenade, swinging a bag of his freshly laundered clothes. It promised to be another lovely day. Even his weekly skirmish with the hatchet-faced old bat behind the counter in Underwood's Laundry hadn't dampened his spirits.

Sparkling blue-green waves, alive with bursting whitecaps and darting flashes of light, were rolling in across the bay with a soothing, sibilant roar. Pennants fluttered fussily at the head of the flagpoles lining the promenade and newly painted beach huts glowed brightly in the sunlight. Further along the beach, Hooky and Bunny Warren were busy issuing

Fairhaven Council's distinctive green and white striped deckchairs and wind breaks to early-birds who were claiming favoured places; their voices and the calls of excited children drifting up from the golden sand. A few hardy souls were already in the water, braving its morning chill to paddle in the breakers or, in the case of one or two of an even hardier disposition, to swim.

What a lovely summer it was turning out to be.

Faces at the windows of arriving excursion coaches were gazing at the beach and the sea with eager anticipation. Fingers pointed and necks craned to look up at multi-coloured bunting and banners strung along the Esplanade, announcing the forthcoming attractions of carnival week: *Grand Carnival Parade ~ Carnival Ball ~ Gymkhana and Fete ~Monster Firework Display ~Miss Fairhaven Pageant.*

The idea of calling a line of shivering girls in bathing costumes 'a pageant' amused David. "I suppose it makes it sound classier," he murmured. It led him to wonder what Jo would look like in a bathing costume. She had been wearing a pair of white shorts when she had cycled to the café a day or two ago, which had made him ponder why it was generally considered that a girl's legs had to be long to be attractive. There was nothing wrong with Nurse Lampeter's legs; nothing wrong at all!

Absorbed by the thought, he was startled by the toot of a horn and the snarl of an engine, as a sports car pulled up at the kerb beside him. Turning his head sharply, he recognised the red MG Roadster and the driver grinning at him.

"Daydreaming again, Little Brother?"

"Rich! I wasn't expecting you! You only said you'd think about Ginny's offer."

"I know," Richard declared. "But I thought I'd come and have a look around; perhaps meet Aunt Ginny and see how the land lies … And visit my kid brother, of course." Opening the passenger door, he pointed to the bag David was carrying.

"Having your clothes laundered? Doesn't your dishy partner do your washing for you?"

"I was going to say over her dead body! But it would probably be over mine, if I suggested it," David replied and eased himself onto the seat beside his brother.

Richard had bought the car over a year ago, but hadn't had long to enjoy it before his illness laid him low. He had offered to lend it to David until he recovered, but although sorely tempted by the glamour of a brand new sports car, David had declined. Bearing in mind his nomadic life and his track record of regular mishaps, some sort of calamity befalling it would have been inevitable.

"Where to?" Richard enquired.

David pointed towards the harbour. "I'd better get back to the café and see how Tilly's coping with the new girl we're trying out. She's Connie's niece. She seems bright enough, but if it's busy they won't have much time to keep an eye on her."

Luxuriating in the comfort and heady, new-car aroma of leather upholstery and plush fittings, David closed the door and settled back to enjoy the wind tugging at his hair, as Richard gunned the engine and they roared along the Esplanade.

He should have guessed that it would take Richard no time at all to charm the girls. Connie's eyes had widened appreciatively when he had complimented her on her victoria sponge; Tilly had fussed with her hair when they had been introduced; and Stella, the new girl, had returned his thanks for bringing him a cup of coffee with a wide-eyed gaze and a bashful smile. Even Gemma, to whom flattery was no novelty now that Chris was on the scene, wasn't immune. She sat with Richard at the yellow table enquiring, with noticeable concern, about his illness and current health.

David shrugged resignedly. What he wouldn't give for his brother's way with women. It seemed instinctive and effortless. Whereas he invariably managed to say the wrong thing and put his foot in it.

His attention was captured by a clatter of crockery and a cry of, "Oh my God! You clumsy little devil! Now look what you've done!" In the far corner of the room, a couple were on their feet; the father continuing to berate his young son, while the mother began mopping the table cloth with a serviette.

"He couldn't help it Alan," she pleaded, as the boy burst into tears.

Glancing around the room with obvious embarrassment, the father exclaimed, "I told him to stop playing with his toys while he's eating! Now look; my tea's gone all over my sandwich and soaked it."

Tilly was in the kitchen and David was about to intercede, but Stella was already approaching the table with a handful of paper serviettes.

"I'm so sorry," the mother said contritely. "It's a bit of a mess. The handle's been broken on that cup, as well. We'll pay for it, of course."

"Don't worry!" Stella replied soothingly. "If you'd like to move to that free table, I'll clean this one up." Looking to David for approval, she added, "I'll get you another cup and a fresh pot of tea."

David smiled reassuringly, and pointing to the sodden sandwich, nodded his assent.

"I'll get you another sandwich, too," Stella declared. Stroking the sobbing boy's hair, she cooed, "Never mind. Will an ice cream help to dry your tears?"

Connie had confirmed that Stella was sixteen, although she barely looked it. She was a little taller than Jo, but almost a head shorter than Tilly, whom she already seemed to hero-worship. Her chestnut hair was drawn back off her face to fall in a long ponytail and, with her delicate features and large, hazel eyes, she reminded David of illustrations of *Alice in Wonderland*. He had half expected a white rabbit to follow her into the café, when she arrived the previous morning. In what looked like a new dress and stiletto heels, with her face powdered and wearing lipstick and eye shadow, she had looked as if she were on her way to a dance instead of starting her first day as a waitress. It had taken Tilly's influence to make her heed Connie's advice to go home and change into flat shoes if she wanted to last all day on her feet.

Watching her help the couple move to another table, David smiled to himself; relieved that she was overcoming her initial nervousness and pleased that she was showing initiative and the confidence to deal with the situation. "You'll do, young lady," he murmured.

"Not another one! How the heck do you do it?" Standing in the doorway, Chris gestured towards Stella who was loading a tray with debris from the mishap. "I presume this is another addition to your harem?"

It brought a ripple of laughter from the customers around them.

"What can I do for my favourite artist?" David chuckled.

Chris replied with a mischievous grin. "Well, you can tell your brother to stop whispering sweet nothings in my girlfriend's ear, for a start. He has to be your brother; one look is enough to tell that! But, since you ask, I'd like a choc ice; one of those Chocbergs, if I may."

"You may. You may also like to know that Tilly has sold another picture."

"Oh, well done, my angel!" Chris exclaimed, as she appeared from the kitchen corridor with fresh linen and cutlery. "Say the word and we'll fly away to somewhere exotic on the proceeds?"

"It was only one of the little pictures," Tilly giggled. "The gentleman who bought it would have preferred a larger one, but it was the only one we had of the harbour."

"Then I shall create more. And perhaps a portrait of you ... as a Greek goddess!"

"Actually, that's quite a good idea," Tilly replied. "Not the goddess part," she tittered. "But, it's Daddy's birthday soon and one has such difficulty choosing something suitable for him. He already has a portrait of Mummy in his den, so perhaps he might like one of me to go with it."

"I'm sure he would," Chris concurred. "I'll do it for you at a special rate; for the sheer joy. A labour of love." Turning his charm on Stella, he added, "What about you my sweet? Wouldn't your daddy appreciate a likeness of you?"

She regarded him with bemused curiosity. "He's got a camera."

It elicited more laughter around the room and the comment, "We've got to come back here, Phyllis! The entertainment's terrific!"

David had to wait until after the lunchtime rush to spend more time with Richard, who had taken a stroll along the seafront with Tilly. The girls had taken it on themselves to rotate and stagger their breaks to ensure that they were all on duty during the busy hour around lunchtime and when the Ocean Queen docked.

When they returned, David was sitting at the white table with a sausage roll and a Pepsi Cola, watching a crowd gather round Chris, who had set up his easel on the mole.

"Don't you take a proper break and get away from this place?" Richard asked, settling himself next to David.

"No, he doesn't," Tilly replied, on her way inside. "We've all tried to persuade him, but he won't listen."

"That's easier said than done," David explained. "Everything's taking off here; the boat tickets; ice creams; Tilly's strawberry sundaes. The café is nearly always busy these days. Chris's pictures are starting to sell, too. I need to be here pretty much all the time. Jo and I are keen to make the most of it while we can. We need to be able to pay the rent and other bills for as long as possible until the harbour redevelopment process starts."

"What are they intending to do?" Richard asked.

"We don't know yet." David waved a hand airily. "But they're planning to knock all this down. They can't touch the pub, it's a listed building, but all the sheds and boathouses behind us will go. We're expecting to get compulsory purchase order notices at some time. Then, I suppose, our landlords will kick us out. The good news is they've got to compensate us."

"Don't they have to offer you alternative premises?"

David shook his head. "Not as far as I know. It doesn't matter anyway. We have no intention of carrying on. Jo's not interested, and her boyfriend is due home from Germany any day now. I wouldn't be surprised if they get married then, which obviously means she'll go with him wherever he gets posted to next."

Richard looked at him searchingly. "What about you? What will you do?"

"I haven't given it much thought. I suppose I'll see what turns up and then move on."

'Richard has obviously made a favourable impression on Aunt Ginny,' David mused, as he descended the long flights of steps leading to the Wintergardens. But when did he ever fail to do so?

"Such a charming young man", had been Ginny's verdict on meeting him the previous day.

At Richard's request, David had visited her to make sure she had no reservations about him staying with her and Jo. But he needn't have worried. She had insisted that she was perfectly happy with the arrangement, and had even enquired about possible dietary requirements relating to Richard's illness.

Jo had been on the telephone to her boyfriend when David arrived. She had greeted him cheerfully afterwards, but had seemed quieter and more withdrawn than normal; as if her mind was elsewhere. 'In Germany I suppose,' David thought gloomily.

Finally reaching the foot of the steps, he looked around, fascinated by the way the Wintergardens was transformed at night. The flower displays and ornamental figures glowed with the colours of concealed lighting, which gave the floodlit floral clock the curious appearance of being animated, like a character from a Disney cartoon. Lights strung between the lampposts and in the trees enhanced the fairytale ambience, providing the perfect mood for romance.

The sight of couples, strolling arm in arm and embracing in the shadows, brought home how little romance there had been in his life. He had imagined himself to be in love during a couple of brief liaisons, but circumstances and his restless, disordered life had prevented them developing into permanent relationships. But none of them had really been love. He realised that, now.

The last time he had walked through the Wintergardens he had been with Jo, on the way to Avril's party. How lovely she had looked in that white dress, with the pink, fluffy cardigan draped around her shoulders. She had seemed to almost bounce along in those high heels, making her flared skirt sway … and his heart beat faster.

Approaching the ornamental fountain, where all the paths converged, he heard music above the background sigh of the sea and the noise of the funfair. On the bandstand, near the floodlit theatre entrance, a group of youngsters were dancing around a transistor radio. He assumed they had it tuned to Radio Luxembourg, because they were jiving to Cliff Richard's '*Move It*'. The driving beat, with its compelling guitar riff, made David feel like dancing, too. But he wisely refrained, remembering the humiliating experience of a youth club dance when he had been fifteen.

Encouraged by Richard and emboldened by the cider smuggled in by his friend, Freddie, he had plucked up the nerve to ask Deidre Mellowes to dance. To his delight and surprise, she had agreed; after which, delight had rapidly turned to pain for her and embarrassment for him. What they had both learned from the experience was that he had two left feet and should avoid venturing onto a dance floor.

'It's a pity they've only got a little radio to dance to,' he thought. 'That's a great place for kids to dance.'

The thought gave him inspiration. Why aren't there open-air dances round the bandstand? As well as the brass band, why not pop singers and groups; trad jazz; country and western? Perhaps he should mention it to Mervin and Dorothy.

Ideas were developing in his mind when he arrived back at the café. Summer dances in the Wintergardens would be great for the kids. But why not pop concerts in the theatre during the offseason, too? Wouldn't that bring in the teenagers, like Dorothy was hoping to do? It would need Mervin's support as well as hers; and more significantly the approval of the council, which was likely to be the biggest sticking point.

He came down to earth later, while he was sitting at the living room window, gazing out at the moonlit harbour. What was he getting excited about? Why should he care what happened to the Wintergardens Palace Theatre; the local teenagers; or anything else? This time next year, Fairhaven, The Rockhopper Café … and his time with Jo … would be no more than a memory.

Reaching for his guitar case, he took out his 'companion' for the past four years. The Gibson acoustic was a twenty-first birthday present from Richard and his most treasured possession. It must have cost a lot of money, but its value to him was beyond price. He had sold his Hofner, albeit reluctantly, but nothing short of total catastrophe would induce him to part with this 'trusty friend'.

He rested it across his knee and ran his hand lovingly over the burnished soundboard, before plucking the strings and adjusting the tuning pegs until he was satisfied. Shaping his fingers over the frets, he coaxed out a few opening chords and began to wistfully croon the Johnny Mathis song: *Chances Are*.

Would he ever feel like this again? Would he have such a longing to make something of his life; for it to have meaning? Would the conviction that he could achieve whatever he set his mind to ever come again? Who would have believed he could run a café without making a complete dog's dinner of it? Not him, for sure! But he hadn't had Jo in his life before.

If only there was a chance for him with her. At first, there had seemed plenty of time before her boyfriend arrived, and he had been able to make himself believe that he would be ready when the time came. But time had run out. It could be any day, now … and he wasn't ready. He never would be.

"Got a minute?" Wally called from the pub doorway.

"Yes; just let me take Rocky and these parasols inside, before I lock up," David replied. "After the busy day we've had, I could do with a drink."

His pint was on the counter waiting for him when he walked into The Mess to take up what he suddenly realised had become his usual place at the bar. Was he becoming that set in his ways; so predictable? Should he buy a Panama hat and a linen jacket … and start smoking cigars?

"What's so funny," Avril asked.

"Nothing," he replied, unaware that he had been smiling to himself.

"Right; we need to agree Monty's plan of action," Wally announced. "He wants to be sure of what to say to the council, when they 'ave their meetin.'"

"Have they asked for one?" David queried.

"Mister Davenport has suggested that we meet after he has

deliberated with his colleagues," Monty proclaimed. "And I deem it advisable to be forearmed."

"In what way?" David asked.

"It is my belief that Mister Davenport is willing to concede that the council does not have the authority to totally prohibit your performances, but I am sure he will wish to impose certain conditions and restraints." Monty drained his glass and overtly placed it on the counter; nodding appreciatively when Avril picked it up to refill it. "What I require from you all is confirmation that you are in accord with my suggested strategy for the negotiations."

Avril replaced his glass in front of him. "How do you mean?"

"My advice is that it may be judicious not to contest those conditions which do not interfere significantly with your ability to provide entertainment for your customers. In the interests of harmony; if you will forgive the pun."

"Whaddya think, David?" Wally asked.

"I don't know," David replied doubtfully. "All I do is sing and play. I don't think anything more than that is any of my business."

"My advice is that we accede to reasonable conditions regarding the volume of noise; the time and length of your performances and the effect on the surrounding environment," Monty suggested. "What I require is your instruction concerning the extent to which I may concede on these conditions."

"I can't see noise being a problem," Wally asserted. "It's only David; not a ruddy great band. We've got t'chuck everybody out at closin' time anyway."

"As far as I'm concerned, they're matters for Wally and Avril to decide," David asserted. "I'm happy to go along with whatever they think."

"Hello! Is it still alright to come in?" Tilly called from the doorway. She was accompanied by Bella and a distinguished looking older woman.

"Hello girls!" Avril called. "Of course it is. Come in; come in!"

As before, every pair of eyes was drawn to the girls, as they entered. Both wore jeans, with Bella in a short-sleeved tennis shirt and Tilly in a light sweater.

"I hope we're not intruding," said Bella. "But we would like to speak with David, if we may."

Wally's eyes twinkled with amusement. "You carry on, my lovely. Don't mind us. I'm sure David don't mind."

"Of course not," said David.

"Thank you. May I introduce my Grandmama?" Bella replied. "Grandmama, this is David ... Wally ... Avril ... and ... where's Hooky?"

"He's not back yet," Avril explained. "He must still be on the beach. It's been a really busy day, so I expect him and Bunny are still clearin' up and puttin' everythin' away."

"I'm delighted to meet you all!" Bella's Grandmama exclaimed. "My family and I have heard so much about you from Matilda and Arabella."

She was slim and almost as tall as Tilly; and although a grandmother, her manner and appearance suggested that she was not prepared to allow age to inhibit her in any way. Her shoulder length hair had mostly faded to grey, but it was immaculately coiffured. She wore a coral pink sweater, with a single row of pearls at her throat, and cream slacks that hugged her neat waist and hips. Her face was carefully made up and, in spite of lines at the corners of her mouth and eyes, she was an attractive woman for her age.

In response to Bella's prompt: "Do you remember this gentleman, Grandmama?" she regarded Monty inquisitively with a gaze that was bright-eyed and penetrating.

Despite his florid complexion, Monty's blush was unmistakable. For once, he was hesitant and anything but eloquent. "I fear your dear granddaughter is ... ah ... perhaps unduly optimistic in expecting Your Ladyship to recall our brief acquaintance," he murmured. "I was but an insignificant junior barrister at the time of your visits to our chambers."

"Let me see," her Ladyship pondered. "One doesn't visit barristers' chambers too often, I'm happy to say. One remembers being given tea while my husband was in conference with Sir Henry Povery." With an engaging smile, she added, "One also recollects that one of the gentlemen who entertained me was a well-dressed young man wearing a rather fetching polka dot bow tie."

"I fear I must plead guilty, as charged," Monty replied quietly.

"Is one correct in recalling that you were about to become engaged to be married?"

The remark evoked astonishment from those around them.

Monty's reply was almost a whisper. "That was my hope."

"Your hope?" she enquired gently.

Monty smiled diffidently. "I'm afraid it proved to be no more than that."

"What happened?" Bella gasped.

"Arabella! Her grandmother admonished. "Don't be impertinent!"

Monty raised a hand to indicate that he hadn't taken offence. "I committed the grave error of introducing my intended to someone I imagined to be a trusted friend. We had known each other since our schooldays. He lived in South Africa, and was here visiting his mother. We arranged a reunion dinner; the result of which was that he returned to Cape Town with a bride, and I resigned myself to bachelorhood."

"Oh, how sad!" Tilly sobbed; her eyes brimming.

"Save your tears, my dear," Monty murmured. "It was long ago and the passage of time has led me to the conclusion that it was the most beneficial consequence for all concerned. I have come to appreciate that matrimony would, in all probability, not have suited me."

The ensuing silence was broken by Wally. "I think we could all do with a drink! Give us yer glass, Monty. What can I get Your Ladyship?"

"Thank you. I must confess to a partiality to Guinness," she replied.

"Right you are!" Wally chuckled. "Pint or a half?"

"Oh, half a pint will be quite sufficient."

"I'll get the girls a glass of wine," Avril called, making her way to the kitchen.

"May one speak about ice cream, David?" Bella asked. "Your ice cream is just heavenly. Tilly suggested that we prevail upon you to provide it for my twenty-first birthday party."

"Of course," David replied. "If you let me know what you need and when you need it, I'll order it specially."

"Thank you. That would be super. And may one also ask if you would be prepared to entertain us with your guitar?"

"Oh, yes!" Her Ladyship exclaimed. "The girls have spoken of your talent, David. One does hope you'll give us some rock and roll."

With Monty going to such trouble on his behalf and Avril and Wally so obviously keen for him to resume his performances, David couldn't bring himself to admit that he no longer owned an electric guitar and amplifier. "I'd be delighted to," he said. "If I can manage it."

"Do you think Daddy will like it?" Tilly asked, holding up her portrait.

David placed his lunch on the red table and sat down between his brother and Chris. Taking a sandwich from the plate, he replied, "I'm certain he will."

"It's a remarkable likeness. I think your father will be delighted," Richard concurred.

There was a murmur of approval from customers sitting at the other outside tables, to which Chris responded with an appreciative nod of his head.

"You're so clever, Chris!" Tilly enthused. "You really should paint more portraits."

"If all my clients were endowed with such beauty, my angel, I would paint nothing else," Chris exclaimed.

"Steady on!" Richard cautioned. "Gemma might hear you."

"My eyes are my own, but she knows my heart is hers!" Chris proclaimed.

"Good grief!" David spluttered, almost choking on his sandwich.

The shoulders of the young man at the next table were shaking. "Is he always like this?" he asked.

"No," David chuckled. "This is one of his better days."

It provoked more laughter from all four of them.

"You may scoff. But we Greeks know how to treat our women," Chris asserted.

"And everybody else's, if they don't keep an eye you!" David countered.

"This place has improved tremendously since the last time I saw it," the young chap observed. "It used to be quite drab and shabby."

He was smartly dressed in a white, open-necked shirt, a navy blue blazer and grey flannels. His honey-brown hair was cropped short and his face lightly tanned. It was an amiable, face that seemed to mirror his personality. David liked him instinctively and had little doubt that girls found him attractive.

"I don't mind at all," David replied. "It was a dump when we took it over. We came up against so many problems that there were times when we didn't think we would ever manage to get all the work done and re-open the place."

The chap smiled and nodded. "So I've heard."

Richard rose from his seat. "Well, I ought to get myself up to Marine Terrace and let them know I've arrived."

"Marine Terrace?" the chap enquired. "That's where I'm off to."

Richard gestured towards the parking bay beside the mole. "My car's just over there. Can I give you a lift?"

"Thank you, but I think I'll walk," the young man replied. "It's not far, and I need to buy some flowers on the way."

"Someone's birthday?" Chris asked casually.

"No; they're to keep an old lady sweet. The old girl can be a bit crusty sometimes. I like to keep on the right side of her."

"Very wise," Chris observed.

The young man rose to his feet. "I really ought to introduce myself before I go." Offering his hand, he said, "I take it you're David? I'm Colin Shuttleworth … Jo's boyfriend."

IX

David wasn't looking forward to the protest meeting scheduled for that evening. An organised protest to the harbour redevelopment might have seemed a reasonable, if futile, response before, but now it meant nothing to him. He just wanted to take his share of whatever they could get for the café and get out of Fairhaven.

Jo's boyfriend turning up out of the blue had been a shock. He wasn't sure he could cope with seeing her with him, yet. Jo would probably bring him to the café to introduce him to everyone, which left David on tenterhooks, wondering if they were about to show up at any minute. He needed more time to come to terms with it and feel capable of hiding his feelings. It didn't help that Colin was friendly and likeable.

Mervin had invited him to sit in on The Jet Stream's audition later that afternoon, so if Jo and Colin didn't arrive beforehand, it would be an opportunity to avoid them. He wasn't proud of himself for taking the coward's way out. He had to face up to reality at some time. But he still wasn't ready.

Soon after lunch, Mervin came back agitated and breathless. "Dorothy's had a phone call from one of your Jet Stream johnnies," he gasped. "Their van's broken down. She's not sure exactly where, because the cretin … her word, not mine …

didn't seem to know. She insists he tried to chat her up. Can you imagine it? Now, don't get me wrong, dear heart; I adore Dorothy! But the poor boy's in for a considerable surprise when they meet, don't you think?"

It could only be Archie, and in spite of what must have been the temptation to leave him there, Dorothy had taken the number of the telephone box he had called from and promised to call him back.

With her father's and her own birthday impending, Tilly had asked for time off to spend a week with her parents. So, after lunch, David wished her bon voyage, with a little birthday present, and went to see how Dorothy was getting on with finding Archie and his pals. She had managed to locate them, but the theatre's van driver had been reluctant to go to their rescue. So David had driven the van and found The Jet Stream, looking less breezy than their name implied, sprawling on a grass verge beside a blue Morris panel van. He was surprised to see that one of them was a girl; even more so when she greeted him with: "Hiyah, David! Remember me?"

In response to his bemused expression, she added, "It's Ruby … Ruby Mitchell! You used to go out with my sister, Sandy. Remember?"

The vague image of her as a freckle-faced adolescent came to mind. "That was what; six or seven years ago?"

"Yes. I've grown up." Her declaration was unnecessary, because she was now an attractive redhead with an engaging smile.

"You're the singer, I take it," he said.

"No; I play drums."

"Never mind that," Archie cajoled. "Let's get our gear moved across to Dave's van. We've gotta get to this Fairford place double quick!" Winking at David, he added, "I smooth-talked that sort, Dorothy, into postponing the audition. She's got a hell of a sexy voice."

Archie hadn't changed since David had last seen him. He was still a stone or two overweight; still garrulous; and still 'full of it'.

"No wonder you're lost," David chuckled. "It's called Fairhaven. And there's no hurry. They'll be getting ready for the evening show by the time we get there. Your audition won't start until that's over."

"You what!?" A greasy haired individual with pock-marked cheeks turned from idly watching the others unload the Morris van. His cheap suit was creased and his patterned brothel-creepers were scuffed and dusty. "It's gonna be midnight by then!"

"The show finishes around ten-thirty," David explained. "I'm sure they'll get you on stage as soon as they can after that."

"That's nae good enough!" the chap barked, with a gravelled accent that suggested Glasgow. "It's taken us all bluidy day tae get here. We're knackered and starvin'. I'm no havin' it!"

"It's your choice." David shrugged.

"This is Malky, our manager," Archie interjected, with exaggerated cheerfulness. "Malky this is my old mate, Dave."

Malky made no attempt at pleasantries and simply glared at David. "So how far away is yer theatre?" he growled.

"It's not my theatre," David said flatly. "I'm nothing to do with it. But Fairhaven is about forty minutes away."

In the event, it took nearly two hours to transfer The Jet Stream's gear to the theatre's Bedford van, arrange for their stricken vehicle to be towed to a garage and then travel to Fairhaven. David could have done without the aggravation, but the look on Archie's face when he met Dorothy made up for it.

"You rotten toe rag, Sheldon!" he growled.

However, Dorothy confirmed the adage: 'looks aren't everything'. Not only did she greet them with beer and sandwiches, she arranged lodgings for them, and for their audition to be rescheduled to the following day.

Dusk was shrouding the last vestiges of daylight when David returned to the harbour, in time to meet a stream of protesters leaving The Packet Boat Inn.

"David; you no come!" Stan exclaimed. "Where you go?"

David thought it best to keep his explanation simple. "A friend's car broke down near Myrtlesham and I went to help him. How did it go?"

Stan pursed his lips. "Ach! This one talk … that one talk … all people talk. No make sense. I sit on hard chair. I turn this way, I turn other way … My arse quick come fed up!"

Victor Sullivan's intervention gave David the chance to smother his mirth. "It was alright, as far as it went. But Stan's right about everybody trying to talk at once."

His wife, Grace, added, "The chap from the council said nothing has been finalised yet, and he couldn't tell us when it would be. He couldn't answer any of Monty's questions, either. So he wasn't much help, really."

"He was probably told not to give anything away." David suggested, and took out his keys.

"The wanderer returns!" Richard called from the pub doorway. "Where have you been, Little Brother?"

"On an errand of mercy."

"I'm dying to hear about it. So is Jo, I'm sure. Colin's getting you a pint."

David's heart sank. "That's all I need!" he murmured disconsolately.

As expected, The Mess was crowded. He was greeted with a raised eyebrow by Hooky, and a cheery, "Hello love. Where have you been?" from Avril.

"Sorry; I had to go and look for a friend and his group. Their van broke down on the way here. They were supposed to audition for the Wintergardens Theatre. Typical of Archie; they got lost."

"You didn't miss much," Wally said dismissively. "A lot of 'ot air bein' bandied about. The bloke from the council was about as much use as a concrete mae west."

Avril pushed a pint across the counter. "That's from Jo's Colin."

The words 'Jo's Colin' stung, but forced to confront what he had spent all day trying to avoid, David turned to the group gathered around the table behind him. Richard, Martin Winsor, Chris and Gemma were sitting around three sides of the table, with Jo and Colin occupying the window seat, facing them. David raised his glass in thanks, hoping his smile concealed his dejection at the sight of Colin's arm draped around Jo's shoulders, and the less than welcoming expression on her face.

"Whaddya think Dave?" Danny Lightwater called from the haze of cigarette smoke shrouding the regulars at the bar. "Reckon the Tories are gonna get in agen?"

"I don't know," David replied, wary of becoming involved in a political argument. "They will if the experts are right. But I suppose things can change by October."

"Super-Mac reckons we've never 'ad it so good!" Hooky chuckled.

"Well, 'e would, wouldn't 'e?" Frankie Laine snorted. "Let 'im try fishin' fer a livin'. That'd make 'im change 'is tune!"

It was greeted with a murmur of agreement from those around him.

"When I started on me dad's boat, there used t'be nigh on twenty skippers workin' out of Fairhaven. Now look at it. Seven of us! An' ol' Jess Shiner's gonna pack it in next year!"

"You sayin' we'll be better off if Labour gets in, then?" Tubby Clayton asked.

Frankie stubbed out his cigarette in the overflowing ashtray in front of him. "Couldn't get any worse could it, Tub? Can you honestly say you're makin' what you used to with your catches?"

"No; it's not what it was," Tubby sighed, without removing his pipe. "Sellin' the catch is tough enough now. It's not gonna get no easier when they knock the fish sheds down."

"Tories; Labour; Liberals; what's the difference?" Danny snorted. "If Labour do get in, what they gonna do different? What've they ever done?"

"There's the National Health Service," David suggested, and immediately regretted it. He had been hoping to learn more about Fairhaven's heritage. But, as usual, the discussion degenerated into triviality with Johnny Cline's comment, "Me mam's under the doctor. She 'ad t'go wiv 'er foot."

David resisted the temptation to ask how she would have got there without it and looked quizzically at Wally, who had placed another full pint in front of him.

Indicating that it was from Danny, Wally asked, "What's wrong with 'er foot, Johnny?"

"Dunno. 'Er big toe's swole up an' gone all funny."

Hooky's quip: "Tell corny jokes, do it?" brought a ripple of laughter, but was lost on Johnny, who looked at him vacantly.

"Thanks for the drink, Danny," David called.

"You're welcome, mate! You're doin' a smashin' job with the Ocean Queen tickets."

The 'debate' moved to Tiny's fallen arches and then to Bunny's treatment for pleurisy in Myrtlesham General Hospital. So, recognising the inevitable descent into the banal, David abstained from further comment and let the sound of their voices wash over him, while he contemplated his uncertain future.

He was roused from meditation when Richard appeared beside him. "So, you'd rather drink with your pals than your big brother?"

David smiled ruefully. "Sorry Rich. Getting dragged into pointless discussions is an occupational hazard in this place."

"Just how much time do you spend in here?" Richard asked mischievously. "You seem to know everybody."

"Everybody knows David," Avril chuckled. "Don't forget he's been singin' for them … and will be again soon. What can I get you, love?"

"Well, I suppose I ought to buy my *popular* brother a drink," said Richard.

"I'll get these, Rich," David insisted. "I owe Danny and Colin one. What are they all drinking over there?"

"Martin had to leave, but I've written it on this beermat. I ought to warn you: I think it'll take more than a drink to get back in your partner's good books," Richard warned. "She's peeved with you for missing the meeting."

"I got that impression," said David, hoping he sounded less concerned than he felt.

Richard went back to others at the table, leaving David to hastily finish his second pint and pick up the metal tray Avril had loaded with their drinks. He put it on the table, with only a cursory glance at Jo, and took Martin's vacated seat.

"Ah; the happy wanderer!" Chris exclaimed, lifting Gemma's shandy and his Guinness from the tray. "I understand we have you to thank for these?"

"You're welcome. It's been a pretty hectic day. A friend of mine and his rock group managed to get lost and their van broke down on the way here."

"We heard you telling the landlady," Colin chuckled. "Jo's been worried about you."

David passed him a half of bitter and placed Jo's Babycham on the table in front of her. She thanked him, but he could see nothing in her unsmiling expression that suggested concern.

To break the awkward silence, he said, "I've got invoices from Delrio and the Corona dealers that need to be paid. There's one from Connie, as well … I'll go and get them."

"There's no need just at this minute," she replied curtly.

But, anxious to get away, he took a long pull at his third pint and stood up. "There's no time like the present."

Rising quickly from his seat, he suddenly felt unsteady. The hastily downed pints and the bottled beer that Dorothy had provided were having their effect. Pretending that something outside on the quay had caught his attention, he waited momentarily for his head to clear. He felt better in the fresh air, but he still had to walk slowly and carefully to the café; fumbling with his keys as he tried to select the correct one. To his surprise, they were snatched from his hand.

"Nurse Lampeter! How neighbourly of you!!"

"You've had too much to drink!" she pronounced, as she unlocked the doors.

"Do you know, nurse; I do believe your diagnosis is correct," he chuckled, as he followed her inside. "That makes us even."

She switched on the lights and looked at him bemused. "What are you talking about?"

"Well, I saw you home when you were tiddly, and now you've done the same for me."

"What on earth's come over you?"

He shrugged. "Light ale and best bitter is my guess. I've drunk several pints, here and at the theatre, and all I've had to eat since breakfast is a chelsea bun."

She glared at him accusingly. "You're not interested in stopping the redevelopment, are you? That's why you couldn't be bothered to come to the meeting."

"No it's not!" he retorted angrily. "I *was* going to come, until Archie and his pals put paid to it. I was foolish enough recommend them, so I couldn't just leave Mervin and Dorothy to sort out the mess they'd got themselves into. But OK; I don't see the point in protesting. There's nothing we can do to stop it happening! And let's face it, we'll be better off getting compensation for the lease than trying to sell this place."

"So, all that matters to you is the money!"

"Don't put words into my mouth! But you know I'm right. I thought that was why we were doing this. Don't you want to get as much as we can for this place … as a nest egg for you and Colin?"

"Yes; I would like to get something out of it," she admitted. "But I'm not prepared to abandon our friends and just walk away! They've been good to us, David. Think of all the help they've given us to get started! This place has to be worth a lot more now than when we took it over. So, if supporting them means letting Charlie McBride and those … those … *greedy sharks* know we're not going to stand by while they destroy people's livelihoods, I'll be happy with whatever we manage to get. If trying to stop them *is* a waste of time, as you're so sure it is, we'll still get the compensation money. But at least we'll have tried and be able to look our friends in the eye!"

Watching her eyes brim with tears, David longed to put an arm around her to comfort her. "Alright, Jo. If that's what you want."

"Right, you two; back to your corners. The bell's gone; fight's over!" Colin called. He winked at David as he and Richard came in. "Time to go my little bruiser," he chuckled, draping Jo's coat round her shoulders.

Richard smiled and looked enquiringly at David.

"Are you sure you'll be able to manage with Tilly away?" Jo asked. "You realise I won't be around, don't you? We're planning to stay with Colin's mum and dad next week, in Leeds."

"Of course he will!" Colin insisted.

Overcoming the urge to tell Colin to mind his own damned business, David said, "Don't worry; we'll manage. I couldn't say no to Tilly. It's her birthday next week. She's been working all hours, so she deserves a break. But Stella's coming along nicely. Tilly's been teaching her and Connie how she does her strawberry sundaes." He forced a smile. "If things get desperate, I can always turn Sammy's charm on the customers and put Richard to work doing the washing up."

It produced a reluctant grin from Jo.

"But seriously. Avril thinks Linda will come in and help out over the weekend."

"Oh, good," she said. "Have you got your front door key, Richard?"

"Yes thanks," he replied.

Colin slipped an arm around her waist as they left. "See yah, fellas!" he called.

Richard waited until they had gone and turned to David. "Give you a hard time did she?"

David shrugged; trying to conceal his despair. "It wasn't anything I didn't deserve." He laughed disdainfully. "She couldn't even be bothered to call me an idiot."

"Well, that's good, isn't it?"

"Not really. It's what she always calls me. It might seem peculiar, but I've come to like it."

"By the way…" Jo's voice from the doorway startled them. Beyond her, on the quay, they could see Colin talking to Chris and Gemma. "…I've been meaning to ask you; where's your speaker box?"

"My what?"

"That loudspeaker thing you plug your guitar into."

"Oh, you mean my amplifier."

"Yes. Where is it? It's not under the counter where you normally keep it."

"No; well. I've … er … I've taken it upstairs. I don't need it at the moment, so I thought I'd get it out of the way."

"Oh, I see. I just wondered." She smiled for the first time. "We'll, good night, then … idiot."

Avril had generously offered to give Stella some support while David attended The Jet Stream's audition, so he sat at the back of the auditorium while they performed very creditable versions of

Peggy Sue and *Good Golly Miss Molly.* It amused him to observe Malky acting the big impresario, leaning back in his seat in the third row of the stalls and ostentatiously smoking a cheroot while he 'conferred' with Mervin and his entourage.

Greeting David as she made her way towards him from the front of the stalls, Dorothy asked "What do think of them?"

"They're not half bad," he replied. He could have done without Des, the vocalist, hopping around, gyrating his hips and batting a tambourine. But the lad could sing. Archie was a competent rhythm guitarist and Vince, on lead guitar, was proficient, if a little unimaginative. What lifted them from being just another run-of-the-mill group was the compelling beat provided by the bass guitar of Joel, a talented lad from Barbados, and Ruby's flamboyant and inspired drumming.

Dorothy nodded her agreement. "I think they'll do. I know very little about this kind of music, but even I can see that girl's got something. It's not Mervin's cup of tea, so he wanted your opinion before we commit ourselves."

"That's quite a responsibility," said David. "I'm no expert, but I think they'll go down well enough with the kids. I must warn you though, if you haven't already found out for yourself; a little of Archie goes a long way. And I wouldn't trust their so-called manager as far as I could throw him."

"I don't need telling," Dorothy replied. "Mister Donachie and I have already crossed swords. He has a ridiculously exaggerated idea of what they're worth. And as for your friend Archie…"

"I use the word 'friend' loosely," said David. "We were billeted together during our national service."

"You have my sympathy," Dorothy murmured. "But tell me more about your idea of music concerts for teenagers."

He was already doubting the wisdom of mentioning it. The enthusiasm with which Dorothy and Mervin had received the suggestion, and their eagerness to seek his advice, made it clear that they assumed he would be involved. He hadn't disillusioned

236

them. Having raised their hopes, he didn't have the heart to tell them that he wasn't planning to stay in Fairhaven. Another time, and in different circumstances, he would have embraced the opportunity wholeheartedly.

Returning to the quay, he was startled by the sudden command, "Hey you; girl!" shouted by a young man sitting at one of the wooden tables outside The Packet Boat Inn.

The chap's fashionable sunglasses and tailored sports shirt and slacks suggested affluence, while his manner bore the hallmark of arrogance. Raising an arm, he clicked his fingers impatiently. Stella looked up from delivering tea and sandwiches to the white table and regarded him circumspectly, unsure how to react.

"You! Over here!" Glancing at the young man and the girl with him, the chap adopted an exaggerated expression of incredulity. "Yes; you! Are you as bloody stupid as you look? We're waiting to be served!"

"It's alright, Stella. Carry on with what you're doing!" David called, as he approached.

The young chap straightened up from his slouch and removed his sunglasses to peer disdainfully at David. "And who the bloody-hell might you be?"

It elicited a snigger from the blonde girl beside him.

David regarded him coldly, holding his gaze. "There's no *might* about it. I *am* someone who doesn't take kindly to my staff being insulted and demeaned."

"In that case, tell *your bloody staff* not to leave people hanging around for ages waiting to be served!" the chap sneered.

"They don't!!" David retorted. "They treat our visitors courteously and promptly."

"We've been here for over a quarter of an hour!" the girl bleated in a nasal whine. "That stupid girl and the older woman have ignored us!"

"I would imagine that's because these tables are nothing to

do with the café," David said flatly. "They belong to The Packet Boat Inn."

"Then why the hell didn't one of your lackeys have the sense to tell us?" the chap barked.

With his hackles rising, David replied slowly and deliberately; his voice low and menacing. "My *lackeys,* as you *so courteously* refer to them, happen to be decent, hard-working people. They have more than enough to deal with, without having to tolerate a bunch of ill-mannered oafs, who don't have the decency to treat them with respect, *or* the intelligence to realise that these tables don't belong to the café."

"Well, *really!*" the girl gasped. "Are you going to let him speak to us like that, Rupert?"

"No; I'm damned-well not!" The chap rose slowly to his feet. "So, we're ill-mannered oafs, are we? I don't take that from anyone; least of all a jumped up little waiter like you!"

David felt his temples throb, as his anger intensified. "Is that a fact … *Rupert?* Well, you and *Pong Ping* and *Tiger Lily* there can get this straight! I don't take insults to my staff … or me … from anyone! *Especially* from a conceited hooray-henry like you!"

The tension was broken by Wally's sharp intervention. "Whass goin' on 'ere, then?" Avril's presence behind him suggested that she had gone to fetch him.

"It's none of your damned business!" Rupert replied haughtily.

"Oh, but it is my business, Sonny-Jim," Wally replied. "This is *my* pub. And you're on *my* property."

"It's alright, Wally. I can deal with this," David insisted, locking eyes with Rupert.

"David! Don't be so stupid!" Avril demanded. "Wally; stop them!"

"Don't, Rupert!" the blonde girl whined. "It's not worth getting into a fight."

"Fiona's right!" their companion cautioned. "Can't you see

he's trying to provoke you?"

"That's enough!" Wally commanded. "I dunno what this is all about, but I'm not gonna risk losing me licence by lettin' you two go at it outside my pub. So pack it in; both of yuh!"

Rupert turned away from David. "You're right Fi. He's not worth dirtying my hands on."

Despite the sneer, David sensed his adversary's uncertainty. Rupert's reluctance to maintain eye contact and the beads of perspiration on his upper lip betrayed his nervousness and suggested that, having failed to intimidate David with arrogance and bluster, he secretly welcomed Wally's intervention.

It surprised David to realise that he didn't. It would have given him great satisfaction to thump the arrogant creep. "You know where to find me if you change your mind … *Rupert*."

Although clearly unnerved, Rupert smirked, "I wouldn't want you to lose your licence, Wally, or get his blood all over your tables."

"I wouldn't be so cock-sure about whose blood it would be, if I was you," Wally growled. "And it's *Mister Jarvis* to you!"

Heads turned, in response to an imperious voice. "Causing trouble again, Rupert?"

"Oh; hello Lady Alice," Rupert replied fawningly. "How lovely to see you."

She was once again the epitome of elegance, in a pale blue cashmere twin-set, dark tailored slacks and a brightly patterned silk scarf draped around her neck. Pushing her sunglasses up onto her hair, she ignored Rupert's blandishment. "What have you been up to this time?"

"Oh, nothing. Just a little misunderstanding."

"There are far too many *misunderstandings, Rupert*," Her Ladyship declared. "Even your father is losing patience with you."

Amused by the way she had so easily deflated Rupert's self-importance, David responded to her enquiring glance with a wry grin. "I suppose you could call it a misunderstanding."

Rupert picked up his sweater from the bench and turned to

his anxious acolytes. "Come on. We've wasted enough time here. Goodbye Lady Alice. It was nice meeting you again."

Watching them leave, Wally murmured. "That's the second time I've 'ad to stop you gettin' into a fight, David-me-lad. You 'ad me worried there. I never 'ad you down fer a brawler, but I could see by yer face you were dying to stick one on 'im!"

"Sorry Wally;" David said quietly; shaken by the intensity of his anger.

"Rupert can have that effect on people," Lady Alice remarked. "I've known his family for many years. Unfortunately, he's the product of his father's indulgence. He's become conceited and disdainful of anyone he considers beneath him. One hears that he's rude and disrespectful to the employees at his father's company, where he works. One has also had the misfortune to witness the abominable way he treats the domestic staff at home; to the point where Simon and Helen are having difficulty replacing those who leave. Unless he mends his ways, one can only imagine it will go badly for him in the end."

"I reckon it would a'done just now, if I'd let young Rocky Marciano 'ere loose on 'im," Wally chuckled.

"Sorry, Wally," David repeated contritely; thankful that the crowd gathered around them was dispersing. "I suppose I made a fool of myself again."

"Forget it, son!" Wally chuckled. "It's allowed now an' agen."

"Don't dwell on it, David," Her Ladyship advised. "I was in the vicinity, so I thought I would take the opportunity to discuss our requirements for Arabella's birthday party; if it's convenient."

"Of course. May I offer you tea or coffee?"

"I'd love some tea, if I may … I say; this is rather pleasant," she remarked, as he led her to the yellow table. "Quite continental."

"Avril!" David called, as she passed the table. "Thanks for helping out here and for preventing something I'd probably have regretted."

"Don't be silly, love," she said. "We're here when you need us; you know that. I can hang on here, while you talk to Lady Alice. So don't worry."

"Thanks; I don't know what I'd do without you and Wally. Could you ask Stella to bring Lady Alice a pot of tea and me a cup of coffee, when she's got a minute?"

"Coming up!" Stella called from the doorway. Approaching the table, she treated him to a sunny smile. "Thanks for standing up for me," she said, blushing as Lady Alice smiled at her. "He was really nasty. He was saying horrible things about me."

"You're welcome. I did no more than I should do," said David. "I like to look after my staff. I wouldn't want to lose you."

Stella's eyes widened. "You mean?"

"Yes I do. Unless you don't want to stay?" he teased.

"Oh; I do! I love it here! Oh; thank you!"

"Stella!" he called, as he watched her almost skip away from the table.

"Yes?"

"Don't forget Lady Alice's tea."

"No; I won't, David."

"And Stella!"

"Yes?"

"You're doing great! Remind me later to sort out a proper wage for you."

Her face lit up with another smile, and he would almost swear that she floated to the kitchen.

"She's a very happy young lady!" Her Ladyship chuckled. "Matilda tells us this is a very happy place to work. If one were much younger, one might be tempted to apply for a position oneself."

"So, who was this chap you nearly got into a fight with?" Richard asked.

David finished serving ice creams and strawberry sundaes to a family at the red table before approaching his brother and Chris, who were standing on the quay waiting for a table to become available. "I don't know; some arrogant twit. But, how do you know about it?"

"I told him," said Chris. "If I hadn't, someone else would have. Gemma saw it. In fact she said you drew quite an audience. I take it this cove was insulting Stella. Gemma felt sure you would have laid into him if Wally hadn't intervened. She's very impressed with you."

"Tut-tut, Little Brother," Richard chuckled. "What would Mum say if she knew her baby boy was indulging in fisticuffs?"

"It didn't get that far," David protested. "But I wasn't going to stand by and let him abuse Stella or anyone else I'm responsible for."

"Quite right," Chris declared.

"Jo hasn't got wind of it, has she?" David asked.

Richard shook his head. "Not that I know of. I only saw her briefly this morning, before she left for work. But she didn't mention it."

"Good; I'd rather she didn't know."

"She and Colin are off to Leeds, as soon as she gets home. So there's not much chance of her finding out," Richard said reassuringly.

"The yellow table's free!" Stella called, as she cleared it.

"Good! Let's grab it!" Chris suggested. "We may as well enjoy a spot of lunch in the sunshine. I'm solvent, so it's on me."

They were distracted by Archie announcing his arrival with, "Dave; me old mate!"

It was one of the rare occasions that David was genuinely pleased to see him. Archie was accompanied by Ruby and Joel, both of whom had their eyes hidden behind the extravagantly large lenses of their sunglasses.

"Take a seat," David suggested. "I'm sure Chris and Richard won't mind if you join them."

"Actually, we came to thank you," said Ruby; removing her sunglasses as she sat down beside Richard. "We made it through the audition, thanks to you."

David waved a hand dismissively. "All I did was put them on to you. You must have impressed them."

"You did more than that," Ruby insisted. "Mervin told us you'd been watching and that he relied on your advice. I'll bet we wouldn't have got it if you'd said no. They're putting us on in just over a week's time, after rehearsals. As well as our own spot, Jenny O'Dell's manager has asked us to try out some new numbers with her. He seems to think she'll have more chance of another hit if she moves away from those weepy ballads. He's dead right!"

"We get twenty-five minutes for the matinees; and twenty for the evenin' shows," Joel proclaimed in his lyrical, Caribbean lilt. Tall and slim, he lowered himself onto a chair with a beaming smile.

"What do you sing, Ruby?" Chris enquired. "Anything I might know?"

"I'm not a singer; I play drums!" she replied curtly. "Why does everyone assume I'm the singer; just because I'm a girl?"

Chris held up his palms in apology. "Whoa! I beg your pardon! You're quite right, of course. This is the twentieth century and we mere males shouldn't expect everything to remain our preserve forever."

Ruby regarded him with suspicion; unsure if he was making fun of her.

"It's alright, Ruby," David chuckled. "He's like this all the time."

"What I mean is: we shouldn't assume that the fairer sex is content to remain chained to the kitchen sink," Chris declared. "After all, our monarch is a woman … and a delightful one, if I may make so bold."

"Who knows; we may even have a female prime minister, one day," Richard suggested impishly.

"Good lord! I wouldn't go that far!" Chris chortled.

"Would anyone like me to get them anything?" Linda asked, as she approached.

"How about excited?" Archie leered.

Linda responded with a glare that, in David's estimation, could have penetrated plate armour. He knew her to be married with children and guessed her to be in her mid-to-late thirties. Although not unattractive, her features were not what he would consider conventionally pretty. They now bore the expression of someone with the battle-hardened experience of working behind the bars of local pubs. Archie couldn't have been more out of his depth.

"For Pete's sake, Archie!" David exclaimed. "You have my permission to spill something very hot in his lap if he gives you any more cheek, Linda," he quipped, although he doubted that she would consider his approval necessary.

David waited for her to take the orders for drinks plus, in Archie's case, a slice of sponge cake, before he came to what was on his mind. "I'm glad you're here, Archie. I want to ask a favour."

"Ask away, buddie!" Archie replied frivolously.

"What are the chances of me borrowing your guitar and amp for an evening, the weekend after next? I've agreed to play at a birthday party, but I had to sell my equipment."

Archie pursed his lips. "Ooh! I dunno, Dave. Like to help you, mate. But I don't like anybody else using my gear, see. Sort of a superstition."

"It would only be for one night," David entreated. "I'll make sure no harm comes to it."

"Archie; you're a selfish pig!" Ruby exclaimed. "It's because of David that we've got this job. It's the least you can do!"

"Hey, man; I got a Telecaster you can use!" Joel announced. "And my Marshall amp will blast it out anyplace you want."

244

"Thanks, Joel; that's great of you!" David replied. "But you may have hit the nail on the head. I'm playing at a twenty-first birthday party for an aristocrat's daughter. Like a fool, I agreed to do it before I knew precisely what they had in mind. I've since found out that there's going to be a full orchestra in the ballroom and they're expecting me to provide the music for the younger ones to dance to in a marquee."

"Sounds great!" Joel exclaimed. "What's the problem, man?"

David grimaced. "To be truthful, I'm getting cold feet about tackling this on my own. It's all very well singing and playing in a pub, or while the guests are eating, as I originally thought. But I don't think there's enough in my repertoire with a beat for jiving!"

"When is it?" Ruby asked.

"Saturday, the eighth."

"Would a drummer help?"

"Do you mean you? How are you going to manage that?"

Ruby took a packet of Kensitas cigarettes and a small Ronson lighter from her bag. "We've got a week of rehearsals and what Mervin calls assimilation before they put us on the bill. I've got nothing on for that evening."

"Count me in," said Joel. "You're gonna need a bass!"

"Hang on! Hang on!" Archie interjected. "We're all committed to The Jet Stream. You can't do other gigs without Malky's say-so!"

"Stuff Malky!" Ruby snapped, lighting her cigarette and exhaling smoke from her nostrils. "Joel and I have had it up to here with him!"

"He's not going to like it," Archie chanted melodically.

"Then, he's going to have to lump it!" Ruby chanted in reply.

"Wait a minute!" David protested. "I don't want to cause trouble between you lot! It's just a one-off job. I don't know what it pays. In fact, I'm not even sure it pays anything! It's just occurred to me that money's never been mentioned."

"Don't worry, David; it's not your fault," Ruby insisted. "I think it sounds fun. And I don't care if it pays or not. Joel and I have made our minds up about The Jet Stream. We'll do the theatre job. But after that, either Malky goes or we do!"

"But … but, you can't!" Archie spluttered.

"Just watch us!" Ruby declared.

David furrowed his brow doubtfully. "If we do this, what are we going to play?"

"Whatever grabs us, man!" Joel chuckled, his dark eyes twinkling.

"That's right," Ruby enthused. "We can rehearse in the evenings, after you close up here."

David was still not convinced. "Suppose we do; *where* are we going to rehearse? We can't do it here; the council are causing enough trouble over me playing in the pub."

She paused while she considered the question. Drawing on her cigarette, she tilted her head back and exhaled a smoke ring. "There's a basement in the building that the theatre uses as a props store. They're letting me keep my drum cases there. That must be soundproof."

"Would they let us use it?"

"I don't know." She grinned mischievously. "It's up to you to sweet-talk Dorothy."

"This young lady seems to have it all worked out; and I don't think she takes no for an answer," Chris chuckled. "And there was I thinking it was only Jo who had you under her thumb."

"Here's Linda with the drinks!" David exclaimed. "Be careful she doesn't spill anything, Archie."

Ruby giggled. "Cheer up, Archie. You look like you've swallowed a wasp. You'll feel better after you've stuffed your face. You always do!"

A drum was beating somewhere in the torpid depths of David's subconscious, as he languorously emerged from the oblivion of sleep. Yawning extravagantly as his eyes focussed, he assumed he had been dreaming about his sessions with Ruby and Joel. The past three days of rehearsals had been enjoyable and exhilarating. But a hectic nine-hour day in the café, followed by another three hours or more in the airless confines of a basement, was draining him mentally and physically.

It was a few moments before his sluggish senses were sufficiently alert to realise that the drumming was continuing and was, in fact, someone hammering on the café doors. His immediate reaction was to assume he had overslept and that the girls had arrived for work. But a glance at the alarm clock revealed that it was only twenty-past-seven; far too early for them to show up. With a groan of anguish, he forced his reluctant body to leave the bed and lifted his dressing gown from the hook on the door.

"Alright; I'm coming!" he shouted, as he half stumbled down the stairs.

Emerging from the corridor, he could see Victor Sullivan peering through a glass pane.

"David! David!" Victor exclaimed, almost before he could open the door. "It's Sammy! He's in hospital. He's been attacked!"

Shock extinguished the last vestiges of drowsiness; instantly restoring David's wits. "Good God! Who by … and why?"

"He was burgled last night. It seems he disturbed them and got beaten up. Grace found out from Miss Forster; she's the nosey old biddy who lives across the street from Sammy and Ivy. She knows everybody's business. Grace gets her a Daily Sketch every day, when she goes out for our papers."

"Burgled!?" David gasped incredulously. "Why would anybody burgle Sammy? What's he got that's worth anyone breaking in for?"

Victor shook his head. "Not much, I should imagine. But, they weren't the only ones burgled. Whoever it was tried to break into one or two other places."

247

"What about Sammy's sister?"

"Ivy's not hurt. But she's badly shaken up. A neighbour's looking after her while the police try to contact a cousin of theirs."

"Could someone let me know if she needs anything?" David asked. "I take it Sammy's in Myrtlesham General? As soon as I'm dressed, I'll ring them and find out how he is."

* * *

"Poor Sammy!" Stella sighed. "We ought to get him a card and some grapes or something."

Connie nodded. "We could, but I don't think he goes much on fruit. Knowing Sammy; he'd probably rather have twenty Woodbines."

"I'm going in to see him this evening," said David. "Richard is giving me a lift to the hospital. So if you think of anything, I'll take it with me."

"They probably won't let him smoke, so I'll get him some fruit when I take my break," Connie proposed.

Sitting on the edge of a table, David stroked his chin thoughtfully. "We'll have to reorganise ourselves to manage with Jo away and without Tilly and Sammy. So, before we open, let's talk about what we're going to do. My suggestion is that Connie carries on as normal in the kitchen; you, Stella, carry on serving the customers, as usual, and I'll back you up when it gets busy. I think it would be a good idea to get the customers to pay at the counter. It will save us running backwards and forwards to the till. I'll work the till and do the boat tickets, and take on Sammy's role of cleaning and washing up … as and when I can. I think we have enough cutlery to manage, but I'll get in some more crockery to make sure we can cope. What do you think?"

"I've got a better idea," Richard called from the doorway. "Why don't I do the washing up? I could clear the tables too."

"You're joking!" David replied. "It's great of you Rich; I really appreciate it. But no thanks. You're supposed to be convalescing."

"And you'll need to, if you carry on burning the candle at both ends!" Richard retorted.

"He's right!" Linda appeared behind Richard and followed him in. Putting her bag on a table, she gave David a determined look. "Stop being pig-headed and have the sense to accept help when it's offered! Avril called me and told me about Sammy, so I've arranged for my mum to look after the kids for a few days. If it helps, I can manage a full day for the rest of this week."

"Come on David; a bit of washing up's not going to kill me!" Richard insisted.

"He's right," Linda asserted. "Richard can take a break if he gets tired. So let him help you, if he wants to! He is your brother, after all."

"Well said, Linda!" Richard exclaimed and clapped a hand on David's shoulder. "Well, Little Brother? Or I should say boss? Where's my apron?"

* * *

The nurse pointed to the half-closed curtain screening the last bed on the other side of the ward. "He's down there at the end, next to the window."

David guessed that she was about his age. She was tall and looked smart and attractive in her little white cap and neatly pressed uniform, which led him to try to imagine Jo in hers. He didn't doubt that she looked just as smart and neat. But cuter … and prettier. 'If only she were here, now,' he thought.

One or two beds were unoccupied, including the one next to Sammy. But most of the patients had visitors around them, maintaining a subdued babble of conversation. However, one woman was absently staring out of a window; she and the equally bored-looking occupant of the bed apparently unable to think of anything to say to each other.

A middle-aged couple sat in silence on either side of a deathly-pale old man, who lay propped up on pillows. His eyes were closed and his mouth hung open, displaying dark, toothless gums. The couple looked up and smiled as David passed them, seemingly grateful for the distraction.

Sammy appeared to be asleep. One side of his face was bruised and swollen, and the flesh around the eye-socket was an ugly mosaic of black, purple and blue.

"Oh, Sammy! What have they done to you?"

Sammy's undamaged eye opened. "That you, Davy?"

"Yes, it's me, Sammy. I know it's a silly question, but how are you feeling?"

"Like I bin run over by a bus." Sammy's attempt at a grin was more like a grimace.

David unloaded the contents of a canvas shopping bag onto the locker beside the bed. "I've got a get well card here from the girls. They send their love and they've sent you some pears and oranges and a bottle of lemon barley water. I would've brought you a bottle of stout, if I'd thought they'd let you have it."

"Rather 'ave a fag," Sammy chuckled. "Open the cards for me, will yuh? Can 'ave a look at 'em later on. Good girls, they are. Tell 'em thanks from me."

David pulled up a chair beside the bed. "What on earth happened?"

Wincing and grunting, Sammy slowly and painfully eased himself upright. "Dunno much … Fell asleep in the chair … Dark when I woke up. Must a'bin late, cos Ivy was in bed … Could 'ear 'er snorin'. Thought I 'eard a noise in the kitchen an' went t'see what it wuz. Soon as I opened the kitchen door sommat 'it me. Sent me arse-over-'ead back in the livin' room. Must a'smacked me 'ead on the sideboard, cause the next thing I know two coppers are bendin' over me; Ivy's cryin' 'er eyes out; an' Mavis from next door's in there tryin' t'calm 'er down."

"Any bones broken?"

"Don't think so. Got pains in me side an' shoulder. Took me down fer an X-ray. Aint 'eard no more about that. Got t'get me leg sorted out agen afore I can come 'ome, though."

"Do they know who it was that broke in?" David asked.

"Nah! Long gone by the time the coppers got there. Could be outsiders; come fer carnival week, so the coppers reckon. Lot a people about then, see? Better chance t'nick stuff. Broke the lock on the back door. Dunno why they picked on us; nuthin' much in our place. Threw stuff about lookin' fer sommat t'pinch. Broke a few plates an' Ivy's wireless ... Loved that wireless, she did. Never misses The Archers an' Woman's Hour. Took the money in the biscuit barrel. Bin puttin' a bit in there t'pay off the rent arrears we owes. Council's threatenin' t'chuck us out if we don't."

"How much do you owe? If you don't mind me asking."

"Got to more'n thirty quid at one time. Paid a bit off since I bin workin' fer you, though."

"Well, don't worry about it, now," David said soothingly. "And we'll see what we can do about Ivy's wireless. Do you need anything else?"

"Nah; don't need nothin'. Worried about Ivy, though. Needs somebody t'keep an eye on 'er while I'm in 'ere. Can't look after 'erself, see. Can't trust 'er with money. Gonna struggle on 'er own with me not bringin' nothin' in fer a while."

"Don't worry about Ivy," David assured him. "Your cousin is looking after her."

"Thass good. Be alright with Rita."

"And don't worry about money, Sammy. You're permanent staff. You'll get paid while you're off. I'll make sure Ivy doesn't go without anything she needs."

"Good lad you are," Sammy sighed. "An' Jo's a smashin' girl. Both bin good to me. Make a good pair, you two."

At the sound of a bell, visitors started to get to their feet; several with barely disguised relief.

"Thass visitin' over," Sammy announced.

David stood up and replaced his chair against the wall. "Sorry I got here late. It's been frantic in the café, today. I'll come and see you again in a day or so, if you're not out before then. I think your cousin is bringing Ivy in tomorrow afternoon. Connie said she'll come and see you in the evening."

"Righto. Thanks for comin', Davy."

"My pleasure, Sammy. Take care. Take your time and get back on your feet again before you think of coming back to work."

Emerging from the hospital's Georgian portico, David took a deep breath to rid himself of the distinctive, and to him, unsettling hospital smell. He had never been able to come to terms with that cocktail of antiseptic, sterilizers and disinfectant, occasionally permeated by other aromas that he preferred not to try to identify.

On his way out, he had noticed a sign pointing to Primrose Ward and, on a whim, had taken a detour to peer through the round porthole in one of its doors. He had been unsurprised to discover that it looked identical to the ward he had just left; apart from the fact that all the patients were women. There was nothing special about it; except that it was where Jo worked.

As he made his way across the car park, Richard's car burst into life with a guttural roar and a puff of blue smoke from the exhaust pipe.

"How is he?" Richard asked.

"He's been knocked about a bit," David replied, settling himself on the passenger seat. "He's badly bruised and his callipers need to be refitted. But there don't seem to be any bones broken."

"I was going to suggest finding somewhere to eat," Richard suggested. "But you look all-in."

"That would be nice," said David. "But what I need first is a pint."

X

The night air was cool and welcoming after the heat and humidity of the basement. Grimacing uncomfortably, David eased the cloying fabric of his shirt away from his back and stretched his arms to flex his cramped shoulders. Ruby Red, as the trio called themselves, had worked hard to make up for the lost evening he had spent visiting Sammy in hospital.

Joel's Fender Telecaster was a pleasure to play and, as all of them were accomplished musicians, they had quickly acquired a basic repertoire of popular songs and instrumentals suitable for dancing. However, David doubted that the two remaining evenings before their performance would be enough for them to widen their range sufficiently to last several hours. Nevertheless, they would have to make do and hope their audience didn't mind repeats; or better still, didn't notice.

It was almost eleven o'clock, and the pubs were closing, but the fairground remained lively and noisy. Light spilled from the windows of the bar in The Grand Hotel, and people were still strolling along the promenade. Sitting on a low wall at the corner of Victoria Street, he could see along the whole length of the Esplanade and hear the sea breaking on the shore with the rhythmic surge that he found so restful and soothing. He was almost tempted to take off his shoes and socks, roll up his trousers and paddle his way home along the beach.

'Home? Don't start thinking of Fairhaven as home,' he cautioned himself. 'It will just make it harder to leave.' The welcome sight of Ruby appearing from Wellington Road prevented him descending into melancholy.

"Just made it before they closed," she announced, handing him an invitingly hot parcel wrapped in newspaper. "It's all freshly cooked. I was lucky; a few other people turned up at the same time as me, so they fried up a fresh batch. You said you were hungry, so I got you rock salmon and a tanner's worth."

"Good lord!" David exclaimed. "It'll take me all night to get through this lot!" Suddenly realising she was alone, he asked, "Where's Joel?"

"He's not keen on fish and chips, so he's gone back to the flat to get settled in and make sure Archie hasn't taken all the shelf and cupboard space."

"Shall we take our supper down to the beach, where it's quiet?" David proposed. But, realising that his suggestion might be misinterpreted, he added hastily, "I didn't mean … I wasn't trying to…"

Ruby replied with a snort of laughter. "It didn't occur to me. But you've put the thought in my head, now."

"Sorry," he muttered. "I could win medals for putting my foot in it."

Giggling, she tugged at his arm. "Come on; I'll risk it!"

"It's good of Archie to share a flat with Joel," David remarked, as they crossed the Esplanade. "But, having been billeted with him, I don't envy Joel being cooped up with him in that pokey little garret."

"I don't think Joel feels he has much choice, she said. "I can't believe those bloody women! How can people be so hateful?"

David nodded in agreement. "What happened, exactly?"

Ruby blew out her cheeks in irritation. "It started, as soon as they arrived at our digs. Two sisters, in their fifties or sixties I'd guess; with their dozy, hen-pecked husbands. Everything was fine until they arrived. Nobody bothered us. Our landlady was as good as gold. She treated Joel the same as everybody else. But then we started hearing comments in the dining room at breakfast. You know; supposedly to each other, but just loud enough for other people to hear."

"Like what?"

"Things like: 'They ought to stay in their own country, where they belong.' I wanted to say something, but Joel wouldn't let me. He told me to ignore it; said he's used to it."

"Sadly, he probably is," David reflected. "There's a notice in one of the windows in Shore Road that says, *No Blacks. No Irish. No dogs.* There has to be something seriously wrong with people like that! What made Joel change his mind?"

"I changed it for him," Ruby declared. "They went on about having to share the bathroom with a blackie, and offensive remarks like that. I gritted my teeth until one of them went as far as to say they wished they'd brought their own cutlery. I couldn't take any more. I let fly and told them exactly what they were!"

"Good for you! What happened?"

"There was an almighty row! You'd have been proud of Archie. He stood up for Joel. As you can imagine, the vile old bags were indignant. I had to laugh in their faces when the sour-faced one came out with, 'Of course, I'm as broad-minded as anybody, but you have to draw the line somewhere.' Broad minded? I don't know how I stopped myself telling her that the only thing broad about her was her backside! It's amazing isn't it? There's always a '*but*' to justify the prejudice of hateful bigots like her. And I told her so!"

"How did she take it?"

"Oh, my God! Both of them were *outraged*. I think that was the word the one that looked like Olive Oyl used."

The mental picture it conjured up made David chuckle.

His amusement brought a smile to Ruby's face. "Well, she did. Thin as a rake, she was; with her hair in a bun. I was told *I'm no better than I should be*. It was obvious what they meant by that. Anyway, the three of us had to find new digs. We were going to anyway; even if our landlady hadn't asked us to. At least she had enough decency to be apologetic about it."

"Are you settled where you are now?" David asked. "I take it you're not at the same place as Malky and the other two."

"No; they're still at that place Dorothy found for them in Lowestoft Road. Colditz by the Sea, as Vince calls it. Apparently, the landlady's pretty strict. I'm fine, though. I've got a bigger room where I am now. It looks out over the Wintergardens ... and I can have a bath whenever I like."

They stopped at the foot of the steps leading to the beach and sat down to eat. "It's funny how fish and chips never tastes this good when you eat it off a plate," David mused.

For a while they sat in silence; enjoying their supper and watching the dark, languid waves roll out of the darkness, to glitter with darting reflections from the lights of the funfair and promenade, before lazily tumbling onto the shore.

Ruby eventually broke the spell. "What are you going to do when the café closes?"

"I don't know. I haven't really thought about it."

"Have you thought about playing guitar full-time?"

"Oh, yes; I've thought about it," David said wistfully. "I'd love to, but it's a tough world. Tough to get into; and even tougher to make any money."

"True; but it can be done if you've got talent *and* you're really determined. And you've got talent, David. You just don't believe in yourself enough."

"So have you! I've been meaning to ask you what made you take up drumming."

"Dad brought my brother, Pete, a set of drums one Christmas. God knows why! But that's Dad; no thought for anything but his pigeons. And Mum gets dozier by the day. Pete wasn't interested, so I started banging away on them. I was about fifteen at the time and I just loved it. Anyway, Sandie knew someone who played the drums in a dance band and he gave me lessons … You *do* remember Sandie, I presume?"

"Yes," David chuckled "How is your sister?"

"Married, with a couple of kids."

"What do your parents think about you going off with a group of lads?" he asked.

She shrugged dismissively. "I'd be surprised if they've really noticed. Everybody goes their own way in our family. Ships that pass in the night, as they say."

David wrapped up the remains of his supper. "I'm afraid that's as much as I can manage, and I don't think I can stay awake much longer. I don't know about you, but it's time I called it a day."

"You mean you got me down here under false pretences?" she giggled and, to his surprise, she leaned across and kissed him.

Although it caught him unawares, it was anything but unpleasant; and he couldn't help responding.

"You had vinegar on your chips," he said, licking his lips. Gratified by her laughter, he added, "Come on; I'll walk you to your digs."

When he arrived home, Wally was sitting at a table outside the pub, puffing on a straight-stemmed pipe.

"Hello, Wally. I didn't know you smoked," David remarked.

"I 'ad a bad dose o'bronchitis two years ago, an' the doc told me to lay off the fags. But I reckon a pipe now an' agen don't do no 'arm." Wally stood up, his expression serious. "Thought I'd better 'ave a quiet word when you got back."

"Why, what's up?" David asked warily.

Wally gestured with his pipe towards the lane between the pub and the café. "Somebody was in the yard outside your place, earlier on. I saw 'im from our bedroom window; pokin' about in your rubbish bins. 'E done a bunk when I came out, so I couldn't collar 'im to find out what 'e was up to. Victor saw 'im, too. It wasn't the same fella that came in the pub, though."

David swallowed uncomfortably. "I wonder if it's the bloke who was hanging about out here."

"Could be. Victor said somebody's bin askin' questions about the boats an' who owns 'em."

"It's all a bit strange," David mused. "And disturbing. I don't want to worry the girls unnecessarily, but I think I'd better warn them; just in case."

Wally nodded his agreement. "It's not a bad idea. Tommy Bowyer said the local nick are gonna make extra patrols round 'ere at night. The boat crews're keepin' a lookout too. So keep yer wits about yuh, an' if you need us just give us a shout."

"Will do, Wally … and thanks."

With carnival week only a few days away, the school holidays in full swing, and the glorious summer weather showing no sign of ending, Fairhaven was becoming crowded. 'The Rocky', as the café was already known to locals, was busy almost from the moment David unlocked the doors. Fortunately, his new system of working was proving effective, although he would admit that much of its success was due to the sterling effort of his staff. For some reason, they had found his warning about the mystery prowler more amusing than disturbing.

Richard was enjoying his role as 'skivvy without portfolio'; a title he had bestowed on himself. He seemed to be everywhere; helping Connie in the kitchen, clearing tables, sweeping and mopping up, in addition to his official duties as washer-up.

Linda was indefatigable and untiring, while Stella remained unerringly willing.

Nevertheless, their ability to cope was tested at lunchtimes or when the Ocean Queen docked. The two occurrences hadn't coincided before. But, to take advantage of the influx of holidaymakers, Danny had shortened one or two cruises and squeezed in an extra one. With everyone working flat-out to serve the lunchtime clientele, the sight of a fresh hoard disembarking onto the quay made David's spirits wilt.

"There are people at the counter waiting to pay, David," Stella announced.

"I know," he replied. "We could do with another pair of hands."

His wish was granted a few moments later, when Linda pointed to a figure dismounting from a bicycle. "I think we're in luck," she called.

David's heart leapt. "Jo!" he exclaimed in sheer delight. "I didn't expect you back so soon!"

Stella and Linda greeted her with the relief of people besieged. Removing her sunglasses as she came in, Jo gazed around the congested café. "It's a good job I came back early. What do you need me to do?"

"You could look after the queue waiting to pay," David suggested. "We're finding it's more efficient than running backwards and forwards with the money."

The till clanged regularly for several minutes as Jo dealt with the queue. It was a while before she and David had time for a proper conversation.

"Aunt Ginny told me about Sammy, when I phoned her yesterday," she explained. "I could hardly believe my ears! She also said that Richard's worried about you."

"Really?"

"Yes; and with good reason, it seems. He's worried about the toll it's taking on you; spending hours practising for Bella's party after a hectic day here."

"He needn't worry. You needn't either. I'm alright. I hope you didn't think you had to come back early on my account." His spirits had been lifted simply by her being there. "I'm glad you did though."

Her enigmatic smile gave him hope that she really had been concerned for him.

"I popped in to see Sammy on my way home," she said. "Thankfully, no bones are broken and there's no lasting damage. He told me you'd been in to see him. He's so grateful to you for promising to keep an eye on his sister and relieved that he'll still get paid."

"If that's that alright with you. Their cousin's looking after his sister. But I thought paying him is the least we can do."

"Of course it is! It's all he's got. At least he doesn't have to worry about Ivy or money while he's recovering. They're moving him to the Hillside, as soon as his callipers are repaired."

"Is that the cottage hospital at the top of the Downs Road?"

She nodded. "Yes. They're hoping to move him tomorrow or the day after. So, at least he'll be here in Fairhaven, where it's easier for Ivy to visit him."

"There's something you ought to know..." he began, but the sound of an altercation on the quay caught their attention and forestalled his warning about the intruder in the yard. Heads were turning towards the sound of raised voices, and people at the window tables were standing up to get a better view.

Linda came in from serving tables outside looking concerned. "I don't know what's going on," she announced. "Stan's yelling at some kids outside his place and threatening them with a stick!"

Hurrying outside with Jo and Stella, David was astonished to find Stan in front of a pile of upturned wicker chairs outside his premises. His features were flushed and his expression one of barely suppressed rage. He was waving a heavy stick threateningly above his head and bellowing in what David assumed was Polish. The head of the stick was solid ball of carved wood, like an African knobkerrie, and looked capable of inflicting a lethal blow. A group of eight boys was backing away from it; one or two of them shouting in a language that David recognised as German, while a young man and an older woman, careful to keep their distance, remonstrated with Stan.

The woman was unmistakably British, but the young man spoke English with a foreign accent. His fair hair was cropped short and he wore dark grey trousers and a black shirt, buttoned at the neck. A silver badge on his breast pocket glittered in the sunlight as he ushered the boys away from danger. The boys were all about twelve or thirteen years old, and most seemed shaken and upset, although one stood his ground and stared defiantly at Stan; even raising a fist.

"Stan! What on earth's the matter?" Jo called, and started to walk towards him.

"Be careful!" Gemma warned. "He's acting like a madman. You never know what he might do!"

"Gemma's right," David cautioned, taking Jo's arm to restrain her. "Look at his face. He's liable to tip over the edge, any minute."

Emerging from his office, the harbourmaster shouted. "What's going on?"

"It's alright. No need to make a song an' dance about it," Wally called back. Pushing his way through the crowd, he approached Stan cautiously. "Come on Stan; put that club down. Whatever the trouble is, brainin' somebody with that thing's not gonna do no good!"

Stan replied with a furious tirade in his native tongue, of which only the word 'Nazis' was intelligible.

"Let's 'ave none o'that, Stan," Wally commanded. "All that's finished with. Bin over an' done with a long time."

"No finish! For me; no finish!" Stan exclaimed, his voice quaking with emotion.

"I'm going to get these boys out of harm's way," Jo announced. "They look bewildered, poor things."

"That's a good idea," said David. "Try and settle them down with some ice cream or something."

"The young man in black turned towards them and smiled appreciatively. "Thank you. You are very kind," he said, before reverting to German to instruct the boys to follow him and Jo to the café.

All but one obeyed. While his companions trouped along beside Jo and Stella, eager to practice their English, he remained glaring defiantly at Stan. It took a second, sharper command to draw him away.

The English woman accompanying the boys gesticulated animatedly towards Stan. "Somebody fetch a policeman. He should be locked up!" she demanded. "What sort of a welcome is this for those children? We invite them here on a goodwill visit, and this happens!"

"Don't be silly, Stan! Put that stick down!" Avril's calm but insistent voice drew everyone's attention as she appeared from the crowd.

Wally stretched out an arm to hold her back. "What're you doin' 'ere? Who's mindin' the pub?"

"It's alright, Wilf's there," she replied and brushed his arm aside.

The crowd watched silently, as she slowly walked towards Stan and held out her hand. "Come on, love," she coaxed. "Put that down and tell me what this is all about."

Ignoring her appeal, he stared at her impassively; his expression dark and menacing.

"That's close enough, Pet," Wally cautioned; his jaw tightening, as he edged forward ready to intervene.

"Don't be silly, Stan! Put it down!" Avril insisted.

Glaring at her, as if in a trance, he mumbled incoherently and began to sway back and forth.

Avril held out her hand. "Come on, love; give it to me."

The hush was almost palpable; as if everyone was holding their breath, while Stan stared at her dispassionately, seemingly unaware of who she was, or where *he* was. Then, without warning, he suddenly took a step forward, prompting a gasp from the crowd and an instinctive reaction from Wally, who darted forward to pull Avril away.

But, as if a spell had been broken, Stan's shoulders sagged and he lowered the stick; the haunted look in his eyes extinguished by the tears coursing down his cheeks. With a whimper and an expression of utter despair, he began to sob.

The crowd's anxious gasp became a murmur of relief, as Avril took the stick and put an arm around him. "Come on, my love," she murmured. "Let's get you away from here and get you a cup of coffee … or somethin' stronger, if you like. Give Wally your keys. He'll lock up for you."

Stan wiped a hand across his weeping eyes and fumbled in his pocket. Handing Wally his keys, he allowed her to lead him through the dispersing crowd as meekly as a child.

"Well; I'll be…!" Wally exclaimed, stroking his beard pensively. "Although I say it meself, I married an 'ell of woman!"

"I'll say!" said David.

"What was all that about?" Ken Rathbone demanded.

"Nothin' much. A storm in a teacup," Wally replied. "It's all over an' done with."

"I shall have to report this!" the harbourmaster insisted.

"You do that," Wally growled impassively.

"He's a madman!" the English woman persisted. "He ought to be locked up!"

Wally glared at her. "What for? Nobody got 'urt."

"No thanks to him!" she snapped. "I'm going to report him to the police!"

"Do what you damned-well like!" Wally replied dismissively. "I'll tell you this, though; it must a'taken a lot to get 'im in that state!"

"I saw what happened," Victor Sullivan said quietly. "And I'm pretty sure I know what tipped him over the edge."

"He seemed to be shouting something about Nazis," David suggested.

"He was," said Victor. "He hates Germans; and with good reason! Grace and I don't know the details; he's never talked about it. But we do know he lost all his family in the war. He was quite young when he came here as refugee. It was in nineteen-forty-six, if I remember correctly. Grace's friend, Florence, and her husband took him in and looked after him for a while. He was even quieter and more withdrawn than he is now."

"I should think so!" Wally murmured.

"It didn't help that he couldn't speak more than one or two words of English," Victor explained. "All they managed get from him was something about the SS and them shooting his father and brother. From what Flo managed to glean from the authorities, we think his mother and sister died in a concentration camp. He was put in a labour camp in Germany. It seems that all his family were shot or died somehow in the war. He was the only one who survived."

A poignant reminder of the pictures on the wall in Stan's office came into David's mind, together with the haunting image of Stan's bleak expression when he had enquired about them.

"So you reckon it was the kids talkin' German that set 'im off," Wally suggested.

Victor nodded. "It could have triggered it, I suppose. I was taking in a delivery and saw the boys messing around with the furniture outside Stan's place. A couple of them were trying to peer in through the window. They weren't doing any harm; it was just boys being boys. I could tell they were foreign, but I never thought any more of it. Anyway, one of them started tapping on the glass and pulling faces. Stan came out to shoo them away and their teacher, or whoever he is, came over and started shouting in German. I think he was telling the boys off. But Stan probably thought he was shouting at him, because he lost his rag. The two of them started yelling at each other and Stan picked up that stick. The rest you saw for yourselves."

"Bein' yelled at in German must a'bin the last straw," Wally observed.

"The chap's shirt could have tipped the scales," Victor reflected. "The SS wore black uniforms, didn't they? It might have brought it all back and sent him over the edge."

"I dunno, I'm sure," Wally mused, as he and David walked back along the quay. "We think *we've* got it rough at times. But we don't know we're born. God-only knows what that poor begger's bin through!"

"I can't imagine what it's like to lose your entire family, David sighed. "And to find yourself alone in a strange country."

"It don't bear thinkin' about," Wally reflected. "You can be sure of one thing, though. Somebody, not a million miles away, is gonna be lookin' out for 'im, from now on."

* * *

David shut the café doors and turned the sign to 'closed', before sitting down at a window table and leaning back contentedly. "Thank God that's over," he sighed. "Let's hope we don't get many more days like this one."

"The German boys seemed happy enough when they left," Jo remarked, as she emerged from the kitchen corridor. "Apart from that conceited kid in the blue shirt."

"I should think they *were* happy!" David said ruefully. "Considering the amount of ice cream and pop they got through! Especially that one in blue you mentioned. A clip round the ear would do that greedy little devil the world of good!"

"You're right," Jo concurred. "The boys' teacher was very grateful though … and quite charming."

265

"Was he?" David teased. "You're not thinking of nurturing Anglo-German relations while Colin's away, are you?"

"Shut up and eat," she commanded and put a plate on the table in front of him.

"What's this?"

"It's what it looks like; ham salad."

"With new potatoes! What have I done to deserve all this?"

She sat down beside him with a cup of tea. "Connie's convinced you're not eating properly. So she and I made it before she left."

"It looks delicious, but I haven't got time. I'll be late for rehearsal."

"Too bad! You're not leaving here until you've eaten it!"

Richard took a seat opposite them. "The kitchen's all clean and tidy, boss!"

"Thank you, my good fellow!" said David.

"I was speaking to Jo," Richard chuckled.

David looked at her enquiringly. "Doesn't Richard get anything?"

"I don't need anything," Richard replied. "There's a meal waiting for me every evening."

"Aunt Ginny will have something ready for Richard when we get back," Jo added. "Richard's eating properly... unlike his brother."

"I *am* eating properly!" David insisted and picked up a fork. "Ruby and I had fish and chips the other night."

"So fish and chips is your idea of eating well, is it?" Jo's forehead furrowed with curiosity. "Who's Ruby?"

"She plays drums in The Jet Stream."

"A girl? Playing the drums?"

"Yes; she's really good. I used to go out with her sister. She and Joel, the bass player, are playing at Bella's party with me."

"Your old girlfriend's sister, eh? How convenient."

David hastily swallowed a mouthful of ham. "Stella's brother is going to run us to Huckfield Hall and pick us up again around midnight. He's got a Standard Vanguard estate. It's a damned-great thing; so there'll be plenty of room for us and our gear."

"Don't eat so fast; you'll give yourself indigestion!" Jo admonished. "I'm sure Ruby won't mind waiting a few minutes more."

"Yes, mother!" he replied. "Look; I'm keeping my elbows off the table!"

It earned him a grudging smile in reply.

"By the way," he said, between mouthfuls. "I meant to tell you, but it slipped my mind with all that hoo-ha with Stan. The order I placed with Delrio for Bella's party has just about caught us up with the target they've set us. So I haven't charged Lady Alice what we normally sell it for. She seemed pleased with the discount I gave her. We've had a cheque from her secretary already."

"Is that allowed? Can we sell it in bulk?" Jo queried.

He shrugged. "I don't know. I didn't ask. No-one said anything when I phoned them with the order. But I'm having it delivered here, anyway. Someone from Huckfield Hall will pick it up, when I let them know it's arrived."

"My goodness; we are getting efficient and business-like, aren't we?" she said mischievously. "I'm beginning to feel surplus to requirements. You seem to manage very well without me."

"I think your timely arrival today gives the lie to that," Richard observed.

"Richard's right," David concurred. "I can't tell you how relieved we were to see you."

Their attention was drawn to the sound of tapping on the doors. "It's not locked, Avril!" David called.

She came in with a cigarette between her long, manicured fingers. "Now you've got a minute to yourselves, I thought you might like know how Stan's gettin' on," she said.

"Yes, we would," Jo replied eagerly. "Would you like a cup of tea?"

Avril shook her head. "No thanks, love. I only popped in for a minute. I'm happy to say he's more like his old self again. He's in our sittin' room, watchin' *Tonight* on the tele." Chuckling to herself, she added, "I don't think he can make heads-or-tails of most of it, but he's glued to it all the same."

"Did he say anything about what set him off?" David asked.

"No; all he keeps sayin' is: he's sorry. We can't get anythin' more out of him. We can guess what caused it, but we can't do anythin' about it. And we can't take away his heartache, poor love. All we can do is keep an eye on him and make him realise he's not alone and can count on us."

"Poor Stan," Jo sighed. "Will it be alright if I pop in and say hello on my way home?"

"Of course! I'm sure he'll be pleased to see you."

David glanced at his watch and got to his feet. "I'm really sorry, but I'm afraid I have to love you and leave you. I'm late already."

"Yes; you'd better go," Jo replied archly. "It wouldn't do to keep Ruby waiting, would it?"

The marquee was spacious, but with so many bodies twisting and twirling energetically on such a warm evening, the atmosphere inside was almost as humid as the basement where Ruby Red had rehearsed. Basking in the clammy glow of the appreciation shown by Bella and her guests, the group members were sitting by an open canvas flap, relishing a break and a cool drink.

"We've done nearly all the numbers we rehearsed," David announced. "We'll have to repeat quite a few in the second half."

"I've been thinking about that," Ruby said pensively. "How do you feel about me padding things out with a drum solo?"

268

"Crazy!" Joel exclaimed. "Great idea Rube!"

"That's fine with me," said David. "How and when?"

She drained her glass and pursed her lips as she thought. "Well; I suggest we start by playing *Guitar Boogie* again, or you could improvise with something like it. When I'm about to break into the solo, I'll give you a signal on the tom-toms … like this." She beat out a rapid rhythm with her fingers on the back of a chair. "You and Joel can cut in with the odd riff as and when you feel like it. When I repeat the signal, I'll wrap it up and we can finish with a few more bars of *Guitar Boogie*. How does that sound?"

"Great! Terrific!" Joel and David enthused.

Ruby pushed her damp fringe off her forehead and swept a stray lock of hair from beside her eye. "Another thought. It's an old trick, as they say in corny films, but we can always justify repeats by saying they've been requested."

"Yeh; everybody uses that scam," Joel chuckled.

"OK. We'll start the second spot the same way we kicked off the evening; with Joel doing *Good Golly Miss Molly*," David suggested. "I'll tell them it's our signature number. You can call the play list after that, Ruby."

"Oh, here you are!" Bella's voice, immediately behind them, made them turn their heads abruptly.

Both she and Tilly looked stunning; Bella in an off-the-shoulder emerald green ball gown and Tilly in ivory-white. It pleased David to notice that she had the silver brooch he had given her for her birthday pinned on her breast. They were accompanied by an immaculately dressed couple, who were obviously Bella's parents.

Tilly bestowed her most captivating smile on David. "Hello," she giggled. "Have you missed me?"

"And how! It's been like a madhouse!"

She responded with an appreciative smile. "I'll be back on Monday."

"Good," he said. "I didn't know you could jive like that! Mervin knew what he was doing when he offered you a job as a dancer."

She laughed girlishly. "I love dancing."

"Did your father like the portrait?"

"Oh yes! He loved it. He wants to meet Chris ... and you."

"Aren't either of you girls going to introduce us?" Although politely made, Lady de Tenneaux's request was an obvious instruction.

She could not have been mistaken for anyone other than Bella's mother, or perhaps an elder sister. Her hair was the same lustrous auburn and her features as attractive as her daughter's. She wore a blue, full-length evening gown, with a diamond and emerald choker at her throat that flashed and sparkled as she moved. She smiled at the three musicians with an expression that bore the openness and geniality of someone totally at ease when meeting people.

"Oh, yes; of course, Mummy!" Bella exclaimed, her cheeks flushed with the heat and, David suspected, more than a little champagne. "This is David ... and..."

Ruby came to her rescue. "I'm Ruby; and this is Joel."

"I'm delighted to meet you!" Lady de Tenneaux replied. "My goodness; haven't you all been working hard? Your prowess leaves one speechless!"

Ruby replied with a modest blush, while Joel signalled his appreciation with a dazzling smile.

"Yes! You're all simply amazing!" Bella concurred "One does so envy those with such talent! Thank you all!" she enthused. "It's all such fun! You're simply wonderful! Thank you so much!"

"You seem to be emptying the ballroom," His Lordship remarked, gazing around the crowded marquee.

He was tall, with wavy chestnut hair, greying at the temples, and a relaxed air of authority. Unbuttoning his impeccably tailored dinner jacket, he regarded the three musicians with a gaze that suggested amused curiosity.

"I'm sorry..." David began.

But Lord Anthony raised a hand to interrupt his apology. "It was meant in jest. However, one cannot help noticing that even some of our more mature guests are gravitating here." He gestured to a group in the far corner. "Including my mother, who, it would seem, is more *with it* ... if that's the appropriate expression ... than some of us."

Noticing the gesture, Lady Alice waved a hand cheerily. David had been amused to observe her on the crowded dance floor with several young men during some of the less lively numbers. In between times, she had been keeping the trio's vocal chords lubricated by ensuring their glasses were regularly refilled.

"I hope you will find this acceptable," His Lordship said, handing David a bulky envelope. "I'm afraid Arabella and my mother were somewhat vague on the subject of your fee. Unfortunately, one has little experience in these matters."

"Thank you very much," David replied, turning the envelope over in his hands. "I don't think we actually discussed it. But this appears to be far too much."

"Not at all," Lady de Tenneaux exclaimed. "However carefully these occasions are planned, one can still only hope all will be well." Her eyes twinkled mischievously. "The young people and, as my husband has suggested, some *not-so-young* are having a marvellous time!"

"Oh, yes!" Bella cried. "Would you sing *Hound Dog* again for me?"

"Of course; especially for you. It's your party," said David.

"Do you know *Living Doll*?" Tilly asked. "I just adore Cliff Richard."

David pursed his lips. "I'm no Cliff Richard, Tilly, and he's only just released that record, so I'm not absolutely sure I know all the words. It's not one we've rehearsed."

"I know it! We'll give it our best shot." Ruby replied emphatically. "Don't look at me like that, David," she giggled.

"There aren't that many words to remember; and only a handful of chords. It's a piece of cake."

"Which reminds me," Lady de Tenneaux exclaimed "Before you girls overwork these poor people, you might allow them to enjoy a little refreshment." Turning to the musicians, she said, "You must be hungry. Come and help yourselves from the supper buffet. And you must have some of Arabella's birthday cake!"

* * *

The chant of, "*We want Ruby! We want Ruby!*" continued to swell until it seemed to fill the marquee, drowning David's attempts to sign off and thank the boisterous throng that packed the dance floor and the area around the dais. Ruby obliged with a roll on a side drum, followed by a rapid paradiddle and splash on a cymbal, which far from satisfying her admirers, only fuelled their demand for more.

Ruby Red had managed to get through the second session with only one or two repeats which were not genuine requests. Supported by the enthusiastic participation of their audience, they had also managed a decent version of *Living Doll,* during which they had briefly stopped playing to allow the balloon-waving dance-floor chorus to perform unaccompanied. The clamorous demand for a conga had also been welcome; taking up time while a long chain of side-kicking revellers bobbed and weaved its way around the marquee, out of the entrance and back in again, several times.

But it was Ruby's 'incandescent' drum solo that had inspired the most fervent and loudest acclaim of the night. Like the revellers, David had been astonished by her skill and virtuosity. In his estimation, the solo had lasted over ten minutes, without her flagging or losing energy and focus. Nor was there a period, as happens in many long solos, when it became overly repetitive and monotonous. It had been a performance all the more remarkable for the fact that it had been made by a young girl, only just out of her teens, who looked as if she would be more at home in a typing pool.

After another unsuccessful attempt to make himself heard, David was relieved to be joined on the dais by Lady Alice. Stepping up beside him, she raised her hands in a plea for calm. "Would everyone please be quiet for a moment!" she cried commandingly into a microphone. "Quiet please!" Waiting for the hubbub to abate, she continued, "I'm sure you will all wish to join me in offering heartfelt thanks to David and his colleagues for entertaining us so splendidly."

It provoked another crescendo of approval. Paddling her hands to demand a reduction in the volume of noise, she beckoned to Bella, who had been dividing her time between the ballroom and the marquee. Bella's arrival on the dais prompted another chorus of '*Happy Birthday to You*'.

Flush-faced, perspiring, and decidedly less well-groomed than at the start of the celebrations, she waited for her grandmother to moderate her guests' clamorous exuberance.

"What a *super, super* evening!" she began, but had to wait for another burst of cheering to subside. Addressing the trio, she exclaimed, "Thank you! You have been absolutely wonderful!" Turning back to the crowd she raised her arms and cried. "Please, everyone; will you show your appreciation for … *Joel!*"

He made and elaborate bow, as Bella's voice was lost in a roar of approbation.

"And *David!*" Acknowledging his own ovation more diffidently, David smiled and raised a hand.

Although more than a little 'squiffy', which was how she had described herself earlier, Bella still retained enough presence of mind to cleverly stage manage the situation. Taking a deep breath, she yelled. "And … *Ruby!*"

The deluge of acclaim seemed to take an eternity to subside, during which Ruby showed her appreciation with another drum roll and a crash of cymbals.

With tears glistening on her glowing cheeks, Bella shouted, "Thank you all for coming! And for making my birthday party *so absolutely super!*"

After another lengthy period of cheers and boisterous clamour, the noisy gathering slowly began to disperse. Draped in streamers and waving balloons that had earlier been released from the canopy, they broke into another ragged chorus of *Living Doll* as they left.

"Good night!" Tilly called from the entrance, where she stood hand-in-hand with the young man who had been her dance partner for most of the night, and who now gazed at her as if he couldn't believe his luck. "You were wonderful!" she cried. "See you on Monday, David!"

Lady de Tenneaux returned as the weary trio were watching the marquee empty. "You poor things. You look all-in!" she exclaimed. "Everyone has had such a wonderful time. Words can't express one's appreciation."

"I can say, with absolute sincerity, that it has been a pleasure!" David replied.

It was only when they were packing up, with caterers clearing away the litter and detritus around them, that David remembered the envelope that Lord Anthony had given him. Lifting the lid of the Telecaster's case, he took it out and opened it.

"What's the problem?" Ruby asked, as he blew out his cheeks.

"What do you think of a hundred quid?" he asked.

"I think yippee!" she cried. "I make that thirty-three pounds, six-and-something each."

David shook his head. "No, it's not."

"Oh Sorry; I assumed we were splitting it evenly," she said. "But it's really your gig, so it's up to you."

David grinned impishly. "We *are* splitting it evenly. I meant a hundred each."

"*What!*" Both she and Joel stared at him in disbelief.

He fanned out the five-pound notes between his hands. "Here; look for yourself."

Ruby clasped her hands to her mouth. "Oh; good grief, David!" Recovering her composure, she exclaimed, "I think we've really got something, here!"

"Whoa; hold your horses!" David chuckled. "How often do you think we'd get bookings that pay like this?"

Joel's laugh was a deep rumble. "Once sure is enough for me, man!"

David divided the money evenly and watched with amused interest as Ruby reached into her shirt and stuffed a fistful of fivers into her bra.

Noticing his amusement, she grinned back at him. "I've got nowhere else to put it. The pockets in these jeans are useless; they're just for show."

He waited for her to snap the catches on her bass drum case and picked it up. "I'll take this and find out where Patrick's parked the car."

Although it was after midnight, it was still warm, with only a hint of a breeze. But after the oppressive heat in the marquee, David relished the comparative coolness of the night air. While he waited for his eyes to adjust to the darkness, he watched the headlights of shadowy limousines snake their way between the trees lining the roadway that led to a distant gatehouse. Light was flooding from the windows of Huckfield Hall, spilling across the raised terrace, where departing guests were still taking their leave of the small group silhouetted in an open doorway.

He thought he recognised the dark outline of Patrick's car parked amongst some trees, and began to make his way towards it. "It's been a night of surprises," he murmured to himself. "And nothing's been more surprising than Ruby."

But another much less pleasant surprise awaited him. As he turned the corner of the marquee, a blow to the side of his head sent him reeling. The drum case fell from his grasp and rolled away towards some shrubbery, as he staggered and fell to his knees. Stunned, with his vision blurred and his ears ringing, he looked up to see the shadowy profiles of four young men gather round him.

"Well what have we here?" The voice was slurred by alcohol, and David's senses were still swimming, but he recognised it nonetheless.

"If it isn't the jumped-up peasant from that crumby café!" Rupert sneered. "I've been waiting all night for this. You were itching for a fight. Well, now you can bloody-well have one … Hold him down!"

David tried to get up, but he was forced back onto his knees from behind by two unseen individuals, who pinned his arms behind him. Grabbing a handful of his hair, Rupert yanked his head back and stared down at him with eyes gleaming with malice. "You haven't got that hairy gorilla to protect you now, have you, *peasant*?" he smirked.

Although fearful and in pain, David's rage welled up inside him. "I wouldn't have needed his or anyone's help to deal with a spineless coward like you!" he spat. "You haven't got the guts to fight your own battles. You need other people to do your dirty work for you!"

Anticipating the blow, he instinctively jerked his head to one side. With his hair still held in his assailant's grasp, he felt an intense burning pain in his scalp and, although Rupert's punch struck him on top of his head, it was enough to make his senses swim for a moment. However, the grip on his hair was instantly released, and he had the satisfaction of hearing Rupert cry out in pain. "Jesus Christ! Hold him still, you idiots! I nearly broke my bloody hand on the cretin's thick skull!"

The grip on David's arms tightened again, only to slacken in response to a shout from the edge of the marquee. "What's the hell's going on? Leave him alone!"

David's assailants froze and turned towards the figure racing towards them carrying a drum case. "Get off him, you bastards!" Ruby screamed.

"It's that ghastly drummer girl!" a nasal voice whined. He couldn't see her, but David was certain it was the blonde who had been with Rupert outside the café.

"Sort her out, Piers!" Rupert commanded, nursing his injured hand.

"Oh; I don't know," an unseen presence replied hesitantly.

"Oh; for Christ's sake!" Rupert exclaimed. "Can't you even deal with a bloody girl?" Turning towards the rapidly advancing Ruby, he shouted, "Stay out of this, you little bitch! Or you'll get…"

It was as far as his warning went before it became a shriek, as Ruby tore up to him and, without slowing her pace, swung a foot at his groin. Rupert's eyes seemed to disappear into his head, as his body jack-knifed and his expression contorted into a mask of agony. Clutching himself, he fell gagging and retching at Ruby's feet, while his girlfriend's scream pierced the night like a siren. Clasping her hands to her mouth, she stared in horror at the figure writhing and mewling on the grass.

"Bloody hell!" one of Rupert's henchman exclaimed.

"Let go of him!" Ruby yelled. "Unless you want the same!"

Her warning and the sound of voices approaching from the direction of the house had the desired effect. David's arms were released and one of his captors exclaimed, "Come on! We'd better bugger off before they get here!"

"What about Rupert? You can't just leave him!" the girl wailed.

"To hell with him! This is all his bloody fault!" was her answer. "Come on Piers. Don't just stand there gaping!"

However, Ruby hadn't finished. "Yes, run; you gutless scum!" she snarled, catching one of them a glancing blow with her drum case as they fled. "Are you OK, David?" she asked, helping him to his feet.

Flexing his muscles to restore the circulation and ease the numbness in his arms, he replied, "A bit woozy, but I'm alright. Boy; am I glad you turned up, Ruby! They took me completely by surprise."

"Who on earth are they?" she asked, glancing down at the still moaning Rupert and the weeping girl kneeling beside him. "What have they got against you?"

"I threatened to thump that cowardly skunk for humiliating Stella outside the café," David explained. "But Wally came out and stopped me. More's the pity!"

"What's going on, here?" an authoritative voice demanded, as a group of people hurried towards them. The voice belonged to a young man whom David judged to be about his own age.

Looking down at Rupert, the chap exhaled audibly. "Oh; it's you Gainsford; I might have known!" With a sigh of exasperation, he turned to his companions. "See what you can do for him, if you will."

Addressing Ruby and David, he said, "I take it Rupert's been up to no good again? My valet, Jenkins, thought he saw someone being attacked and came to fetch me. Allow me to introduce myself; I'm Edward de Tenneaux, Arabella's brother." Noticing that David was holding his head, he added, "I say; are you hurt? Let me have someone look at that."

"No; I'm OK thank you," David replied. "No real damage done. Just a bit of a headache. I was caught unawares by our friend there and two or three of his pals."

Edward de Tenneaux grimaced. "No-one in their right mind regards Rupert Gainsford as a friend. Fiona must have brought him. He certainly wasn't invited."

He gazed at Rupert disdainfully, as two men gently raised him, groaning and whimpering, to his feet. "You appear to have received the come-uppance you undoubtedly deserve, Gainsford. You were an odious toad at school and you still are … Oh do stop snivelling Fiona!" he snapped at the weeping girl. "He treats you dreadfully. No-one with any self-respect would stand for it!"

The harsh words prompted another burst of sobbing, but ignoring her, Edward de Tenneaux returned his attention to David. "Allow me to apologise for this unpleasantness. It's David isn't it? Bella and the rest of my family will be distressed to learn what's happened; especially when you've been so instrumental … no pun intended … in making tonight such a memorable occasion. I'll happily call the local bobbies, if you wish to press charges against Gainsford."

"No, that won't be necessary," David insisted. "And there's no need for an apology, or for your family to be concerned. Apart from this little incident, we've had fun."

"That's awfully good of you, David," Edward said, bursting into laughter as he watched Rupert, still whimpering and clutching his damaged manhood, being lowered onto a gardener's truck. "Now there's sight for sore eyes. You appear to have dented his pride, shall we say?"

"Actually, it was Ruby," David chuckled. "I was pinned down by his pals."

"One of them was called Piers," Ruby declared.

Edward nodded knowingly. "Oh, that will be Torbury-Price. Piers is easily led and not terribly bright. I'll need to have a word with him. I'm sure my father will speak to Gainsford's parents, too. They're awfully nice people, but Rupert's their only child and frightfully spoiled. He's a complete ass, I'm afraid."

"That's not how I'd describe him!" Ruby declared. "He's a spineless thug!"

"Yes; you're quite right, Ruby!" Edward conceded. "I must say one is even more in awe of you, now … as, I am sure, is

Gainsford." Looking closely at David's head, he added, "I'd feel happier if you would allow me to arrange for someone to have a look at that."

"Thank you, no. I'm perfectly alright," said David. "To tell the truth, I'd just like to go home to bed."

"Are you absolutely sure you're alright, David?" Ruby queried, as Edward de Tenneaux took his leave. "You should have let him call a doctor."

"There's no need; I'm fine. I've got a headache that's all. Come on, let's find your bass drum."

She pointed to a clump of bushes. "I can see it in there."

"I'll bet poor old Rupert needs attention, though," David chuckled. "I hope there's plenty of ice left in the champagne coolers."

"Pointed-toe boots come in handy, sometimes," Ruby giggled.

"I'll tell you what," he said, when they had stopped laughing.

"What?"

"Remind me not to upset you when you're wearing them!"

"That's an impressive looking wound," said Chris, pointing to the dressing on David's head.

"It's Nurse Lampeter's handiwork," David replied. "I told her it's only a graze … probably from the ring Rupert was wearing. But she insisted it's a gash and put this on it. She even shaved a patch of hair off. I feel like I've been scalped."

"It seems you were lucky not to be more badly knocked about," Colin suggested.

David nodded. "I would have been if it hadn't been for Ruby!"

"She sounds a bit of a spitfire," Colin chuckled.

"Oh she is!" Chris exclaimed. "She's a sparky little redhead. There's not much of her, but she can obviously take care of herself. She put me in my place the other day. I consider myself fortunate that she didn't rearrange my valuables, like she did for that cove who set about David!"

It took a few moments for Colin and David to control their laughter.

"I couldn't believe it!" David exclaimed. "She came tearing up to him and put the boot in … on the run! No-one expected that. Least of all Rupert!"

"I take it you're discussing Ruby," Richard suggested, as he appeared in the doorway of the café. "Tilly says she was the big hit of the evening … on stage, too."

"She was!" David agreed. "Boy; can she play those drums! I wish you'd been there. Her solo was amazing."

"Is it alright if I take my break now, boss?" Richard asked, taking his coffee to join Chris and Colin at the red table.

"Do you have to call him boss?" Chris enquired impishly.

"Only when Jo isn't here," Richard replied.

Chris smiled reflectively. "Now, there's another determined young lady."

"She certainly is," Colin said wistfully. "I wanted us to spend a week with my mum and dad; for them to get to know her, and for her to meet the rest of my family. But when she heard about the problems here, she was adamant that she had to come back straight away. Mum and Dad were ever so disappointed. But none of us could talk her out of it."

"It was none of my doing!" David insisted.

"I know. I'm not suggesting you had anything to do with it," Colin assured him. "Jo found out about the old boy being in hospital and how busy you were when she phoned her aunt. Apparently, her Aunt Ginny had a fall while we were away. Something to do with arthritis, I believe. I don't think it was anything serious; the old girl seems indestructible. I did my best to convince Jo that she would be fine and that you'd manage for a few days, but there was no changing her mind. Ginny seemed alright when I saw her this morning, so I have my suspicions that she may have been laying it on a bit thick."

"That's a shame," David murmured, hoping he sounded more sympathetic than he felt. "Jo's earned a break. I told her she needn't have cut it short, but she insisted on pitching in here as soon as she got back."

"Well; that's Jo," Colin sighed. "She's back at work now, so everything I'd planned has gone by the board. Mum and Dad were really upset when she left like that. They'd been looking forward to having us both there. So I stayed on after she'd gone, as we'd originally intended. Mum was planning a family celebration … for this." Delving into his pocket, he took out a small box covered in crimson satin.

David's heart missed a beat even before the lid was lifted to reveal a ring, set with a row of three matched diamonds and seated in a blue velvet cushion. The diamonds sparkled in the sunlight, as Colin held out the box. "My godmother gave it to me, for Jo. It was her mother's. I'm told it's worth a pretty penny."

"It's beautiful!" Richard exclaimed.

Chris took the box and whistled appreciatively. "Very classy! So, you're going to plight your troth to the fair Josephine!"

"Yes; I didn't get the chance at home, so I thought I'd surprise her on her birthday."

David couldn't say anything. It was as much as he could do to control his expression.

"Are you planning to stay in the army?" Richard asked.

Colin nodded. "For the time being."

Chris looked enquiringly at David. "What about you? What do you have in mind? Something musical and involving a red-headed drummer, perhaps?"

"That was something I wanted to speak to you about, David," Colin interjected. "I was wondering what your plans are."

"My plans?"

"Yes; I wondered how long you intend staying on here."

Chris got to his feet. "Well; I'll leave you to your deliberations. I think I'll take my easel onto the mole and create another masterpiece."

"Mind if I come with you?" Richard asked. "I could do with stretching my legs for a few minutes."

"I'd be delighted," Chris replied. "Might I suggest you peer over my shoulder occasionally and gasp in admiration? You know; to draw a crowd. *Pour encourager les autres,* as our neighbours across the channel would have it."

"He's quite a character, isn't he?" Colin chuckled, as he watched Chris and Richard leave.

David simply nodded.

Colin put the ring back in his pocket and indicated a vacant chair. "Can you spare me a minute?"

Waiting for David to settle himself, he began, "My reason for asking about your plans is this: I've decided to quit the army, but not immediately. For various reasons, one of which is financial, it's better if I don't leave for at least six months. Jo doesn't want to join me in Germany, but there's a private clinic near where my parents live. It's advertising for nurses; and Jo's a damned good one. Her ward sister thinks the world of her. She can stay with my mum and dad until I leave the army … and earn really good money. A hell of a lot more than she's getting slaving away on the wards at Myrtlesham General."

Finally finding his voice, David enquired, "What has all this got to do with me?"

Colin drummed on the table-top pensively with his fingertips. "You and Jo have done wonders with this place. I saw how well you're doing when she was making up the books. She tells me that this Monty chap thinks that, even though the protest won't stop the redevelopment, it will probably be delayed by legal complications. In his opinion, it might be months before the council act on the compulsory purchase orders."

"Monty's probably right," said David. "He usually is."

Colin paused, as if unsure how to continue. "The thing is, David; you don't seem to have any plans for the immediate future, and it will be next year before Jo and I are married, I'm back on civvy street and we've settled down somewhere. It seems a shame not to make the most of this place while we can." He rubbed his hands together nervously. "So, I wondered how you'd feel about staying on to manage the café in the meantime."

Taken aback, David glared at him indignantly. "*You* wondered? What about Jo? Is that what *she* wants?"

"We haven't discussed things in detail yet," Colin conceded warily. "But I'm sure she'll see the sense of it. It's the ideal solution for all of us."

"Is it?" David replied flatly. "Let me get this straight. You're expecting me to carry on running this café for you, as long as it suits you? It may have escaped your notice Colin, but *I own* half of it. Jo and I are equal partners!"

"Don't misunderstand me!" Colin protested. "Of course you are. I expressed myself badly. I didn't mean it to sound like that. Let me put it another way."

"Don't bother!" David snapped. "It makes no difference which way you put it. As soon as the season's over, I'm off. That's what Jo and I agreed. What happens to this place after that is between us."

Colin took a deep breath. "I see. I didn't mean to upset you, David. I just thought it was something that would benefit all of us. But the undeniable truth is: when Jo and I are married, she and I will make decisions together ... about everything ... including what we think should happen to the café."

In spite of rising anger, David made himself reply calmly. "I understand that, Colin. I would expect Jo to discuss what's best for her with her husband. But, when it comes to it, the decision about what happens to this café will be made by *her and me*!"

XI

Wally cleared dirty glasses from the bar and looked at David enquiringly. "You don't look all that thrilled about it. I thought you'd be pleased with Monty's news."

"I am!" David insisted. "Sorry; my mind was on something else."

"As expected, the council wishes to impose conditions on their agreement not to prohibit your musical performances," Monty pronounced. "Which, in the circumstances, I considered acceptable and in our best interests not to challenge."

Avril lit a Pall Mall and inhaled deeply. "You did well, Monty!"

"Yes; well done! Thanks," David concurred. "A large one for Monty, please, Wally."

Monty smiled appreciatively. "Most gracious of you, dear boy."

Picking up his glass, Wally pushed it under an optic. "So, if I've got it right; David can only perform on 'is own, and not so loud as to annoy the neighbours; we can't 'ave music more'n once a week, and not on Sundays; no dancin' in the bars or on the quay; and we've got t'knock it on the 'ead before closin' time. Is that right?"

"In essence, that is so." Monty drew on his cigar pensively. "However, I felt obliged to draw Mister Davenport's attention to the difficulty in restraining members of the public who may feel the compulsion to dance. I reminded him that jurisdiction of the actual quay is the prerogative of the Harbour Authority, which limits the ability of you or Fairhaven Town Council to intervene."

"What did he say to that?" Avril asked.

"He had to concede that my premise is correct, of course. However, we came to an amicable agreement that your obligation, in this respect, would be satisfied by a notice prominently displayed outside these premises, to the effect that: *dancing on the quay is prohibited*, together with your undertaking to discourage your patrons from so doing."

"I can't see us gettin' many complaints from the neighbours, such as they are," Hooky observed. "Most of 'em will be in 'ere. But, if anybody starts jitterbuggin' out there, it'll be Adolph Rathbone's 'eadache."

Monty raised his glass in thanks to David. "Within the limits of the harbour, perhaps. But it is my belief that he and his superiors will have difficulty in trying to exercise their authority over the area immediately outside this public house."

"It won't stop 'im tryin' though," Hooky chortled. He looked meaningfully at David. "So when're you gonna start singin' agen?"

Caught off guard, David hesitated. "Um … I'm not sure … I'll need to think. It'll have to be when it suits Avril and Wally, of course."

Wally shrugged his shoulders expressively. "It's up to you, son. Whenever you're ready."

David was spared the necessity of answering directly by the appearance of Bella and Lady Alice in the doorway of The Mess.

Greeting everyone warmly, Lady Alice exclaimed, "David; we are most dreadfully sorry! One would, of course, have apologised at the time, but you left before I was informed of Rupert Gainsford's appalling assault on you."

"Your poor head!" Bella cooed, gently brushing David's hair with her fingertips. "Does it hurt dreadfully?"

Ignoring the smirk on Hooky's face, David replied, "Not really. I had a headache the next day, but Jo put the dressing on it. As you know, she's a nurse. She thinks I'll live."

"One does so abhor gratuitous violence," her Ladyship declared. "Rupert's behaviour these days is simply beyond the pale! Arabella and I would have offered our apologies sooner, David. But having so many people to stay made it impossible to get away … and you're not on the telephone."

"Please; there's no need to apologise. No permanent damage has been done. At least, not to me."

It elicited a titter from Bella. "Edward told us what Ruby did. One would so love to have seen it! No-one has seen or heard from Rupert since."

Lady Alice stifled a smile. "He and his parents will certainly be hearing from Arabella's father! Now, David; I hope you will permit my family and I to make amends in a small way and invite you dine with us. One does, of course, appreciate how busy you are at present, so would the second Friday after the bank holiday be convenient? Please bring your young lady. Might one be correct in assuming it's Ruby?"

Surprise and awareness of the difference in their social standing made David hesitate. "Oh! That's very kind of you. But there's no need; really," he stammered.

Sensing his dilemma, she added, "It will be quite informal, I can assure you. Perhaps we might prevail upon Matilda, or Tilly, as she insists on being called, to join us." She sighed impatiently. "Why do young people insist on shortening the perfectly good names they were christened with?" Regaining her train of thought, she continued, "I believe Edward's wife is the only member of our family you haven't met. Monique is French; she plays the piano quite beautifully. I understand you play too, David. So no doubt you and she will have a great deal to talk about. I'm ashamed to admit that we, as a family, are not musical. If it weren't for Monique, the Steinway would never be used. Perhaps you would care to play it when you visit us?"

The thought of playing a Steinway grand piano took David's breath away.

"Please say you'll come, David," Bella implored. "It'll be such fun!"

"I understand your brother has been seriously ill," Her Ladyship observed. "Do you think you could persuade him to come, too? We would all be delighted to meet him."

Realising that they were sincere, David felt unable to refuse without appearing ungrateful. "Thank you. It's very kind of you. I'm sure Richard would love to meet you."

"What's it to be, Your Ladyship?" Wally enquired. "Guinness?"

"I really shouldn't, but alright. It's *my round*, though; if that's the correct expression. I insist. And perhaps we might dispense with formalities, don't you think? Please call me Alice. And may I call you Wally?"

"That's far enough … *Alice*. One Guinness comin' up." Wally chuckled. "What about you, young lady?"

"I'll get Bella a glass of wine," said Avril.

"May one leave the rest to you, Wally?" Lady Alice proposed. "I'm sure you are familiar with everyone's preference." Picking up a leaflet from the counter, she asked, "What is this?"

"It's a notice about the next meetin' of the 'arbour redevelopment protest," Hooky explained. "They've already 'ad one. The council and some local bigwigs wanna knock all this down an' put up sommat more modern. Blocks of 'oliday flats an' a lido, so somebody said. Nobody knows for sure. Whatever it is, the people round 'ere don't wan' it. But what *they* want don't count."

"The harbour is subject to one or more historic statutes," Monty explained. "I am currently exploring the possibility of a legal challenge on that basis. Though I fear the procedure may be lengthy and prove too costly to pursue."

Lady Alice fished a pair of horn-rimmed glasses from her bag and perched them on her nose to inspect the leaflet more closely. "Who is the chairman of your campaign committee?"

"I don't think we've got one," Wally replied. "It's bein' run by Martin from the chandlers, an' Gemma from the jewel shop."

"To whom are they speaking at the council?"

Wally's brow creased as he thought. "Nobody, as far as I know; apart from the bloke that was at the last meetin'."

"Which was, if I may say so, a fruitless exercise," Monty interjected. "The council's representative did not seem inclined to listen. However, our objections were not expressed lucidly. Sad to say, the meeting became rather heated and ill disciplined. The two young people leading the protest are undeniably dedicated and committed, but I think it fair to say that very little was achieved."

"A bit out o'their depth, if you ask me," Wally suggested.

Lady Alice eased herself onto a bar stool. "Tell me more about your proposed legal challenge, Monty," she said. "Do we know who these *bigwigs* are?"

"So there's an old lady in the café," David remarked. "They're not that unusual."

"This one is!" Stella insisted. She had hurried into the kitchen with a tray of dirty crockery and a concerned expression. Lowering her voice to barely a whisper, she added, "I think she's a bit dotty. She said someone's been drawing pictures on the window and told me to wipe them off. Then she started trying to serve the customers! I didn't know what to do. Luckily the man with her stopped her."

"Is it a man in a white coat?" David teased.

It elicited a giggle from Connie, but Stella replied earnestly, "No; he's dressed nicely. He asked for you. The man outside is frightening, though … and ever so big. I nearly fainted when he smiled at me. He's got a funny uniform on; like the ones you see German soldiers wearing in war films."

"It sounds like that chauffer you told me about," Richard suggested.

"It must be," David muttered nervously. "Which means Charlie McBride's here again. What the devil does he want now?"

Thankfully, the café was quiet. It was late afternoon and only two inside tables were occupied. A family of four got up from one of them as he arrived and the father approached the counter to pay.

"Was everything alright?" David asked, glancing apprehensively at the 'old lady', who was standing in the centre of the room, swaying her hips to the rhythm of *Swingin' Shepherd Blues* that was playing on the radio.

"It was very nice," the mother replied. Steering her children to the doorway, she called, "Goodbye and thank you."

The old lady beamed and waved to the children. "Bye-bye. Come again soon."

She was slim, but not frail. Her floral dress fitted her snugly, although it was of a style that had last been fashionable in the thirties. Tresses of grey-white hair had escaped from beneath a wide-brimmed straw hat that was tilted jauntily on the back of her head and secured by a large silver-topped hat-pin. Belying her lined features, her eyes were clear and bright, as she greeted David with an amiable smile. "Hello; you must be Charlotte's boy! How is she? We never hear from her these days."

Taken unawares, David smiled awkwardly and mumbled, "Hello." His attention was fixed on Charlie McBride, who rose from his seat at a table behind her. On the quay, Horace was standing beside the Daimler.

"Don't mind Veronica," Charlie murmured quietly. "Her mind wanders, but she's quite harmless. She and her sister, Lillian, had this café before Ralph. During her more lucid moments, she has a remarkable memory for family history. She wanted to come and have a look at the old place. I didn't think you'd mind."

"No; I suppose not," David replied dubiously.

"Lillian passed away four years ago," Charlie explained. "And, in case you're wondering, Charlotte was their other sister. She died a long time ago; before the first war. Veronica's looked after in a home, these days. Now that Ralph's gone, she's the last of the Ellery brood." In response to David's arching eyebrows, he added, "Yes; Ralph was her brother. This is your Great Aunt Veronica."

Nonplussed, David replied, "I had no idea. I know hardly anything about my dad's side of the family. We've never kept in touch and Dad hasn't spoken about his relatives all that much."

"This is Aunt Elizabeth's great grandson, Veronica," Charlie said deliberately. "His name is David." Gesturing to Richard, as he appeared from the kitchen corridor, he added, "And this is his brother ... Richard, isn't it?"

Visibly perplexed, Richard replied, "Yes; that's right."

The old lady's smile vanished and she suddenly became animated. "Poor Aunt Lizzie!" she cried. "Mother told us she *had* to get married ... *to a travelling salesman*! And you know what they say about *them*!"

It evoked a stifled titter from the two remaining customers, as David and Richard gazed first at her and then at Charlie in bemusement.

"Herbert!" she announced. "Hebert Sheldon; that was his name. The baby was a boy. Now, what did they call him?" She put a finger to her lips as she thought. "Leonard! That was it!" she declared. "Yes; Leonard."

Richard's eyes widened. "Leonard was Grandpa's name!"

Interpreting Charlie's smile as complacency, David snapped, "What's this all about, Mister McBride?"

"I told you," Charlie replied calmly. "Veronica was reminiscing about the café during one of her lucid periods. I told her it was still in the family and she mentioned she'd like to see it again; that's all."

As they spoke, the old lady began to remove plates from the table where the remaining couple sat. "Can I tempt you with our home-made cakes?" she asked cheerily. "They're all freshly baked by my sister and me, here on the premises."

Handing the plates to Stella, she exclaimed, "You're not Florence! I don't think I know you; are you new? You must remember to wear your lace cap and apron, dear," she admonished. "My sister will be very cross if she sees you without them."

Stella smiled apologetically to the couple, as Charlie put a comforting arm around Veronica's shoulders. "I don't think Lillian will mind, just this once," he said affectionately. "It's Florence's day off."

Veronica smiled indulgently at Stella. "Oh, I see! I didn't know Lillian had taken you on. I suppose you've got to wait for your uniform to come." Pointing to Stella's ponytail, she said, "You have lovely hair, my dear. But you must put it up when you're serving the customers."

To David's surprise, Stella did so; winding her ponytail up onto her head in a top-knot, which she secured with her hair band. "Sorry ma'am," she said, and grinned at him impishly on her way to the kitchen.

Accepting payment from the couple, David watched Aunt Veronica follow Stella, who now seemed happy to humour her.

At the sound of voices in the kitchen, Charlie looked anxiously along the passageway. "I hope Veronica's not getting on the wrong side of that lass of yours. She's a spirited little piece, that one, isn't she?"

"Jo's not here … and she's not *my lass*," David retorted. "We're business partners. I'd never met her before I came here. It's a mystery to both of us why Uncle Ralph left her half this place."

Charlie chuckled, as if enjoying a private joke. "It's no mystery, son. Ralph had a thing for Ginny Broughton … or Trafford, as she became when she married Ernie. Ralph and Ernie met in a POW camp in the first war. Sometime after that, they hooked up again when Ernie moved here. Both of them took a fancy to Ginny. I'm told she was a bit of a looker in her younger days. Anyway, Ernie had charm and the gift of the gab … as well as a few bob in the bank … so poor old Ralph never got a look in." Charlie chuckled again. "But he still carried a torch for Ginny; for all the good it did him. So I suppose that led to him developing a soft spot for the young girl she took in, after Ernie died; your lass … sorry, business partner."

"Jo's aunt can't have told her about that," said David. "Because she hasn't a clue why she was left anything in the will."

"I doubt Ginny realised that Ralph still fancied her," Charlie suggested. "He was a funny beggar. He probably never let on."

"We had no idea Uncle Ralph had any other family; least of all sisters," said Richard. "We knew very little about him. I don't remember any of the others being mentioned, either."

"I don't suppose you did," said Charlie. "Veronica told me your great grandma was shunned by most of her relatives. Her own mother and father disowned her. In those days it disgraced the whole family if a girl had a nipper out of wedlock."

"But I thought Aunt Veronica said our great grandpa *did* marry her," Richard contended.

Charlie nodded. "He did; but it was too late. The damage had already been done. Apparently, Herbert was away travelling a lot and Elizabeth was sent away. He did the honourable thing and married her when he found out, though. But Elizabeth was never forgiven and, according to Veronica, it was forbidden to mention Herbert's name."

David blew out his cheeks. "It sounds like a Victorian melodrama. So, when did Uncle Ralph's sisters take this place on?"

"They came to Fairhaven towards the end of the last war. They were both war widows by then. They had this place until Ralph bought it from them; so they could retire in comfort … or so he claimed."

"What do you mean *so he claimed*?" David queried, as the probable reason for Charlie's visit dawned on him. "Are you suggesting that Uncle Ralph didn't really own this café?"

Charlie smiled knowingly. "No; you've got nothing to worry about. The sale was all above board according to the documentation I've seen. But it's hard to see where the money went that Ralph is supposed to have paid for it. Veronica doesn't remember … Lillian was more of a businesswoman. After they left here, they lived in a little bungalow just outside Myrtlesham. They got by; but you couldn't call it living in real comfort. This place was thriving when they had it. It makes you wonder how much Ralph actually coughed up for it."

"May I ask how you know so much about our family?" Richard asked.

The answer was forestalled by Aunt Veronica approaching from the kitchen. Taking a sip from the cup in her hand, she replaced it in the saucer and tapped on the door of the cupboard by the stairs. "Teddy!" she called. "Tell Ralph to wash his lobster pots properly before he puts them back in here."

"Alright, I will," Charlie replied, and grinned self-consciously at David. "She thinks I'm her late husband, sometimes."

"You can smell fish when you open this door." Veronica declared. "We don't mind him storing his pots under the stairs … if they're clean." As an apparent afterthought, she added, "And tell him Lillian doesn't like him hiding all those cigarettes and bottles in there. She says we'll get into trouble as well, if he gets caught."

Thankful that there were no customers in the café, David gazed at Aunt Veronica in astonishment.

But she pointed to Horace who was sitting at an outside table. "I'd better take that gentleman his tea," she said, hurrying past the three of them. "We mustn't keep our customers waiting."

Charlie's grin broadened and he burst out laughing. "So *that's* where the crafty old beggar hid his loot! It's perfect! Who'd suspect two respectable middle-aged ladies of sitting on a load of smuggled fags and booze?"

David stared in surprise. "Didn't you know?"

"No; I didn't … But I do now!"

"So, why have you been having this place watched?"

It was Charlie's turn to look bemused. "What the hell are you talking about?"

"I'm talking about whoever you've had out there at night, watching this place!"

"Watching this place?" Charlie snorted. "You've got to be kidding! If you think I can be bothered to have you watched, think again!"

"Then who…?"

"I don't know. But, if you ask me, it's likely to be somebody Ralph was involved with."

"I thought you said *you* were involved with him," David declared.

Charlie waved a hand towards the cupboard. "Not with that lark! So you can forget it. I did a bit of business with Ralph, but I had nothing to do with bringing the stuff in. It was too risky, and I had my own contacts. I left all that to Ralph and Ernie."

"What; Ginny's husband!?" Richard gasped.

Charlie nodded. "It was Ernie's boat. I guessed they used lobster pots to smuggle the stuff ashore amongst whatever Ralph managed to catch. It was good cover. But I didn't know where they hid it."

"Surely Ginny wasn't involved?" Richard exclaimed.

Charlie shook his head. "No; I doubt she knew anything about it. Ernie was smart enough to get out at the start of the war. Ralph started up again when it ended, but as far as I know, Ernie never got involved again."

"How do you know all this ... and so much about our family?" Richard challenged.

"Yes; *I* was wondering that," David exclaimed. "As well as why *you* brought Aunt Veronica here."

Charlie sat on the edge of a table. "Let's just say I've always made it my business to know what goes on around here." He regarded them silently for a moment before continuing. "If you must know; *I* brought Veronica here because she wanted to come ... and there's nobody else. She didn't have any children. Lillian's daughters are both dead; one died before the war and the other was killed in the blitz. Veronica's other sister, Charlotte, was only seventeen when she died; and Ralph never married." He shrugged resignedly. "So, who else was there to make sure Veronica and Lillian were comfortable? Who looked after them when they left here? Not Ralph, I can promise you! He never cared about anybody but himself." Spreading his hands expressively, he declared, "Who do you think visits Veronica and takes her out? Who makes sure she's comfortable ... and pays for her care?"

"But why?" David asked.

Charlie held his gaze. "Because I believe families ought to look after each other."

"Families?" Richard queried. "Are you suggesting you're related to our aunt?"

Charlie's gold filling glinted as he smiled. "I'm not *suggesting* it, son; I *am* related to her, like I was to Lillian ... and Ralph. Their mother married again after their father died. She and her second husband had a son ... and here I am."

The brothers stared at him dumbfounded, until Richard found his voice. "So..."

"That's right. I'm your Great Uncle Charlie!"

It was several moments before David regained his composure, and the anger welled up within him. "So, why the hell haven't you said anything before!?" he demanded. "I suppose you thought if you kept quiet, Jo and I might fall for that derisory offer you made!"

"I didn't really know who you were then," Charlie replied calmly. "Other than you must be Ralph's distant relative. I shouldn't think Ralph was all that sure, either. He never bothered about his family; especially me. He was prepared to do business with me, but he never acknowledged me or accepted me as his brother."

"So, how did you find out about us?" Richard asked.

Charlie took a deep breath. "Well; first of all, I didn't know Ralph had made a will. Before he died, he promised me the business at a knock down price; in consideration for some money I'd lent him. Ralph was a chronic gambler; he couldn't help himself. It was cards; the gee-gees; the dogs; back-room gambling dens … you name it. So, it was a nasty shock to find out he'd made a will and left this place to somebody else."

Charlie's lisp had become more pronounced with frustration. "I didn't know anything about you two until Veronica started reminiscing one afternoon, and I put two and two together." Charlie fixed his gaze on David. "But the offer I made you wasn't derisory. It was a decent offer for a business that was worth next to nothing! I didn't think a couple of green youngsters like you would last five minutes trying to run this place. I offered you a retainer to give you time to think … and come to your senses."

"But you knew there would be compensation for the compulsory purchase!" David contended. "And I'll bet you knew how much it was likely to be!"

"I was pretty sure I'd get back at least what I paid you," Charlie conceded. "But that's business, son. And you could have lost your shirt before you ever saw any compensation. You still could!"

"We'll take our chances!" David growled.

"That's your choice." Charlie gazed around him. "You've done alright, so far. Fair enough; you don't trust me … and we don't have to like each other just because we're related. But the only reason I brought Veronica here was because it was her wish to see it again. It's her last chance before it goes. We may have had different fathers, but she's still my sister … and that means something." He looked deliberately at the two young men. "You're brothers; surely you can understand that."

The ensuing silence was pierced by Veronica's strident cry: "Florence! What's this horrible penguin-thing doing out here?"

* * *

"What's the matter?" Richard asked, as David pushed his plate away. "You've hardly eaten anything."

David gazed absently around the busy restaurant. "Nothing; I'm just not hungry. I'm probably too tired to eat. I've got a lot on my mind at the moment."

"I can believe that," Richard chortled. "There's never a dull moment with you, is there? Fancy finding out we had a smuggler in the family and relations we never knew about; all in one day!"

"Ralph's smuggling is no surprise," David replied. "But I still haven't got over finding out we're related to Charlie McBride. You should have seen Avril's face when I told her and Wally. She was sorry to have missed Aunt Veronica though. She and Wally remember her and her sister fondly. But they didn't know Ralph was their brother."

"He must have been a rum sort," Richard mused. "Difficult to get to know."

"And to like, from what we hear," David suggested.

Richard chuckled to himself. "Aunt Veronica's a sweet old darling, isn't she? Despite what you've told me about our uncle, you have to give him credit for looking after her. It was quite touching to see how the café brought back memories for her. Connie and Stella were lovely with her, and it was kind of you to go along with her thinking she still owned it."

"She might have sacked me if I hadn't."

Richard sighed despairingly. "Why do you always hide behind a joke when people praise you?"

David deliberately avoided a direct answer. "She's probably forgotten she came. Charlie was right; she's got a good memory for the past, but she doesn't remember what's just been said to her."

"I wonder what Jo will say when she finds out that Charlie's our great uncle," Richard pondered.

David's answering smile vanished, as a thought came to him. "Don't mention what Ginny's husband was up to with Ralph. There's no point in upsetting her and spoiling Jo's engagement celebrations."

"Don't worry; I won't." Richard set his knife and fork down on his plate. "What an interesting family we have. Fancy Grandpa Sheldon being born on the wrong side of the blanket. Do you think Dad knows?"

"He must do. Perhaps it's why he never talks about his family."

Richard decided it was time to change the subject. "So we've been invited to dine with the aristocracy. My word; you are going up in the world, Little Brother."

"And I may get the chance to play a Steinway."

"You said you had a lot on your mind," Richard prompted. "What else is there?"

David sighed wearily. "Well, for starters, Ruby's pushing me for a decision about carrying on with Ruby Red after The Jetstream finishes at the Wintergardens Theatre. Apparently, she's been in touch with an agent in London."

"And you're not keen?"

"To be honest, Rich; I don't know. But there doesn't seem to be much else on offer at present."

"What else is bothering you?"

Fearing that his brother knew him well enough to guess, David replied hastily, "Wally and Avril are expecting me to start playing in the Packet Boat again soon."

"And that's a problem?"

"I need an electric guitar and an amp to be heard over that noisy crowd."

"Oh; of course," said Richard. "I remember you saying you've sold yours. I could lend you the money."

"Thanks; but that's not really the problem," David replied. "I could buy another one with the money I got from Bella's party, or I could borrow Joel's Fender Telecaster again. But you know how busy we are in the café, especially this week. I'm just not in the mood to perform after that."

Richard nodded sympathetically. "I can appreciate that. It's been frantic at times, hasn't it? Especially when the Ocean Queen comes in."

"All the uncertainty over the harbour redevelopment doesn't help, either," David groaned. "It's getting on my nerves. I just wish they'd damned-well get on with it!"

"What about Colin?"

"What about him?" David replied defensively.

"Well, are you still stewing over him asking you to keep the café going?"

Relieved that Richard wasn't alluding to what was really dispiriting him, David replied, "No ... Well, not as much. He's got a flaming nerve, though! Fancy expecting me to dance to his tune, when he hadn't even talked it over with Jo!"

"I shouldn't think she'll be too pleased," Richard reflected.

"Probably not. But I imagine he'll been forgiven once she sees that ring."

Richard nodded in agreement. "You're probably right. Colin told me he's taking her to somewhere called The Bartlett Grange Hotel, this evening; ostensibly as a birthday treat. He thinks it's a suitably romantic setting to pop the question."

"I believe it's a swish place somewhere near Myrtlesham," David explained. "I'm told it costs an arm and a leg to eat there." He glanced at his watch. The ring was probably already on Jo's finger.

"He obviously thinks she's worth it." Richard toyed with a dessert spoon. "I think it's only fair to warn you that I'm hoping to be given a clean bill of health the next time they examine me. My appointment's next Thursday. So I won't be able to stay on as your pot washer. I really have to get back to work as soon as they give me the all clear. My bosses have been wonderfully supportive, but I can't go on taking advantage of their generosity much longer."

"I understand. I'm really grateful, Rich. I don't know what I'd have done without you. I wish you'd let me give you something for it."

Richard waved a hand airily. "Don't be silly. It's given me something to do, and done me good."

"You're looking so much better."

"I feel really well. I'm putting on weight too. It's all the good food and care that's being lavished on me."

"Good for you!" David chuckled. "Let's hope they sign you off, so we can all stop worrying. Sammy will be pleased, too. He's due out of hospital today, and he can't wait to get back to work. I think he's worried you'll want his job permanently."

"I've enjoyed it, but you can put his mind at rest. You've got some terrific people working for you, but it's too much like hard work. I've got to hand it to you, David; you've done a great job!"

"I've had a lot of help, and I've been lucky to have a partner like Jo. She's taken care of the finances and all the paperwork. I'd be hopeless at that. She's done a fair stint in the café as well, on top of her regular job."

"She's quite a girl," said Richard. "Colin's a lucky man." Picking up a menu bearing the Blue Lagoon Restaurant emblem, he asked, "What do you fancy for dessert?"

"Nothing for me, thanks. But don't let me stop you."

Richard shook his head. "No; I'm not bothered." Smiling at the approaching waitress, he said, "Nothing else, thank you Miss. Just the bill, please."

The tinkle of a telephone bell prompted David to remark, "That reminds me, I must ring Mum and Dad. I haven't spoken to them for over a week."

"I told them how busy you are," said Richard. "I put them in the picture about everything you've got going on here when I saw them last Sunday. They understand and they send their love. They're dying to see you, of course. Mum wanted to come and visit you, but Dad said it would be an unnecessary distraction for you, this week. The Old Man's tickled pink by what you're doing."

"I should think it's come as a bit of shock," David snorted. "I'll bet he never thought me capable of it … or anything much. I've always been a disappointment to him."

"Don't talk such rubbish!" Aware of inquisitive glances from other diners, Richard lowered his voice. "You're wrong, David. You don't understand him; that's why you're always at odds with him. It's not just Mum who worries about you. You don't know the way he talks about you. The first thing he asked was, 'How's David getting on?' I had to tell him all about the café; you playing at the twenty-first birthday party; and everything else I could think of. I missed out your little altercation, of course. How's the head by the way?"

"It's fine. I could have done without Minnehaha Lampeter scalping me, but my hair's growing back."

"About you and Dad," Richard persisted. "Give him a chance, David. He's proud of you; he really is."

They were interrupted by the waitress returning with the bill. "This is on me," said David, but Richard snatched it off the plate and took out his wallet. "Your turn next time."

"Well, at least let me buy you a pint. Not in the Packet Boat, though. I'd rather go somewhere else tonight."

* * *

It was almost midnight when David arrived home, to find a stack of metal barriers near the entrance to the quay. Signs fixed to lampposts proclaimed: "*In the interests of public safety, access to the quay will be restricted to boat owners and the proprietors and employees of harbourside businesses between 9am and 1pm on the day of the Carnival Parade.*"

According to Wally, the corner outside The Packet Boat Inn was a popular spot for people to watch the parade, as it made its way down the hill and onto the Esplanade from its start at Crokers Park. The restriction had been put in place for the past few years and was intended to prevent spectators congregating on and around the mole and impeding people using the harbour. The business proprietors affected were understandably less than happy, but their objections had fallen on deaf ears.

Wally didn't open the pub for the ten-til-two session on carnival day, but he had acquired a special licence to open from four o'clock until midnight. Likewise, David saw little point in opening the café while the barriers were in place. His girls wanted to watch the parade, so he had told them not to come to work before midday. 'At least I'll get a lie-in,' he thought wearily.

He took out his keys, but drawn by the rhythmic surge of the sea, he turned towards the mole. Gleaming like a luminous globe, the moon bathed the ancient stones in a pallid glow, as he climbed the steps and made his way towards the harbour entrance. Within its benign shelter, small craft rocked gently at their moorings and lights glowed in the cabin windows of one or two larger vessels. Except for the groan of fenders, the creak of rigging, and an occasional ripple of water against a hull, only by the restless sigh of the sea broke the stillness and quiet.

Struggling to cope with despondency, David leaned on the harbour wall and gazed out at the ribbon of iridescent moonlight shimmering on the languorous swell of the dark ocean.

"So, what now?" he asked himself.

Being part of Ruby Red would be fun at first, and life with Ruby would be anything but dull. But few, if any, of the venues they were likely to play would be anything like Huckfield Hall. The likelihood was that many would be smoky dives and clubs, where they would find themselves consorting with individuals who, in any other circumstance, they would give a wide berth.

The thought reminded him of his only experience of such places; a seedy nightclub off Wardour Street in Soho. He had stared, wide-eyed with amazement, at what was going on in the semi darkness beyond the edge of the tiny stage, while he and his fellow musicians played for a sparse and indifferent audience. It still embarrassed him to recall how, watching a girl inject herself with a hypodermic syringe, he had assumed that she suffered from sugar diabetes; until, amused by his naivety, she had disabused him.

He wanted no part of that. Nor did he want Ruby to be mixed up in it, although he suspected that she would cope better than him. It was sobering to think that she was probably about the same age as the girl in the Soho nightclub, and frightening to think of her being drawn into a nightmare world of junkies and alcoholics. Ruby wasn't Jo, but he'd grown fond of her; perhaps more than fond, although he couldn't be sure of her feelings for him. She obviously liked him … and there was that kiss. But experience had taught him not to take too much for granted.

If he had asked himself what he wanted from life only a few months ago, it certainly wouldn't have been the aggravation and sheer hard work of running a café. But it was different now. He and Jo had achieved so much; overcoming the problems and pitfalls of refurbishment, getting the place ready to open, and actually making a success of it. Who would have believed him capable of sustaining the motivation and perseverance to accomplish something like that? Certainly not him!

But he should have known it couldn't last, and anticipated that, when he finally found what he wanted, fate would snatch it from him. Perhaps it was no more than he deserved for wasting opportunities that had come his way in the past.

Struggling to shake off his melancholy, he looked up at the stars glittering in the purple canopy of the night sky. It brought to mind a television programme called *The Sky at Night* and, with a chuckle, he mimicked the staccato delivery of its irrepressible presenter, Patrick Moore: "Will a man ever stand on the moon? Well, we just don't know!"

He had read that the Russians had sent something called Sputnik into space on a rocket. Some people even claimed to have seen it shining as it orbited overhead. But shooting what looked like a giant ball bearing around the earth was a far cry from spaceships taking men to the moon and distant planets, like the fantasy voyages Jet Morgan and his crew made in *Journey into Space,* on the wireless.

It was no use; he couldn't get Jo off his mind. He had managed a cheerful response to Richard's toast: 'to the happy couple' in the saloon bar of The Golden Lion, and raised his glass to them with a forced smile and the thought: 'I don't suppose *they're* toasting each other with Simonds IPA. It's probably champagne.' It reminded him of Avril's party and Jo's animated confession that she had never had champagne before. He remembered the sparkle in her lovely eyes, as she had exclaimed, "I like it!"

"Happy birthday, Jo!" he murmured wistfully.

He was yawning extravagantly when he returned to the café. Locking the doors behind him, he made his way towards the stairs, only to curse as he stubbed his foot against something solid in the entrance to the passageway. Reaching out, he flicked on the light switches and stared in amazement at the Marshall amplifier on the floor at his feet and his Hofner guitar propped against the counter.

His hands were trembling as he retrieved the envelope from under its strings, and recognised the handwriting that spelled out his name. Swallowing to clear the lump in his throat, he took out the note.

Dear David,

I saw this in the window of a music shop in Myrtlesham. I thought it looked like yours, because I recognised the crack in the inlay at the top. When I went in, a chap called Benny told me he had bought it from you. He said to say hello and tell you he is sorry but he has sold your amplifier. But he assured me the one he sold me is just as good. He was kind enough to deliver it for me.

The penny has finally dropped. Why didn't you tell me you had sold them to pay for the kitchen? I am very cross with you. We need to have a serious talk. Love, Jo

He sat on the corner of a table and rested his foot on a chair to balance the guitar on his raised knee. Not bothering to plug it into the amplifier, he carefully tuned the strings and, with bittersweet memories of the precious weeks spent with Jo, coaxed out a few melancholy chords.

Having time for a leisurely breakfast was now a rare treat in David's busy life. Sitting in the morning sunshine, savouring his toast and marmalade, he sang along contentedly with Pat Boone, who was crooning *April Love* on the café radio. Unable to contemplate daily life without music, he had bought the old

Pye valve set, with its bakelite knobs and heavy wooden cabinet, from a second-hand shop to replace the little Grundig transistor radio he had given to Sammy's sister.

He had decided to deny himself the pleasure of joining the crowd beginning to line the Esplanade for the carnival parade. An hour or two to himself was more appealing than being penned in and jostled on what promised to be another very warm day. Groups of people gathering beyond The Packet Boat Inn were merging into a sizeable throng, but thankfully the barriers and the ample figure of PC Tommy Bowyer prevented his tranquillity being disturbed; or so he thought.

It didn't take long for him to be disillusioned. His first uninvited guest was a persistent wasp that wouldn't be persuaded that his Golden Shred wasn't for sharing. After fruitless attempts to swat the annoying intruder away, he settled their dispute with a rolled-up copy of The Myrtlesham Argus.

"Oh, it *is* you!" Chris exclaimed, as he appeared at David's shoulder. "For a moment, I thought it was Errol Flynn."

David put down the paper. "I was trying to stop that irritating little pest helping himself to my marmalade."

"He appears to have lost his appetite," Chris observed, nudging the crumpled corpse with his shoe. "The little blighters can get quite aggressive at this time of year. It wouldn't surprise me if one or two of his pals turn up looking for him."

"Thanks; that really cheers me up! Being stung by a horde of angry wasps will make my day!"

"A Reckitt's Blue Bag is the thing for wasp and nettle stings," Chris declared. "That's what dear old Nanny Pickles used to dab on it if my sisters or I got stung."

"I haven't got a Blue Bag … or a Nanny Pickles."

"In which case, I suggest you avoid duelling with any more wasps. Are you bringing your little drummer-girl to the carnival ball?"

David shook his head. "No; I'm not going."

"Oh dear, Cinders. Is your wicked stepmother making you stay at home?"

"I haven't got tickets," David replied. "I can't dance, and Ruby will be on stage with The Jetstream."

Chris shook his head. "No she won't. There's no show tonight. Gemma tells me there never is on parade day. I suppose it's because of everything else that's going on. Getting tickets for the ball is no problem, though. And don't worry about your lack of dancing skills. You can bet there'll be plenty of clodhoppers stumbling round the dance floor."

"I assume you're taking Gemma?" David asked.

"Of course! Colin asked me to get tickets for him and Jo, as well. He thinks Jo is going to try and set Richard up with one of her colleagues from the hospital. If you bring Ruby, it'll make up a nice little party."

"No thanks, Chris. I really don't fancy it."

"What a shame. Well, if I can't persuade you, I'll leave you to your solitary breakfast. I'm off to set up my easel, ready to portray the procession in all its majesty. A few more masterpieces might help to fill the empty coffers of a poor starving artist."

David watched Chris make his way onto the mole, puzzled that Richard hadn't mentioned going to the carnival ball, or Jo finding him a date. It was something he normally had no trouble managing himself. Having someone else find one for him was the sort of thing he would normally joke about.

"It's Colin's idea, I shouldn't wonder," he surmised. "Well, if trying to exclude me is part of his plan, I can save him the trouble."

He was looking forward to trying out his new amplifier. He had only managed to strum a few chords the previous night, before fatigue had forced him to seek his bed. His privacy was disturbed again when a shadow fell across the table.

"There's a young lady at the barriers, sir; askin' for you." Although the harbour was part of PC Bowyer's regular beat, he and David had not yet acquired the familiarity of being on first name terms.

David followed the policeman's pointing finger to where Ruby was waving to him. He waved back. "OK. You can let her through."

"Looks like we've got another lovely day," PC Bowyer remarked, signalling to Ruby as if he were directing traffic. "It'll be a relief for the carnival organisers. It was a real washout last year; it rained all week. Chucked it down on the day o'the parade."

"Well, there's no chance of that today," David declared. "They're forecasting this good weather to last for some time."

"I'll leave you to it, then, sir," said the constable, as they watched Ruby vault nimbly over a barrier.

Dressed simply in an emerald green blouse worn over blue jeans, she came towards the café with a leather shoulder bag swaying at her hip and the cuban heels of her ankle boots clacking on the paving stones. Her eyes were hidden behind the large lenses of her sunglasses; and with no makeup and her titian hair pulled back in a ponytail, she looked fresh and appealing. Responding with a little wave to a wolf-whistle from the harbour, she seated herself beside David and greeted him with a peck on the cheek. "Hello. Taking the day off?"

"No; it's not worth opening until after the parade."

"I thought I might find Archie here," she announced.

"Why would he be here?" David asked.

"Haven't you heard?"

"Heard what?"

She took off her sunglasses and fished a packet of Kensitas from her bag. "There's been a bust up, and Archie's gone missing."

"What's he done?" David exclaimed.

"It's what's been done *to him*!" Lighting her cigarette, she inhaled deeply. "They've done the dirty on him."

"Who has? And how?"

"The Jetstream, or what's left of it. We got a call from Malky yesterday afternoon. He wanted us to meet Busty Bertha and her boyfriend."

"Who?"

"The singer, Gloria Whassname. You should've seen what she had on. Talk about June is bustin' out all over! Her sweater couldn't have been any tighter or low-cut; with it all on show … And there's plenty to show! Malky was all over her like a bad dose of the measles. She's full of herself, too. Gives me the impression she's hard work. She wanted to rehearse a couple of numbers; to see how it panned out. That's when Malky dropped the bombshell."

"What bombshell?"

Ruby blew out a plume of smoke before answering. "Gloria won't join The Jetstream unless her boyfriend comes too. And he won't come unless he's lead guitar. Malky knew that from the start, but didn't tell us. He'd persuaded Vince to move from lead to rhythm guitar before the rest of us got there … which leaves Archie out in the cold."

"They can't do that!" David asserted. "It's Archie's group; he formed it! It used to be called The Meadowlanders; after him, Archie Meadows."

"Well, they have!" Ruby declared. "Archie's been stitched up! Malky's as mad as hell because Joel and I are leaving when this booking ends, so he claims that we don't get a vote on the new line-up. We weren't even there when he and Vince and Des are supposed to have voted for the change. Nor was Archie."

"What a lousy thing to do!" David exclaimed. "What did Archie say?"

"He called them back-stabbing bastards and all the other names he could think of. Joel had a word with him … I tried to, but he stormed off, practically in tears. Joel says he didn't go back to their flat last night. I thought he might have come here."

David shook his head. "No; I haven't seen him. But there's nothing I could I do about it, if he did."

Ruby gazed at him meaningfully. "You can guess what he'll do when he calms down."

"What's that?"

"He knows we're reviving Ruby Red when we finish here. He's your mate, so he'll expect to join us. Joel has already hinted at the possibility."

"We were billeted together during our national service, but I wouldn't really call him a mate," David insisted.

"OK; but do you want him in the group?"

David sighed and eased back in his chair. "If I'm totally honest; no. He can follow a chord sequence well enough, but he can be a pain in the neck. He's unreliable and he'll chase anything in a skirt."

"I know. Don't forget I've had to put up with him for the last few months."

David sighed heavily. "Despite that, I don't feel happy about leaving him out in the cold. He's had the stuffing knocked out of him ... when everybody else is making plans."

Ruby blew a smoke ring as she contemplated. "OK, mister softy. Suppose we give it a try? *And I mean a try!* Will that make you happier?"

David looked at her questioningly. "Are you sure? What about Joel?"

Ruby grimaced. "No, I'm not sure. But neither are you, are you? I'm willing to give it a go, but with conditions. He needs it spelled out: if he plays up, he's out on his ear!" Her expression softened, and she added, "Don't worry about Joel. He's the most easy-going fella I know. Believe it or not, he seems to get on well with Archie."

A surge of cheering from beyond The Packet Boat Inn and the measured thump of a bass drum signalled that the carnival parade was on its way.

"Shall we go up on the mole?" David suggested. "We should be able to see over the heads of the crowd on the promenade."

"If you like," Ruby replied, with little apparent enthusiasm.

"Do you want to take a drink with you?"

"OK; thanks. Have you got raspberryade?"

The parade was much like others David had seen, although it was bigger than many and, he would admit, more entertaining than most. Brightly adorned vehicles of all types, sizes and vintages passed by displaying the names of local businesses and bearing tableaux depicting themes as wide-ranging as nursery rhymes, fairy-tales, maritime scenes and events from history and folklore; as well as one or two whose significance escaped him. The Wintergardens brass band, together with those from the Salvation Army, the Sea Scouts and the Boys Brigade contributed to a musical cacophony constantly being overridden by amplified music from the floats and the echo of announcements booming from loudspeakers mounted on lampposts. All along the cavalcade, individuals in fancy dress – from cowboys and indians, comic book heroes and cartoon characters, to a strange assortment of wild animals – waved and cavorted, dousing the crowd with water and tossing sweets to excited children. Attended by her 'court' of scantily clad mermaids, the glittering carnival queen smiled serenely and waved to her subjects from her throne of giant seashells.

'Parochial, quaintly amateurish and uniquely British,' David thought, as he watched the tail of the parade recede along the Esplanade. But he had to admit that, like everyone else on that glorious English summer day, he had thoroughly enjoyed it.

Perched on the sea wall, Ruby had been more interested in watching Chris at work. To her delight, he presented her with a portrait of herself sketched in charcoal.

"I've been trying to persuade David to bring you to the ball tonight," Chris told her. "But he tells me he's not a dancer."

"Nor am I," she said. "You won't get me trussed up in yards of taffeta and tulle."

"Not an old-fashioned girl ... like Eartha Kitt," Chris mused.

"Who?"

"Never mind. Where's David taking you instead?"

"If I'm lucky, I might get another fish supper on the beach," she giggled.

Chris whistled through his teeth. "My word! Prince Charming here certainly knows how to sweep a maiden off her feet!"

Ruby patted David's shoulder. "Don't worry about Archie; he'll turn up ... like a bad penny. Are you happy for me to try and sort things out with him if I see him first?"

"Yes. How do you fancy a proper meal at the Blue Lagoon?"

"You bet!"

"OK. It'll be busy, so I'll reserve a table." David looked at his watch. "I ought to go back and get ready to open up. Shall I call for you about half-past seven?"

Ruby hoisted herself back onto the sea wall and lit a cigarette. "That's fine. I'm going to stay here for a bit and watch Leonardo at work."

The doors were open when David arrived at the café, which meant that Jo was there. How would things be between them now that she was engaged to Colin? Feeling strangely nervous, he went in and found her in the kitchen, washing up his breakfast things.

"I was going to do that as soon as I got back," he declared.

"It's alright; I don't mind. Thanks for your card and the bouquet."

"You're welcome. Happy birthday for yesterday. I didn't know what to get you, so I thought you might like some flowers."

"Thank you; they're lovely"

"Thank *you* for the guitar and amplifier," he replied awkwardly. "I'll pay you back."

"You'll do no such thing!" she insisted. "I paid for part of it out of the takings, as you should have done! But consider the rest *your* birthday present."

"That's not until November." He swallowed hard. "I don't know what to say."

"You could start by explaining why you sold them without telling me."

"We needed to get the work done quickly. I was pretty sure they'd fetch good money, and I didn't think I'd need them anymore."

"Couldn't you have discussed it with me first?"

He shrugged dismissively. "I didn't want to worry you with it. And I knew what you'd say. I've told you before; I don't want you risking your savings in this place."

"I wouldn't have needed to," she countered. "At least, not for long! Benny told me how much he paid you. What we made on the Delrio order for Bella's party came close to that. So, I assume it was enough to do the kitchen."

"Was it really?"

"Yes; of course. And this place is making good money now. With everything else you've taken on, we're starting to build a decent balance at the bank. That's after paying the bills and the running costs and wages!"

"That's marvellous! Why didn't you tell me?"

"I thought you knew! Didn't you see the last statement from the bank?"

David returned her gaze sheepishly. "You know I avoid things like that. I didn't read it. When I realised where it came from, I just left it for you."

She sighed heavily. "You're hopeless! That reminds me; how much have you taken from the till for your own use? Aunt Ginny thinks the tax man might want to know."

"Well; ah … I don't know exactly," he mumbled uncomfortably. "I haven't kept tabs on it, really."

"Well, roughly," she persisted. "Have you had the same amount each week?"

"Well; let me see. I think it's probably about ... something like ... say, a fiver."

"You're lying, David; I can tell!" Her intense gaze seemed to penetrate his thoughts. "You haven't taken much, if anything, have you?"

"Alright; no."

"I thought not. What on earth have you been living on?"

"There's the leftover food!" he protested. "It just goes bad and gets thrown away if it's not used up. Sammy takes some and I use the rest. Why waste it?"

"But that's not a proper meal!"

"I manage. I make proper meals out of it, and I go out to eat sometimes. I had dinner at The Blue Lagoon last night ... Richard treated me," he added awkwardly. "But I've got money. In fact, I'm pretty flush at the moment. My tips from playing in the pub have kept me going, and I found some money in a jacket pocket that I'd forgotten about. On top of that, we got *a hundred quid each* for playing at Bella's party!"

Jo shook her head in frustration. "One meal at The Blue Lagoon isn't eating properly! Connie said you're weren't having proper meals!" She dried her hands on a tea towel and threw it at him. "You're ... you're..."

"An idiot?" he suggested.

"How's your Uncle Charlie?" she asked, her eyes twinkling mischievously.

"So Richard told you."

"Yes; he told me all about your aunt's visit. What a surprise!"

"More of a nasty shock where Charlie's concerned," said David. "I take it Richard also told you that Aunt Veronica confirmed our suspicions about the hidey-hole."

"Yes, he did. I saw Avril and Wally just now. They had no idea that the ladies who had this place were your Uncle Ralph's sisters. They said it was never mentioned. Not that they ever saw much of Ralph before he took over here. But Wally said it was no surprise that your uncle never let on about the family connection. Apparently, he wasn't very sociable and never spoke about his family or his private life."

"What amazes me is that Ralph's sisters knew what he was up to and kept quiet about it!" David exclaimed.

"Me too," Jo concurred. "Apparently your aunts were very respectable ladies. But Wally said it explains why Ralph sometimes brought his boat in late at night."

David would have liked to avoid referring to her engagement, or even thinking about it, but knew he ought to congratulate her. However, he was distracted by rhythmic beating on the café doors and a voice calling, "Hello; anybody home?"

Jo followed him into the café, where they found Ruby sitting on the edge of a table.

She held out her empty raspberryade bottle. "I thought I'd better bring this back. Do I get thruppence back on it?" she asked mischievously.

David took the bottle from her. "I don't think you two have met, have you? Jo; this Ruby from The Jetstream … Ruby; meet my business partner, Jo."

Ruby stood up, revealing that, in her cuban heels, she was a head taller than Jo, who was wearing sensible low-heeled pumps. The girls gave each other an appraising look as they exchanged 'pleased to meet yous'.

"I'd better go and see if I can find Archie," Ruby declared. "See you later, David. I'll make an effort and wear a dress. Don't be late!"

"I'm taking her to The Blue Lagoon. It's a sort of thank you…" David began.

But Jo interrupted him with a terse, "There's no need to explain. It's none of my business, is it?"

Tilly and Stella appeared in the doorway, giggling and chattering animatedly. "The policemen are just moving the gates for Connie to get her car through," Tilly trilled. "Did you see the parade?"

Jo shook her head. "Not much of it. But I've seen it plenty of times before."

"I did," said David. "It was good fun, wasn't it?"

"Avril was soaked by water balloons," Tilly chortled.

Jo grimaced expressively. "Good grief! I'll bet she blew her top. Especially if they ruined her hair!"

"No; she didn't!" Stella squealed. "She joined in with all the fun."

Connie's Morris Minor drew up outside, and she and Linda began to unload cakes and confectionery from the boot; overseen by PC Bowyer, who removed his helmet to wipe the brim and mop his brow with a large handkerchief.

"We could do with a drop o'rain," he remarked ruefully. "Me lawn's parched. It looks more like thatch than grass. Me roses're feelin' sorry for themselves, too." He sat down, with a gentle groan of relief, and placed his helmet on the yellow table. "They reckon we'll be in for water rationin' if this goes on much longer." Gazing up at the almost cloudless sky, he added, "It's thirsty work on a day like this."

Taking the less than subtle hint, David asked, "Can I get you a cup of tea or coffee? Or perhaps a cold drink?"

"That's very kind of you. A cup o'tea would do nicely."

People began to stream onto the quay as soon as the barriers were removed, and it wasn't long before all but one or two tables were occupied. Richard hadn't arrived yet, so David took on the role of washer up and Connie's assistant, while Jo took care of the ice cream hatch and the till. Its distinctive *clang* could be heard continuously amid the rattle of crockery and the babble and hubbub of fifty-odd voices.

"Listen to that," David exclaimed. "Jo's going to end up with arms like Popeye, at this rate."

It brought a chuckle from Connie and the comment, "It must be music to your ears."

"A symphony on the keys of a till," David proclaimed exuberantly.

Fully occupied with trying to keep pace with customers' orders, they didn't immediately notice when the clamour in the café suddenly moderated to almost a hush, broken only by a few unrestrained voices. It was a cry of, "My God! What's that fool doing!?" followed by a rising tide of shouting and shrieks of alarm, that led David to drop the knife he was sharpening and rush from the kitchen.

He found nearly everyone in the café on their feet, clustered around the window and in the doorway, obscuring his view. He was about to ask Jo what was gripping their attention, when a crash and the sound of splintering wood reverberated across the harbour, immediately accompanied by the cries and screams of horrified onlookers.

XII

Linda stood motionless in the middle of the room, her expression frozen in horror. Beside her, Tilly wrapped her arms around Stella, who had burst into tears. Shocked into indecision, David stared around him at the almost deserted tables, until he was brought to his senses by a shout from Jo. "Don't just stand there! Where's the first aid case?"

"The big one's behind a box under the counter!" he shouted. "I'll get the other one!"

Rushing back to the kitchen, he pulled off his apron and yanked open a cupboard door to drag out a satchel with a red cross stamped on the flap. "I think there's been an accident in the harbour!" he called to a startled Connie.

He had to force his way through the crowd blocking the café doorway and milling around the tables outside. There was no sign of Jo, but PC Bowyer and another constable were attempting to bring order to a scene of turmoil and confusion, exacerbated by the growing number of onlookers crowding onto the quay and clambering onto the wooden furniture outside the pub for a better view.

"Come along now! Move back! Make room there!" PC Bowyer commanded, spreading his arms wide to usher people away from the water. "Get back, sir; please!" he barked to a young man who was balanced precariously on a bollard, taking photographs.

"What's goin' on, Tommy?" Wally called from the pub doorway. Barging his way through the mêlée, he stared in horror at the figures thrashing in the water and calling for help amid the wreckage of a boat, whose overturned keel revealed a jagged hole in its splintered bows. "Jesus! It's them German kids!"

"Some idiot in a speed boat just went out of the harbour like a bat out of hell!" one spectator shouted. He pointed to the stricken vessel. "That boat was coming in and had to swerve to miss it."

"The first I knew about it was when it smacked into one o'the pillars at the entrance," the constable explained. "Gave it a right ol' whack an' swung round into that rusty old barge."

"Who was the ruddy fool in the speedboat?" Wally demanded.

PC Bowyer shrugged his shoulders. "Dunno. 'E went round the point … never even stopped. The engine in that boat there was still runnin', an' it went full-tilt into that concrete buoy. Smashed the bows in like matchwood … an' over it went!"

The current was running in through the harbour entrance in a series of rhythmic surges that rose up the walls and eddied back, creating a constant swell. Tossed amongst boats swinging at their moorings and the debris swirling around the stricken vessel, the helpless victims of the collision were desperately trying to swim to safety or cling to anything that might keep them afloat.

Turning to David, Wally pointed to a boat tied-up to the quay. "See that skiff; the blue one with four oars? I'm gonna grab that. It's Cyril Taite's; 'e won't mind. Too bad if 'e do. You fetch the lifebuoy by the 'arbourmaster's office."

Taken by surprise, David asked, "Will one be enough?"

"Thass all there is," Wally replied ruefully. "You run an' get it, while I get the skiff ready; an' we'll see 'ow many we can fish out, eh?"

"But I've never rowed a boat before!" David protested.

"Never mind, you'll get the 'ang of it. But don't worry; I'll be doin' most o'the rowin', while you pull 'em out. Got that?"

David nodded and gave Wally the first aid kit. "This might come in handy."

Wally patted his shoulder. "Good lad! Off yuh go then."

David's heart was beating like Ruby's bass drum, as he forced his way through the edge of the crowd, which was now three or four deep. Ken Rathbone was nowhere to be seen when he reached the harbourmaster's office, but the desperate cries from the water stiffened his resolve and, after several attempts, he managed to break the lifebuoy's retaining brackets and tear it loose. He didn't speak German, but there was no mistaking what *hilfe* meant.

Forcing his way back through the bystanders, he was relieved to see that some people were prepared to do more than just watch and shout unwanted advice. Some were throwing ropes and calling instructions, while one or two had jumped into the water and were trying to shepherd victims to safety.

He watched Jo kneel beside a motionless figure who had just been brought ashore with what looked like a serious head wound. It was a relief to notice that he wasn't one of the boys, but the profusion of blood suggested that his injuries were more than superficial.

Harbourmaster Rathbone, apparently under the impression that the situation would be improved by him bellowing through a megaphone, was standing on the mole yelling, "Stand off! Stand off!" to the skipper of a small cabin cruiser approaching the harbour entrance.

The skiff had gone. David was surprised to see two men rowing it towards a group of boys clinging to a mooring buoy. For a moment he imagined he was seeing things, when he recognised the tall figure in the boat with Wally. "Stan!" he gasped in amazement.

A man in the water was struggling to support a panic-stricken youngster, who was screaming and flailing his arms, so David ran along the quay and threw the lifebuoy to them. Wrapping the long retaining rope around his waist, he dug in his heels and towed them towards a group of people waiting on the slope of the launching ramp.

Amid the clamour of voices, he thought he caught the jingle of distant bells and prayed that it heralded the approach of much needed help. He knew it would be a welcome sound to Jo. She was now treating four casualties, aided by Gemma and Tilly, who was cradling a sobbing boy in her arms and murmuring gently to him in his native tongue.

Stan's distinctive voice echoed across the water. "Come … come! Take hand!" he called, leaning over the side of the boat to reach a lad who was clinging to a splintered plank.

With his own charge safely in the hands of people on the ramp, David looked around to see if there was anything else he could do to help. But unable to identify anyone he could reach, he watched spellbound as Stan hauled three more boys and an adult into the skiff, while Wally deftly worked the oars to manoeuvre it close to the mooring buoy. He couldn't help wondering which of them was more surprised, when he recognised the rescued adult as the tutor with whom Stan had had the altercation.

David was sure he wasn't the only one to breathe a sigh of relief when a black Wolseley saloon, with its bumper-bells ringing insistently, nosed its way through the crowd. It was followed by two ambulances and a black van, which disgorged half a dozen policemen to assist the hard-pressed bobbies on the quay.

PC Bowyer touched his fingers to the brim of his helmet, as a dapper, grey-haired officer stepped from the police car and donned a braided peaked cap. "It looks a bit of a mess constable," the officer remarked, gazing around him.

"That it is, sir," PC Bowyer replied. "Some idiot in a speedboat caused it. That boat, or what's left of it, swerved to miss it and came a cropper. I'm told it's a charter boat from Ecksom Sands that was cruisin' just off the beach to let the passengers watch the parade go along the Esplanade. It was just comin' in to let them spend the afternoon in Fairhaven."

"Who was in the speedboat?" the officer enquired.

"We don't know yet, sir," a sergeant replied. "We're still making inquiries."

"Casualties?"

"No fatalities, as far as I know, sir. It was mostly kids on board; on a school trip from Germany. We're just checkin' to make sure we've got 'em all."

"I shall be reporting the incident to the Coastguard and the Harbour Authorities, Inspector," the harbourmaster announced, hurrying towards them.

"I should imagine so," the inspector replied. "But we'll be making our own enquiries. Can you tell us who was in the speedboat?"

"I'm afraid not. It's not one I recognise."

A shout of, "Look; there's another one!" from someone in the crowd, provoked another chorus of yelling and gesticulating. All eyes followed arms pointing to the harbour entrance, where the head of a diminutive figure could just be made out bobbing on the swell, as he clung precariously to a weed encrusted mooring ring.

"My God! He'll be swept out!" the harbourmaster exclaimed. Raising his megaphone to his mouth, he called, "Ahoy the skiff! There's another one! At the harbour mouth!"

Alerted by the amplified voice, Wally and Stan hurried their bedraggled and shivering charges out of the boat and into the care of people on the launching ramp. Wally waved an arm in acknowledgement and gestured to Stan, apparently indicating what he wanted him to do. Reaching for the oars, they carefully turned the skiff around and pulled for the harbour entrance; Wally's voice echoing across the water, as he called the timing of each stroke to Stan.

"They won't make it!" Ken Rathbone shouted helplessly. "That kid's not gonna hold on much longer!"

To everyone's horror, his fear was realised. With the skiff still yards from the boy, he was suddenly dragged from his slimy handhold by a surge of the tide. Someone screamed and an agonised groan rose from the crowd, as the boy was lifted on the swell before disappearing beneath the surface. Shocked and horrified, the onlookers watched a tall figure stand up in the skiff and remove his jacket, before plunging over the side.

After what seemed an eternity, two heads appeared above the water at the harbour entrance, close against the mole. "I got! Wally come! I got!" Stan spluttered urgently. "Come quick … I not hold!"

Any animosity that David felt towards Ken Rathbone was swept away, as he watched the harbourmaster race along the mole, his cap flying from his head as he dived into the water beside Stan. Together, they held the limp figure of the boy afloat, keeping his pale face above the surface until Wally reached them.

David suddenly realised he was shivering, although he was standing in bright sunshine. The spontaneous torrent of applause and cheering irritated him. He appreciated that it was prompted by relief, but he couldn't help feeling that it was somehow inappropriate; even disrespectful. As if the tragic event had been as much a spectacle for the onlookers as a harrowing and traumatic experience for the victims and their rescuers.

He heard a policeman make his report, somewhere behind him. "We're still taking statements from eyewitnesses, sir. But, from what we know, everyone's been accounted for. The skipper of the wrecked boat's in a bad way, so we can't confirm that with him. The boys' teacher reckons there were twenty-three on board;

that's him and eight boys, eleven other adults, the skipper and two crew. One of the crew confirmed that. He said everybody was up on deck, ready to disembark, when it happened. So we're sure nobody's trapped in the boat."

"That's something to be thankful for, sergeant."

"Yes, sir. I don't think anyone's been killed, but the doctor here can tell you more about that."

"Thanks for your help, doctor," said the inspector. "It's fortunate you're here. What casualties do we have?"

"Four need hospitalisation; one critical and one or two with broken bones, but no fatalities." He pointed to Jo. "There might well have been if it hadn't been for that young lady; she's a nurse. She was already treating casualties when I arrived. The chap they're putting in the ambulance has serious head and neck injuries."

"That's the skipper of the wrecked boat, sir," the sergeant added.

"He can thank his lucky stars the nurse was here!" the doctor declared. "If it hadn't been for her, he might have bled to death."

David gazed at Jo with renewed admiration, as she wearily gave her version of events to the burly policeman towering over her. He smiled wistfully. He'd never known a girl like her.

Avril had appeared, with blankets and towels, to do whatever she could to help; as David had never doubted she would. Her hair was tidy and held in place by an alice-band, but no longer immaculately lacquered and coiffured.

"Avril has arranged for the doctor to make sure the boys are alright in the pub, David," Tilly called. "She thought it would be more comfortable for them and might settle them down. Is it alright if I go with the boy in the ambulance? I speak German … It might help."

"Of course! That's really kind of you, Tilly."

The boy's tutor raised a hand from his blanket to signal his gratitude, while Tilly rewarded David with a smile.

A puddle was spreading at the feet of Stan and Ken Rathbone, who were standing together on the quay, with blankets draped around their shoulders. They were gazing into an ambulance, where the boy they had rescued was receiving attention. Noticing their concern, one of the attendants gave them a thumbs-up and called, "He's swallowed a lot of water, but he'll be good as new."

"I'd better get into some dry clothes and start sorting this mess out," Ken Rathbone declared."

"D'you need a hand?" Wally asked.

"I'd appreciate it," he replied. "You being a naval man. The Ocean Queen's due in soon. Can you take charge and warn the skipper and any other boats coming in about the hazard, while I'm away?"

"Yeh; of course," Wally replied. "The Emerald Star's on the way back, by the look of it. I'll get Frankie to tow this wreck out o'the way, if yuh like."

"That'd be champion, thanks … er."

"It's Wally. Over by the barge be alright, will it?"

"That'll do nicely." The harbourmaster offered his hand. "Call me Ken. Thanks Wally."

Catching David's eye, Wally winked; a broad grin appearing amid the tangle of facial hair. "Alright, son?"

David nodded; dazed and awed by what he had seen. Watching the police and ambulance crews relieve exhausted and emotionally drained rescuers, he reflected on having witnessed the very best of humanity. Outwardly unexceptional people, living in an insignificant little seaside resort, had instinctively rallied to the aid of those in peril.

Among them, a young nurse had skilfully and determindly saved the life of a badly injured man; a publican had been an oasis of calm, drawing on his naval experience to avert a crisis; someone he had dismissed as a preening martinet had proved himself resolute and courageous when the need had arisen; and the humanity of a solitary exile, embittered by the savagery of merciless oppressors, had transcended hatred and led him to rescue the children of his persecutors.

"And I called Fairhaven a dump," David murmured.

"What was that, David?"

"Nothing, Connie; I was talking to myself."

"Oh, I see." She was holding a tray bearing cups and beakers of strong tea. "We thought this might help."

"Oh, good. Well done! Go ahead and hand it round. I'm sure they could all do with it."

When he returned, the café was already full again and noisy with the boisterous chatter and laughter that ensues from the release of tension. Stella's eyes were red and swollen, but she had recovered her composure and was hard at work.

"We're giving the customers fresh tea and coffee. I hope that's alright," Linda announced.

"Yes; of course. That's very thoughtful." He smiled affectionately at her and Stella. "Thanks for holding the fort, girls. I really appreciate it." On his way to the kitchen he called, "If any kiddy's ice cream has melted, you can replace that too."

A welcome surprise was waiting for him when he got there. "Sammy!" he exclaimed. "How are you? It's great to see you!"

"Fit as a fiddle," Sammy replied and hung up his coat. His movement appeared a little stiff and his eye socket was still discoloured, but the swelling had subsided. "Knew you'd be busy. Come in the back way cos of all that palaver out front."

"Are you sure you're ready to come back to work?"

"Course I am! Give us that apron. Got a letter from the council this mornin', sayin' the rent arrears 'as bin cleared up. Ivy's figured out 'ow to work that little wireless you sent 'er, too. Tickled to bits with it, she is."

"You're both welcome."

"Bin good to us, you 'ave. Won't forget it; neither of us."

"Good grief!" David gasped, as Jo came in through the rear door. "Look at you!"

"Look like you bin slaughterin' pigs, girl," Sammy chuckled.

"Oh, thanks! You two really know how to flatter a girl, don't you?" Putting down the first aid case, she said, "Hello Sammy. You look so much better."

Beads of perspiration dotted her forehead and a lock of unruly hair hung over one eyebrow. Her skirt and sweater were rumpled and stained with blood, and there was a smudge on her face where she had wiped her cheek. "Looking like this, I thought I'd better come in this way," she said with a grimace.

David blew out his cheeks. "You did a heck of a job, Nurse Lampeter! The doctor said you saved that bloke's life."

"I only did what I've been trained to do," she replied. "Avril asked me to tell you that Richard's just called her and asked her to pass on a message. He didn't come to work because his boss phoned, wanting to take him out to lunch. It was out of the blue and Richard didn't think he could say no, so he arranged to pick him up from the station in Myrtlesham."

David shrugged. "It doesn't matter; Sammy's here, now. Why don't you get off home? You look all in."

"I suppose I'd better," she said. "It won't do much for our reputation if the customers see me in this state. But Tilly's gone to the hospital with the German boy, hasn't she? Are you sure you can manage without both of us?"

"Yes; we'll manage. The fete will be in full swing in the rec. The parade finishes there, and the Miss Fairhaven contest starts at the Wintergardens bandstand shortly, so it should start to calm down here, soon. Go home and put your feet up. You've earned it."

"OK; I will in a minute, after I've cleaned myself up a bit … But I've got something to tell you…"

She wasn't given an opportunity, because Linda's head appeared round the doorframe. "Hello Sammy! Lovely to see you!" she called, before turning her attention to David and Jo. "Sorry to interrupt, but there's a queue at the till. One or two are getting a bit impatient … Sorry; gotta dash; somebody's ringing the bell at the ice cream hatch."

"Sorry Jo; I've got to go!" David declared, narrowly avoiding a collision with Connie as he hurried out of the kitchen. "Can whatever it is you want to tell me wait?"

"I suppose it'll have to," she murmured. Retrieving her handbag from a worktop, she called, "Yes; alright. See you tomorrow. Have a nice evening with Ruby!"

David was opening the café doors, to take Rocky out and open up the parasols, when Grace Sullivan appeared, waving a newspaper. "Have you seen this, David? We're on the front page of this morning's East Coast Herald!"

She came in and laid it on a table to reveal the banner headline: *Disaster in Fairhaven Harbour.* Beneath it, was a picture of the capsized boat and figures in the water. The accompanying article was headed: *An Eyewitness Account by our reporter Warren Gradsley.*

It began: *Yesterday afternoon, I was among the holidaymakers packing the small seaside resort of Fairhaven to enjoy the annual carnival celebrations. But no-one in the excited crowd cheering the colourful parade could have anticipated that the celebrations would be marred by disaster. The Puffin, a small cruise boat that was entering the picturesque harbour with a party of German schoolchildren, was wrecked while avoiding a collision with a speedboat…*

David skimmed over the following paragraphs, which contained an embellished, but reasonably accurate, description of The Puffin's demise. It concluded with: *more exclusive pictures on pages 6 and 7.* "I see the police haven't caught the idiot in the speedboat yet," he remarked.

Grace's announcement brought Tilly hurrying from the kitchen, where she had been making up a batch of strawberry sundaes. While he waited for her to read the article, David found himself reflecting on the previous evening.

Ruby had kept her promise and made a very pleasing 'effort'. In a sleeveless summer dress, with her hair brushed into burnished waves and her pretty face carefully made up, she had looked anything but a tomboy. Archie had telephoned her at her digs that afternoon, in a mood she had described as bolshie. She had related their conversation in her usual uncompromising manner. "He played hard to get when I said we'd be prepared try him out with Ruby Red," she had snorted dismissively. "He seemed to think he was doing us a favour. But when I told him it was take it or leave it, he came down off his high horse and said he'd think about it … He'll say yes; you know he will."

At her insistence, David had related the events of the accident as briefly as he could, despite her frequent interruptions for more detail. Her spirit and vivacity had been just what he had needed after such a trying day. As they had left the restaurant, she had sprung a surprise on him with the suggestion, "Do you fancy a coffee at my place?"

He smiled, remembering her impish grin when he had asked, "Are you allowed visitors in your room at night?"

"Not a fella on his own," she had giggled. "But it'll be fun sneaking past my landlady."

He hadn't believed that 'a coffee' meant much more than that, but his heart had still been fluttering as they had walked to her digs. However, there had been no chance to find out, for two reasons; the first of which had been her reaction to his chance remark that he wondered what it was that Jo had wanted to tell him.

"Didn't you say she's getting married soon?" Ruby had inquired.

"It's not planned for a year or so, as far as I know." he had replied. "Why do you ask?"

Ruby had smiled mischievously. "I just wondered if it suddenly has to be a rushed job."

She couldn't have chosen a more effective way to dampen his ardour. Shocked and dismayed, he had retorted, "Trust you to think of that!"

His anger and the sharpness of his reply, had surprised her. "Alright; no need to bite my head off! It was just a thought."

"Well, keep your grubby thoughts to yourself!" he had growled irritably.

The second reason was the young chap they had found in the rustic bus shelter, outside Ruby's digs. Tall and good-looking, he had been snappily dressed in a pale blue jacket and fashionably-narrow, grey trousers. To David's surprise and regret, Ruby had greeted him warmly and introduced him as Russ, from The Rocking Redwings.

Russ had explained that Gloria had kicked him out of their campervan after 'another ding-dong', leaving him with the near impossible task of finding somewhere to sleep at that time of night, during carnival week. David's suggestion that Gloria might have calmed down by then had been dismissed with the comment, "You don't know Gloria!" Knowing her all too well, Russ had resigned himself to a night in a draughty bus shelter.

Any chance of 'a coffee' had disappeared, when Ruby had noticed her landlady's curtains twitch. But its appeal had already been tarnished by her unwelcome insinuation. So, cutting his losses, David had offered Russ the use of his couch as an alternative to the spartan hospitality of the Myrtlesham and District Motor Traction Company.

Russ had left a few moments before Grace arrived with the morning paper, more in hope than with conviction that Gloria's mood might have improved.

David's meditation was interrupted by the rustle of Tilly turning the pages of the newspaper. One of the pictures inside was of Wally and Stan pulling a young lad from the water; another was of Jo tending to the skipper of the wrecked boat. There was more narrative, including a piece which began: *Amid the chaos and confusion in the aftermath of the accident, Nurse Joan Lambert was an angel of mercy administering to the injured.*

"The Rockhopper Café got a mention, too," Grace exclaimed excitedly. "Your customers were singing your praises; saying how you all pitched in to help and gave everyone a fresh pot of tea afterwards."

"I'm surprised they got the café's name right," David replied caustically. Pointing to Jo's misspelt name, he said, "They didn't manage it with Jo's ... They're as bad as the Argus!"

"Oh my goodness!" Grace gasped. "I didn't notice that! What a shame; it's such a lovely picture of her."

Although he had scorned Ruby's uncouth insinuation, it still lingered in David's mind. Surely that couldn't be what Jo had wanted to tell him! According to Colin, they weren't planning to get married for another year. But what if they were trying to pull the wool over his eyes? Was that the real reason Colin had tried to persuade him to stay on and run the café? Were they hoping to scurry off somewhere and get married before the baby was born? And why had the possibility that Jo was expecting occurred to Ruby? He knew that women were perceptive about things like that; so had she sensed it when they met?

He shook his head, trying to clear the flood of irrational thought and speculation from his mind. What was he thinking? Jealousy allowed him to believe Colin capable of such deceit, but he couldn't believe it of Jo. So, had she tried to tell him that she was expecting?

Grace was taking her leave and Tilly had returned to her ice cream sundaes, when Richard bounded in a few moments later. "Morning boss! I'm really sorry about going AWOL yesterday. I hear you had a lot to contend with. But I really couldn't put my chairman off. He'd brought his wife with him, too."

David waved away the apology, "Don't worry; Sammy's back!"

"So I hear. Jo told us about the accident when she got home. She looked as if she been in a war."

"She was wonderful!" David proclaimed. "She saved a chap's life."

Chris's grinning face appeared around the doorframe. "I take it you're talking about yesterday's excitement. I'd already gone when it happened. Gemma said our Stan was the hero of the hour!"

"He was," David affirmed. "So was Ken Rathbone. It makes you think. It's so easy to misjudge people and get things wrong."

"That's true," Chris said solemnly. "I'm sure Colin would agree with you about getting things wrong."

David felt his chest tighten. "Why?"

"I'm not sure David knows yet, Richard suggested. "I don't think Jo's had a chance to tell him."

"Tell me what?" David asked, hardly able to breathe.

"I don't think we should be the ones to tell you," Chris said hesitantly. "Perhaps it ought to come from her."

"For Christ's sake! Stop playing silly buggers … and just *tell me*!"

"Alright; alright. Keep your hair on!" Chris replied soothingly. "It's all over between Jo and Colin. She's given him the boot."

David suddenly realised he was holding his breath, and had to lean on the counter to steady himself. "What; for good?" he gasped.

"It certainly looks that way," said Richard. "They never went to that posh hotel. According to Ginny, Colin was going on about Jo changing her job, moving in with his parents, and wanting her to persuade you to keep the café going … and she hit the roof! Letting on that he'd already spoken to you about it only made matters worse. Apparently, it all got very heated. Ginny said he accused Jo of being ungrateful and claimed he was doing it for their future. But Jo laid into him about being controlling and manipulative, and taking it for granted that she would just go along with whatever he decided."

Struggling with his emotions, David murmured, "So *that's* what she wanted to tell me yesterday."

Richard nodded. "I expect so. She's coming in later. It might be better if you didn't let on that we've told you."

"I agree," said Chris. "Well, I'm off to the art shop. See yah later alligator!"

With his spirits soaring, David became businesslike. "Right! Time we got ready to open up."

"What do you want me to do now that Sammy's back?" Richard enquired.

"It's Stella's day off, so would you mind standing in for her and giving Connie a hand, if needed?"

"My pleasure." Returning Gemma's wave as she passed the window, Richard called, "You've just missed the king of the jive!"

She came to the doorway giggling delightedly. "I've just seen him. You'd never guess Chris could be so light on his feet, would you?"

"How did you get on with the girl Jo fixed you up with, Rich?" David asked.

Richard looked bemused. "What are you talking about? What girl?"

"I thought Jo set you up with one of her colleagues for the ball. At least, that's what Colin told Chris she was going to do."

"Are you sure Chris wasn't having you on?" Richard chuckled. "You know I'm not keen on blind dates. I took Jo to cheer her up. She's had a rough time recently."

"Would someone help me open this jar?" Tilly called.

"OK; coming!" Richard replied, and made his way to the kitchen.

"Your brother's a good dancer," Gemma enthused. "It was just what Jo needed to take her out of herself. They made such a lovely couple on the dance floor."

The harbour redevelopment protest meeting had been in progress for little more than half an hour, but David was already regretting his offer to make the café available as a venue. Martin Winsor had not turned up, and controlling the unruly gathering was clearly beyond Gemma's capability. People were shouting and talking over her and Monty, who was on his feet attempting to glean information from the nervous chap representing the council's planning department.

Seated beside the harassed young man, Councillor Bentley gazed up at the ceiling; his expression betraying his barely restrained frustration. An abundance of wavy hair and relatively unlined features belied his age, which David knew to be fifty-something. He was dressed in a dark tailored suit, a white shirt and a striped tie bearing an emblem that suggested membership of an exclusive club or association. From the start, his attitude had indicated that he was not there from choice.

"Please be quiet!" Gemma pleaded, holding up her hands in supplication. But her words were lost in a tide of angry voices.

"Stow it; the lot of yuh!" Wally's commanding bellow reduced the noise to a hush and drew faces towards the doorway, where he stood with Lady Alice. "You're worse'n a load o'kids!" he snarled.

"I couldn't agree more," said Councillor Bentley, signalling his disdain by inspecting his fingernails.

"This lady's given up 'er valuable time to come all the way over 'ere an' give us 'er support," Wally announced. "An' when she gets 'ere, what does she find? You lot bawlin' and carryin' on like a boatload o'jacks in a Pompey ale 'ouse! We could 'ear you outside my pub! Show a bit o'respect fer Gemma! She's gone out of 'er way t'set this up, so we can try an' find out what they wanna do with the 'arbour. So why don't you all shuddup an' listen!"

"Thank you, Wally," said Gemma, with palpable relief.

The hint of a smile played at the corners of Lady Alice's mouth, as she accepted the chair David offered her. Wally folded his brawny arms and remained standing with his back to the doors, as if daring anyone to question his authority.

"Is this lady a property owner or the proprietor of a business affected by the harbour redevelopment?" Councillor Bentley asked loftily.

"No, she's not," Gemma replied.

"Then, may I ask why she is becoming involved if she has no interest in these proceedings?"

Lady Alice's frown and pursed lips signalled her displeasure. "It would be appreciated, Councillor, if you would refrain from referring to one as if one were not present."

"I beg your pardon, madam. I was speaking through the chair," he replied condescendingly. "But if you'd care to give me your name, it will enable me to address you directly?"

"This is Lady Alice de Tenneaux," David interjected; his voice conveying his irritation. "She has *become involved*, as you put it, because she has kindly offered us her advice and support. It may have slipped your memory Councillor, but this is *our* meeting, and we have the right to invite whoever we choose!"

It was greeted by a rumble of accord from around the room. "Well said, David!" Victor Sullivan called.

The councillor's obvious annoyance was tempered by deference. "I beg your pardon, My Lady. I assure you no disrespect was intended. I'm here in response to the invitation made to Fairhaven Town Council. As their representative, I was merely trying to discover the purpose of this meeting."

"I would have thought that was obvious," Jo replied curtly. "We don't know what you intend to do; or when. We haven't been told much beyond the fact that you're going to compulsorily purchase the harbourside properties."

The councillor's young colleague fiddled nervously with the papers on the table in front of him. "The developer's plans have yet to be finalised, but they'll be published as soon as they're available," he offered hopefully.

"But where does that leave us!?" Jo retorted. How do you expect us to make plans to deal with it, if we've got nothing to go on?"

"That's right!" an elderly man in blue overalls concurred. Taking his pipe from his mouth, he flourished it to emphasise his point. "I build boats. My boatyard's been in the family for over two hundred years. I've got a half-finished ketch, a cabin cruiser undergoing repair and an ex-navy MTB conversion job on the stocks. At any given time, I can have three or four boats being built or repaired. How do you expect me, or any of these people, to pack up and start again somewhere else; just like that!?"

The volume of voices rose again in protest, to the Councillor's undisguised frustration and his colleague's apprehension.

"Quiet!" Wally growled, as Monty rose from his seat.

"Would it be correct to presume that problems with establishing clear title to certain areas included in your planned development are contributing to the delay?" Monty suggested.

It evoked a murmur of anticipation from the meeting and a nervous glance at the councillor from the planning representative.

"I'm afraid I am unable to answer your question," Councillor Bentley replied guardedly. "I'm not involved in the negotiations being conducted by the development consortium and their representatives."

"It's also my understanding that there are two historic royal charters appertaining to Fairhaven Harbour." Monty added.

The councillor stood up slowly and buttoned his jacket. "As I've just explained, I am not a party to the negotiations and, consequently, I don't believe I can be of any further assistance to you." To his colleague's surprise and obvious alarm, he added, "I'm sure Mister Townsend here will be pleased to answer any further questions you may have."

"One moment if you please, Councillor!" Lady Alice's voice cut through the intensifying volume of disapproval, reducing it to a murmur of anticipation. She rose to her feet and donned her spectacles; studying him over the lenses before opening the manila folder she held. "Before you leave, there are one or two matters with which one is confident you *are* able to assist us."

Councillor Bentley hesitated. "I'm afraid I'm in rather a hurry," he began, but transfixed by her determined gaze, he subsided onto his chair. "But, as you have gone to the trouble of coming here…"

"One is led to believe that the proposed redevelopment is planned as a joint venture between Fairhaven Town Council and a development consortium consisting of…" Her Ladyship paused to refer to her folder. "The Harding Gudrun Development Corporation; a company called Questholme Construction Limited; and another called McBride Enterprises."

There was a murmur of unrest from the meeting at the mention of McBride Enterprises, although everyone was aware of Charlie McBride's involvement.

Lady Alice regarded the councillor questioningly. "May one assume this to be correct?"

Clearly caught unawares, he replied, "Yes; that is correct. May I ask where Your Ladyship obtained this information?"

"One would hope it would have been in the public domain, in view of local authority involvement." Her curt response was received with exclamations of accord from the meeting, but

339

she continued without pause. "To enlighten you, Councillor; my son, Lord Anthony de Tenneaux, has associates in the City of London, as well as in political circles. Alderman Sir Francis Laughton is a close friend. One assumes you are acquainted with him?"

Councillor Bentley remained expressionless. "I am indeed," he said calmly. "I presume Your Ladyship is also about to reveal that I am a director of Questholme Construction Limited, which is well known to everyone at Fairhaven Town Council … including Sir Francis. I have made no secret of the fact."

If the admission was intended to disconcert Lady Alice, she gave no indication that it had succeeded. "One would hope so," she replied flatly. "But it is not the involvement of your company or McBride Enterprises that suggests cause for concern."

"You speak for yourself!" a gruff voice shouted from a corner of the room.

She ignored the ensuing laughter. "One would suggest that what *is* of concern is the involvement of The Harding Gudrun Development Corporation, which is presumably providing much of the necessary finance."

"That was not my choice, nor is it my affair," the councillor insisted dismissively.

"Perhaps you might consider making it so," Lady Alice suggested curtly. "My son informs me that there is suspicion that a certain Daniel Nielson is involved with this corporation, which conducts its banking transactions in Zurich, where he now resides."

"I wasn't aware that there is anything illegal about having a Swiss bank account," Councillor Bentley countered.

"Of course there isn't. But I'm sure you are aware of the protection from scrutiny that the country's banks afford. One is not revealing anything that isn't in the public domain by pointing out that a government project was seriously compromised by an organisation with which Mister Nielson was associated. My son had lunch with one of Mister Macmillan's advisors the other day, during which he learned a good deal more about Mister Nielson's dealings. One is not at liberty to divulge details, but suffice it to say that he has a reputation in the City for what my son referred to as *cutting corners.*"

Councillor Bentley remained impassive. "Thank you My Lady. This is all extremely interesting. But I'm not acquainted with this person. I believe you said his involvement with Harding Gudrun is no more than suspected. But, even if it should prove to be the case, he would remain on the periphery of our arrangements and would not be directly involved."

"One wonders if Alderman Sir Francis Laughton shares your lack of concern," Lady Alice suggested. "As chairman of the local branch of his political party, one cannot imagine he, or Central Office, would appreciate the press asking awkward questions about the possibility of his council being involved with someone with Mister Nielson's reputation; especially with a general election approaching."

Councillor Bentley rose to his feet once more. "Thank you, My Lady. Your information and advice is appreciated; although I'm sure your concern is unwarranted. There is no evidence to suggest that Mister Nielson is involved with this development. Now; if you will excuse me, I'm already late for another appointment." With his anxious colleague close on his heels, he made his way to the entrance. Collecting his trilby from the hat stand, he inclined his head to Lady Alice. "Goodnight to you all."

Wally blew out his cheeks, as several conversations broke out at once around the room. "Well, what are we supposed to make o'that?"

"We don't seem to be any closer to finding out what they're intending to do," Jo sighed.

"Thanks to Lady Alice, we know there's a shifty character involved with them," David remarked.

"You mean as well as your Uncle Charlie?" Wally chuckled.

"Lady Alice said the newspapers are snooping around this Nielson chap, so perhaps that might put them off," Jo suggested hopefully.

Her Ladyship interrupted her conversation with Monty to disabuse her. "One was merely suggesting that, with the approach of a general election, the government would not wish the newspapers to associate the party with nefarious dealings with which people like Mister Nielson are involved. I have no idea if that really is the situation, or if the press has any interest in him at all."

"Nonetheless, we really appreciate your help," said Victor. "You have obviously gone to a great deal of trouble."

Other voices endorsed the sentiment, to which Lady Alice replied with an appreciative smile. "It was my pleasure. I doubt it has made a great deal of difference, but one does so hate to allow such high-handedness to go unchallenged."

Monty drew on his cigar. "The redevelopment plans are almost certainly being delayed by difficulties the consortium hadn't anticipated. But, I fear it's nothing that can't be overcome by the quality of legal representation that such an organisation is able to afford."

"So where do we go from here?" Gemma sighed. "It's all so dreadfully depressing."

"I would suggest the pub!" said David. "To drown our sorrows."

"Oh, don't give up yet," Her Ladyship advised reassuringly. "Remember Robert the Bruce and the spider."

* * *

"So you're footloose and fancy-free again, Miss Lampeter." David hoped his ostensibly casual remark hadn't sounded as jubilant as he felt, but he'd been able to think of little else since

Chris had told him of her breakup with Colin. It had been difficult to hide his pleasure and feign surprise when she had told him herself.

She looked up from setting chairs around the tables they were rearranging after the meeting. "Yes; I'm off men for good. They're more trouble than their worth!"

"So, where's Colin, now?" he asked.

"At home with his mother and father."

"For good?"

"I suppose so; at least until his leave ends. I have no idea, really."

"But surely he'll try to make it up with you, won't he?"

"He already has. He called me last night, wanting to meet me and, as he put it, *patch things up* between us. Why do you ask?"

"Oh; no reason. I just wondered."

"I told him there's no point. There's no chance of me changing my mind! It's over; finished! I have no intention of marrying him. Is that what you want to know?"

"No; no! I wasn't being nosey!" David insisted. "I just wondered … Poor Colin."

She turned sharply and glared at him. "That's just typical of you men isn't it!? You all stick together. Poor hard-done-by Colin!"

"Hang on! That's not what I meant!" David protested. "There's no need to fly off the handle! I wasn't suggesting that, at all! I meant he must be pretty upset now he realises what he's lost." He wanted to add, 'I would be'. But caution warned him that it wasn't the right moment.

"Trust you!" Her expression softened and her eyes sparkled. "I'll say this for you. You know how to talk your way out of trouble."

"It's something I've had to learn from necessity."

"You seem to have changed your mind about the harbour redevelopment," she suggested. "You were quite aggressive with that councillor. If I didn't know better, I'd swear you didn't want it to go ahead, after all."

"He really got on my wick!" David snorted. "His kind think they can walk all over people like us." He waved a gesturing arm around the café. "We've put a heck of a lot into this place, haven't we? I never thought we'd achieve anything like what we've managed here. From what I heard this evening, I'm even more convinced those shysters are not being honest with us. Probably to get away with paying the bare minimum in compensation. I'm fed up with their sort getting their own way all the time!"

Jo's eyes widened. "Steady, Tiger!"

Embarrassed by his outburst, David grinned sheepishly. "You know what I mean."

"Yes, I do. I never thought I'd hear you talk like that."

"And it's not just the business owners it affects, is it?" he exclaimed. "The people who work for us will suffer too. Sammy and the girls have put their hearts and souls into this place! I'd hate it all to be for nothing; just to line the pockets of people like Councillor Bentley and Charlie McBride."

"Shouldn't you say *Uncle Charlie*?" Jo teased. Becoming more serious, she added, "I couldn't agree more! But it's so different to what you've said before."

"I know. We can't win; we don't stand a chance against them. But if I had my way, this place would go to someone who really wants to keep it going. Stella's been in tears. She loves it here, and it's all Sammy and his sister have to live on. Remember how they treated him at that boatyard? Where's he going to find anyone else who'll pay him more than a pittance?"

"We can't be sure a new owner would have kept him on, anyway," Jo cautioned. "Or Stella, for that matter."

"I suppose not," David conceded. "But whatever happens, I'm going to do all I can to find them somewhere they'll be appreciated!"

Jo leaned on the back of a chair and gazed out across the harbour. "What do you suggest we do while we're waiting for the council to issue the compulsory purchase order?"

"The season's nearly over," he mused. "The kids are back at school in a week or so. I don't know if it'll be worth staying open for very long after that."

Jo sighed heavily. "Why does life have to be so complicated?"

"I don't know," he said. "Too much thinking gives me a headache. Why don't we give it a rest and join the others in the pub?"

She shook her head. "I'm not in the mood, but you go ahead. I think I'll go straight home, if you don't mind."

Swallowing his disappointment, he replied, "No; of course not."

Jo retrieved her handbag and made her way to the entrance, giving him a wan smile as she opened a door. "I suppose it will all sort itself out in the end."

"Yes; I suppose so," he murmured.

David couldn't resist a smile of satisfaction, as he sang the opening lines of Ricky Nelson's *Never Be Anyone Else But You*. It felt good to be performing again. Fairhaven was still packed with holidaymakers, so Hooky's posters on the promenade lampposts had guaranteed a large and appreciative audience that filled both bars and overflowed through the entrance lobby onto the quay. The tables and benches outside the pub and the café were crowded and the rails overlooking the beach were once again lined with David's teenage fans. No-one seemed concerned that couples were ignoring the newly erected sign prohibiting dancing.

Behind the bar, everyone was at full stretch to satisfy the thirst of David's enthusiastic, though less than pitch-perfect, 'choir'. Only Avril seemed unaffected by the heat and humidity. Her hair was once again carefully styled and lacquered and her face immaculately made up. However, Wally, Hooky and Linda were constantly fanning their faces and mopping perspiration from their brows.

David laughed with unashamed pleasure, as the raucous crowd joined him in the chorus. Leaning to one side, he looked across the overcrowded Mess, trying to see beyond the groups sitting at the window tables for a glimpse of Richard and Jo. For a short while they had sat at the bar. But, with The Mess becoming ever more crowded, concern for Richard's health had led Jo to persuade him to leave the humid, smoke-laden atmosphere and join Gemma and Chris outside. He couldn't see Richard or Jo, but he did notice Mervin arrive on the quay with Bernard, who was on crutches. He had also spotted Lance, the man from Delrio, with a willowy girl whose face was shadowed by the wide brim of a white sunhat.

While his audience was still applauding and shouting their appreciation, he launched into his own version of *Guitar Boogie*, accompanied by rhythmic clapping and drumming on tables and chairs. Hooky pitched in, beating on the ship's bell with a wooden spatula, while in the narrow confines behind the counter, Wally twirled Avril in an ungainly pirouette.

Could life be any better? He was doing what he loved for an appreciative audience that included so many of those he had come to regard as good friends. What a glorious summer it had been; in so many ways. He had proved, not least to himself, that he could persevere and achieve things he would once have dismissed as impossible. He had found happiness and purpose … with a wonderful girl!

However, the sight of the scantily clad girl waving from the calendar on the pillar beside him was an unwelcome reminder that August was coming to an end, and that this glorious summer and the Rockhopper Café would soon be no more than cherished memories. *Don't think about it now! Enjoy it while it lasts.*

Acknowledging the rowdy ovation as the final chord faded and died, David rested his guitar on its stand and switched off the microphone. Hooky tossed him a bar towel and he wiped the perspiration from his face before taking a pull at the refreshing pint Wally had placed at his elbow. His clammy shirt, clinging to his shoulders, was all the encouragement he needed to make his way across the congested bar to enjoy the intermission outside in the cooler, fresher air.

A dusky haze was beginning to veil the horizon when he stepped out onto the quay. Beyond the headland, the blue of the sea was deepening to almost indigo; seemingly alive in its relentless surge to the shore. Lamps on the quay glowed like amber jewels against the darkening sky; their reflections dappling the dark water of the harbour. Spilling across the crowded tables outside The Packet Boat Inn, the harsher light from its windows deepened shadows; creating stark, unworldly profiles of the people sitting around them. While, along the promenade, the illuminations shone ever brighter in the gathering twilight; glittering like a necklace of coloured pearls as they followed the contour of the bay towards the blazing light of the fairground.

David gazed around him contentedly. He could think of nowhere he would rather be. Acknowledging compliments and the approbation of those around him, he scanned the large crowd seated at the rustic tables and standing in groups all around him. But he couldn't see Richard or Jo. He found Tilly and Bella on the edge of the quay, sitting on a crate beside Bernard, whose plastered leg was stretched out in front of him. Though simply dressed in sweatshirts and jeans, the girls drew the attention of almost every adult male in the vicinity.

"Have you seen Richard or Jo?" he asked.

Tilly shook her head. "No; I thought they were inside with you."

"What happened to you?" David asked, gesturing to Bernard's leg.

Bernard smiled coyly. "I'm kinda embarrassed to say. I fell down the steps in front of the theatre. But I was *stone-cold sober*," he insisted. "It was a quarter after ten in the morning. I thought I'd dance down them; you know, like Gene Kelly. I didn't know they'd just been cleaned. They were wet and kinda slippy. I guess you could say I came down them faster than I figured."

"No serious damage done, I hope?" David enquired.

"Nothing broken. The doc said my ligaments are damaged. Gonna be out of action for a while."

"Here we are, dear hearts!" Mervin called, as he gingerly weaved his way through knots of people, carrying a metal tray loaded with four brimming glasses. He was wearing his ubiquitous yachting cap and a gaudy silk shirt patterned with New Orleans jazz caricatures, which seemed to glow of its own accord in the fading light.

"*Simply merveilleux*, David!" he exclaimed. "I just had to come and catch your act! Look at all these people! It's amazing! You must, *simply must*, help with our rock and roll concerts! In fact, you have to take part! Let's talk about starting them, soon!"

"Thank you," David replied, avoiding a direct reply.

Tilly and Bella each took a glass of wine from the tray. In response to their thanks, Mervin exclaimed, "Mon plaisir! I had to burrow my way through all those beef-cakes to get to the bar. But hey-ho! The landlady's a dear. She saw you girls out here and asked if the wine was for you. I don't think she charged me for it."

"I expect it's her own," Tilly suggested. "Avril is so kind!"

"Oh rather!" Bella concurred. "Everyone is so friendly."

"Coca Cola for you, Bernard," Mervin announced solemnly. "No alcohol allowed with those tablets you're on. The poor boy slipped on the theatre steps," he explained. "Calamity for him, and *disaster* for us! Darling Gareth is doing his best to understudy for him in our *South Pacific* routine, but the dear boy just doesn't have the flair or the pizzazz! His arabesques are not exactly a coup de maître!"

While commiserating, David gazed around the quay.

"Are you looking for someone?" Mervin asked.

"Yes! My brother and my partner, Jo."

"Oh, I can help you there. I saw her when Bernard and I were on our way here. She was with another girl and two rather good-looking boys. They were on the other side of the promenade, and it was too crowded to see clearly. But one of them did rather remind me of you."

"Thanks; that explains it," said David.

"They've probably gone for a walk," Tilly suggested. "It's hot inside and almost impossible to find anywhere to sit. We were lucky Bella found this box, so that Bernard could rest his leg. I'm sure they'll be back soon."

"Do you know *Love Me Tender*?" Bella asked.

David ran through the opening bars in his head. "Yes, I think so. I'm fairly sure I know all the words."

"Will you sing it for me?" Bella implored. "Although it does make one cry. The end of the film was so sad."

"I can't promise to do it justice, like Elvis," he cautioned. "It will probably be the sound of my voice that makes you want to cry. But, I'll do my best."

Taking a hopeful, but fruitless, look towards the promenade, he glanced at his watch. "Well, I suppose I'd better get back to work."

XIII

A glass of Andrews Liver Salts was not the ideal start to the day. But neither were throbbing temples and an unpleasant taste in the mouth that suggested the sweepings of a rabbit hutch. David doubted that it would do much good, but catching sight of his haggard reflection in a kitchen window, he reluctantly swallowed the effervescing liquid.

He hadn't meant to drink so much the previous evening. It had happened almost without him being aware of it; the result of conflicting emotions. He hadn't counted the notes and coins crammed into the dimpled beer mug on his bedside table, but Hooky had been convinced that his audience's appreciative whip-round had to amount to thirty quid or more. Although exhausted, Wally and Avril had been delighted with what Wally had described as, "The best ruddy night we've ever 'ad!"

However, David's elation had been overshadowed by the disappointment of not having Jo and Richard there with him. While he might have hoped that Jo would appreciate its importance to him, he had *expected* Richard to understand. They hadn't even told him they were leaving, and had simply drifted off with Gemma and Chris.

As always, David's regular fan club had been vociferous and boisterous with its acclaim and he had been grateful for support from Tilly and Bella, as well as Mervin and Bernard, who had been generous with their praise; as had Laurence and his girlfriend. Grace and Victor Sullivan had stayed for a while and Stella had arrived with her boyfriend just after the start of his second session. He had also spotted Johnny Cline and several others from the boat crews and nearby businesses among the crowd. Even Danny Lightwater had turned up to wish him well and let him know that he intended to keep the Ocean Queen cruises going for another week.

But the two people who, with his parents, meant most to him hadn't bothered to stay.

Two aspirin tablets, allied with the 'dose of Andrews', were beginning to alleviate his headache, although they weren't having much effect on his unsettled stomach. The charred slice of toast he had forced down had done little more than replace the taste of rabbit litter. Careful to avert his eyes from the sun, he opened the doors to let the fresh morning air fill his lungs and pervade the café.

The sea was calm, with only a gentle breeze ruffling the advancing ranks of blue-green rollers and, beyond the harbour wall, a flock of wheeling gulls signalled the return of a fishing boat. The gin tubs were beginning to leave or be cosseted away for the winter, so the working boats would soon have the harbour mostly to themselves again. Secured beside a rusting barge, the wreckage of The Puffin was a sobering reminder of how hazardous seafaring could be.

The call, "Excuse, pliz!" drew his attention to a small, grey-haired man in a dark blue blazer and grey flannels, who was waving to him from the quay. He was accompanied by a tall, slim woman wearing a white linen jacket over a flowered summer dress. Silvery blonde hair fell to her shoulders from beneath a red beret, which was tilted fetchingly over one eye.

As they came closer, David noticed the track of a jagged scar, almost hidden beneath makeup, running across the woman's forehead from her shadowed eyebrow to her hairline. The breeze lifted her hair to reveal the line of another scar reaching from her jaw to just beneath her ear. Her features suggested that she had known trauma and suffering, although they still retained evidence of her former beauty.

"I'm afraid we don't open for another hour," David explained.

"Pliz," was all David understood, because the rest of what the man said was an impenetrable jumble. He thought he caught the word 'look', and moved aside, gesturing for them to enter.

"You're welcome to come in and take a look around, but if you're looking to buy a café, I'm afraid this one's no longer for sale."

"We do not want café." The woman's voice was low and husky and, although accented, her English was better than that of her companion. Her piercing blue eyes gazed at David intently as she spoke. "We look for person. Maybe you know?"

The man held out his hand with a slight bob of the head and addressed David again. Failing to understand, David smiled and grasped the extended hand. His expression obviously betrayed his difficulty, because the woman explained, "He say his name; Ludwick Krawiec."

Feeling his cheeks flush, David replied, "Oh; I see! I'm David Sheldon. I'm pleased to meet you Mister…"

"Krawiec," the woman repeated, pronouncing it slowly. "Ludwick iz my brother. I am Jolanta…"

Her brother interrupted before she could continue. "Zis; look zis, pliz!" He produced a copy of the East Coast Herald, opened and folded at pages six and seven. Pointing to one of the pictures of the harbour incident, he said, "Zis … zis man!"

"Oh, you mean Stan!" said David.

The man's brow furrowed with bemusement.

"Stan is how we know him around here," David explained. "I believe his proper name is Stanislav."

"Stanislaw! His name iz Stanislaw?" the woman prompted. "Stanislaw Mierzejewski?"

"Yes; I think so. That sounds about right."

"Iz Stanislaw?" the man exclaimed excitedly.

"Yes; he's my neighbour." David gestured along the quay. "You see the building with the closed shutters, just before the ramp. That's his place."

"Jolanta; Jolanta!!" Grasping his sister's hand, the man babbled animatedly in what David presumed was Polish, and tried to pull her towards where David was pointing. But she resisted and admonished him sharply in their native tongue.

"Iz true?" the woman asked earnestly. "Iz man in picture?"

"Yes; that's him." Unable to supress a chuckle, David added, "He's something of a local hero. Do you know him?"

The woman was looking at him, but her eyes suggested her thoughts were elsewhere. "My husband was brother of Stanislaw."

* * *

"Where did you get to last night?" David asked casually. He had waited a while before mentioning it; not wanting it to appear important to him.

Jo looked up from tallying the bookings for the previous day's boat trips. "We went to the funfair."

"The funfair?"

"Yes; it was Chris's idea. The pub was so crowded. It wasn't much better out on the quay, and you had to fight your way to the bar, so he suggested 'all the fun of the fair'."

"Oh, I see. I hope you had a good time."

"We did; it was fun! I hadn't been in there for years; not since… Well, never mind." Tapping her pen rhythmically on the counter, she looked at him archly. "You were surrounded by your adoring public when we left."

"It was a good night," he replied. "Wally said it was the best night they've ever had." He couldn't help adding, "Tilly and Bella came; so did Stella. Nearly everybody did; even Lance, from Delrio."

"That's lovely! We didn't think you'd miss us. All that smoke wouldn't have been good for Richard; and we couldn't talk to you with that din and so many people around you."

"So my music's *a din*, is it?"

Jo's eyes sparkled. "That's not what I meant, and you know it! You didn't mind, did you?"

"No; of course not," Avoiding eye contact with Tilly, he added, "I didn't notice you'd gone until Mervin mentioned seeing you on the promenade."

It appeared to satisfy her, because she said, "Tell me about Stan's family. It's exciting, isn't it?"

"Yes; but there's not a great deal to tell. They're his sister-in-law and her brother. They didn't know that Stan had survived the war until they saw his picture in the paper. Apparently he's the image of his dead brother; the woman's husband ... By the way, the East Coast Herald got your name wrong; just like the Argus."

Jo shrugged dismissively. "It doesn't matter. It's wonderful for Stan ... and his family. Where do they live?"

"I don't know."

"Why not? Didn't you find out anything about them?"

"Not much. It's none of my business; and the bloke's English wasn't that good. His accent was thicker than Lyle's Treacle. I could hardly understand a word he said."

"You said *her* English was good, though," Jo persisted.

"Yes, it was pretty good. But I didn't ask questions in case she thought I was prying and getting too personal."

"But Stan wasn't there?" Jo prompted. "Does anyone know where he is?"

"Avril might know, or perhaps the Sullivans. But it was too early to start banging on doors to ask if anyone knew where he was. Avril and Wally must have had a really late night after all the clearing up, so I didn't want to disturb them. I offered the couple tea or coffee but they declined and went off into town.

They're coming back later. I suggested they ask in the pub, if Stan's still not at home."

Jo nodded her approval. "That's a good idea. Avril's been keeping an eye on Stan, lately."

David chuckled mischievously. "Well then; she'll be able to tell you everything you want to know after she's interrogated them."

"Are you implying we're nosey?"

"Aren't all women?"

She poked out her tongue in response. "No; we're not! We take an interest; don't we Tilly?"

Tilly smiled, but said nothing and carried on re-stocking the shelves with soft drinks.

"Oh, you do that alright!" David declared. "You *take an interest* whether it's any of your business or not."

Jo pointed her pen at him accusingly. "That's better than you men! You never tell each other anything!"

"We do! We warn each other never to bet on anything that Frankie's put money on!"

Her bottom lip quivered. "Why are you so stupid?"

"I don't know. It must be a gift."

Their banter was interrupted by PC Tommy Bowyer tapping on the window.

"What have you done now?" Jo chortled. "Why are the police after you?"

"Didn't you know?" David exclaimed. "I'm on their most wanted list!"

"What for?"

"Oh; not having a dog licence … Riding a bike without lights…"

"Idiot!" she snorted, as Tilly started to giggle.

Enjoying their amusement, David opened the doors. "Good morning, constable. What can we do for you?"

PC Bowyer glanced enquiringly at the giggling girls and removed his helmet.

"Take no notice of them," said David. "I've tried hiding the gin, but they keep finding it." It prompted a stifled squeal from Tilly, who covered her mouth with her hand and scurried along the passage to the kitchen.

Struggling to keep a straight face, Jo asked, "Would you like a cup of tea?"

"No thank you Miss," the constable replied. "It's very kind of you, but I can't stop. I thought you'd like to know we've caught the mad devil that was drivin' that speedboat."

"Oh good!" Jo exclaimed. "That's good news."

"Yes; thanks for telling us," said David.

"It's a bit of a rum do," PC Bowyer mused. "I'm told somebody's been smugglin' in booze and tobacco from the continent."

Wide-eyed with alarm, Jo stifled a gasp.

PC Bowyer carried on, unaware of her anxious glance at David. "They've been operatin' out of that derelict warehouse behind Timpson's boatyard. Customs an' Excise blokes 'ave been keepin' surveillance on the harbour for the past few weeks, but when they closed in on the culprits, one of 'em made a run for it in that speedboat and … well, you saw the upshot of that."

"So it's Customs and Excise who've been watching the harbour?" Jo remarked deliberately.

"That's right, Miss."

"Was one of them that little dark-haired bloke I reported?" David enquired.

PC Bowyer shrugged. "I don't know, sir. I've never seen any of 'em. Most of us knew nothin' about it until Superintendent Chesney came over from Myrtlesham and briefed us yesterday. It was all hush-hush before that. The customs men kept under cover an' made their own enquiries. All I know is what the Super told us. It don't look like they were interested in you."

"Then why were they asking questions about us?" David asked. "Wally said someone was asking about us in the pub. He saw somebody poking about in our rubbish bins, too."

"Whoever did that was tryin' to cover their tracks, I expect," the constable conjectured. "I was there when a call came in from the firm that collects your rubbish. They asked to speak to DI Wigmore, but 'e was out on a case. Nobby Clarke, the desk sergeant, took the call. They told Nobby they'd been asked to report anythin' suspicious they picked up from around here. Apparently, they'd picked up a load of cardboard boxes with foreign writin' on 'em from the yard at the back. They were empty o'course, but they'd obviously had foreign cigarettes and tobacco in them. Brandy, as well."

"I think we…" Jo began hesitantly, but stopped as she saw the cautionary shake of David's head.

Thankfully, PC Bowyer failed to notice. "They must've been tryin' to hide the evidence by dumpin' the boxes in with other people's rubbish," he suggested. Replacing his helmet on his head, he said, "I'll leave you to it, then. I expect you're waitin' to open up."

"Thanks for letting us know," said David.

"Yes; thank you!" Jo called, as PC Bowyer took his leave.

For a moment they looked at each wordlessly, until Jo found her voice. "Why didn't you want me to tell him where those boxes came from?"

David hesitated. Was there any point in upsetting her by revealing what he knew about Ralph and Ginny's husband? "It could open a can of worms," he said. "They obviously don't know about that cubbyhole, or what Ralph was up to. We'll have customs men all over us if they find out. It's all in the past and they're going to pull this place down. So why don't we just let sleeping dogs lie?"

There was no sign of the fine weather ending. Fairhaven was still basking in unbroken sunshine, as David came out of the Wintergardens and crossed the Esplanade. Green and white deckchairs and windbreaks dotted the sand and the sea sparkled and glistened like molten glass. There were fewer holidaymakers now that the bank holiday was over and schools were about to reopen, but those still sunbathing and cavorting in the waves seemed determined to make the most of the last dregs of summer.

Ruby had been her usual exuberant and forthright self during lunch, but he had sensed that she had something on her mind that she hadn't mentioned. Recently opened between the theatre and the bandstand, 'Barnacle Bill's' specialised in locally caught crab and lobster. It consisted of a wooden cabin, with metal tables and chairs arranged beneath the trees on either side. It was a delightful way to enjoy a leisurely lunch on such a lovely day, although David doubted the viability of the business when inclement weather forced it to rely on the relatively few tables inside. The thought made him smile. "You're thinking like a real businessman, David."

He had learned from Ruby that Malky's plans for the new-look Jetstream were not progressing smoothly. Russ was having second thoughts about joining the group and had confessed to Ruby that he would be glad to see the back of Gloria, who had been acting the prima-donna and tormenting Malky with her demands. To further upset his applecart, Jenny O'Dell's manager had decided to relaunch her career with a more upbeat image and was trying to poach musicians to accompany her.

The Jetstream had only a week left of its contract with the Wintergardens Palace Theatre, but Ruby had shown none of her previous impatience over David's uncertainty about when he would be available, and had seemed uncharacteristically vague about what she planned to do in the meantime.

The sound of Russ Conway's *Side Saddle,* playing on the Beach Café's newly installed jukebox, brought to David's mind his Aunt Catherine; a classically trained pianist, who had given him his first piano lessons and nurtured his love of music. He chuckled as he remembered how she would sometimes delight him by suddenly switching from Chopin or Debussy to ragtime and honky-tonk.

He couldn't resist a sardonic smile as he noticed the banner draped across the open doorway, proclaiming: *Best Ice Cream Sundaes in Fairhaven*. "Good old Uncle Charlie," he chuckled. "You never let up, do you?"

It was also a reminder of how often the other Russ's name had cropped up during lunch. It seemed that Ruby was still in touch with him, even though he and Gloria had returned to Manchester.

David gazed around him contentedly; his spirits lifted by the sights and sounds of a sunny summer's day by the sea. It made the prospect of life as an itinerant musician less than appealing. He was tired of always moving on. The Rockhopper Café and Fairhaven felt like home, and the friendships he had made were precious. Most of all, there was someone in his life who made him want to stay.

It was Tilly's last day, and she was taking a late lunch break when he arrived back at the café. However, Stella and Jo were coping with what afternoon trade there was. Tilly had stayed on as long as possible but, understandably, she wanted to spend time with her parents before returning to finishing school. The customers would be sorry to see her go; and not just the young lads. Everyone would miss her amiable nature and eagerness to please. But no-one would miss her more than Stella, to whom she had become a mentor; almost a surrogate big sister.

It was amusing, but touching, to observe how Stella tried to copy the way Tilly dressed and emulated the way she dealt with customers; sometimes even the way she spoke. Tilly was obviously fond of Stella, too. Despite their very different backgrounds, they had become noticeably close. David sighed;

dreading the flood of tears he knew would accompany their parting. Despite her youth, Stella was gaining confidence and learning to cope with difficult and demanding customers on her own. It would break her heart when the café closed, as it would his to have to let her go.

"Can I leave you to manage while I pop home and get Tilly's cards and leaving present?" Jo asked.

David nodded. "Yes; go ahead."

Stella didn't seem to need any help looking after the few tables that were occupied, so he wandered outside and found a distinguished looking chap sitting at the red table, gazing with obvious amusement at Rocky and the specials menu chalked on his torso.

The man's white shirt was open at the neck and the cuffs were turned back, revealing what appeared to be an expensive gold wristwatch. A blue cashmere sweater was draped casually around his shoulders and his sunglasses were pushed up onto brown, wavy hair that was greying at the temples and brushed back in wings that touched the tips of his ears. In David's opinion, his appearance and bearing were those of someone to be reckoned with.

Suspecting that he may have something to do with the harbour redevelopment, David approached cautiously. "Good afternoon. What would you like, sir?"

"Good afternoon." The man's voice was modulated and cultured. "I rather think I'd like to try one of Tilly's exotic strawberry sundaes." He pronounced it deliberately and looked up with a smile; his eyes half closed against the glare of the sun. "Would I be correct in assuming you're David?"

With his curiosity aroused, David replied, "Yes; I am."

The man stood up and offered his hand. "I'm delighted to meet you, David. I've heard a great deal about you. Allow me to introduce myself. I'm Geoffrey Dennison; Tilly's father. I'm aware that I'm a little early to collect her, but I thought it would give me a chance to meet you and thank you."

His handshake was firm and steady, and David relaxed. "It's a pleasure to meet you, sir," he replied; adding with a chuckle, "Tilly's taking her lunch break at the moment. But I'm sure you'll enjoy the strawberry sundae. It's our speciality and Tilly's own recipe. I can promise you it will be delicious … and unique. There are hardly ever two the same."

Mister Dennison laughed heartily. "Knowing my little scatterbrain, I can believe it." Becoming serious, he added, "Allow me to thank you and your partner, David. We've heard so much about you all. Tilly has told us how kind you've been and how much she has enjoyed her time here."

"It's been a pleasure," David insisted. "I don't know what we would have done without her. She's been such a help getting the café up and running. She's worked so hard and stayed cheerful and helpful, no matter what. The customers love her."

"It's kind of you to say so. Thank you for looking after her. I must confess that Tilly's mother and I were more than a little concerned when we learned that she was working as a café waitress, but it seems to have been the making of her. We're delighted with the way she has matured during her time here. She's so proud of having earned her own money, for the first time in her life; and paying her own way." Mister Dennison grinned mischievously. "Up to a point, I might add. But I'm sure you know what I mean. She's told us of your kindness. I know she'll miss you all very much."

"And we'll miss her," said David. "Especially this young lady." He gestured to Stella, who was approaching with tea and scones for the white table.

"You must be Stella!" The exclamation startled her, and she looked at David enquiringly.

"This is Mister Dennison, Stella; Tilly's father."

Blushing deeply, Stella delivered the tea and scones and greeted Mister Dennison with what, to David, looked like a little bob. "Pleased to meet you," she said shyly.

"I'm delighted to meet you, Stella," said Mister Dennison. "I understand you and Tilly have become great friends. I know she'll miss you terribly."

Noticing tears well up in Stella's eyes, David came to her rescue. "Would you be an angel, Stella, and bring Mister Dennison one of Tilly's special sundaes?"

"Of course!" Her reply was almost a sob, as she turned away and hurried inside.

"*Daddy!*" Tilly's excited cry turned heads, as she skirted the tables outside The Packet Boat Inn and ran towards him. With a squeal of delight, she launched herself into her father's welcoming arms.

Watching father and daughter embrace, David reflected on how mistaken his notion of her parents had been. They were obviously very well off to be able to afford her fees at a Swiss finishing school; from which he had imagined they might be somewhat strict and authoritarian, as well as perhaps a little stuffy and snobbish. But Mister Dennison was none of those things. He seemed a friendly and likeable man, who clearly adored his daughter.

Stella returned with a strawberry sundae; her eyes betraying that they had shed tears. Taking her hand, Tilly exclaimed, "This is my friend Stella, Daddy!"

"We've already met," her father chuckled. Drawing a small package from his pocket, he winked and slipped it into Tilly's hand.

"This is for you," Tilly said quietly and handed it to Stella.

"Oh; thank you! I've got something for you. It's in my bag in the kitchen," Stella exclaimed breathlessly; her hands trembling as she unwrapped a small velvet covered box. Lifting the lid, she gasped as she gazed at the gold locket and chain.

Tilly giggled and lifted her own locket from her throat. "It's exactly the same as mine. Shall we put our photos in them? Then you won't forget me."

"I won't; I won't! I'll never forget you, Tilly!" Stella sobbed, clutching the locket as they hugged each other with tears coursing down their cheeks.

Feeling tears prick his own eyes, David was relieved to see a couple leave their table and move to the counter to pay. While he was at the till, Stella scurried past to the kitchen; returning almost immediately with her gift for Tilly. When he went outside again, Tilly's father was tucking into his strawberry sundae with obvious relish, and Tilly was helping Stella fasten the clasp of her locket chain. He recognised the silver charm bracelet glinting on Tilly's wrist as one she had admired in Gemma's window. David guessed it must have cost Stella, what to her, was a considerable amount of money.

Tilly dabbed at her eyes with a paper napkin. "I really must get back to work."

"Why don't you sit down with your father and let me bring you something?" David suggested. "Your duties are officially over Miss Dennison. Consider yourself an honoured guest of the establishment."

Tilly replied with a giggle and an angelic, if watery, smile.

Mister Dennison pointed his spoon towards the mole. "That chap with the easel. Would he, by any chance, be the artist who painted Tilly's portrait?"

David nodded. "Yes; that's Chris!"

"I'd very much like to meet him. Our friends greatly admire it. I'd like to congratulate him."

"When you're ready, I'll introduce you," said David.

Mister Dennison patted his stomach. "I'm ready now. I don't think I can finish this; delicious as it is."

David tapped Stella on the shoulder. "Things are pretty quiet here, and Jo will be back any minute, so why don't you sit down and keep Tilly company, while I introduce Mister Dennison to Chris."

As they walked towards the mole, David heard Tilly say, "Here's my address in Switzerland. Will you write to me sometimes and let me know what you're doing and how you're getting on? I know your address, so I'll do the same."

'I hope they do keep in touch,' he mused.

Unaware that he had said it out loud, he was startled when Mister Dennison replied: "I'm sure they will."

"Well; if it isn't Fairhaven's own Elvis!" Chris exclaimed, as he saw them approach. "And who have you brought to worship at the feet of the master?"

David grimaced at Tilly's father and shrugged. "I'm sorry; I should have warned you."

After the introductions, David left them and returned to the café. He hadn't expected Jo to take long to cycle home and collect Tilly's leaving presents, but she was still missing and Tilly and Stella were serving customers.

Another half an hour passed before she arrived with Richard, giggling girlishly, and with her eyes twinkling.

"You took your time! What kept you?" he asked tersely.

A look passed between her and Richard that started them both laughing.

"What's so funny?"

"I'll tell you when my nerves stop jangling," Richard chortled. "Right now I could do with a drink!"

"Help yourself," said David tetchily.

"No; I mean a good stiff drink!"

It prompted another peal of laughter from Jo. "Richard has just given me a driving lesson!" she exclaimed, her eyes sparkling with mirth. "I almost scared him to death!"

Laughter from Tilly and her father irritated David even more. "Couldn't you have done that some other time?" he growled.

"It was only for half an hour or so!" Richard insisted. "I think Jo spent less time driving than it took to adjust the seat so that she could reach the pedals."

It prompted more laughter from everyone, except David.

"What do you drive?" Mister Dennison asked.

"I've got an MG TF," Richard replied. "Jo had problems with the clutch. I'd swear we left the ground more than once. It felt more like being on a bucking bronco than in a car."

It elicited another giggle from Jo, and a chuckle from Tilly's father.

With a meaningful look at David, Richard said, "It looks like *I'll* have to introduce us. I'm Richard; David's brother. And this is Jo, his business partner … the sensible half of the partnership."

Swallowing resentment, David moved away to greet some arriving customers. It was the same old story: Richard, charming and witty; the centre of attention, and *he* the butt of the jokes. Even more galling was the fact that Richard's 'magic' worked on Jo.

As David had feared, Tilly's farewell was protracted and tearful. Throughout the rest of the afternoon, friends, acquaintances and a few of their regular customers came to wish her well. Mervin, Bernard and a few more dancers called in, as did Grace and Victor Sullivan, who presented her with a bag of her favourite sweets and sticks of rock with *Tilly* and *Rockhopper Café* running through them. Avril and Wally brought her a bouquet of flowers and a fluffy toy penguin that was instantly christened Rocky. Gemma gave her a necklace made of delicate silvery leaves, while Chris provoked another flood of tears when he surprised her with a little watercolour of The Rockhopper Café. Sammy seemed no less affected than everyone else. He had 'chipped in', as he put it, with Connie and Linda, towards a silk scarf. His response to a farewell peck on the cheek was an embarrassed, "Look after y'self, girl."

Tilly's gift from Jo and David was a bonus in her pay packet and a transistor radio. The idea came to Jo when she remembered how Tilly used to sing along to David's little Grundig.

In return, Tilly had a gift for each of her colleagues; David's being a pair of enamel penguin cuff links. Like everyone else, he was near to tears when she and her father finally took their leave.

Later, when the café had closed for the day, he sat outside in the evening sunshine. His throat tightened as he remembered Tilly and Stella clinging to each other in a final heart-breaking embrace; and Stella standing outside the pub, sobbing and waving, until Mister Dennison's car had turned off the Esplanade and disappeared from view.

Amid the flow of tears, Tilly's parting words to David and Jo had been, "I've had such a *wonderful* time! I'm so sorry this lovely café has to close. *It's so unfair!*" Handing David a card bearing her address and telephone number, she had pleaded, "Please keep in touch. Let me know how you are and what you're all doing. And ... and, if you open another café, will you let me come and work for you again?"

"Of course!" he had replied, although there wouldn't be another Rockhopper Café. Accepting that his hopes and dreams had crumbled to dust did nothing to ease David's despondency. Nor had watching Richard and Jo leave together, with Richard continuing to tease her about her driving, while she gazed up at him, laughing delightedly; for all the world like ... he could hardly bear to think it ... like a girl in love.

It was to be expected that it would feel strange without Tilly's irrepressible cheerfulness and amiability. To David, it seemed odd not to hear her polished accent and the infectious giggle that brought a smile to everyone's face. Stella was polite and helpful to the customers, but her usual sparkle was missing. The strawberry season, prolonged by the long, sunny summer and Ginny's green fingers, had finally come to an end. But having been taught by Tilly, Stella could still concoct other varieties of ice cream sundae. In an attempt to cheer her up, David had replaced the 'special' chalked on Rocky's chest with *Stella's Tropical Ice Cream Sundaes.*

However, Tilly's departure was an unwelcome reminder that the café's days were coming to an end; bringing down the curtain on one of the happiest times of his life. The clientele now included a sizeable number of local regulars; perhaps enough to justify staying open until the compulsory purchase order arrived. But his heart wouldn't be in it. There was no point in putting off the inevitable, and he didn't think he could bear to watch the breakup of the harbour community that was now so dear to him.

Ruby Red no longer seemed so appealing, but he had no other option and he couldn't keep Ruby hanging on much longer. So it was better to make a clean break from Fairhaven … and soon.

That wasn't all that was troubling him. When Mister Dennison had asked Richard what he did for a living, he had explained that he was the general manager of an engineering company, based in Earls Court. It had prompted Jo to ask if that was anywhere near Bayswater. She had explained that Colin had left behind a brochure about the private clinic in Leeds, where he wanted her to work. Her remark, *It says they're opening a new clinic in London … in Bayswater*, hadn't registered as anything other than a casual comment at the time. But the more David thought about it, the more it played on his mind; especially after watching her and Richard leave together. Was she planning to follow him to London?

David's thoughts were interrupted by Avril's sudden arrival. "Can I have quick word with Connie?" she asked. "I want to ask her if she'll make a cake for me."

"Of course," said David. "Have a seat and I'll get her. Do you fancy a cup of tea or coffee?"

Avril smiled appreciatively. "Thanks, love. I'll have a coffee, please."

She and Connie were sitting in the sunlight at the white table when David brought their coffees. Placing them on the table with a theatrical flourish, he adopted a comic French accent to enquire, "Would ze belles mademoiselles like somesing else?"

"No thanks," Connie giggled.

"I was just thinkin' how odd it feels without Tilly," Avril observed. "But I can see you're determined to keep everybody's spirits up."

"It'll take a while to get used to not having her around," David said ruefully. "We all feel it; Stella most of all."

A little later, when the other outside tables were unoccupied and he was sure that Stella could cope with the customers inside, he asked, "Could you spare me a minute, Avril; if you and Connie have finished your business?"

"Of course, love!" she replied.

Connie picked up her cup and saucer and started to rise.

"No; don't go, Connie," he said. "This concerns you, too." He sat down with them, making sure Stella wasn't within earshot before he began. "You and Wally have a lot of friends and business acquaintances around here, haven't you, Avril? I was wondering if you'd help me try and find something suitable for Stella, when we close up here for good. I'd like to help Sammy find something too, but I know that'll be more difficult."

Avril patted his hand affectionately. "Of course! She's a smashin' kid, and a real worker! I'll ask around for her; and Sammy, as well."

"Thanks. I can't just leave them in the lurch. They've been absolute bricks! We'd never have managed without them. I'd like to help them find somewhere they'll be happy … and appreciated."

Turning his attention to Connie, he added, "I'm not forgetting you, but I realise you may have different ideas about what you want to do. Let's face it, you never intended to work all the hours you have, did you? "

To his surprise, Connie's eyes brimmed with tears. "Don't forget there's someone else you need to look out for. Just make sure you look after yourself, as well!"

"Don't worry about me," he said airily. "I'll manage. I always do."

"Will you?" Connie challenged. "We both know what you want, and it's not traipsing around the country with a rock and roll band!"

Caught off guard, David resorted to his customary method of self-defence. "You never know; Ruby might beat some sense into me."

"You can joke all you like, but I'm right, aren't I?" Pulling a handkerchief from her sleeve, Connie dabbed at her eyes. "Why do you think Stella and Tilly … and Sammy … have worked so hard? Why do you think I've been working damned-near full time? We've been well paid, but that's not the reason. We've done it *for you*!" Wiping her eyes again, she continued, "Jo's done her share, on top of her job, but it's *you* who made it such a happy place to work. You've looked after everybody. Sammy will never forget what you've done for him and his sister! You kept us all cheerful; encouraged the girls and gave them confidence … and made us laugh. We've been like a family. It's been a joy to work here!"

"Connie's right," Avril concurred. "We've all seen it. Wally was only sayin' the other day what a lift it gave the harbour when you and Jo opened this café again. People have commented on what a lovely atmosphere there is in here."

Taken aback, David replied, "I don't know what to say. I can't claim to know what I was doing. Jo and I made it up as we went along."

"You two have done wonders with this place!" Avril insisted. "We hoped you might become more than business partners."

The whine of an approaching milk float gave David an excuse to avoid a response. Hastily getting up from his seat, he said, "Sorry, ladies. Will you excuse me? The milkman needs paying."

"So, tomorrow's the big day," Chris declared, spooning sugar into his tea. "I must say you look as fit as a butcher's dog."

Richard smiled appreciatively. "Thanks; I feel it. I just hope to God they sign me off and let me get back to work. As much as I've enjoyed spending a few weeks with my little brother, I'm raring to get back into harness."

"It can't have been bad having a dishy little nurse to look after you, either," Chris chortled.

Richard smiled. "It certainly hasn't. Jo and Ginny have looked after me very well. I'm nearly back to what I weighed before my illness. Another few months and I'd be a real porker!"

"Lucky you!" David hadn't meant to speak his thoughts. It had been an instinctive reaction, born out of resentment and, he had to admit, jealousy. Wishing his remark hadn't sounded so bitter, he continued to clear the red table.

Chris raised his eyebrows. "Oh dear; do I detect the green-eyed monster rearing its ugly head?"

Richard unwittingly forestalled David's intended suggestion that Chris should keep his trap shut for once, with the observation, "They'd have done the same for you, David."

"Do you think so?" he replied, trying to appear indifferent.

"Of course they would. What makes you think they wouldn't?"

"Well, for a start, Aunt Ginny's not exactly my biggest fan."

Richard looked bemused. "What makes you think that? I've never heard her say anything derogatory about you!"

"She doesn't need to!" David retorted and emptied an ashtray into an old ice cream carton. "It comes over loud and clear. I'm the last person she'd have as a lodger."

"That's nonsense!" Richard refuted. "I can't imagine where you get that idea from."

"Can't you?" David exclaimed. "How many times do you think they've offered *me* a meal? I'll tell you; *none!* I've only ever been in the house twice; when I picked Jo up to go to Avril's birthday party, and when you asked me to make sure that Ginny was happy for you to stay there!"

"I'm sure it's not intentional." Richard insisted. "I'm positive they never meant you to feel unwelcome. You've always got something going on. Rehearsing for that swish party; playing your guitar in the pub; sorting out your pal's group at the theatre; seeing Ruby…"

Embarrassed by his outburst, David mumbled, "Forget it, Rich. It's not important. I'm grateful to them for looking after you." Adopting a more conciliatory tone, he asked, "What's your new flat like?"

Pleasure replaced concern in Richard's expression. "It's in Richmond upon Thames."

"I know Richmond well," Chris declared. "I used to share a houseboat on the Thames with several other impoverished coves during my student days. Delightful in summer, but brass monkeys in winter!"

Richard nodded. "I can imagine. I had a look at one or two flats the other day, when I visited my colleagues at work. To see if they still remembered me," he added flippantly. "The flat I've gone for is well equipped, with a view of the river. It comes with a lock-up garage at the rear, which is a boon. The landlord seems pretty decent, too."

"I can recommend a few pubs," Chris proposed.

Richard chuckled. "That'll come in handy." Turning his attention back to David, he said, "I'll be off for good on Saturday morning, regardless of the hospital's verdict. I can't move into my new flat for another week or so, but I don't feel I can impose on Ginny's hospitality any longer. I'll stay with Mum and Dad, and sort out all the stuff they've been keeping for me."

"I'll bet they can't wait to get their spare bedrooms back," David quipped. Picking up his tray and the carton of rubbish, he left Richard and Chris discussing the attractions of Richmond upon Thames.

* * *

Richard was helping Stella look after the customers while David snatched a few moments for a late lunch, when Archie appeared with a cheery, "Watcha, Dave!" and an expression that suggested he was far too pleased with himself for comfort; David's in particular.

"Hello, Archie. Nice to see you. What can I do for you?" David enquired warily.

"That's very civil of you, mate," Archie replied. "I'll have a Tizer and a cream slice."

David rose from his seat stifling a smile. It was almost possible to admire Archie's cheek … almost.

"I'll get it," Richard called.

David sat down again. "So what's put that smile on your face? Got a hot date with Dorothy?"

"Leave off!" Archie growled, before his face broke into another broad grin. "Guess what!"

"I can't," David replied. "Surprise me."

Archie leaned forward conspiratorially. "Well; Declan, that's Jenny O'Dell's manager, wants to liven up her act and get her doing a bit more upbeat stuff. He's forming a group to back her."

"I know; Ruby told me."

Archie held up a hand. "Wait! Here's the best bit. Guess who Declan's asked to help him get her backing group together?"

Unable to resist it, David replied, "Colonel Parker?"

"Who?"

"Colonel Tom Parker; Elvis's manager."

"No, yuh prawn! *Yours Truly!* We're gonna be…" Archie paused dramatically. "Jenny O'Dell and the Meadowlanders! Whaddya think of that?"

"I'm really happy for you, Archie."

"Sorry, mate. It means I'm not gonna be able to help you out with your group," Archie declared, with all the remorse he could feign. He looked up with a cocky grin as Richard brought his pastry and Tizer. "Cheers, squire."

Exchanging a sardonic smile with his brother, David replied, "That's a shame. But don't worry; I understand. I'm sure Joel and Ruby will too."

"Yeh; they're fine with it," Archie declared and took a large bite of his cream slice. Brushing a shower of pastry flakes from his shirt, he swallowed noisily before adding, "Especially now Russ Pakenham's joining your group."

"You what!?" David sat bolt upright and stared at Archie in astonishment.

Archie looked genuinely surprised. "Didn't you know? Russ has jacked it in with The Rocking Redwings. He's given Gloria the elbow, too. Mind you I can understand that. She's a real belter; but a right pain in the khyber!"

"Who *says* he's joining Ruby Red?" David demanded.

"Ruby told me," Archie mumbled through a mouthful of cream slice. Washing it down with Tizer, he added. "If you want my advice, you wanna watch that Russ. I reckon he's got his eye on Rube."

* * *

David left the telephone box and returned to the café with his thoughts and emotions in confusion. Contrary to his expectation, Ruby hadn't reacted aggressively when he had phoned her at her digs. In fact, she had been apologetic when he had challenged her about inviting Russ to join the group without consulting him. Her explanation, that a duo consisting of just bass and drums would find it difficult to find work, had made sense.

She had also explained that Russ knew the owners of a lot of clubs and dance halls in and around Manchester. So her idea was that the three of them would keep Ruby Red going until David joined them. As a sweetener, she had added the flattering suggestion that, as he had a better voice than Russ, he could do most of the vocals.

It had all seemed logical. David had wanted to be convinced; and he almost had been, until he had made himself ask, "What about you and Russ?"

"Me ... and Russ?" she had replied hesitantly.

"Yes. Is there anything between you two that I should know about?" Interrupting the ensuing silence he had insisted, "Tell me the truth, Ruby."

The catch in her voice had given him the answer before she replied, "Sorry, David. It just sort of happened. I was going to tell you, but I didn't know how ... I'm *so* sorry!"

The voice had seemed to come from elsewhere, as he heard himself say quietly, "OK; I just needed to know."

"Are you still coming?" she had asked tearfully.

"I don't know, Ruby," he had murmured. "I just don't know."

Hooky picked up David's glass and held it under the best better tap. "How much longer d'you reckon on keepin' your place open?" he asked.

"That's the sixty-four thousand dollar question," David sighed. "I'll need to discuss it with Jo, but there doesn't seem to be much point in keeping it open much longer. I'd like to try and get Stella and Sammy settled somewhere first, though."

Hooky frowned thoughtfully. "It won't be easy in Sammy's case."

"I know," David conceded. "But I owe it to him to try. I realise his leg is going to be a problem. But he's smartened himself up a lot recently, and I can hand-on-heart give him a good reference. He makes sure the kitchen and the equipment are left clean and tidy these days."

Hooky placed a full pint in front of David. "So 'e should after all you've done for 'im. You know Wally banned 'im, don't you?"

David stared at him in surprise. "No, I didn't! Sammy's never mentioned it."

"Yeh; it was before you came. Made a ruddy nuisance of 'imself; tryin' to cadge fags and drinks off the boys."

"That's a shame," said David, as it dawned on him that he had never seen Sammy in The Packet Boat Inn. "Things can't have been easy for him. He and his sister were living from hand to mouth when I came here. His sister can't work; she relies on him for everything. Losing even the pittance my uncle probably paid him must have been a blow for them."

Wally's head appeared above the cellar hatch. "I take it you're talkin' about Sammy Althrop."

"Yes," said David. "I didn't know you'd barred him."

"Yeh; it was a while ago now." Wally closed the hatch behind him and stroked his beard pensively. "Might 'ave t'see what we can do about that, if 'e promises to behave 'imself."

"Any news of Richard's hospital appointment?" Avril called from the Wardroom.

"No; I expected him to show up before now," David replied. "I'll go and phone to see if he's back when I've finished my drink."

Wally nodded in the direction of the living quarters. "Use the one upstairs."

While he waited for his call to be answered, David's attention was drawn to the framed photographs on the sideboard next to the telephone. The largest was of Avril and Wally, arm-in-arm and smiling outside what appeared to be a register office, on their wedding day. As always, Avril was immaculately dressed in a pale, two-piece suit with a little lacy hat worn rakishly at an angle. Wally was impressively attired in naval uniform. They looked young and happy, and in love; something that David was beginning to wonder if he would ever experience.

"Hello; Virginia Trafford speaking."

Aunt Ginny's voice startled him. "Oh ... um ... It's David; David Sheldon. Would it be possible to speak to Richard, please?"

"I'm afraid they're not back yet, David."

"I see. I was hoping to find out how his examination went," David explained, before his mind registered that she had said *they're* not back.

"Well, I can put your mind at rest," Ginny replied. "Jo called earlier. She said it was very successful. He's been cleared to go back to work. Jo thinks her interview went well, too. I believe they're calling in to see your parents on the way home."

David felt his scalp tingle. "Her *interview*?"

"Yes." Ginny hesitated. "Didn't she tell you? She's applied for a position at a private clinic in London."

"No; she didn't tell me." Afraid that his voice would break and betray him, he mumbled, "Thanks for letting me know about Richard."

He replaced the receiver and stood there, trembling and staring vacantly into space, while he struggled to control his emotions. Somehow, he had to hold on and hide his distress from Avril. If he couldn't, she would demand to know the reason. So might Hooky and Wally. He didn't want their sympathy or their pity. Neither would take away the heartache nor help him come to terms with losing Jo … to his brother.

After a restless night, David felt as if he were sleepwalking through the day. Tired and demoralised, he was wearily serving customers, operating the till and dispensing ice cream with almost robotic detachment. Thankfully, Stella had recovered some of her exuberance, which prevented the mood in the café resembling a wake.

He wasn't in the right frame of mind to speak to her and Sammy about closing the café, although he couldn't put it off much longer. They both knew its days were numbered, but it was only fair to warn them that, come what may, he intended to close the place for good in a week or two. Sammy would probably accept it stoically, but David didn't doubt that it would open the floodgates on Stella's grief. All he could do to soften the blow was assure them that he would do everything he could to help them find new employment.

The morning came and went without a visit from Richard, but David had no intention of phoning him again. Aunt Ginny must have mentioned that she had passed on the good news, but he would still have expected his brother to want to tell him personally.

It was late afternoon and Jo would be off duty, but he didn't expect to see her before the café closed; if at all. Not that she was needed. Linda had agreed to help out in the afternoons while they remained in business. The school holidays were over, so she and Stella were coping quite comfortably without much help from him. With little to do, he decided to take a stroll along the promenade in the hope that it might help him clear his mind.

The sun was still shining, but the breeze had died, leaving the atmosphere heavy and sultry. Illuminated by the sun, a bank of menacing cloud shrouded the horizon. Glowing in angry shades of black and purple, it dimmed the shimmer of the tranquil waves out beyond the headlands; threatening to end the weeks of unbroken sunshine with one of the heavy storms that so often follow spells of very warm weather. So, he would probably leave Fairhaven as he had arrived; in the rain.

The almost unnatural stillness was suddenly shattered by a heart-stopping roar, as two Hawker Hunter jet fighters streaked low overhead and out to sea, with sunlight glinting from their cockpit canopies. David hadn't particularly enjoyed national service, but he felt pride in their grace and power; the RAF roundels arousing a momentary pang of nostalgia.

A shriek of, "Oh my Gawd! I thought me number was up!" from a woman collecting photographs from the Happy Snaps kiosk brought a smile to his face. With his curiosity aroused, he stopped to look at the snapshots displayed in the glass-fronted panels all around it. They included the usual family groups, couples strolling arm-in-arm and individuals striking comical poses; all taken by an annoyingly persistent *Flash Harry* whose trademark was a pork pie hat and a variety of fancy waistcoats. Prowling the sea front, he took unsolicited snaps of holidaymakers, which he then tried to cajole them into buying from the kiosk.

David was about to walk away, when the photograph of a couple kissing caught his eye. It had been taken from behind the girl, whose hair masked the chap's face, which she was cradling between her hands. Something about them looked familiar and, taking a closer look, he held his breath. There could be no mistake … it was Richard and Jo.

Dazed, and with his emotions in turmoil, he leaned on the promenade railings and gazed out to sea. There was no longer any possibility that his fears might be unfounded. What a fool he was to have allowed himself to hope when Jo finished with Colin. Had he really been stupid enough to believe he stood a chance with her? Especially with his brother around. Admitting it did nothing to assuage his misery, but somehow he had to come to terms with it... if only for their sake. Although God-only knew how!

It occurred to him that perhaps Richard had been waiting until Jo finished work, so that they could tell him *all their news*, together. A sudden thought elicited a bitter snort of self-mockery. Neither Jo nor Ruby had really *been* his, but even so, 'losing' two girls in as many days was some going; even for him.

Richard's car was parked in the bay beside the mole when David arrived back at the harbour. One door of the café was open, but the 'closed' sign was displayed on the other, despite normal closing time being fifteen minutes away. Jo and Richard were the only ones inside; both with their backs to the entrance. Jo was sitting on the stool at the counter, with Richard standing beside her, looking over her shoulder at something she appeared to have in her hand.

David's heart was pounding, and he paused to control his breathing before going in. Both of them looked up sharply; Jo twisting round and greeting him with a welcoming smile.

"Hello, Little Brother; where have you been?" Richard called cheerily.

"I was about to ask you the same question."

"Sorry, David. I would have come before, but it was too late when we got back last night. The car's radiator sprang a leak on the way. I managed to nurse it back here, but there was a puddle under it this morning. I need it over the weekend, so I had to get it seen to in a hurry."

David nodded understandingly. "Is it OK now?"

"Yes; for the time being. Ginny's neighbour put me on to a garage in Myrtlesham. The chap there said that if I got it to them straightaway they'd patch it up until I could get it repaired properly. I had to stop a couple of times on the way to top up the rad, and it took longer to fix than I expected. So, when the car was ready, I hung on and picked Jo up from work." Taking a sip from his glass, he added, "If you were on the phone, I could have rung you and let you know."

David shrugged. "There's no point bothering for the short time we're here. But even if we'd applied for one, you can bet the Post Office wouldn't have got round to installing it yet."

It brought a smile from Richard. "You're probably right. But Ginny said she'd told you they've given me the all clear. So it wasn't as if you didn't know."

"Yes; I'm really glad, Rich … and relieved. We all are." He gestured towards the doorway. "Why have you closed early?"

"We only closed a few minutes ago," Jo said defensively. "There were no customers and Stella wanted to get away early, so I let them all go. You don't mind, do you?"

"No; I just wondered."

They were distracted by Avril appearing in the doorway with the greeting, "Hello, my loves. Sorry to interrupt." Looking meaningfully at Richard, she said, "Could I have a word with you, when you've got a minute?"

"Of course. How about now?" In response to her conspiratorial nod, Richard looked at Jo and David and raised his eyebrows before following her out onto the quay.

"I wonder what that's all about," Jo giggled.

She was wearing a primrose summer dress; and with that raven hair, her radiant smile and those sparkling, doe eyes, David thought she had never looked lovelier. He had to swallow to clear the lump in his throat before he could speak. "I hear you're moving to London."

"Possibly." She pursed her lips. "If I get the job at The Hugo Levingarde Clinic. I've had an interview. I've just got to wait for them to check up on me and decide if I'm suitable."

"Your aunt said your interview went well. Where are you going to live?"

"That depends." She hesitated. "Richard's promised to help."

David managed a weak smile. "I see. It's expensive to live in London."

She nodded. "I know; but the money's really good. Much better than the National Health Service pays; and I'll get a London living allowance."

David's deepening despondency wouldn't allow him to let it rest. "How does Aunt Ginny feel about it?"

Jo clasped her hands in front of her. "She understands. She's been thinking of getting somewhere smaller, anyway. It was in her mind when she thought I might marry Colin. The house is too big for the two of us, so it certainly will be for her on her own." As if anticipating his next question, she added, "I just feel it's time for a change. I thought about it a few years ago, but did nothing about it. Now seems the right time."

Breathing rapidly, and with his pulse racing, David croaked, "At least you'll have Richard to look after you."

"I suppose so," she murmured, and held out the photograph she had been holding. "What do you think of this?"

"It's a car."

"Clever you," she chuckled.

"A shooting brake," he added. "It looks like a Morris Traveller. Are you thinking of buying it?"

"I was thinking of you, actually," she replied. "One of the anaesthetists at Myrtlesham Gen is selling it. It belonged to his dad, who died recently. He'll accept a reasonable offer. He says it's in good condition and it's been serviced regularly."

"Well, he would wouldn't he?" David replied peevishly. "What made you think I'd want it?"

Jo ignored his touchiness. "Richard said you can drive, so I thought it might be handy for you and Ruby to carry all your equipment around in. The extra room and the doors at the back would make it easy for you to get everything in, wouldn't it?"

"I would have thought it would be more use to you," he answered moodily. "Now you're having driving lessons."

Jo's smile faded. "What's that supposed to mean?"

"Nothing; I was just saying…"

"It isn't *nothing*, is it?" she asserted. "You're obviously still annoyed because I was late getting back the other day!"

"No I'm not! But you knew it was Tilly's last day!"

Jo exhaled audibly with exasperation. "How was I to know her father was coming early? She wasn't ready to go when we got here, anyway!"

David shrugged dismissively. "Forget it."

"Forget it? *You* obviously haven't! Richard offered me a lift to save me having to carry Tilly's presents, and I happened to mention that I'd never driven a car. Just for fun, he let me have a go on that unused road behind the empty furniture warehouse. It was a bit of fun … for a few minutes; that's all!"

"Alright; alright." Taking her change of mood as a warning, David was ready to draw a line under the issue.

But Jo wasn't easily appeased. "And another thing. What's all this about you complaining that I've never invited you home for a meal?"

Taken by surprise, David's immediate instinct was to deny it. "I've done no such thing!"

She looked at him searchingly. "That's not what Gemma told me. She said Chris thinks you're feeling left out."

David felt his cheeks flush. "Well, Chris should mind his own damned business! So should Gemma. Richard was going on about how well you've fed him. All I said was: lucky you. That's all." His protestation didn't sound convincing, even to him.

"We weren't leaving you out!" she insisted. "You're always doing something. But you're welcome to come for a meal, if you want to."

"I don't!" His reply had been sharper than he intended, but increasing despair was fuelling resentment. "Can we change the subject?"

"Suit yourself," she replied flatly. "Alright; changing the subject. Can I ask when you're thinking of leaving?"

"Soon!"

"That's a fat lot of help! How *soon* is soon? There's a heck of a lot to do. We've got to make our minds up about when we're going to close this place; and we ought to give Stella and Sammy proper notice … and Connie!"

"Oh; thank you *so much* for enlightening me!" David snorted. "Of course, that never occurred to me!" He sighed with irritation. "Do you honestly think I haven't considered all that, and what it'll do to Stella and Sammy; especially Sammy? How is he going to get another job in a hurry with that gammy leg?"

"I wasn't suggesting you hadn't thought about it!" she snapped. "But we've got to get things straight in our minds and decide what we're going to do … and when. There's a heck of a lot to think about, David!"

"I know that. I don't need telling!"

Jo continued undaunted. "What I'm saying is: we've got to run down the stock. And we need to know where we stand with Delrio and the other wholesalers. There's all the kitchen equipment, the tables and chairs, the till and all the other odds and ends to get rid of. Then there's…"

"I know! I know! *I've* been running this ruddy place all summer; in case you haven't noticed!"

Jo stared at him, her eyes flashing angrily. "Yes; I have noticed! And I've done as much as I can! *I've* taken care of the paperwork and kept an eye on our finances. *I've* done the banking and paid the bills, as well as working here when I can. But I've got a full-time job, in case *you* haven't noticed! I can't work twenty-four hours a day!"

"I'm not suggesting you can!" David retorted. "But it hasn't been a picnic for me either. I know what I'm doing. I have no illusions about how much there is to do before I can *get the hell out of here … and away from this godforsaken place!*"

Jo's eyes brimmed with tears. "So that's how you feel, is it?

"*You bet!* I can't wait to get away from Fairhaven … and everything to do with it! I've worked my tail off-seven days a week … ten hours a day; damned-near every day since we opened. So the last thing I need is a lecture from you!"

"I'm not lecturing you. I…"

Tormented by anguish and heartache, David gave her no chance to continue. "OK; you asked me when I was planning to leave. So, let me ask you when *you* plan on leaving. You obviously didn't think I had the right to know that you intended to. But now I do, it would be nice to be given an idea when!"

She paused before answering. "I was going to tell you. But I wasn't sure I wanted the job … and I don't know if I've got it yet. I thought you'd probably go before me, anyway. So, to answer your question, *I* don't know either."

"Well; now we've started the ball rolling, let's suppose *you do* get the job. When do you *think* they'll want you to start?"

Jo hesitated. "I don't know. They mentioned the beginning of next month, but…"

"*Next month?* Just who do you suppose is going to sort everything out when you've gone swanning off to London with my brother? Me; Billy Muggins, I presume!"

Jo's response was swift and furious. "I'm *not* expecting you to do it all! And I'm *not* swanning off to London with your brother!"

"Oh, really?" What would you call it, then?" David demanded. "You're as bad as Colin; expecting me to dance to your tune, while you do whatever you want to!"

"*How dare you!*" Tears streamed down Jo's cheeks while her eyes blazed with fury. "Just shut up about Colin! I thought we could talk sensibly about how we were going manage it all. But you … you never listen; *Mister Know-it-all*! You shout your big mouth off and start bandying accusations around … about things you know *nothing* about!"

Stung by the vehemence of her outburst, David yelled, "Don't I? I know when I'm being taken for a fool!"

"So you should! I'm sure you've had plenty of experience of it. Because that's just what you are!"

"I was a fool to trust you!"

"*Shut up! Just shut up!*" she shrieked. Picking up her bag, she slid off the stool. "I don't want to hear any more! *I've had enough!*" Sobbing uncontrollably, she ran to the doorway. "Do what you like with this place. *I don't bloody-well care!*"

Her distress brought him to his senses. "Come on Jo; that's not going to solve anything is it?"

"*Drop dead!*"

The door slammed behind her with a crash that threatened to break the glass panes and loosen the hinges. It was still reverberating when Richard opened it again.

"What going on?" he exclaimed. "What the hell have you done? Jo just ran past me crying her eyes out!"

Fighting back his own tears, David growled a warning. "Not now, Rich. Now's not the time."

Richard shook his head. "You really are a prize chump, David! You never learn, do you?" He sighed resignedly. "I'd better go and catch up with Jo. I'll see you tomorrow morning, before I go."

David waited for his brother to close the door behind him before subsiding onto a chair. Resting his elbows on a table, he held his head in his hands and gave way to grief.

XIV

It was still dark when David woke, aware that something had roused him from fitful sleep. For a few moments he lay still, listening intently. But all he could hear above the comforting sigh of the sea was the rapid ticking of his alarm clock and the occasional slap of water against the hull of a vessel in the harbour. As his eyes adjusted to the gloom, the shadowy outlines of his bedroom furniture took shape in the glimmer of pallid light seeping through the curtains. But there were no shadows in his mind to dim the memory of Jo's anguish as she had fled from the café.

In the words of the song: you always hurt the one you love, and lashing out in despair with those cruel and spiteful accusations was exactly what he had done. There was so much he wanted to say; wished he had said. Telling her he loved her would only have embarrassed both of them, and sown the seed of future awkwardness if she became Richard's wife. But he could have tried to explain in other ways how much his time with her meant to him, and that he would always treasure what they had achieved together.

A flicker of intense light lit up the window, followed seconds later by a dull rumble somewhere out at sea. The brewing storm was finally heralding the end of 'the endless summer' and sweeping away the last remnants of his hopes and dreams. There was no silver lining to the clouds that darkened his future. This time his stupidity had surpassed all previous folly.

He couldn't blame Jo for falling for his brother. Richard charmed everyone with effortless ease. He was charismatic, steady and dependable, and had a well-paid career that would assure his wife and family the good things in life. Whereas David was all too aware that he had nothing to offer, and that his 'talent' was to unerringly say or do the wrong thing, at the wrong time. He certainly couldn't blame Richard for falling in love with Jo.

Another flash of lightning lit up the room; followed almost immediately by a clap of thunder that resounded across the bay in a rolling, sonorous boom. In its wake, a patter of raindrops quickly became the hiss of a downpour, before intensifying into the sibilant roar of a deluge. The billowing curtains and the splatter of rain on the bedroom floor prompted David to get up and close the window. As he did so, he was startled by another blinding flash that illuminated the rain-lashed harbour in a spectral glare; momentarily silhouetting vessels bucking at their moorings and masts spiralling against the blackness of the sky. The accompanying crack of thunder was ear-splitting; rattling windows and reverberating like a broadside of cannon fire. Blowing in ferocious gusts, the wind buffeted the buildings; hurling rain against the windows in torrents, and sending anything not tied down clattering and careering across the quay.

David switched on the light and glanced at the clock; nearly half-past two. Haunted by shame and remorse, and with the storm raging outside, he knew it was no use trying to go back to sleep. So he went down to the kitchen and made a pot of coffee. Returning with it to the living room, he settled himself at the table and tore open the envelope he had found on the counter after Jo and Richard had left. Associating brown envelopes with trouble, he had ignored it. But looking more closely, he noticed that this one simply had his name hand-written on it. Taking out the letter, he smiled ruefully at what he supposed could be called a 'Dear John'. Ruby wrote as she spoke, almost without pause and with the minimum of punctuation.

Dear David

> *Joel and I are off to Manchester to join Russ tomorrow after the last performance of The Jetstream and I haven't been able to stop thinking about you and your phone call. I know I should have explained things to you to your face. I wanted to but I knew it would be too hard to do. So I chickened out and got one of the stagehands to deliver this letter for me. I am sorry if you think I have been devious. But it just sort of happened between Russ and me before we knew it really. I think it might work out for us I really hope it does. The offer to join Ruby Red still stands anytime you like. There is an address and telephone number where I can be contacted on the back of this letter. I would love you to join us but I don't think you will. You were never serious about you and me were you? I could tell by the way you talked about her and I saw the way you looked at her when you introduced us. Well you know what they say about faint heart and fair lady Go get her David. Well, that's about all. A million thanks for everything I have loved the time we had together. We made some good music together didn't we? I really hope everything works out for you. Please keep in touch.*
>
> *God Bless*
> *Ruby x x x*
> *PS Joel says Hi*
> *PS2 Wring every penny you can get out of the greedy sods who are after your cafe*

"God bless you too, Ruby," he said quietly. "I will keep in touch." He chuckled to himself as a thought came to him. "I hope Russ doesn't think he's going to get a quieter life with you."

* * *

Sunshine was lighting up one wall of his bedroom when David woke the second time. Rousing himself wearily, he yawned and stretched before looking out in dismay at the splintered crates, broken creels and other debris littering the quay and harbour. One or two small craft were wallowing half-submerged at their mooring buoys, and a large inflatable dinghy had been picked up by the wind and tossed onto the mole.

He could see one of his chairs floating at the foot of the launching ramp, and another caught between a bollard and the mooring ropes of a lobster boat; two of its legs reduced to splintered stumps. Thankful that he had remembered to bring Rocky and the parasols inside the previous evening, he dressed quickly and went down to see if the café had suffered any more damage.

Stepping outside, he found the rest of his coloured chairs scattered across the quay and trapped beneath the wooden furniture outside The Packet Boat Inn. The red table was on its side under the window and the other two were overturned and lay with their legs in the air, like stricken beasts. David's cursory inspection suggested that they had only incurred a few scratches and some chipped paintwork. But it no longer mattered. He could see no point in taking the trouble to repaint them.

"That was a wild night," Wally called, as he emerged from the doorway of the pub. Gazing at the mud and pools of murky water beneath his wooden tables and benches, he shook his head. "What a mess! It looks like ol' Dan Norris is gonna be kept busy."

"Who's Dan Norris?" David asked.

Wally pointed to the broken slates scattered across the quay. "Dan's bin repairin' roofs an' chimney stacks for donkey's years. Must be well into 'is sixties, but it don't stop 'im gettin' up on a roof. Don't use scaffoldin', neither."

"Rather him than me," David murmured.

Wally stared up at the roof line. "I can see one o'my ridge tiles is missin'. It looks like you've got a few slates loose, too."

"You're not the first person to think that." David remarked.

Wally's chuckle rumbled in his chest. "Some're missin' an' loose on Victor's an' Gemma's roofs, as well. Can't see no damage on Stan's or the chandlery. But I'll give Dan a bell an' get 'im to come over an' take a look. It might not be straight away; there'll be plenty more in the same boat after last night. In the meantime, let's see what we can do about your tables an' chairs."

David looked up to see the sun disappear behind an ominous bank of dark cloud, as he deposited the remains of two broken chairs in a corner of the yard behind the café. On the quay, people were beginning to clear up and repair the damage to their boats, while Wally helped Ken Rathbone clear debris from the harbour. Wielding a long-handled gaff, he was hooking lobster pots and fishing nets from the water. There was no sign of life in Rolfe's Chandlery, but Victor and Grace Sullivan were sweeping up broken tiles and litter, which Gemma was shovelling into a large oil drum.

David was about to lend a hand, when Stan appeared from his emporium, wearing a grey trilby, a gabardine raincoat, and carrying a scuffed leather suitcase bound with a webbing strap. Looking around at the damage, he grimaced as he came towards David. "Burza blastiks bad, ya?"

Assuming that he was referring to the storm, David replied, "Yes; it was very bad."

Stan took a postcard from his pocket and pointed to the address written on it. "How say zis place?"

"It's called Beccles," David explained, pronouncing it slowly and carefully.

"Bec … culs," Stan repeated. "I stay Jolanta house. She wife my brother, Stefan. Stay maybe one week."

"I met her the other day," said David.

"Jolanta say that." Stan smiled wistfully. "I think she dead when blastiks Germans come. She think I dead; same like Stefan."

"I'm really happy for you, Stan," said David. "We all are."

Stan chuckled to himself. "Avril happy. She cry; she laugh same time."

"Do you know how to get to Beccles?" David asked.

"I go in train to Norwich." Stan pronounced it Noorvich. "Jolanta go there in car; take me to house."

"That's nice. I expect you'll have a lot to talk about."

"Ya." Stan frowned and stroked his chin. "She have bad time. Germans come my brother house." He hesitated, before tugging at his jacket. "Zis … black."

"You mean black uniforms; the SS?" David prompted.

"Ya; Jolanta like slave. She run away … they find. Cut Jolanta face." Stan hesitated. "She think maybe all good when Germans go." He shook his head despondently. "Then Russians come."

Unable to think of an adequate response, David said, "Well, I hope everything's better for both of you, now."

Stan nodded. "Ya; all good now. England good place; good people. You … Jo … Avril … Wally. All *good* people here."

"Thank you," said David. "You're a good person too, Stan. I'm grateful for your kindness and generosity."

Stan pursed his lips. "Iz nothing. You; Jo make nice place here." Waving an arm towards the quay, he asked, "What you do when all finish?"

"I'm not really sure," David replied vaguely. "I'll probably make a living here and there, playing piano or guitar."

Stan looked surprised "No stay Fairhaven?"

David smiled ruefully. "No; Stan. There's nothing left for me here."

Picking up his suitcase, Stan shook his head. "I think maybe you make mistake, David."

* * *

Apart from loose or missing roof slates and broken furniture, David appeared to have suffered no other damage. He had joined in the clearing up operation, but it would be a while before the quay and harbour were free of wreckage and debris. There seemed little point in opening the café until the harbour had been cleared up, so he decided to ring Connie and explain that she wasn't needed until later, and ask her to let Stella know. Sammy usually didn't put in an appearance until mid-morning, anyway.

Making his way back from the telephone box, he saw a familiar grey limousine glide into the parking bay beside the mole. "What the devil does he want, now?" David groaned.

Despite his suspicion and apprehension, he couldn't help watching with amused fascination as Horace performed his pantomime ritual of opening the rear door. However, his amusement was short lived. Charlie emerged from the Daimler and, with a frown, gazed at the quagmire outside The Packet Boat Inn, before beckoning for him to approach.

David did so, albeit reluctantly. Hopping around the mud and puddles, he greeted Horace with a circumspect nod of the head, before asking tersely, "What can I do for you ... *uncle*?"

"It's more a case of what I can do for you, son," Charlie replied calmly.

"Waving a hand at the harbour, David retorted, "You and your pals have grabbed my café and everything else round here. Don't feel obliged to do any more for me!"

Charlie's smile revealed a glint of gold. "That's one of the things I want to talk to you about, David." Looking up at the threatening clouds, he said, "It looks like rain; shall we sit in the car?"

"What for?" David demanded, flinching as Horace reached across him to open the car door.

Charlie chuckled. "There's nothing to worry about. You've been watching too many George Raft films, son." He gazed at the café and nodded appreciatively. "You and Ginny's lass have done alright. I never thought you had it in you. But you've proved me and a lot of other people wrong." Feeling the first spots of rain, he gestured towards the open car door. "Shall we? I've got some news for you … and I've got a proposition to put to you. The least you can do is hear me out."

* * *

David's contemplation of his uncle's visit was interrupted by the sound of someone rattling the café doors. Looking out of a living room window, he saw his brother's car parked by the mole, and went down to let him in.

"How are you this morning?" Richard enquired guardedly. "In a better mood, I hope." Observing the scuffed tables and chairs outside the doors, he remarked, "That was a heck of a storm last night. Did you suffer any other damage?"

David shook his head. "Not much. Only a few roof slates."

Richard held out a bunch of keys and a bulging school satchel. "Jo asked me to give you these. Apparently, all the café's paperwork and what-have-you is in there. She said to tell you to do what you like with this place. She doesn't care anymore."

Struggling to hide his anguish, David took them and dropped them onto the counter. "Are you off then?"

Richard nodded. "Yes. If you need to get hold of me, I'll be staying with Mum and Dad until I move into my flat." He handed David a slip of paper. "That's my new address. I'll let you have the telephone number when I know it. You're welcome any time; to stay if you need a bed."

"Thanks, but I don't expect I'll get to Richmond all that much."

"I see. Like that is it?" Richard settled himself on the high stool. "Feeling sorry for ourself are we, Little Brother?"

"What if I am?"

"There's no point in wallowing in self-pity," Richard observed bluntly. "Jo wants nothing more to do with you; and you've only got yourself to blame. You had no reason to treat her like that, David. You've really hurt her!"

Tormented by guilt and remorse, David responded angrily. "Don't come it with me, Rich! You're the blue-eyed boy, aren't you? Just like always! All I've ever got from everybody is: Richard's such a lovely boy; and so successful. Why can't you be more like your brother?"

Richard's expression darkened. "Don't talk rubbish! Your problem is: you never stick at anything. You always give up or find a way to lose what you already have! Shall I tell you why? Because you're never satisfied. The grass always looks greener somewhere else doesn't it? Then off you go chasing rainbows. But there's never a pot of gold at the end, is there David? Until you realise that, you'll always lose out!"

"Here endeth the lesson! Is that it ... finished?" David replied cynically.

"Pretty much. I've never tried to outdo you, David. I'm your brother, for God's sake! But you're your own worst enemy. You and Jo have done wonders here. Be proud of what you've achieved. Why don't you build on that? Open a new Rockhopper Café somewhere!"

David shrugged dismissively. "There's no need; this one's not going ... at least, not to the developers."

"Really? What's changed?"

"Uncle Charlie was here earlier. Apparently, he and his cronies have suddenly lost interest in the harbour. Their lawyers have found that legal complications and overturning restrictive statutes going back centuries will be more difficult and a damned sight more expensive than they predicted. According to him, the council's got cold feet, too. One of the national dailies has picked up the Herald's story about the accident in the harbour. Their reporter has been poking around and asking questions about the redevelopment. His paper is thinking of running an article along the lines of a David and Goliath struggle between us and the developers. And Lady Alice was right about concerns over the development consortium. Apparently, Myrtlesham and District is a marginal constituency, and our councillors' political masters are worried about something like this rocking the boat with a general election coming up."

"That's great! Stick with it, then!" Richard enthused. "You've shown a lot of grit and determination to make a go of this café!"

David's laugh was laden with bitterness. "Stick with it? You must be joking! I couldn't give a damn about this place! They can knock it down or blow it up for all I care!" He took a deep breath. "You might as well know, if you haven't already worked it out for yourself. Jo's the reason I stuck it out here. She made it all worthwhile." He turned towards the window to hide the tears pricking his eyes, and looked out at the slanting rain spattering on the quay and dimpling the water in the harbour. "There's no way I could face it here, day after day, without her. Knowing it's all for nothing."

"Didn't it occur to you to tell her?" Richard suggested gently.

"What good would that do? She doesn't feel that way about me. I know that … and I've had to accept it. Telling her would only have made things worse … especially now!"

"You could hardly have made things any worse than they are," Richard asserted.

David subsided wearily onto the corner of a table, willing his brother to leave him to his misery. "I didn't know what I was saying. I was mad with her … with you … with myself. I've never cared about a girl like this before. It's been like a ride on

The Big Dipper at Blackpool! Up and floating on air one minute; down and miserable the next."

"I think you'll find it's called love," Richard chuckled.

"Go ahead; laugh! I've lost out again, haven't I? But it's different this time, Rich. She's not just another girl. This time it matters! It really matters!"

"And whose fault is it for messing things up?" Richard snorted. "You've got no-one to blame but yourself, Little Brother. You managed that all on your own!"

"Rich; if you call me *Little Brother* once more, I swear…!"

They were silenced by the strident command, "I've told you before! Keep these doors closed if you don't want the whole world to know your business!"

Ginny was silhouetted in the entrance, shaking water from her umbrella. Propping it against the doorframe, she came in and closed the doors. "Now, young man; I suggest you stop this nonsense, and listen!" She looked at David determinedly, as if expecting him to challenge her.

Knowing better than to try, David braced himself for the expected onslaught.

"Would you please explain to this nitwit…?" Richard began.

Ginny held up a hand to silence him. "In a minute! There's something I want to make clear first." Taking off her raincoat and headscarf, she hung them on the coat hooks beside the doors. "May I sit down?"

"Of course," said David nervously. "Would you like a cup of tea or coffee?"

"No thank you." Ginny settled herself at a table and took a deep breath. "It wasn't just the storm that kept me awake last night. I don't know if Richard told you, but for much of it I was trying to comfort my distraught niece. It's something I hoped I'd never have to do again."

"I'm sorry; I never meant to…" David began, but got no further.

"Just listen; please!" Ginny insisted, before continuing more calmly. "As I'm sure you know, Jo is like a daughter to me. Her happiness and welfare matter more than anything. My dearest wish is for her to find happiness and fulfilment with someone who'll love and cherish her as she deserves."

"It's *mine*, too!" David declared.

"Alright." Ginny replied. "I doubt that Jo's told you herself, so let me tell you something about her. She was fifteen when she came to live with me. Her father was killed in the war. Her mother remarried, but Jo didn't get on with her step-father. He wasn't cruel or abusive; they just never got on. She was unhappy at home and headstrong, so when her mother died, her stepfather was as glad to see the back of her as she was to go. Jo's not really my niece, as such. Her mother and I were second cousins. But living on my own, after Ernest died, I was the only one, of what family we have, who was willing to take on a fifteen year old girl."

Ginny steepled her fingers under her chin, as she appeared to marshal her thoughts. "She could be difficult and uncommunicative at first. But as we got to know each other, and she learned I wasn't going to put up with any nonsense, she settled down and revealed herself to be the lovely girl we both know. She eventually decided that she wanted to be a nurse, and found she had a real calling for it.

"I'll say!" David declared. "I've seen her in action."

Ginny smiled for the first time. "There were one or two boyfriends along the way, but nothing serious until about four years ago, when Duncan appeared on the scene. I forget why he was at Myrtlesham Hospital. I believe it had something to do with his training as a surgeon. Jo was nineteen. He was six years older than her; handsome and more worldly than anyone she'd been involved with before. She fell for him completely. She started talking about marriage; where they might live; their future together... Then, all of a sudden, he was off! He hadn't told her his appointment was only for a few months. All she'd been was a temporary amusement … which he was cruel enough to tell her when she begged him not to leave her."

David felt his fingernails digging into his palms. "What a callous swine!"

"Quite!" Ginny continued unperturbed. "He broke her heart. I could hear her sobbing, night after night. It took her a long time to get over it. Then, just over a year ago, she met Colin, when they were both taking part in a Civil Defence exercise. She saw him as solid and dependable; perhaps a little too serious and careful, but after what happened with Duncan, I think she was willing to accept that. I don't believe she was deeply in love with him. I'm of the opinion that she was content with their relationship as it was, with him in Germany. They were only together for a day or two at a time when he came home on leave. The last time was just before you arrived here."

"I didn't know she had a boyfriend at first," said David. "It was quite a while before she mentioned him."

Ginny nodded, but continued without comment. "They wrote regularly and phoned each other quite often; he even sent her a dedication on Family Favourites. But I'm pretty certain she wasn't desperate to marry him. I think she had her doubts, even before they went to Leeds. I could tell she was in two minds about going, which is why I offered her excuses to come home. I wasn't surprised when she jumped at the opportunity! If she hadn't made up her mind before, she certainly did when she saw, first hand, the influence Colin's mother had over him, and realised that she'd play second fiddle to both of them."

"He tried to persuade David to keep the café running for another year, before he'd even spoken to Jo about it," Richard explained. "We didn't think she'd be happy about that."

"She was livid!" Ginny said flatly. "Especially when she found out that he had their future planned without any thought for what *she* might want. Jo has quite a temper when she's roused."

"Don't I know it!" David murmured ruefully.

Ginny rummaged in her copious bag and retrieved a packet of Senior Service. She lit a cigarette and drew on it deeply before continuing. "I'm sure Jo wouldn't have gone through with marrying Colin; even if *a certain someone* hadn't come into her life. I could see what was happening. Her old sparkle was back, and it's been lovely hearing her laugh so much; the way she used to. I could tell she was falling in love, despite herself."

Ginny's words cut as brutally as a knife. Taking a deep breath, David marshalled what was left of his self-control. "She deserves it," he croaked. "She's a wonderful girl. I wish her all the happiness in the world." Turning to his brother, he said, "You too, Rich. I've been a damned fool. That's nothing new, I know. I should have realised what was happening. Tell Jo I didn't mean what I said … I'm happy for both of you." He swallowed to clear the tightening in his throat. "I was going to say: look after her. But I know you will."

Richard slid off the stool and grabbed him by the shoulders. "Wait a minute, David!"

"Don't, Rich," David pleaded; his voice quavering. Determined not to break down in front of them, he murmured, "Do me a favour. Just leave me alone; both of you … please."

"Let me finish," Ginny insisted.

"There's no need," David murmured. "I understand."

Richard shook his shoulders gently. "No you don't, David…"

Wiping his eyes with the back of his hand, David took a deep breath. "I do, Rich. I've seen the photo."

"What photo?"

"The one of you two kissing. It's in that photo booth on the promenade."

"*What?* You're nuts! It's not us … it can't be! I've never kissed Jo!" Richard turned to Ginny in desperation. "Help me knock some sense into his thick skull!"

Ginny sighed resignedly. "I'm beginning to think we ought to knock their heads together." She stood up and looked at David meaningfully. "I don't know anything about a photo, but it's not Richard I'm talking about." Patting his arm, she smiled affectionately. "Don't you know how Jo feels about you?"

David's dumbfounded stare elicited a chuckle. "All I've been hearing these past weeks is: 'David this; David that. You'll never guess what he's done now! Guess what he came out with today'…"

David took a deep breath in an effort to control his turbulent emotions. "But she's always kept her distance! She made it plain, right from the start, that we were just business partners!"

Ginny tapped the ash from her cigarette into a metal ashtray. "She thought you were only interested in getting as much as you could from this place. You gave her the impression it was all that kept you here. You appeared to be planning your future with that other girl. I don't think Jo could face having her heart broken again. I think it triggered painful memories and became too much for her. She seems to have made up her mind to make a fresh start in London."

David's senses were reeling. "But I don't care about the bloody money!" he bellowed. "And I'm not planning anything with Ruby. Jo's all I care about! *She's* the reason I stayed here! None of this means a damned thing without *her*!"

"Then, why the hell didn't you tell her?" Richard demanded. "I knew you were fond of each other, but I didn't realise you were *in love*! None of us did! How could we, when you didn't even let on to each other how you felt? *You* certainly had me fooled. You even seemed to get on well with Colin. As Ginny said, we thought you were keen on Ruby. So how was Jo supposed to know how you felt about her?"

David waved his arms in exasperation. "I've just told you; I thought that was what *she* wanted! Colin seemed like a nice bloke, but I was friendly with him for her sake. Do you imagine I'd have spent all summer trying to hide my feelings, if I'd thought I stood any chance with Jo? When Colin turned up, I was just hanging on; trying to make the most of every day I had left with her."

"I have to admit that I didn't know what to make of you at first," Ginny declared. "I didn't think you'd stay long, either; or take much interest in the place. But then I began to suspect I might be wrong. After a shaky start, I could see you were putting a great deal of effort into making a success of this café. I didn't mention it to Jo in case I was mistaken, but you genuinely seemed to care for her. She told me how you sold your guitar rather than let her dip into her savings, and how little you took from the business for yourself. As for Colin; I think he loved her in his own way. But he wasn't right for her, and she knew it."

Richard squeezed David's shoulder. "Jo's right; you *are* an idiot. A twenty-four carat, fully hallmarked idiot! There's nothing between Jo and me except friendship … and, it seems, our love for my dumb kid brother."

"It's been delightful having Richard with us," Ginny said quietly. "But Jo wanted to look after him for you … because he's *your brother*. She knew how worried you were about him."

"Are we getting through to you, bonehead?" Richard chortled. "Forget what's been stewing in whatever you use for a brain. There's *nothing* like that going on between Jo and me!"

David couldn't stop himself trembling. "Well; what was I supposed to think? You seemed to be together all the time. You took her to London … and home to Mum and Dad."

"I gave Jo a lift because she had an interview at that private clinic. I had to go to London for my hospital appointment, so it saved her a difficult journey on busses and trains. I wanted to call in and tell Mum and Dad the good news on the way home. Surely you can understand that! We were late back because the car's engine was overheating and I had to nurse it all the way. It might interest you to know that Jo and Mum spent most of the time talking about *you*. Jo couldn't stop laughing when we were telling her about some of the scrapes you got into to as a kid. I think her words were: 'Why am I not surprised?'... Mum and Dad thinks she's the bee's knees."

It brought a wistful smile to David's face. "Didn't they pump you to find out if you were thinking of 'settling down' with her, as Dad would say?"

"No; they didn't," Richard chuckled. "Although their eyes did light up when Jo was talking about a cottage in a little village a few miles from here. I think it's called Foxley, or something like that. Jo pointed it out when we passed it on the way to London. The cottage looks as if it hasn't been lived in for some time, so I reckon it would take a lot to make it habitable. But Jo seems to have fallen in love with it."

"I think you mean Floxley St Peter," said Ginny. "My late husband's nephew, Giles, lives there; at Floxley Grange. He took over as chairman of Tralford Estates when Ernest died."

"Tralford? Isn't that who we pay our rent to?" David queried.

Ginny nodded. "Yes; that's right. I happen to hold shares in the company."

"So, you've been our landlord, all along!" David exclaimed. "Why didn't you or Jo tell me?"

"Jo doesn't know. And I'm not your landlord! I don't own the company. I'm just a shareholder. I don't have any say in the business. I didn't tell either of you, because I didn't think you needed to know." Ginny smiled knowingly. "I knew about your lease from when my late husband, Ernest, was chairman of the company. He and your uncle formed Tralford Estates before the war. I'm surprised neither of you twigged that Tralford is a combination of my married name, Trafford, and Ralph. Ernest bought your uncle's interest in the company when he ran up substantial gambling debts and needed money in a hurry."

"We've heard about the gambling," said David. He almost added: "And what Ralph and your husband were up to." But he stopped himself. Why open old wounds, especially when she had looked after Richard so well, and came to his and Jo's rescue in their hour of need? Why not let it rest?

Ginny continued, unaware of his deliberations. "Ernest also arranged for the company to buy the freehold of these premises from Ralph, and lease them back to him on the extremely favourable terms you know about."

"Presumably, that's why Uncle Ralph left half the café to Jo," Richard suggested.

Ginny pursed her lips. "It could be. I didn't know he'd made a will. But, despite his cantankerous nature and hardly knowing Jo, I think Ralph had a soft spot for her. He seemed quite upset when he heard about the way Duncan treated her."

"Who wouldn't?" David declared. "How could anybody treat her like that?"

"You mean apart from you?" Richard replied deliberately. "You've really hurt her, David; and it might be too late to make amends. She had a phone call from that clinic this morning. They've offered her a job and asked her back to make arrangements."

David's stomach lurched. "Well, I'm damned-well gonna try! Where is she?"

"She's got the day off again today," Ginny replied. Looking at her watch, she added, "I think she's probably at the bus stop. There's a bus due any minute. I would suggest…"

But David was no longer listening. Wrenching the doors open, he rushed outside; heedless of the rain and the fact that he was in his shirtsleeves. With no time to avoid the mud and puddles outside the pub, he splattered through them; gasping as water flooded his shoes and soaked his socks and trousers. Head down, he ran along the almost deserted promenade, narrowly avoiding a couple huddled beneath an umbrella. In the distance, through the slanting rain, he could see the shelter … and the bus approaching it.

With his chest heaving, he tried to put on a spurt. But he had never been a sprinter and his legs refused to oblige.

Through the dripping strands of hair, plastering his forehead and blurring his vision, he saw the brake lights of the bus flare as it pulled up at the shelter. In desperation, he gasped, "Jo!" But he was too far away and his plaintive cry was snatched away on the breeze.

His hopes were raised when a group of people emerged from the shelter and began boarding the bus. "Take your time," he urged them breathlessly.

He sensed rather than saw a car draw up beside him and heard Richard shout, "Get in!" But unwilling to risk unnecessary delay, David kept running. Too breathless to reply, he pointed frantically at the bus.

The MG snarled and roared away in a cloud of exhaust fumes and, for a moment, it seemed that Richard might make it in time. But the bus pulled away as he swung in behind it. Flashing his headlights and blasting his horn, Richard followed, but the bus driver ignored what he must have assumed was an impatient hothead. Richard had to brake suddenly, when a boy, head down and oblivious to danger, darted across the road in front of him, and the MG's engine stalled. To compound David's misery, the traffic lights changed as the bus passed through them and turned off the Esplanade. Any thought Richard may have entertained of ignoring the red light was banished by the police car that pulled away from the kerb behind him.

Panting and wheezing, David staggered to a halt at the shelter and grasped the bus stop pole for support. With his chest heaving and his legs shaking uncontrollably, he watched helplessly as the bus disappeared behind the buildings in Victoria Street. His shoes were awash, his thighs ached and his lungs were on fire. Rivulets ran down his neck from his saturated hair, and his shirt and trousers clung to him like a sodden shroud.

His anguished wail of, "Oh, Jo!" was greeted with bewildered stares from an elderly couple sitting in the shelter, and ribald mockery from two lads passing on a BSA Bantam. Doubled over and fighting for breath, all he could manage was a two-fingered response to their chant of: "Hey Joe; whaddya know?"

David lifted his head and groaned despairingly, "I love you Jo."

"What did he say?" the elderly woman asked.

"Take no notice," her husband replied awkwardly. "I think he's one o'them."

The rain was stopping; no longer spattering in the gutter at David's feet. But he wouldn't have cared if a monsoon had deluged Fairhaven. Summer was over ... gone forever.

"Look at the state of you! What on earth do you think you're doing?"

The voice came from the shelter behind him and, for a moment, David thought he was hearing things.

"Jo?" Turning his head, he saw her peering round one of the weather screens; her lovely face framed by the brim of a yellow rain hat and her eyes wide with amazement. Stumbling into the shelter where she sat, David knelt at her feet; uncomfortably conscious of his wet clothes and the cold concrete beneath his knees. "Thank God!" he panted, almost dizzy with relief. "I thought you were on that bus."

"Of course not! It's the pensioners' monthly outing."

"What!?"

She brushed strands of dripping hair from his eyes. "This is a pickup point for the local Pensioners Association excursions. The Myrtlesham bus is nearly always late."

"I've just run myself ragged ... in all this rain!" he gasped. But, overwhelmed by relief, he spread his hands in a gesture of helplessness.

Her sparkling eyes held his gaze. "Why? What do you want?"

"You! I have to talk to you."

"You said more than enough yesterday!" she replied curtly.

"Listen, Jo; please!" he pleaded. "I've been a complete ass! I never meant what I said. I was going out of my mind. I thought you were going away with Richard!"

405

"*With Richard?*"

"Yes! You've been spending a lot of time with him."

"He's been living with us. I could hardly avoid it, could I?"

"I know. But I thought you and he…" David shook his head, unable to give voice to his heartache. "You went to London with him … and I saw a photo in the Happy Snaps booth."

"Oh that!" Jo waved a hand dismissively. "I've seen it too. That annoying creep in the tartan waistcoat took it. Lovely shots of you an' yer fella, miss. Four for three-an'-a-tanner, two for 'alf a crown," she mimicked acidly.

"So, *I am* right!" David exclaimed. "Richard swore he's never kissed you! But I knew…"

She grasped his head and jerked his chin up.

"What are you doing?" he gasped in alarm.

"I'm going to roll your eyelid back."

"What the heck for?"

"To show you what I was doing when that photo was taken. It was blowy on the prom, and Richard got grit in his eye. I had to get close … like this … to wipe it off his eyelid."

David pulled his head away abruptly. "I'll take your word for it!"

"I suppose the photo did make it look as if we were kissing," she admitted. "But we weren't, and you owe Richard an apology."

"And you," he murmured. "You most of all! I'm sorry; so sorry! What I said to you wasn't true … and not fair! You've worked so hard to make the café a success. I didn't mean it! I was going crazy. I thought I was losing you … I love you Jo."

"You've got a funny way of showing it," she said, her voice trembling. "What brought this on, all of a sudden?"

"It's not all of a sudden. I've wanted to say it all summer."

"So, why didn't you?" she demanded; her eyes moist and glistening.

"How could I? I thought you were going to marry Colin. But I wouldn't have dared, anyway. I didn't think you wanted to hear that from me. I thought you'd keep away from me if I told you how I really felt." Conscious that the seconds were ticking away, he started to panic. "Please listen, Jo! You've got to believe me. I wouldn't have said the things I did if I hadn't been going out of my mind ... I love you. I wouldn't hurt you for the world!" He knew he was babbling, but desperate to make her understand in the little time he had, he tried again. "Please, Jo. Your bus will be here any minute ... and there's so much I want to say. But I don't know how to say it properly ... If I was Richard, I'd know the right words."

Her eyes overflowed with tears and she took his face between her hands. "We both said things we didn't mean, yesterday. But you don't need to be like Richard. You've just said what I wanted to hear. You've can have all the time you like ... if you mean it."

"Of course I do! I absolutely adore you!" He was trembling uncontrollably, but not because he was cold. "You don't know how much I've wanted to say that."

"You don't know how much I've wanted you to." Tears tracked down her cheeks, as she stroked his face. "I love you, too. But I didn't think I meant that much to you. I didn't think you wanted me in your life."

"You are my life!" he sighed, gently brushing tears from her cheek. "You mean the world to me! The café ... the music ... my whole life. They don't mean a thing without you!"

Fresh tears streamed down her cheeks, as she rested her face against his; oblivious to his dripping hair.

"Don't cry, Jo; please!" he pleaded, taking her in a soggy embrace as she began to sob.

"I thought you wanted Ruby," she whimpered.

"Of course not! There was nothing serious between us; honestly. She knew it's you I want. She's gone off to Manchester with a bloke called Russ."

With his own tears merging with rivulets running from his hair, he held her; savouring the delicate fragrance of her perfume, until her shoulders stopped heaving and she lifted her head.

"Can I get a hanky out of my bag?" she sniffed.

Her rain hat had fallen off onto the bench, and he stroked her hair. "Alright. But promise me you'll phone that clinic and tell them you're not coming today."

She dabbed at her eyes with the back of her hand. "I wasn't going today. My appointment's not until next Thursday. I was going into Myrtlesham for a new pair of shoes."

"They never told me that!" he spluttered indignantly. "They let me run myself ragged … in all this rain!" But he had to admit that, once again, he was the victim of his impetuous nature. "Never mind; I've got a nice pair of brown suedes you can borrow!"

"Idiot," she giggled, drying her eyes with a linen handkerchief. "Look at you; you're soaked! We need to get you home before you catch your death of cold."

"I'm not cold," he insisted. "Come on; no more tears. Those beautiful eyes shouldn't cry. I want you to be happy … as happy as you've made me. You're everything I've ever wanted; perfect."

"*Perfect?*" she snorted and flipped open a silver powder compact to inspect the damage to her makeup in the mirror. "I'm certainly not that!"

Feigning a solemn expression, he said, "Alright then; nearly perfect … Except for your name, perhaps."

She smiled self-consciously. "I know. I don't like it either. I was told it was my dad's idea to call me Josephine."

"It's a lovely name, for a lovely girl," he said softly. "I meant the Lampeter bit."

"Sorry; I can't do much about that, either."

"You could change it to Sheldon." He had blurted it out without thinking; and froze, with his heart in his mouth, as her eyes widened in surprise.

"What?"

"Sorry; I shouldn't have said it." Convinced he'd put his foot in it again, he avoided her gaze. "Sorry, Jo. I didn't mean to spring it on you like that. It's much too soon, I know. But…"

"Do you mean, what I think you mean?" she asked deliberately.

With his courage deserting him, David fixed his gaze on the puddle forming around his knees. "I know I'm not much of a catch. We both know you can do better … a lot better. So; if it's no, just tell me. It won't change the way I feel, but at least I won't hold out any false hope." Despite her unnerving silence, he made himself carry on. "But if there's a chance it *might* be yes, when you've got to know me better, will you think about it?"

"Are you sure that's what you want?" she murmured.

"Yes; completely sure. I've never wanted anything so much."

Jo dabbed at her eyes again with her handkerchief. "Alright. In that case; yes."

"Thank you." David's heart was pounding so hard that he could hardly breathe. "Take all the time you need. I won't try to rush you or pester you for an answer."

She took his face between her hands again and kissed him. "That's not what I meant. I don't need more time … or to get to know you better. You haven't actually said it, but if you're asking me to marry you, the answer's *yes* … As long as you're sure it really is what you want."

Dizzy with euphoria, he gasped, "What; *really!?*"

"Yes; of course! If you're *absolutely* sure."

The voice from the other side of the screen was a sudden reminder that they were not alone. "I think you should, dear," the woman called. "I don't think he's safe to be left on his own."

"She's right!" David exclaimed. "I need looking after! I need my own nurse! Look at me! I might get pneumonia … or even *old* monia!"

Jo's peel of laughter echoed in the confined space. "You're an idiot!" she squealed. "But you're *my* idiot, and I love you."

"You're not going to take the job at that posh clinic, are you?" he implored.

She shook her head. "No; not if you don't want me to. I don't really want to go. This is my home, and I feel I'm doing something worthwhile at Myrtlesham Gen."

David took her hands between his. "You are." Rising stiffly to his feet, he said, "They need you. We all do. You're special."

The swish of tyres on rain-drenched tarmac announced the arrival of the Myrtlesham bus, prompting the elderly couple to move out from the shelter. With its diesel engine rumbling and rattling impatiently, the bus pulled up at the kerb and, grasping the pole, the woman carefully stepped up onto the open platform. Turning to Jo and David with an amused smile, she called, "Congratulations!"

Jo stood up and the conductor winked at her as he rang the bell. "Thank you!" she replied, returning the couple's wave as the bus whined and growled away from the kerb. "Goodness knows what they must be thinking," she mused.

"They're obviously convinced you're marrying a nutcase," David suggested. "But I'll change! I'll be more sensible from now on."

"No you won't," Jo chortled.

"I will! I can change; honestly."

"*Don't you dare!*" She reached up and drew his face to hers. "You've got a wet nose, like a little dog," she giggled. "I don't want sensible. I love you just as you are: clever; funny; kind … *bonkers!*" She kissed him again gently. "And just wonderful!" Tilting her head, as if in serious deliberation, she murmured, "Hm; Jo Sheldon … Yes; I like that."

"So do I!" David sighed and hugged her closer. "That *is* perfect."

Richard's car roared to a halt beside them with a squeal of brakes. The rain had stopped, but Richard's expression was anything but sunny when he got out. Staring at Jo, he said, "So you're still here!"

"Yes; it would seem so."

He glared at David. "I've just had a hell of a job convincing two coppers that I wasn't some modern-day highwayman trying to hold-up a bus!"

David grinned mischievously. "Tut-tut, Big Brother. You should drive more carefully. You could have given some of those old folks a heart attack." Enjoying the puzzled look on Richard's face, he added, "Wrong bus. That was a pensioners' outing."

"I thought it was you!" Jo tittered. "But I couldn't make out why you were driving like a madman and sounding your horn like that."

Richard threw up his hands in exasperation. "David; you really are..."

"May I introduce my fiancée?" David interjected airily.

Richard's anger crumbled and he burst out laughing. "You're a nightmare, Little Brother! But you've finally got it right ... at last!"

Jo started to unbutton her raincoat. "You're shivering, David. Put this round your shoulders."

"Hang on; I've got a blanket in the car," said Richard. He returned with a thick, tartan car rug and a towel, which he tossed to David for him to dry his hair. With Jo's help, he draped the heavy blanket round David's shoulders. "Come on Sitting Bull; let's get you back to the café. I take it you've changed your mind about selling it now."

"You bet! If my wife-to-be agrees, of course. Victor Sullivan told me that, before all the recent hoo-ha, he was thinking of converting his upstairs into a holiday flat. It's not a bad idea now the harbour redevelopment's off."

Jo stared at him in amazement. "What do you mean: the harbour development's off!? Are you saying they're not going to knock us down, after all?"

"That's right; they've changed their minds. It'll be too expensive and too much trouble, so they've lost interest in the harbour. Uncle Charlie told me this morning."

Jo threw her arms around his neck. "Oh, David! That's wonderful! And you don't want to sell our café?"

"Of course not! Whatever gave you that idea?"

She slapped his arm. "Be serious! Tell me what's happened!"

David winced. "Ouch! You pack quite a wallop for a little 'un. With that temper, being married to you is gonna be dangerous."

"You'd better believe it!" she giggled. "Come on; tell me!"

"Right; pin back your lugholes," he said, enjoying Richard's amusement at his more than passable impersonation of Cyril Fletcher. "The Council's got cold feet over redeveloping the harbour. We're all getting official letters telling us they're not going ahead with it. Charlie-boy explained everything when he turned up this morning to sound me out about the American diner … He's retiring to Jersey, by the way."

"What American diner?"

"My brain's too soggy to go into too much detail at the moment. But the gist of it is: Charlie knows some people who are thinking of opening one of those American style diners in Fairhaven. You know; hot dogs, hamburgers and milk shakes. He's not involved personally, but the people who *are* involved are looking for someone with the knowhow to run it; and he's recommended me. There's no rush. It won't happen for at least a year; if at all."

"So, we'll have to sell the café, then?"

"No! Whether the diner happens or not, let's keep it, shall we? It's ours! We did it together! But if we decide this deal is right, whoever these people are will build the diner and equip it; and I … we … will stock it and run it."

Jo's eyes widened. "Could you cope with running both?"

"No; but *we* could! We can do anything, together! The hospital needs you and you love nursing, but if you can carry on looking after the paperwork and our finances, I'll manage both places, day-to-day."

"Really?"

"Yep; piece o'cake! But there's something more important to deal with first. We've got to get you an engagement ring. It won't be a priceless antique like Colin's, but it *will* be a proper diamond ring. You can choose it."

"Nearly everyone seems to have seen that ring except me!" she said. "But I don't need an engagement ring. Even a simple one will be expensive."

"I can afford it!" David insisted. "I've still got the money from Bella's party and my tips from playing in the pub. And if I take up Mervin's offer to help him and Dorothy produce music concerts, I'll get consultancy fees."

"Good grief!" Jo gasped. "You really are my little business typhoon aren't you?"

"You bet. You're the boss, but I think it'll be well worth keeping the café open during the winter. We've got quite a few local regulars, and one or two boat crews have asked if we'd do them a fry-up when they get back from fishing. I'm sure I can manage with Connie, Stella and Sammy … at least until next summer. I'm pretty sure Linda will help out, if we're really busy."

Jo picked up her rain hat. "So will I."

"Get in the car!" Richard commanded. "Ginny will be wondering where we are. You can carry on planning your business empire later. It's stopped raining, so I'll put the top down. Jo will have to sit on your lap, but I don't suppose that will bother either of you, will it?"

"By the way; is that Morris Traveller still for sale?" David asked, as Jo wriggled her way onto his lap.

"I expect so."

"Good! If you think we can afford it, something like that would be ideal for picking stuff up from our suppliers. It'll save on delivery charges."

"You *can* afford it!" Richard declared, wiping rain off the MG's hood as he stowed it away.

David stared at him in surprise. "How do *you* know?"

"Because it'll be a wedding present from your big brother. A thank you for a convalescence I wouldn't have missed for the world, and for being looked after so well by my sister-in-law!"

"Oh, Richard; you can't!" Jo exclaimed.

"Yes I can!" he insisted. "I've been looked after wonderfully by you and Ginny; for a pittance. And you've put a smile on my little brother's face you couldn't wipe off with sandpaper!"

David chuckled delightedly. "Thanks Rich. It's been great having you here. Seeing that a certain little nurse seems to fancy giving Sterling Moss a run for his money, the car would be handy for her to get to and from work, as well."

"Slow down, Tiger! You're giving me a headache," Jo chortled.

But David's exhilaration kept him in full flow. "When we get back, ask Aunt Ginny about Tralford Estates."

"Why?"

"Just ask her. I think you'll find it interesting … And you're having an engagement ring! If only for one reason. When you were getting those wolf-whistles on the way to Avril's party, I could guess what all the fellas were thinking: 'How did *he* get a gorgeous girl like that?' And there was I thinking: '*If only!*' Well, from now on, they'll see a ring on your finger … and I'll be thinking: 'Eat your hearts out!'"

Jo's laughter warmed him more than any blanket. Wrapping her arms around his neck, she nestled against him. "And I'll be thinking: 'Hard luck girls. Find your own idiot.'"

David answered with a delighted grin. "By the way; I hope you haven't got to work next Friday evening. We've all been invited to dinner with Lady Alice's family, at Huckfield Hall. I'm looking forward to showing off my fiancée and finding out how much Lady Alice had to do with stopping the harbour redevelopment."

"But, I've got nothing to wear!" Jo exclaimed. "I'll need a new dress, as well as new shoes."

"What's wrong with your white dress? You look terrific in that."

She pulled a face. "I'm not wearing that old thing to meet Lady Alice's family!"

David chuckled contentedly. "Speaking of white dresses; I'm gonna need a best man, Rich."

Richard settled himself behind the wheel and turned the ignition key. "I'm honoured. Just let me know where and when."

"Don't know where. I'll let my fiancée decide that. But it's gonna be soon. Before she comes to her senses and changes her mind."

"Not a chance!" she murmured in his ear. "You needn't think you're wriggling off the hook."

The clouds were shredding like torn curtains in the stiffening breeze, revealing ragged patches of blue through which shafts of golden sunlight brought the dull, blue-grey rollers to life in a blaze of darting lights.

As they pulled away from the shelter, David pointed to the rainbow arcing across the harbour. "You're wrong about there being no pot of gold, Rich! I've found mine!"

Richard responded with a burst of delighted laughter. "Alright; you win! But promise me you'll ring Mum and Dad as soon as you can. They're going to be thrilled to bits!"

"Will do, Rich. Why don't you bring them down for a day and we'll have a little celebration with Aunt Ginny."

"That's a good idea!" Richard replied. "That reminds me; you'd better let Avril know pretty soon, too! I suppose there's no harm in telling you, now. She's planning a farewell do for you. I was supposed to find out when you were likely to go, and tip her the wink." He laughed, as another thought occurred to him. "But what am I worrying about? When she comes down off cloud nine, you can bet your life she'll just change it to an engagement party."

Freeing his arms from the blanket, David hugged Jo closer to him; hardly daring to believe he wasn't dreaming. How could he have imagined, on that rainy March day, that the little seaside resort he had dismissed as dull and dreary would be the place he would call home; that the unwanted legacy of a shabby, run-down café would give his life purpose and meaning; or that his mysterious business partner would turn out to be the love of his life?

The rain-washed air felt fresh and clean as they sped along the Esplanade. With the breeze in his hair, the comforting sigh of the sea in his ears, and the girl he adored in his arms, David felt that his heart would burst with happiness.

Lifting his face to the sun, he shouted for joy. "God bless you, Uncle Ralph!"

APPENDIX

UK currency in general circulation before 1971

Denomination	Value	Commonly known as
Copper Coins		
Farthing	¼ penny	
Ha'penny	½ penny	
Penny	12 = 1 shilling	Copper(s)
Threepenny bit	3 pennies	Thruppence/threppence
Silver coins		
Sixpence	6 pennies/pence	a tanner
1 Shilling	12 pence (20=£1)	Bob *(eg: three bob)*
2 shillings	24 pennies	Florin / Two-bob bit
Half a Crown	2 shillings & 6 pence	Half a dollar
Crown*	5 shillings	Dollar
Notes		
10 shillings	2 = £1	Ten-bob note
1 pound (£1)	20 shillings/240 pence	a quid
5 pounds (£5)**	5 pounds/100 shillings	a fiver

Coinage was commonly referred to by just numbers – eg: one-and-six (written as 1/6 or 1/6d)

*Although legal tender, the coin was too large and heavy to be in general circulation

** Until 1957 the £5 note was very large, measuring approximately 21 x 13 cms and known as a 'white fiver'. They were not commonly encountered by much of the population, as £5 equated to something close to a week's wages for many working men and women

Legal and other professional fees were usually charged in 'Guineas' (21 shillings), although the equivalent coin was not in general circulation

Music mentioned in the story
(versions listed are those generally popular
in the UK at the time of the story)

Song Title	Recording Artist	Written by	Released	Record Label
A White Sport Coat	Marty Robbins	Marty Robbins	Jan 1957	Columbia
April Love (3))	Pat Boone	Sammy Fain/ Paul Francis Webster	Oct 1957	Dot
Bird Dog	The Everly Brothers	Bordleau Bryant	Jul 1958	Cadence
Chances Are	Johnny Mathis	Robert Allen/Al Stillman	Aug 1957	Columbia
Everyday	Buddy Holly	Buddy Holly	Sep 1957	Coral
Good Golly Miss Molly	Little Richard	John Marascalco/ Robert Blackwell	Jan 1958	Specialty
Guitar Boogie Guitar Boogie Shuffle	The Rambler Trio Bert Weedon	Arthur Smith (Various adaptions)	1945 1959	Super Disk Parlophone
Hang Down Your Head Tom Dooley	The Kingston Trio	Traditional	1958	Capital
Hound Dog	Elvis Presley	Jerry Lieber/ Mike Stoller	Feb 1953	Peacock
It's Only Make Believe	Conway Twitty	Jack Nance/ Conway Twitty	July 1958	MGM
Living Doll (1)	Cliff Richard	Lionel Bart	July 1959	Columbia
Love Is A Many Splendored Thing (2)	The Four Aces	Sammy Fain/ Paul Francis Webster	1955	Accord

Love Me Tender (3)	Elvis Presley	Ken Darby/ George R Poulson	Sep 1956	RCA Victor
Moonlight Serenade	Glenn Miller Orchestra	Glenn Miller	1939	Bluebird
Move It	Cliff Richard & The Drifters	Ian Samwell	Aug 1958	Columbia
Never Be Anyone Else But You	Ricky Nelson	Thomas Baker Knight Jnr	Feb 1959	Imperial
Peggy Sue	Buddy Holly	Jerry Allison/ Norman Petty	Sep 1957	Coral
Poor Little Fool	Ricky Nelson	Sharon Sheeley	Jun 1958	Imperial
Singing The Blues	Guy Mitchell Tommy Steele	Melvin Endsley	Oct 1956 1957	Columbia Decca
Walking My Baby Back Home *	Nat King Cole Johnnie Ray	Roy Turk/Fred E Ahlert (1930)	Sep 1951 Feb 1952	Capitol Columbia
Who's Sorry Now *	Connie Francis	Ted Snyder/ Bert Kalmer/ Harry Ruby (1923)	Nov 1957	MGM
You Always Hurt The One You Love*	The Mills Brothers Connie Francis	Allan Roberts/ Doris Fisher	1944 1958	Decca MGM

(1) From the movie 'Serious Charge'
(2) A later version of the theme of a movie bearing the same name
(3) From the movie of the same name
*. Various other versions were recorded before and afterwards

ALSO BY
TONY HOPES

A YEAR AT NETHERCOMBE LEY

ISBN 9781783061419
tony.hopes@hotmail.co.uk

When Harry Simmond's wife left him for a career and a new love, his comfortable, suburban life came to a shattering end.

Without the support and steadying influence of his daughter, Debbie, who is at university, he sought solace in self-pity and alcohol.

His eighteen year old son, Adam, tired of bearing the brunt of his father's drunkenness and depression, has left home and fallen under the unsavoury influence of an old school friend.

Realising that he is on the brink of an abyss, Harry has taken the decision to make a dramatic change to his life. To give himself time and space to seek redemption and renewed purpose, he moves to a quiet Dorset village, where he is befriended by the local vicar, and the influence of three women transforms not just his way of life, but his whole attitude to living; during the course of **A Year at Nethercombe Ley**.

 Matador